"With the eye of a poet and the rectitude of a historian, Paulette Jiles travels the back roads of the American Civil War and returns with a story that is both gripping and gorgeously rendered. Adair is destined to find a place of honor among the great heroines of modern fiction."
—Geraldine Brooks

"Jiles is a gifted Missouri historian who brings to light many overlooked Civil War facts and acutely portrays Missouri's logistic misfortune as a hotbed of both Union and Confederate violence."
—*Booklist*

"[A] powerful debut novel. . . . The writing is, at times, poetic."
—*San Diego Union-Tribune*

"[S]he is a poet by training, which is evident in the novel's tight focus and carefully crafted sentences that eschew all but the most necessary of words. . . . A subtle narrative that invites the reader to contemplate the extraordinary peeking from within the ordinary."
—*Civil War Book Review*

"[S]tarlight perfectly captured."   —*Christian Science Monitor*

"Hey, what's wrong with you, poking around out here when what luck has purchased for you is Paulette Jiles inside? You know what it means when there is Paulette Jiles inside? You have any idea what the boon is when this woman's sentences are anywhere in sight? Be smart. Open the book. Don't bother with the title and all that. Go right to the crux of the matter—Blackwater, Missouri's impudent gift to the impossible art."   —*Gordon Lish*

"Compelling. . . . A poet and memoirist, Jiles writes in blunt, lovely prose. . . . Comparing *Enemy Women* to *Cold Mountain* doesn't quite do Jiles's novel justice." —*Washington Post Book World*

"*Enemy Women*, as all of Paulette Jiles's work, has a Homeresque feel to it. Like something written by an old soul. The wandering—not just over earthly miles, but through zones of sensuousness, epiphany, intuition, creatureliness, homely integrity, all that old, old true human stuff. . . . This is an ageless story that casts a different shadow. . . . There are ageless truths. All is fair in love and war, as they say." —Carolyn Chute

"Jiles's novel is fascinating because it's an exciting and generous story with sympathetic characters and more than its fair share of exquisite language and intriguing dialogue." —*Orlando Sentinel*

"An enthralling narrative." —*Library Journal* (starred review)

"Many passages read like prose poems and yet move with the pace of a thriller." —*BookPage* magazine

"Flawless. . . . Her heroine negotiates that vast plain between meaninglessness and myth. Like all courageous people, Adair discovers her own truth." —*Montreal Gazette*

"*Enemy Women* is a book that will not be forgotten." —*Dallas Morning News*

"A remarkably engaging story. . . . [T]he power of [the] writing, setting, and historical context raises this novel from the tedium of a predictable romance. Jiles's description is memorable and evocative." —*Denver Post*

"Beautifully written passages. . . . A real page-turner." —*Milwaukee Journal Sentinel*

Frank E. Brooke

About the Author

PAULETTE JILES is a poet who has published several volumes and is also a memoirist. Born and raised in the United States, she now has dual citizenship with Canada. It was there that she won a Canadian Governor General's Award, Canada's highest literary honor, for poetry. Her previous book, *Cousins*, "a sort of memoir," was published by Knopf in 1992. She lives with her husband in San Antonio, Texas.

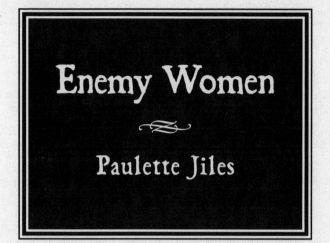

Enemy Women

Paulette Jiles

Perennial

An Imprint of HarperCollins*Publishers*

A hardcover edition of this book was published in 2002 by William Morrow, an imprint of HarperCollins Publishers.

First Perennial edition published 2003.

Designed by Debbie Glasserman

The Library of Congress has catalogued the hardcover edition as follows:

Jiles, Paulette.
    Enemy women / Paulette Jiles.
        p. cm.
    ISBN 0-06-621444-0
    1. Missouri—History—Civil War, 1861–1865—Fiction. 2. Young Women—Fiction. I. Title.

PR9199.3.J54 E5 2002
813'.54—dc21

                                                                2001040200

ISBN 0-06-093809-9 (pbk.)

03   04   05   06   07   ❖/RRD   10   9   8   7   6

For my cousin Susan Jiles Lawson and, as always, for Jim

Acknowledgments

My deepest thanks to my agent, Liz Darhansoff, whose encouragement, persistence, and skill are the reasons you have this book in your hands. Thanks to my cousin Susan for all those years of finding the way on Ozark trails, for her hospitality and love of Civil War history, and for her noble horses Whiskey, Cowboy, and Buddy, who carried us so many miles through the mountains. Without the excellent works of Jerry Ponder, historian of southeastern Missouri, I could not have told this story. He has persisted for many decades in the face of indifference and has meticulously set down the facts of the war, and his books will be groundwork for many writers in the years to come. The following were also helpful in my research into the Civil War era: *Inside War: The Guerilla Conflict in Missouri, 1861–1865*, by Michael Fellman, Oxford University Press, New York, 1989; *A History of the 15th Missouri Cavalry Regiment, C.S.A.*, by Jerry Ponder, Ponder Books, Doniphan, Missouri, 1994; *The History of Ripley County, Missouri*, by Jerry Ponder, 1987; *Camp and Prison Journal*, by Griffin Frost, reprinted by the Press of the Camp Pope Bookshop, Iowa City, Iowa; *The Civil War: A Narrative*, by Shelby Foote, Random House, New York, 1963; *Civil War in the Ozarks*, by Philip W. Steele and Steve Cottrell, Pelican Publishing Company, Gretna, Louisiana, 1998; *The Civil War in Carter and Shannon County, Missouri*, by J. J. Chilton, Eunice Pennington, David Lewis, Esau Hewett, et al., West Carter County Genealogical Society, Van Buren, Missouri, 2000; *The Little Gods: Union Provost Marshals in Missouri, 1861–1865*, by Joanne

Chiles Eakin, Two Trails Publishing Company, Independence, Missouri, 1996; *Likeness and Landscape: Thomas M. Easterly and the Art of the Daguerreotype*, by Dolores A. Kilgo, Missouri Historical Society Press, St. Louis, Missouri, 1994; *War of the Rebellion*, Official Records, U.S. Government Printing Office, Washington, D.C., 1880–1901; *Ozark Tales and Superstitions*, by Philip W. Steele, Pelican Publishing Company, Gretna, Louisiana, 1998; various reminiscences of the Civil War from old diaries, letters, and other material published in the *Daily American Republic* of Poplar Bluff, Missouri; *Lost Family, Lost Cause*, by Ivan N. McKee, Pine Hill Press, Freeman, South Dakota, 1978. I will be forever grateful to Lois Glass Webb for her encouragement and especially for sending me the photocopies of the OR reports on southeastern Missouri and a great deal of other rare material, taking time off from writing her own novel to do so. Thanks to my cheerful and efficient editor at Morrow, Jennifer Brehl, for an excellent editing job on a complex manuscript. Many thanks to Dr. Deborah McCormick for teaching me to ride sidesaddle. Thanks to Rick and Kristan Casey for the use of the jacal. Many thanks to Sky and Tim Lewey of the Open V ranch in Uvalde for all their hospitality and good conversation and for the use of the other house in a lightning storm, when the power blew out, where I finally finished this manuscript by hand and by candlelight. Thanks to Rocky Sisk for guiding us up the Devil's Backbone and over to the old military graveyard on the Trace. A special thanks to Bob and Nancy Shivers for their help in printing out manuscripts, putting up with my odd hours in the office, and their encouragement. Thanks as always to Gordon himself for being the literary genius of discernment and acumen he is and having the wisdom not to miss the Second World War. Thanks to friends Naomi Nye, Wendy Barker, Nan Cuba, Trish Maloney, Janice De Lara, Karen Janny, and Bob and Jean Flynn for their faith in the book and for reading first drafts. Appreciation is due Genevieve Kile, Carter County history buff, for her unpaid years of work in rescuing primary source materials. Special thanks to Jim for his close editing, advice on military matters, and his patience.

Enemy Women

Prologue

There will be trouble in Missouri until the Secesh are subjugated and made to know that they are not only powerless, but that any attempts to make trouble here will bring upon them certain destruction and this . . . must not be confined to soldiers and fighting men, but must be extended to non-combatant men and women. [Emphasis in the original]

—BARTON BATES TO EDWARD BATES, ST. LOUIS, OCTOBER 10, 1861, EDWARD BATES COLLECTION, MISSOURI HISTORICAL SOCIETY, ST. LOUIS

November 15, 1864: Last night there were ninety more arrivals [prisoners] from St. Louis. One lady also with them; she is a Mrs. Martin, formerly a Miss Blanerhassett, they tell us that in St. Louis one of their female prisoners is wearing a ball and chain, "and still they come." The wonders of this progressive age still continue to announce to an astonished world similar brave feats. We are in the full blaze of the nineteenth century. Women wearing balls and chains, as political offenders.

—GRIFFIN FROST, CONFEDERATE PRISONER IN ST. LOUIS, *Camp and Prison Journal,* PRESS OF THE CAMP POPE BOOKSHOP, IOWA CITY, IOWA, 1994, ORIGINALLY PRINTED IN 1867, QUINCY HERALD BOOK AND JOB OFFICE, QUINCY, ILLINOIS

YOUNG MEN JOINED UP BY THE THOUSANDS IN THEIR EAGERNESS TO GO to war for the state of Missouri; they would go to war and come home with stories to tell as their fathers had come home from the Mexican

War with tales of faraway places and cannon fire and the bold charge
the Missourians had made at Saltillo. At Doniphan Courthouse, down
in the Ozark mountains, a rally and fish-fry was held in the early summer of 1861, with crowds coming into town in wagons and on horseback. The Missouri State Guard officers sat behind a plank table and
signed them up one after the other, yelling, *No, man, you can't join the
cavalry if you don't have a horse! Here, here, you want to be a cannoneer!* It
was in May 1861 after the Federals in St. Louis had fired into a hostile
crowd and killed thirty people, including several women and a year-old
baby, that young men from the southern part of the state joined the
Missouri State Guard in droves. The rally at Doniphan Courthouse
drew a large crowd from the Ozark hills and settlements nearby. A long
fire pit glowed under fifty skillets of frying fish. There was a brass band
and a large banner painted by the Misses Parmalee and Newnan
depicting a plump Greek woman in a robe holding out a laurel wreath
with one hand and in the other hand an object that was either a skewer
of some kind or an infantry sword. The legend stated *O for Thee Missouri to the Tyrant I Shall Never Yield.*

The Misses Parmalee and Newnan had got into fierce arguments
about how much of her breasts should show. Lucinda Newnan wanted
one breast escaping entirely from her toga or whatever it was she was
wearing and said that was how they dressed in those days, and Amanda
Parmalee said that their mothers would kill them if she was exposed in
that manner and it didn't matter how they dressed in those days. They
probably dressed all kinds of ways in those days. So they painted her
robes over the offending flesh. Adair Colley's father would not let her
go to help paint the banner at all because, he said, they would be going
to the fish-fry and rally and two trips into Doniphan Courthouse in
three days was too much. So Adair and her sisters made small State
Guard flags from a worn sheet, and painted on Missouri's bears and the
state motto, *Salus Populi Suprema Lex Esto*, and waved them from the
carriage in the stream of people going into town.

The band played "Maryland, My Maryland" commendably well.

The ladies of Doniphan brought fresh bunches of quill pens to the recruiters. They seemed to bear in their hands bouquets of goose feathers like formal presentations, and an urchin was employed to sit on the ground at the boots of the cavalry recruiter to cut the quills and hand them up. Ink flew.

The men of the Missouri State Guard soon found themselves attached to the Confederate army and sent to the east to fight. The newly elected officers stared in dismay at their orders, but orders were orders. All locally raised units, one after another, were loaded on steamers and ferries to cross the Mississippi and the new soldiers marched on into Virginia and Tennessee, and the only people at home in the southeastern Ozarks were the women and the children. In the meantime the Federal forces moved thousands of troops into the Ozarks, other state troops from Illinois, Indiana, Colorado, Wisconsin, Iowa, Minnesota, and Kansas.

The Union command also sent down from St. Louis the newly created Missouri Union Militia, and so these forces came down upon the southern counties unopposed. The Militia was made up in the main of dubious characters from the St. Louis riverfront, and their officers knew where to send stolen goods and stolen horses and they began to enrich themselves and also to fight among themselves. With all the young men gone, the Missouri Union Militia began to take what they wanted from the people of the southeastern counties.

Many of the young men who had joined up with the Missouri State Guard returned home after their six-month enlistment and were determined never again to leave. They had had enough of war and somebody was needed to protect their homes against the Union Militia and the other troops from the midwestern states. They began to organize other veterans to counter the raids of the Federals.

One of these units was Reeves's Independent Scouts, which attached itself to the CSA in order not to be regarded as guerillas and therefore not under the protection of the rules of war. They determined to keep some semblance of order in the southeastern counties. Instead they were once again sent off to fight with the Confederate Army at the battle of Perryville, Kentucky, in 1862, and there is evidence that the entire unit mutinied, threatened to shoot their officers, and then returned to the Ozarks en masse.

At home, Timothy Reeves once again organized a unit of volunteers and called it the Fifteenth Missouri Cavalry, CSA, having extracted a promise from the Confederate command that they would never again be sent out of southeastern Missouri. He got that promise and it was kept.

Throughout 1861 and 1862, small units of the Union Militia and Reeves's men clashed at the rivers and the crossing places, they fought among the rocky bluffs and the dense pines. The Militia made forays and then retreated to the Union garrison at Iron Mountain, shut the doors of the fort behind them and barred it. Reeves's men dispersed to their homes in the hills. The railroad came south from St. Louis as far as Iron Mountain so that the Union Militia could be supplied with all they needed from the city's army depots. Reeves's men were supplied by the women. They wore homespun uniforms and ate what they could shoot or grow.

The Misses Parmalee took the plump Greek lady with her laurel wreath and her skewer and her brave motto and buried her beneath the manure pile, for if the Federal soldiers found the banner in their possession they would set the house on fire. Adair Colley took the homemade State Guard flags and burned them in the fireplace.

Then the regular Union Army came at the Christmas season of 1862 and at that time the Federal troops numbered ten thousand men. This was an army with infantry, artillery, and cavalry, a medical corps and commissary wagons, and a brass band.

They came down from the garrison at the railhead at Iron Mountain, which was 120 miles to the north. The rattling, clanking column fed itself uneasily southward into the hills to dispense with the Confederates of the Ozarks once and for all. They were disciplined men with responsible officers, but around them at the edges of the column the irregular Union Militia floated and canted and harried the people like hawks.

This army of ten thousand men under General Davidson camped at Doniphan Courthouse and stayed for two weeks and ate up and burnt up everything in the country. Some were regular U.S. Army and some were state troops from Iowa or Illinois or Wisconsin. The people of the southeastern Ozarks were astonished at this great army and the irrefutable power of the Union. Adair Colley, who was then seventeen, rode out to see them passing along the Military Trace and knew then that the Northern armies were more powerful than anyone had imagined.

Her father and her brother buried their supplies under the house; casks of honey and lard and cornmeal.

The Fifteenth Missouri Cavalry waited for the lines of this great army at the river crossings. They fired on the Union Army as it crossed in the hard, glassy currents, so that men and horses snared and tangled with one another. The snorting mule teams floundered as their drivers were shot out of their wagon seats to sink beneath the surface, and when Union cavalrymen came to rescue the wagons they too became targets of Reeves's old Mexican War smoothbores.

As soon as the dense gunpowder smoke drifted away, Reeves and his men drifted too, back into the mountains. The great Union Army bogged down at the river crossings and the men slept in tents in the hard, cold rains, and by January 1863 the soldiers wondered why they had come, and so did the officers. In late January an eight-foot rise in the Black River swept away everything in the main camp but a barrel of medicinal whiskey which was emptied by troops of the Thirty-third Illinois Infantry who then began to fight among themselves. As they marched down the muddy roads an Iowa soldier wrote home that the local people were but weeds in the garden of humanity. The army became lost, finally, and wandered through the mountains without direction. This great army of Union troops and machinery paid themselves through the Ozarks like whey through muslin, and when they were gone it was as if they had never been.

So they straggled back to Iron Mountain, and the Regular U.S. Army troops were sent elsewhere. And then the Militia went out raiding again. On Christmas Day, 1863, Major James Wilson, of the Union Militia, went out looking for Reeves. He was exhausted and furious and stung by an enemy that did not show itself, by men who ambushed and then melted away, by women and children who knew nothing about the Fifteenth Missouri Cavalry, had never heard of Timothy Reeves, whose men weren't here right now but were all out looking for strayed cattle.

Timothy Reeves and the men of the Fifteenth Missouri were having Christmas dinner with their families at Pulliam Springs. Major Wilson caught them with their turkey lifted on their forks. He wanted Reeves so badly he did not care that there were civilians in the way. He lined up his men and called fire. Reeves escaped with his life, but Wilson killed sixty civilians—men, women, and children—and an unknown number of the men of the Fifteenth. He took 150 prisoners. Colonel Reeves, who at one time had been a man of the cloth, said there was no hole deep enough to hide Major Wilson, nor any far wasteland wherein he might conceal himself, that he was marked for death with the mark of the Beast.

In the heat of September 1864 the Confederate General Price came up from Arkansas with an army of twelve thousand men to retake Missouri for the Confederacy. These men in gray also passed through in the thousands. General Price came with infantry and artillery and medical corps and commissary wagons and a brass band.

The Union Militia fled the southeastern counties as Price swept through, but they burnt down the town of Doniphan Courthouse on their way out. Reeves's men caught the arsonists at Ponder's Steam Mill on the Little Black River. Adair Colley and her sisters could hear the firing from the farmhouse; it went on for hours. Later the people of that neighborhood came to bury the Confederate dead and the Union dead both, and there they lie to this day. The graves have no names carved upon them. Stone slabs piled one upon the other mark their places deep in the oak forest like nameless and forsaken Iron Age monuments.

Reeves and his men followed Price's Confederate Army all the way through the Ozarks and up to Iron Mountain. It was the first time the Fifteenth had left its home ground, but they were after Major Wilson, and nothing could stay them. Price's army attacked the Union garrison at Iron Mountain and drove them out. It was later told that on the night of the retreat Major Wilson gave his watch to his sergeant, saying, Take this for my son, for I will not see the dawn of another day. Thus it proved to be. On the road to St. Louis the Union forces were scattered and retreating, and it was there that Colonel Reeves caught him. He read Wilson and six of his cohorts the charges of the murder of sixty civilians. He lined up his men and called fire. They left Wilson's body for the hogs, lying to one side of the road to St. Louis.

Then it was with the Confederate general Price as it had been with the Union general Davidson. They paid themselves through the Ozarks as whey through muslin. The great Confederate Army went up the Military Road singing, never to be seen again.

Afterward the Union Militia came back and built their fort at Iron Mountain all over again. Then they came down raiding with an even greater fury than before.

Oct. 29, 1864

Dear Wife and Children; I take my pen with trembling hand to inform you that I have to be shot between 2 & 4 o'clock this evening. I have but few hours to remain in this unfriendly world. There are 6 of us sentenced to die in retaliation of 6 Union soldiers that was shot by Reeves men. My dear wife don't grieve after me. I want you to meet me in Heaven. I want you to teach the children piety, so that they may meet me at the right hand of God. . . . I don't want you to let this bear on your mind any more than you can help, for you are now left to take care of my dear children. Tell them to remember their dear father. I want you to tell all my friends that I have gone home to rest. I want you to go to Mr. Conner and tell him to assist you in winding up your business. If he is not there then get Mr. Cleveland. If you don't get this letter before the St. Francis River gets up you had better stay there until you can make a crop, and you can go in the dry season.

It is now half past 4 a.m. I must bring my letter to a close, leaving you in the hands of God. I send you my best love and respect in this hour of death. Kiss all the children for me. You need have no uneasiness about my future state, for my faith is well founded and I fear no evil. God is my refuge and my hiding place. Good-bye Amy

Asey Ladd

—Asa Ladd, a Confederate prisoner of war in Gratiot Street Prison, St. Louis, who was selected along with five others by the Union command of that city to be executed in retaliation for Reeves's execution of Major James Wilson of the Union Militia. Ladd was from southeastern Missouri.

I<small>T WAS THE THIRD YEAR OF THE WAR AND BY NOW THERE WAS HARDLY</small> anybody left in the country except the women and the children. The men were gone with Colonel Reeves to live in the forests, and many families had fled to Texas or St. Louis. Abandoned house places looked out with blank windows from every hollow and valley in the Ozark mountains so that at night the wind sang through the disintegrating chinking as if through a bone flute.

Adair Colley had just turned eighteen in early November of 1864 when the Union Militia arrested her father and tried to set the house on fire. Her sister Savannah saw them first; a long line of riders in blue trotting in double column as they turned into the road that led to the Colley farm.

All through the last three years of the war Adair's father had tried to keep his children close to home. Because he was a justice of the peace, he was called Squire, and the newspapers he subscribed to came addressed to Squire M. L. Colley. Her father had determined to stay out of the war and keep his children out of the reach of soldiers of either army and he had succeeded in this for three years. He read in the Little Rock paper that the Missouri Union Militia was being thrown together out of troops dredged up from the riverfronts of St. Louis and Alton, from the muddy Missouri River towns. Men who joined up for a keg of whiskey and five dollars a month.

The trained and disciplined Union troops had long ago been sent to the battlefields of the East, to Virginia and Tennessee, while the hastily recruited Militia had been sent down into the Ozarks to chastise the families whose men had gone to the Southern Army, to catch and arrest them when they returned from their six-month enlistments, and to punish those who might be suspected of harboring Southern sympathies.

Adair's father did not know what the law was on this matter, concerning men who had been in the Southern Army and had returned home and were soldiers no longer, or those who had never joined up at all but had no means of proving it. But it was no matter, for the Union

Militia knew no law. After they burnt down the courthouses they then began to ambush the mail carriers, so the southeastern Ozarks seemed a place cut off from the entire world.

Adair's father read to them in the evenings out of the rare newspaper he managed to acquire, the Memphis *Appeal* and the St. Louis *Democrat*. Adair sat on the clothes trunk to stare at the fire and listen to the inflamed prose of the *Democrat*. She would rather he read the racing news from the Nashville paper, for she wanted to hear if Copperbottom's sons were running but the war consumed everything, even human thoughts and horse races.

There are four main rivers coming down out of the southeastern Missouri Ozarks into the Mississippi. They are the Eleven-Point, the Current, the Black, and the Saint Francis. For three years Adair had seen at a distance soldiers of both armies riding up these river valleys in search of one another. Her brother, John Lee, rode to the ridges to stand watch for them every morning, for the Fifteenth Missouri Cavalry under Colonel Reeves would take your horses as quick as would any Militia. He watched for their smoke, at dawn when the soldiers would be lighting their breakfast fires. He did not go to war himself for he had a withered arm. So the Union Militia raided and set fire to the outlying places all around the Colley farm but continued somehow to miss them.

All through this time Adair's father remained absorbed in his books of law, his newspapers passed from hand to hand down the Wire Road or the Nachitoches Trace by neighbors or one of the few travelers. The light fell from the twelve-paned windowlights onto the harvest table as he wrote, arguing to editors the causes and the Constitutional points of the war in letters that became harder and harder to mail.

As the war dragged on, Adair began to hear from her cousins and from what neighbors remained to them that women were being taken by the Union Militia and sent to prison for disloyalty, that the women were accused of supplying clothing and food to their brothers, their fathers, husbands, sons, or cousins who rode with Timothy Reeves.

That the Union had arrested and sent away the Blakely sisters and the Sutton girls and old Mrs. Holland from Jack's Fork. Nobody seemed to know where it was that the women were being held in that far city, but after a while word came back that it was in places called Gratiot and the St. Charles Street Prison for Women.

In stained coats of Federal blue the Militia came upon the towns of Doniphan Courthouse and Alton, the Crites homestead and all the house places down Pike Creek and the Current River, carrying away jewelry and horses, quilts and silver, to be sold on the black market in St. Louis. They burned houses and shot whoever got in their way. They beat Adair's father in the face with such force Adair thought they had put his eye out. They used a wagon spoke and afterward they threw it away stained with his blood and hair.

The Militia got the horses and then broke their way inside the house. One soldier started shoveling the coals from the fireplace out over the floors and onto the big harvest table, while another tipped over the china cabinet and started dancing up and down in the dish fragments, singing, *Oh sinner, come view the ground, where you shall shortly lie. . . .*

There was a thin November snow coming down at that time from behind the Courtois Hills, light skeins of snow unwinding themselves over the valley of Beaverdam Creek. Then it turned to a hard rain. It was this that saved the house. The cold rain came down driving like hail, and steam blossomed hot out of the fireplace where water was streaming down the chimney. A strong wind came up out of the south-west and blew off Adair's bonnet and tore at her bonnet strings until she thought they would cut her throat.

While the girls fought the fire the Militia carried out everything from the house in the way of food or valuables that they found. They came out of the house with their coat collars turned up against the rain, their arms loaded, and between the door and their wagon was a trail of spoons and bobbins and trodden paper. Then they went on, taking her father away in their commissary wagon with his arms tied behind him and without a hat. The rain beat into his face, and the blood ran draining down in thin streams. Then the tilting wagon and the soldiers went off into a world of hammering water and the iron tires were surrounded by a thin halo of spraying mud. By evening the Little Black River had risen to flood stage.

So it was in the third year of the Civil War in the Ozark mountains of southeastern Missouri, when Virginia creeper and poison ivy wrapped scarlet, smoky scarves around the throats of trees, and there was hardly anybody left in the country but the women and the children.

2

Sixty-nine years ago last week [September 1863] the people of Shannon County [southeastern Missouri Ozarks] were thrown into grief over the murder of John West, Mrs. Sam West, Louis Conway, James Henry Galvon, Wm. Chilton, Henry Smith, Sam Herring, Jack Herring, John Huddleston, John Story, and Joshua Chilton. . . . As the story is told by relatives of the victims . . . a company of Federal soldiers came over from Rolla to the vicinity where the Chiltons lived and the drive on the various homes was made in the dead of night. . . . [The Federals; i.e., Union Militia] started their raid going for the Chiltons. . . . Joe Butler and Alex Chilton were at the home of the latter's mother, and just as they were mounting to leave, eight Federal soldiers came in sight. The soldiers dashed in pursuit, but Mrs. Susan Orchard, sister of Alex Chilton, stepped into the road in front of the oncoming soldiers and flaunted her apron in front of the horses of the soldiers, until they stopped, and by the time the pursuers got around her the fleeing pair were too far gone to be caught.

—J. J. Chilton, from the *Current Local*, November 12, 1931, reprinted in
The Civil War in Carter and Shannon Counties, West Carter County
Genealogical Society, Van Buren, Missouri, n.d.

In the year before the war began Adair's father brought home a horse early on a winter night. Adair saw her father coming down the road on Highlander with the lineback dun on a lead following behind, and the two horses were spraying up snow in a froth all around them—

selves. The lantern he carried shone in moving bars between the oaks and then onto the rails of the yard. She ran behind her father through the drifts with her skirts lifted while he led Whiskey into the barn. The dun horse stared at everything about him, alert and suspicious. Her father put him in the end stall away from Gimcrack and Highlander and Dolly. His color was unusual and burnished; the body color was mixed, of pale straw-colored hairs mixed with black hairs, which made a glistening gray-gold, and as he moved restlessly in the stall the color shifted in the lantern light, as if his coat was of twill or taffeta. His mane and tail and legs were black. There was a line of black up his spine, and faint tiger stripes on his legs where the black faded into the body color. His head began dark and then trailed off to gold around the muzzle. He had a strong body, a high-arched neck, and his long black tail was set high.

Is he mine? She reached out to stroke his neck. His winter coat was thick and healthy.

He's yours, daughter.

Adair held up the candle-lantern to see the blue lights that shone in his corneas, and the dun horse stared at the yellow flame for a moment, and then turned again to look around him and called out to Highlander. His nostrils were large and full and she could see every eyelash over his dark eyes. Before they went back into the house Adair took her saddle from the junk stall rail and put it on his back to see if it would fit, and it settled well on his withers.

Now come in and leave him be, said her father. He's in a new place and I suspect he is uneasy, so leave him be awhile.

Adair went inside to the drawing room and sat down on the clothes trunk by the fire. She didn't want anybody to talk to her so she could think about the trails she and Whiskey would ride on in the morning. With a horse like that she could attempt the crossing of the Current River and ride on to Slayton Ford. She could make it all the way to the Eleven-Point. She could be gone most of the day without tiring him. There were only a few years left to her before she would have to marry and be closed up in a noisy house, trapped by domesticity. Adair dreamed often of the waste places and their silences. Places where nobody lived and so there would be no smoke and dirt and ceilings and mindless talking, only herself and the clean snow and the way the world went at every cant and turn of the seasons, and herself riding through it.

You can't be riding that horse out at all times of the day and night, her brother said. I need that horse sometimes too.

I'll ride out whenever I want, said Adair. She laid out her heavy stockings and lace-ups in front of the fire. And when I say I'm going, don't stand in the doorway.

Savannah, get rid of that skunk, said Little Mary. It does its business in the corners. There's some over there now. I can smell it.

Savannah sat on the upturned churn with a skunk kitten in her hands. It was born out of season, she said. The skunk turned its triangular head to look in amazement at the fire, and then gazed up into Savannah's face. Its paws moved in erratic, vague motions. And the cats got the other ones. Just left heads and feet lying there around the milk vessels. All it can eat is milk.

Well, get it out of the family room anyhow.

It's hungry, poor baby. Savannah got up and went into the kitchen. She was nearly fifteen and all her maternal instincts were in full bloom.

Adair, you listen to your brother, her father said. It's your horse but he gets to borry it sometimes. Her father was reading. He didn't want any arguments. He'd do anything to get out of an argument when he was reading. The pamphlet was "Missouri Report: *Dred Scott vs. Emerson*." He said, Be kind to one another. We are about to go to war. It's going to be the great American war. Bigger than ary war we had yet. They've invented right smart of new kinds of armaments. Be kind to one another. He slowly turned the pages by the light of a coal-oil lamp.

He had endured them all with a great deal of patience. Adair's mother had been taken from them with a fever in 1855. Because their brother was a hunter and the three girls had few skills at weaving or

cooking, they lived an untidy life and were improvident and argumen-
tative and content.

You bought that horse for me. Adair got to her feet. This isn't fair.
You give Whiskey to me.

I can't believe you are talking to Pa like that, said Little Mary. She
sat across from Pa wrapped in her heavy knitted shawl. She was braiding shoestrings. He is the only parent we got. You were supposed to
take over milking April when she come fresh and you never did. Little
Mary was a twelve-year-old martinet, a person Adair thought was
already fit to be running a girls' seminary.

I ain't here to do your bidding, Mary.

Girls, said her father. He turned a page.

And her brother said, Girls! Girls!

You just lay a hand on my horse, John Lee, said Adair.

The fire raided the interiors of the hickory logs thrown on it, and
their faces turned to it. The smell of hickory and the sharp smell of
oak. The moon looked briefly in the window and then the snow started
up again.

Well, when are you riding? said John Lee. We could study out how
to share the cussed horse if we could come to an agreement.

You're behind in all your work, said her father.

Well, what? said Adair. There's nothing that needs doing tomorrow
morning. Savannah can milk. She just loves that sorry old cow to death.

She looked in the clothes trunk for some kind of gloves. She found a
pair of crocheted lace mitts, and although they were very old and formal and raveling loose, she thought they would do as well as anything
else. The old clothes trunk Adair sat on was filled with quilts and odd
leavings. Her mother had saved everything and was extremely prudent,
for in this wilderness, who knew when she could replace clothing or
women's tools? It contained a Log Cabin quilt of great age and almost
every discarded piece of clothing her family had worn since 1819. The
Log Cabin was made from the remnants of clothes of family long gone
on before, from their Sunday and wedding clothes, pieces of figured

silks and velvets. Their mother had said there were stories in it, some of them scandalous. When she died, she had taken most of the scandals to the grave with her unspoken.

I need him tonight, said John Lee. He was sitting in front of the fireplace, his heels out on the hearthstones, his leather leggins smoking. To himself he said, Shit fire and save the matches. He held his shrunken left arm in his right. He had stood the smoothbore in the corner. Either me or Pa are on Highlander all the time, he's about wore out. John Lee turned in the chair to look at his father. The pockets of his hunting coat were full of .58 caliber conical balls, and they thudded together when he turned.

You can't have Dolly, said Savannah. She had come to the doorway from the kitchen. Dolly is very emotional.

John Lee snorted and turned back. His black hair fell in his face. Adair can't ride that horse all day ever day.

All the time, said Adair. And I am going to start at first light tomorrow.

When the Dipper's handle had turned under the mountains she went to the outhouse where the frozen shit down in the vault was piling up into a rigid peak until it nearly reached the seat but her father would not do anything about it and John Lee was going hunting so everything was left up to the girls. She turned over a gourd of fireplace ash into the pit. In the kitchen she filled the wooden bucket with hot water and washed herself under her nightgown and thought she would rather live in the woods than put up with people like this.

Upstairs, Savannah lay asleep with two kittens and the pet skunk so Adair pulled her own feather tick onto the floor and slept there.

ADAIR GOT UP AT SIX THE NEXT MORNING IN THE DARK AND PUT THE girls' hand mirror in her dress pocket. Then she took a pinch of salt out of the salt box and sprinkled it on the coals of the fire. She watched the sparks but saw no message in them of the man she was to marry. She did it once again and thought she might have seen the face of a soldier. One of the young men of the county.

Outside, as she passed the kitchen window, she watched her breath appear before her in the lamplight and then it died away in moist clouds. This was the smoke of her internal fire and her soul. Every breath was a letter to the world. These she mailed into the cold air leaning back with pursed lips to send it upward. She stood and listened to the black wolves on Courtois singing up and down the scales. She held a candle in her hands and it shone in bars through her fingers on the snow.

She went to the barn and put the candle in its sconce against the crossbeam of the main stall. The girls' sidesaddles were lined up on the rail of the junk stall. She put her saddle on Whiskey. His taffeta coat shone in different colors as he moved, from gold to tobacco to gray, and he was anxious to get out of the stall. Adair knew he was a horse of great courage and amiability by the way he cocked his ears toward her and listened to her when she spoke to him.

She led him out to the yard rails and the world was silent, and this silence was a coin to be spent very carefully. She wadded up her skirts so she could get her knee around the leaping horn and put her left toe into the stirrup. She wore her brother's long johns under her skirts and heavy stockings rolled down over her light shoes. Then Adair and Whiskey rode out into the dawn along Beaverdam Creek, and the snow was as pale as mist and the pack that belonged to the black wolf was running through the pines on the ridges above them.

They began to gallop and the snow flew up around her in waves. It was the winter of 1860–1861, before the war had begun. Whiskey charged forward, she could hardly hold him back, he wanted to leap out into the world and find out what was in it. Adair braced her weight on her right thighbone, gripped the leaping horn with her right knee against the surge of his gallop. They ran straight through the glassy black pools of Beaverdam where new snow massed white on the banks. The water spouted around her in fountains and her skirts billowed out behind her.

They rode down the valley of Beaverdam Creek, on to where it narrowed. They charged up the ridge trail at a full gallop and passed her mother's grave and its armor of flat limestones. When they gained the top of the ridge, even from that distance she could hear the percussive grinding of Ponder's Steam Mill on the Little Black River. There while they stood the sun came up. It boiled up molten in the cold pines and lit every massive trunk as they stood in their ranks. Struck the top of the mountains, and made mists in the valleys.

Whiskey stepped out eagerly, his ears up, his neck arched high, looking for the next new thing. They came to the Blue Hole spring. The spring sprawled out of a bluff of limestone and was caught in a mossy dam someone had made. You were supposed to lean backward over a well and look at the well water in the mirror to see the face of your future intended. But there were so many rivers and creeks and springs in the hills that nobody dug wells. The pool of the Blue Hole spring would have to do. Her cousin Lucinda Newnan said these devices told only what your own desires were, and these tricks of descrying the future just revealed a girl's own intentions and not a thing else. But Adair wanted to know somehow, for the wrong man could shut you up in a house, he could take your horse away from you if he proved to be cruel, and put him to a plow, and beat you with a broom handle and no one could rescue you. She had not heard of anyone who hadn't married, except the Witch of Slayton Ford. She had to know. Perhaps she was asking to see the wrong man so she could be forewarned. Could see his dark intentions even though they were hidden behind a handsome face.

She tied Whiskey to a low limb, and then sat at the foot of a sycamore that leaned out over the pool. She sat down in the snow, with her head tipped back and the hand mirror held overhead. Leaned farther and farther back, trying to bring the pool's surface within the small moon of the hand mirror. And at last it appeared. The rocks below the surface formed a face, and the reflection of the back of her own head made it seem that the face was surrounded with dark hair, and a small fish swam out of the teeth. Well, who is it? She thought. Who is it?

Her breath clouded the mirror and she wiped it on her sleeve and looked again. She thought of the boys of Ripley County and Carter and Butler, almost all of them ready to go away to war, and could recognize none of them. What lay beneath the water was the face of a stranger in limestones the color of bone with topside minnows floating through his head like intentions that she could not decipher. Her fingers in the crocheted gloves were cold. A brown, dry oak leaf fell into the water and the stranger smiled. Adair gasped and the mirror fell out of her hand into the pool. It flashed and wavered into darkness. She beat the snow from the back of her skirt and although she tried to find the little mirror with a sycamore rod, and later with a cant hook, she could never recover it.

But in general, and whenever they wished, Union troops shot or hanged their prisoners, as did their guerilla foes. Many soldiers alluded to this widespread practice, but few so matter-of-factly as Private Edward Hansen . . . who had joined the Union Second Missouri Light Artillery. On July 19, 1864, near Patterson [southeastern] Missouri, Hansen noted in his diary, "Up to this day we had done but little skirmishing and catched several fellows, very mistrusting figures, which we had orders to take with us as prisoners, but no sooner did we find one in arms we just hung them to the next best tree."

—FROM *Inside War: The Guerilla Conflict in Missouri, 1861–1865,*

BY MICHAEL J. FELLMAN,

OXFORD UNIVERSITY PRESS, NEW YORK, 1989

The Federals came to our home two or three days later and began to try to persuade Mother to have Father come in and surrender and go to Pilot Knob [Iron Mountain] and take the oath of allegiance. Meantime, while mother was discussing the matter with them, two of them took me up on a hill west of the house and out of sight of mother, and one of them took a belt from around his pants and buckled it around my neck, then bent a small sapling over and tied the end of the belt around it and hung me up for a minute or so. I had told them where father was, as mother had told them, and when they let me down I told them he was down in the field, which they knew was not so for they had come by the field. The hanging hurt my throat so that it was sore for several days. I was seven years old at the time.

—J. J. CHILTON, FROM THE *Current Local*, MAY 26, 1932, REPRINTED IN

The Civil War in Carter and Shannon County

A give-and-take war developed between Reeves' 15th Missouri Cavalry, CSA, and the Missouri Union Militia units in the area. Many families were forced to refugee, some as far north as St. Louis.

—FROM *A History of the 15th Missouri Cavalry Regiment, CSA*, BY JERRY PONDER,

PONDER BOOKS, DONIPHAN, MISSOURI, 1994

THEIR FATHER WAS TAKEN ON NOVEMBER 16, 1864.

Well, here they come, said Savannah. She stood at the door with a handful of quills and the penknife. I don't know why we thought they'd keep on missing us.

John Lee, go on, said her father. Cut the horses loose and get up the hill.

Her brother John Lee ran, going straight up Copperhead without bothering about the path, for they were taking prisoner all young men of military age whether they were crippled or no.

Then Savannah ran to the fields to chase Dolly into the hills. The ground was hard frozen as stone and she fell down and then got up again and kept running. Adair shoved the clothes trunk out the front door and threw the washing over it.

They wore dark blue. They were young men from St. Louis or from the river towns. Their horses were ganted, rake thin, and the blue coats torn and faded, for they had been long in the field and the Ozark mountains were a geography that could beat men and equipment and horses all to pieces. The fenders and girths of their saddles were scarred and repaired with whang leather. They were hungry-looking and cold and rank, jangling loose in their saddles at a hard trot. They watched from one side to the other in a nervous, habitual searching stare, as if looking for the rebel bullet that might strive toward them

out of the deep woods of the southeastern Ozarks and blow them out
of their saddles.

Their father stood at the front-yard rails to meet them.

A captain on a sorrel horse pulled up and asked Marquis Colley what
unit he had joined.

He said he had never joined any military unit and that they had no
business messing with him.

The captain asked him who taught the common school, and Adair's
father said that he himself did, except it had been burnt down and a
new one had not been built because of the war and the hard times that
had come on everybody.

What were you teaching them? asked the captain.

Geography and the structure of the Constitution, he said. And their
arithmetic and their spelling.

Adair and Little Mary stood behind their father. Adair could not see
Savannah but she was fairly certain that Savannah had come back from
chasing Dolly away, to the back of the house to run the pigs out over
John Lee's tracks.

I bet you are teaching them about the advantages of human bondage,
said the captain. You are instructing them in disloyal thoughts.

I am not instructing anybody in anything, said Judge Colley. At
present.

Where's your boy? Ain't you got a boy?

He's gone to Cape for flour.

Well, we are levying a tax on you for the war effort, said the captain.

The Militia took everything the Colley girls had garnered and spun
and sheared and gathered into casks. They took the butternuts in their
split-oak baskets, they loaded their commissary wagon with the corn. A
sergeant cut ten yards of jeans twill out of the loom. They shot the
dogs and took as many chickens and geese and pigs as they could catch.
They tied the chickens and geese by their legs to the ringbolts of the
wagon. The gander and several hen geese got away by taking to the air.
The rooster beat his way into the blackberry thickets; two soldiers
kicked at the brambles and thrashed at them with their rifle butts but

they could not dislodge him. Another came out of the barn pen leading the milk cow and her calf. Two other soldiers seized the horses, including Whiskey.

Adair fought with the soldier who had Whiskey and tried to wrench his hands loose from Whiskey's halter. His fingers were very hairy, and they locked hands and turned and turned in the wintry front yard. They tore through the red honeysuckle vines. It was sensual and cruel, and Adair would not let go. She held on even when he slammed her knuckles up against the yard rails.

They fell over the soap-boiling fireplace, Whiskey was snorting with such force he was whistling like a stag and he flung his head up and down, and backed up away from them, dragging them with him. Finally another soldier came up behind her and struck her across the shoulders with something, and knocked her down.

When she got to her feet, she saw other soldiers setting the house on fire. They threw as many objects as they could into the fireplace and then shoveled coals all over the floor and table. The smoke expanded inside, thick and yellow. Adair let go of Whiskey in order to help her sisters drag things out of the house. So the soldiers tied Whiskey and Gimcrack and Highlander to the back of their wagon. One soldier had set the barn on fire and it was well on its way to making a great November bonfire, the smoke pouring upward into the oaks and the crows flying overhead.

The Union Militiamen also dragged things out of the house and went through the kitchen to take what seemed to them desirable or valuable. They smashed the Tennessee looking glass just to be smashing it. They took her mother's cut-glass decanter. They threw the girls' bonnets in the fire and the family Bible as well. They took a nail bar to the spring wagon and jacked the swivel off the striker plate, and knocked the wheels off their hubs. Adair began to scream that the house was afire, as the outside walls of the house took on a layer of flames, rippling upward in the increasing wind.

Then the rain came in sheets. It stormed through the open windows and soaked *The Horse Fair* in its frame, and the fire began to sizzle like frying bacon and then the flames diminished.

The captain and a sergeant bent Marquis Colley's hands behind him, tied them with rope. They said they were taking her father in for disloyalty. A man was never too old to be disloyal. The captain struck Marquis Colley several times in the face with a wagon spoke. Adair and Little Mary tried to put themselves between the captain and their father, but the sergeant kicked Little Mary's legs out from under her and then kicked her again in the ribs when she was down.

Don't touch my girls, said Marquis. Leave my girls alone.

The captain grabbed Adair by the hair and threw her to one side.

If you keep on, I'll shoot him right here, he said.

I know you, Tom Poth, her father said to the captain.

And I know you, Marquis Colley, said the captain. He was a red-headed man. I don't know how you got elected justice of the peace. Tom Poth had teeth that were very white and small. You gave aid and information to Price, didn't you?

I never spoke to any of his men or officers, said her father.

Yes you did, said Captain Poth and raised the wagon spoke and struck Marquis Colley in the face again and again, and then began to beat him in the head and the sound of it was as if he were striking a melon. Blood sprayed. Adair ran to the tailgate and tried to climb over it. Her father's head fell forward and began to drain blood all down the front of his coat and striped shirt. A soldier shoved her off the tailgate.

We're back, said one of the others. Several men laughed. We're just cleaning up the last few here. You all are about all that's left.

The driver of the wagon raised the long reins and slapped them on the horse's rumps and they surged forward into their collars.

Adair and Little Mary ran after the Union Militiamen in the rain, holding to the gunnel of the wagon where Marquis Colley sat with his arms bound, his face looking like a mask made of red stuff that began to run pinkish in the heavy cold rain. Gimcrack and Whiskey and the tall, dark Highlander were being dragged behind and their long necks stretched out in resistance. Whiskey's changeable coat had turned a sodden tobacco color in the rain and he kept trying to turn his head to see where Adair was, and called out furiously to her.

Then Little Mary's skirts grew heavy in the rain and she had to let go of the gunnels. Adair tried to climb up on the running board to lay hold of the brake and throw off its catch, but one of the men guarding her father banged her fingers with the butt of his rifle, and Adair had to let go and fall back.

JOHN LEE CAME BACK DOWN THE MOUNTAIN AFTER THE MILITIA WERE gone. They all stood inside the house among the wreckage and the smoke. Savannah and Little Mary ran around and closed the shutters again. The barn was still burning for some reason, taking with it the girls' sidesaddles and the harnesses.

John Lee said he had best get clear of the house before they came back again. He sat with the smoothbore in his good hand and the withered arm tucked in his belt.

I'll get Pa loose from them, he said. I think you should head north toward the Yankee garrison. At least they ain't fighting up there. I don't think they will hurt women. That's what Father said. I will be looking for you on the road. Just get moving.

Adair said, Can't we follow them and talk to their commander? Let's go and speak with their superior officer. That's what the Laphams did. Adair fastened her bruised hands together in a hard grip. She wiped her face on her shoulder and her shoes gritted on the broken glass. They got Mr. Lapham back.

John Lee, can't you follow them and shoot them? Savannah said. You could lay up somewhere and get that captain in the head.

I don't have the firepower, said John Lee. And I'm on foot. I will try to get to Doniphan Courthouse and get old Mrs. Carter to enquire for Father. If they see me they'll take me. He wiped his right hand across both eyes to sear off his tears. Where's Dolly?

Savannah said, I ran her up Copperhead.

All right. I'm going, girls.

He struck off on foot with the old smoothbore. He carried it as always in the crook of his right arm. He was bent against the driving winter rain, and his hat brim was drooped and streaming water.

So Adair and Little Mary and Savannah gathered what they could from what was left in the house. They couldn't do anything about the barn, it was burning despite the rain. As they stood there part of the hayloft floor came down on the barrels of pitch and lard below, and crushed the big barn loom and the hand gin.

In the house, Adair found that their bonnets were burned up, both the winter ones and the summer straw ones. She threw the washing off the clothes trunk and dragged it back into the house. She found her good embroidered mandarin jacket and put that on, then wrapped herself in her mother's plaid shawl, and put woolen blankets around the girls. She found in the clothes trunk a pair of her brother's old ankle jacks that he had worn when he was ten years old, and they looked as if they would fit her. She changed shoes because her own black shoes were not sturdy.

In that trunk she also found a pair of men's smallclothes, the old style knee britches, and made Little Mary put them on under her skirts to keep warm. The knee britches came down to Little Mary's ankles. Adair found a black velvet bonnet that must have been made in 1820, as it had a crown like a top hat and was turned up in front. It still had a jaunty feather. The tag inside said it was made by Elizabeth Nighswonger in Charlotte, North Carolina. She put it on Savannah. Savannah threw it off on the floor and said she would die before she wore it.

Well, you will die of the cold, then, said Adair. I ain't got no use for you whining and sick. Just wear the blanket, then.

Savannah made a sobbing sound, but she picked up the old bonnet and put it on. Adair went again through the clothes trunk, and there in the very bottom she found a coin purse beaded in black bugle beads, and in it, five silver shillings dated 1779. She was very surprised and closed her hand around them. She took up the satin-and-velvet Log Cabin quilt in its linen wrapping. It had to be used. There was no help for it.

Adair got down on her hands and knees on the charred floor and started going through all the litter. She found the sapphire-and-diamond earbobs lying beside the overturned dish cabinet. The earbobs appeared to be just more fragments of china. She took a round tin that once had held the crystalline medicine called blue mass and filled it with soft soap from the crock, and jammed the earbobs inside. She took up her beaded bag in which she had kept *Friendship's Offering* and small articles of sentimental value and put it in the carpet sack as well.

Take two dresses apiece, girls, she said. And wad up the others and put them under the mattresses. If we're going to be talking some Militia commander into letting Pa go then we can't be looking like white trash.

Can we talk them into letting him go? Little Mary stood breathing out fog in the corner, watching the rain come in.

I don't know.

They're going to kill him, said Little Mary. She stared at Adair, as if she had become frozen with the thought.

Shut up, they are not.

Then Adair went to where the coats were hanging on pegs in the kitchen. Adair found her father's short-brimmed felt hat, the one he called his tavern hat. It had a low crown and at some time he had stuck a turkey feather in it. That must have been before he took the temperance pledge. She put it on, feather and all. They looked like circus clowns in their peculiar headwear.

So at that time Adair and her little sisters had decided to walk north 120 miles to Iron Mountain where the Yankee garrison was, and it was a long cold walk. At least they would be out of the way of the warring. Adair could not take her little sisters south for they were warring all the way down to New Orleans, and all through Arkansas.

That night Adair and her sisters slept in the half-burnt house in their parents' bed, listening to the black wolf and his pack singing up on Courtois. By midnight the weather cleared, and the barn was burnt to a glowing structure, still resolutely standing. It stood like a frame of thin wires of light, an architect's drawing in fire. Like the luminous outline of a barn drawn in phosphorus against the dark hills. Their neighbors did not come to them, for Adair and her sisters could see the smoke of their neighbors' houses as well, and toward the burned town of Doniphan Courthouse they heard the pop of rifle fire and then the crisp hiss as it echoed from hill to hill. The road was shining with broken fragments of light reflected from puddles and at a long distance they heard it again; a sharp report. A moon came up, detached and bony, journeying through the early winter stars. Then the moon was gone and there was only the Milky Way and its deep river.

THE NEXT DAY ADAIR AND HER SISTERS BEGAN WALKING. THEY BEGAN TO walk in the streams of refugees afoot as if they were white trash. It was in that stream of walkers lone and frozen every one that someone denounced her to the Yankees.

4

Diary of Private Timothy Phillips, Nineteenth Iowa Infantry Regiment, Ozark Mountains, February 25th; "Refugees continue flocking to us and dare not return to their homes." February 28; "Plenty of women in camp begging for rations." March 19; "We have now here some two dozen women and not less than a hundred children—more or less—varying in age from two weeks to fifteen years." March 5; "Refugees are coming in daily. An order has been given to build a stockade around the court house . . . every two or three days we find a body floating in the river."

In April, receiving orders to join the Vicksburg campaign, the Nineteenth pulled out of [the Ozark town of] Forsyth, burning the town, stockade, courthouse and all. Phillips made no more mention of the refugees.

—FROM *Inside War*

October 1, 1864—Some fifteen or twenty women and children were brought in this afternoon, and are now quartered in a building opposite Gratiot [military prison, St. Louis]. I do not know whether they are prisoners or refugees, but one thing I am certain of—they are the raggedest and dirtiest set I ever saw; some of them have not sufficient clothing to hide their nakedness. They were picked up in the southwest (part of the state). Some of the women would be really goodlooking if they were properly dressed, but they are a pitiful looking crowd in their present condition.

—GRIFFIN FROST, *Camp and Prison Journal*

UNION CORRESPONDENCE

Special Orders, No. 270 Saint Louis, Mo., October 3, 1863

VIII. Hereafter all issues of subsistence stores to suffering and destitute refugees &c., will be confined strictly to loyal persons and such only as can prove, by reliable witnesses, that they are, and have been, loyal to the government of the United States since the breaking out of the present rebellion, and that they are, at the time the issue is made, in actual want and danger of starvation if not temporarily relieved. In all cases when "after careful examination," it shall be deemed advisable to issue subsistence to indigent loyal refugees, the issue will never exceed half rations of meat, bread, beans and hominy. . . . The commanding officers of districts, posts, and where these issues are authorized, will be held responsible that this charity of the Government is not abused. The Chaplain will be held accountable that none but really indigent persons in danger of starvation shall receive the allowances.

By command of Major-General Schofield:

J. A. Campbell, Assistant Adjutant-General

—OFFICIAL RECORDS OF THE WAR OF THE REBELLION (OR), CH. XXXIV, P. 601

THEY WALKED UP THE MILITARY ROAD NORTHEASTWARD, INTO THE HIGH Ozarks. They walked one foot in front of the other. They left behind them their grave-places and their dancing places and their animals.

They went past the ruins of the Parmalee place. A spotted mastiff sat at the ash hopper and watched them going past. Wrecked things from the Parmalee house were scattered around the yard. The light wind made the snow in the road lay out in lines like windrows. Adair promised her sisters she would find their father and then go and find Whiskey and Dolly. She would steal Whiskey back. That the Militia would be made to account for everything.

Little Mary doubted this and said so. The copper-colored leaves on the oaks beside the road made a metallic sound in the wind. Adair carried a large carpetbag containing her other dress, and a side of bacon and a book of poetry, the Log Cabin over her shoulder in its linen wrapping like a soldier's bedroll. Little Mary carried a smaller roll of bedding. Savannah trudged along in the snow lugging a pair of saddlebags containing the frying pan and cornmeal.

What about Highlander and Gimcrack? asked Little Mary. You have to keep them in mind.

I got to get Whiskey first, said Adair. So then I won't be afoot and I can locate them.

That Log Cabin was to be my wedding quilt, said Savannah. Mama said.

All right, said Adair.

If we could get up ahead of them and we had the smoothbore we could kill them, said Little Mary. But we're on foot.

Savannah started crying in long, wavering tones. They're going to kill him, she said. They're going to kill him.

Where'd the clock go? said Little Mary.

Adair said, They didn't get it. It had a different kind of time, it was on past time and it wasn't there, it shot itself back into the past, to the year 1859 when it was bought. Savannah, hush up, baby.

They left the Snider boy's corpse lying in the field for three days, said Savannah.

Now hush and listen to me, said Adair. She walked on with a fast, driving stride. Thou shalt not be afraid for the terror by night, nor for the arrow that flieth by day. All things are foreordained. Adair did not know whether she believed this or not, or if she did, whether the foreordainment would be to their advantage at all, but for her sisters she attempted to appear confident of the Lord's good intentions toward them.

The girls were silent. They were thinking this over. The wind came down the hills and they could see it as it moved over the matte surface of the pine forests. They could see it as they stood on top of Anvil Mountain, bent against it. The wind seemed made of iron. It struck Adair full in the face so that she could not get her breath and she felt as if it had bruised her. Then they walked on, anxious to get off the ridge.

Line after line of scudding clouds now came down from the northwest in shades of gray. It began to snow.

As they climbed yet another mountain, and came out on top of Beauford Barrens, they could see a good ways north over the rolling ocean of blue ridges. Adair looked at the distant pine dark hills in the snow and saw that they were very beautiful.

Then up the stony red-dirt road came a man riding a pale cream-colored horse. Adair recognized Greasy John. He came riding up out of the forest onto the Barrens looking around him uneasily and then he spied them.

Greasy John wore a round-topped hat with a short brim. Everyone knew him. He lived in a cave under the bluffs above the Current River. He was entirely greasy, in worn homespun. His feet stuck out sideways in strapped gaiters. He wore an ancient buckskin shirt and a gray blanket over that. He had at one time, they said, been a lawyer in Portageville, had read law somewhere in North Carolina. But he had become enslaved to a depraved appetite for forty-rod whiskey and was content to live his life out in a mess of blankets and furs, tobacco pipes and blackware coated with mutton grease in his limestone cave.

Dear me, said Greasy John. He pulled up and regarded them in the thin winter atmosphere. Their skirt yardages rolled in waves as the breeze took the hems up. He took off his battered hat and tossed his greasy curls as if he were a darling boy, fetching as a pup. You girls are afoot and wandering the roads like orphans.

We're heading north, said Adair. They come by and burnt the barn and took about everything. They took Daddy. We're just going on north.

On north. Where to?

Iron Mountain, nearby to the Yankee garrison. She put up her hand to Greasy John's reins. Ain't you run into the Militia? Tom Poth's men? Where are you wandering to?

Me a-wandering! Girls, the roads are alive with invaders from the distant prairie states. Snow built a sparkling white rind on the edge of his hat brim. We have been invaded by Buckeyes, Hoosiers, and the ice people of Illinois. He lifted a forefinger. We are at war with *Indiana*, of all things. Very shabby state of affairs. He leaned over and spit on the frozen ground and the spit smoked. They is nothing in Doniphan since they burnt it up. I'm going on to Poplar Bluff to see if they don't have some supplies there at the store. I heard they didn't get the Stricklands' stillhouse.

Adair said, Well, I wouldn't know about stillhouses.

No, no, of course not, you all are the Judge's girls.

Adair said, And the Militia took him. Have you seen him?

Your father? You can't hardly recognize anybody these days. He distributed his thin and scholarly hands about in the air, making gestures of amazement. They're either in a uniform or they been beat up.

Well tell me if you have seen him or not! said Adair. She gave the reins a shake as if to knock sense into either him or his horse. The cream-colored horse tipped his head to one side and swung his rear end around to evade her.

I wouldn't have recognized him if I did, he said. They are harrying their prisoners northwards in lines of them. Covered with snow. Up to Iron Mountain to send them here, there, or yonder. He patted himself on the chest. I didn't even know Doniphan had been burnt. Scared the blue Jesus out of me. I had only come into town to locate some saleratus for my biscuits. I absconded on my only horse. Let go them reins.

Adair held on. Trade me this horse for some sapphire earbobs, she said.

Sapphire earbobs. Now wouldn't I be fetching in sapphire earbobs? He laughed with delight. Let go them reins.

Adair let go. Greasy John gazed around him into the rattling dry leaves of the roadside brush, then the other way, leaned down out of the saddle and said,

They are taking some women prisoners. Just go to the Yankee commander if you can tell where he is at this particular moment in time, and tell him you are a Rebel spy, and you won't have to walk all the way to Iron Mountain. You'll be taken there in a *wagon*, in chains.

Adair hit at his cream-colored horse with her fist. Go on, she said.

Greasy John laughed and rode on. He rode through the short grass of the high Barrens and then downhill into the dim snowy columns of the pines. He turned, and called out,

They's a mule running loose near Ten-Mile Creek if you can catch him!

THEY DESCENDED THE HILLSIDES AND WALKED ON INTO THE VALLEY OF Ten-Mile Creek. The pines gave way to oak and sycamore in the bottoms. In the heavy cold shade of the oaks that lined the road, their rusty leaves still clinging, Adair strode on. She told her little sisters that their father would be held in the Yankee camp right now out of the cold. If you thought about it, he would likely be warmer than they were.

So they camped that night in the wind shadow of an upturned maple tree root before a raveling fire. They piled up heaps of leaves and curled up in the piles like canines, covered with their shawls and blankets and the Log Cabin. They lay their heads on the old carpetbag and the saddlebag. All Adair could think of was to get the girls and herself somewhere safe until the war was over, and then come home and see if her father would not be released and come home too. It snowed intermittently in the night and then cleared.

Adair and her sisters saw refugee wagons going past even late into the dark, and the lanterns tied to the backs of the vehicles cast long, revolving shadows on the stony road. The bodies of the immense old water oaks and sycamores of the creek bottom threw their shadows forward into the pouring snow, and then as the wagons passed, the shadows swung around behind the trees and then drained off back down the road and then fainted away into the dark again. Adair lay wrapped in all they owned with her little sisters and watched. It made the old trees seem animate, as if the shadows were their thoughts, and these great woody thoughts came out and took place in the world only when human beings passed by in the night with lanterns. The wolves did not sing that night but to Adair it seemed they conversed among themselves in low voices just outside the blaze of their fire.

The following morning they walked on. They walked wrapped in their heavy plaid shawls, beneath the great iron trees whining in the wind, and they fell in with the other people of the Ozarks in their long retreat. Women also afoot, and old men. They were in the midst of a refugee army carrying quilts and books and burlap-wrapped sides of bacon. The children walked sturdily and did not cry for the war had been going on for three years and they had endured many things.

At Ten-Mile Creek the girls saw wagons lined up to cross, and that someone else had laid hands on the loose mule. He was tied to the ringbolt of a buckboard.

At noon on the road ahead of them, Adair saw a group of refugees stop for a moment and stare off to the right-hand side and then go on. Then in their own line of stragglers Adair and the girls came past three dead Union soldiers laid in the snow, and the snow drifting over their open eyes. One man lay on his back with his hands stiffly in the air and his fingers curved downward. Another was a black soldier and he was almost completely covered with snow. They seemed like dismal piles of rags or trash barely recognizable as having once been human. She couldn't see what had killed them.

Don't look, said Adair. She took her sisters each by a hand and gripped their hands hard. She jerked their arms. Don't look. Look straight ahead and keep walking.

Who shot them? said Savannah.

Nobody, said Adair. They just froze.

They don't look froze.

They were caught in a deer snare. They're not from here, they don't know where the snares are.

The Colley girls bent their heads and walked on, on that stretch of the road between Ten-Mile Creek and Cane Creek, a deeply cut path hardly wide enough for a wagon, which turned and sliced through the red earth of the hills. They walked through drifting tissues of snow.

Savannah, hold hands with me, she said. My hands are cold.

By and by Adair and her sisters came upon Jessie Hyssop, the Witch of Slayton Ford.

Ma'am! Ma'am! said Adair. She ran forward down the road. They were just coming to where a trail turned off the Nachitoches Trace toward Cane Creek Fields.

Well, here you all are, said Jessie. She was a strong woman of no more than forty-five, with heavy hips and thighs and a good-looking face. Her slick brown hair showed under her enormous straw hat. It was not a bonnet but a daisy-wheel hat, with a flat crown. Her skirts were made of gores of all different materials in various patterns. She wore a cloak with a shoulder cape and carried an empty tow sack. Around her danced a pack of feist dogs, shaggy terriers with square ears and bright, mean eyes.

Well, I am glad to see you, said Adair. Last year I wanted to come and talk with you. One of the terriers dashed at her and barked. Adair pulled back her skirts and spat at the dog. Get!

Well, that time has gone, ain't it? said Jessie. I've got these dogs here, and that one has puppies back at the tavern. You wouldn't want to take one to raise, would you? She kept on walking.

No, ma'am, said Adair. Are you burnt out? Adair hurried to walk beside her.

They started to, Jessie said. A big fat sergeant was running around with a torch. But we make good whiskey there at the tavern. The captain says, that's Hyssop's Rest, boys. Leave it be. So this fat sergeant went and shoved the torch under the back kitchen, where the captain couldn't see him do it. The fanatic element has taken over, she said. She marched on. I prayed for rain. I guess the Lord heard me. I was loud enough about it. The Lord sent a general rain over the entire county and it put out the kitchen fire. And I have walked all the way from Slayton Ford in the Irish Wilderness to here for turnips and potatoes.

Yes, ma'am, said Adair. The rain saved our house.

Then how come you are on the road?

They took Pa. They said he was disloyal. Adair kicked at a rock in the road. Disloyal to what?

Jessie reached down and stroked the ears of one of the dogs. Her hand was surprisingly young-looking and rounded with muscle. The small dog stood on its hind legs with its paws on her skirt and stared up into her eyes as if taking in some vital substance.

They'll think of something, said Jessie. I guess they just wanted your horses. That Captain Tom Poth is selling them up to St. Louis. He is a mercenary son of a bitch.

Savannah jabbed her knuckle into Adair's waist and asked, Can she cuss like that?

Little Mary whispered, She's a witch, Savannah, she can cuss if she wants to.

Adair said, Can you tell where he is at?

Your pa?

Yes, ma'am.

By witching? Better ask the Yankee commander.

I thought you could tell things by looking in a pan of water or something.

I am turning off here, said Jessie. To Cane Creek Fields. Then back home. I am going to dig up some of these potatoes from Fursey's old place. Some people can tell things by looking in a pan of water, but I don't care to look anymore.

They are going to kill Pa, said Savannah. She started crying again. She dropped the skillet and Adair picked it up.

A person should really learn the telegraph alphabet, said Jessie. You could talk to people in Georgia if you knew the telegraph alphabet.

Savannah bent her head down and looked at her shoes and continued to cry in low, persistent strangling noises.

We have come to the end of days, said Jessie Hyssop. Whatever kind of days it is we been in. The courthouses are gone and so are records and ain't you seen those men laying dead beside the road? Now we have a world of devices and not of witching.

Well, Jessie, can't you help a person? Adair was so angry she was near tears. I have an old shilling I could give you. Fix it so that I could speak to a horse and he would throw his rider in the Current River and drown him. So I could call Whiskey to me, and he would break his reins and come to me.

That is another matter, said Jessie. Horses are another matter. They are already mostly in the witch world because they eat no meat. You have spent half your life wandering in the woods horseback by yourself or with Lucinda and them girls. Don't you know anything? Jessie's flapping straw hat winged up and down like a sailing crane. I know you, Adair, and I know you'd be gone in the hills for all of your natural life if you could. Your mother used to have to sit watch on you ever second, you were a trial to her.

I was? Adair kept walking beside Jessie.

Yes.

Her sisters came silently behind, and down in the valley of Cane Creek the wind became confused and turned the falling snow into spirals.

Well, Jessie, we are just looking for somewhere to sit out until this war is over, and if a person had the second sight like you do, they could see where other people's loved ones had been carried away to, and their horses too. Do you see spirits?

Yes, but I don't pay any attention to them, said Jessie.

But they come to tell us things.

No they don't. People ain't smart just because they're dead.

Well what are they?

Just mournful. They've lost something and can never leave off looking. Such is the power of desire even beyond the grave. They are trembling with want.

Adair struggled along against the wind with the carpetbag in one hand and the skillet in the other. I don't know how I'd learn the telegraph alphabet. Can't you look in a well, or when you throw out coffee grounds?

Jessie stared into the snowy aisles of the woods for a while. Then she said, I don't know if I could or not. I myself have asked old women for what they knew, and the old women at that time remembered things from old women they had known and so on until the beginning of the world. What they knew didn't always please me.

Jessie had come to the turnoff. The trail to Cane Creek Fields wound through the valley lands now curtained with snow flurries. The wind whistled. Adair came close to hear what she was saying.

We are in the middle of many changes, and this endless changing is become disorder and people cannot long endure disorder. They'll do anything rather than put up with it. Desperate things. Things that they don't want to remember later. Jessie drifted into the snowy air, eastward down the small trace. She turned. Her breath came in clouds.

She waved her hand. The dogs ran around her skirts smelling at the road.

At every crossroads you come to, she called back, pile three stones one on another. For the Father, the Son, and the Holy Ghost. This is to prevent the spirits from coming next behind you.

Adair stood and watched her disappear down the Cane Creek Fields road, among the great valley trees, their limbs crested with snow.

She's just a common woman, said Adair. She runs that tavern over in that town called Wilderness right there in the middle of the Irish Wilderness and there are riotous things that go on over there. She's just a public woman.

What? Savannah raised her head.

Nothing.

You better shut up, Adair, said Little Mary. She'll hear you and do something. Little Mary knocked the drops of moisture from her shoulders. Something you won't like.

Adair stood discouraged and hurt for a while, looking at the ground. She was trying to remember the last time she had put her arms around her father and told him she loved him. How long ago had it been? Until finally her sisters said for them to go on. But before they went on, Adair piled three stones one on the other, for the Father, the Son, and the Holy Ghost.

At Cane Creek Adair and her little sisters found a place to cross where they had to wade only up to their knees. The water numbed them. They took off their shoes, held their skirts up in wads and their bundles overhead in one hand. They forged through.

A wagon came up the Trace behind them, heading north like everybody else. It was driven by a man with a hard face and beside him two women; behind, three half-grown children sat backward, leaning against the seat. The children were staring glumly at the Trace receding away from them and then at the water as the wagon came across. The wagon trundled through the ford, spraying crescents of water from its wheels. The children turned their heads all in unison to look at the Colley girls and then turned back again. The girl had a white eye and both boys had long hair tied back with boot strings. In her shawl the girl held a squirrel head and after staring long at Adair and her sisters, went back to eating on it. Turning it in her fingers to see what meat was left on the bone. The wagon jangled with household goods. Baskets, a clock, a bale of blankets.

Adair said, Good day, and the man with the reins in his hands said, That's the damndest hat I ever saw.

Adair didn't know which hat he was referring to, but she said, You don't look so good yourself. She and Savannah and Little Mary sat down and tried to dry their legs and cotton stockings without being indiscreet.

Who are you all?

Upshaws.

From where?

From the Irish Wilderness. Near Jessie Hyssop's tavern, town of Wilderness on Slayton Ford.

The man had a pair of jaws like church pews, augmented by a curling brown beard. He said, Reeves burnt us out because we went into the Union Army camp to trade horses. Said we were collaborating.

Well, said Adair. If you been trading for our horses I'll go back and burn down whatever's left. She stared at them with furious black eyes. If you've collaborated for my horse. Whiskey is his name. He's a line-back dun with tiger stripes on his legs. They took him two days ago. And a heavy horse, brass colored, and a dark seal brown with no white on him. Our names are Colley. My father is Judge Marquis Colley.

Well, you ain't nothing special just because your daddy is a squire, said the man.

I never seen horses that looked like that, one of the women said. And don't you go threatening us.

I ain't threatening, said Adair. I am going to find our horses again and anybody who took them will pay for it. The three children, two boys and a girl, turned again all together in a single movement to stare at Adair and kept on staring. I need them to go find my father.

Hush up, Adair, said Savannah. You'll get us taken in.

The horses leaned into their collars and the wagon creaked as it moved forward. The horses had U.S. Army brands on them. The Upshaw children continued to watch her and her sisters as they went off down the road.

Did you see the brands? asked Little Mary.

Also they had a U.S. Army ammunition box in there, said Savannah. The girl was sitting on it.

After another mile the girls came upon them once again. One wobbling wheel had bent itself off the nave and collapsed. The front end had dropped onto the singletree. They were standing in the red dirt of the road and the wind took up the women's skirts and pressed them against their legs and shoes. It scattered the snow in light sprays.

Looks like you're afoot, said Adair. She smiled.

We got these horses to ride, said the woman. You're the ones that are afoot.

Adair and her sisters walked on. They came to the Military Crossing of the Black River and joined the lines of refugees and vehicles waiting to cross on the ferry. Nobody talked much for all they had to speak of were tales of misery and fire, and all these tales were alike, but instead inquired of one another for missing relatives. Mostly the missing were the men but also children had gone astray, and old people.

As they neared Iron Mountain the road became disordered with broken gray basalt. The stones were the size of a skillet and the road had two shallow ruts through a jumbled bed of black stones. On an uphill stretch where the right-hand side fell off into a deep ravine, and the refugees' wagons crashed and battered on the stones, a sign said THE STONY BATTERY: WORST STRETCH OF ROAD MADE BY MAN. Alongside, Adair saw the remains of wheel hubs, broken spokes, horseshoes, and sections of iron tires. Down in the ravine were broken bottles and chairs, things that had fallen from the wagons and that no one cared to climb down and retrieve. The noise of the wagons was deafening.

The following day at noon they found themselves alone on a long stretch of road going up the Saint Francis River valley. Walking between walls of standing dry grasses, big bluestem as tall as they themselves were, bent over as if pointing downwind toward something that had escaped.

At this place their brother rode out of a stand of cane and stood waiting for them. He had a good Union carbine stood up on its butt on his thigh and the reins wrapped around his bad hand.

He sat his horse and nodded to them, and smiled a thin smile. He rode a dwarfish gray horse that had stout legs and a head like a cheese cask. His uniform was of homespun and drawn up by hand, for the Confederacy had long ago abandoned the hopeless task of provisioning any troops whatever north of Little Rock. He had on a pair of laced-up boots that were nearly new, and Adair knew they were U.S. Army issue as well.

Yo, girls, he said. His eyes were watchful. His jaw worked as he searched both ways up and down the Trace.

Adair reached up and took her brother's arm briefly and then let it go. He swung down and put his withered arm around her. Then in turn around Little Mary and then Savannah. He did not let go of the carbine.

Adair heard then the long grinding complaints of alarmed fox squirrels. Somebody was coming up the road. Crows scattered among the treetops like black quarter notes. Then she saw the Upshaw family who had been in the broken wagon coming up the road. The women were riding the harnessed horses sitting sideways and the children riding behind. The U.S. brand stood out clearly on the horses' jaws. The women's bonnets billowed out in the wind. The man was afoot.

John Lee stared at them out of his black eyes without cease until they passed by. They took in the sight of John Lee's uniform and then turned away. They gazed straight ahead, for the whereabouts of a Confederate soldier was a dangerous thing to know. They went past with strange blank countenances as if they had been temporarily struck blind. John Lee bent over and spat on the ground.

Who were those people?

Upshaws, Adair said. They said they were from the Irish.

They said Reeves burnt them out, said Savannah.

For what?

They claimed he caught them going to the Militia to trade horses.

I bet they done more than trade horses.

Where'd you go after you left the house?

I went to Ponder's Mill on the Little Black after the Militia pulled out, he said. You could see the Militia going north along the Military.

Where were you looking from? Adair asked.

Stanger's Steep. He pulled his hat brim down against the stinging light snow. Colonel Berryman was there gathering up men. I bet there was three hundred men there. He stayed about as long as you can hold a hot horseshoe. Then he was off after them. Me along with them. People said they took Pa on north with some other prisoners. Carters said.

Adair bent over against the wind and tucked her hands inside the shawl.

What are we going to do?

John Lee thought about it for a while.

Go on north. They're raiding down here till hell wouldn't have you. Now, I don't want you all living anywhere near the Yankee garrison.

He paused and cleared his throat and spit in the snow. There are women that fall into bad habits in refugee camps. Pa wouldn't want you all near women like that. Go and live with the Daltons at the store on the Saint Francis River. Stay out of the way of everybody.

All right, said Adair. She and her sisters stood around him.

John Lee nodded and watched the tree line. Now look here, what I got. It's a new kind of rifle, what they call a repeater, a Spencer. I can almost shoot it with one hand. But it's hard getting ammunition for it. It takes rimfire cartridges.

Where'd you get that uniform?

The Chilton girls still have a barn loom. I'll be all right. But you all stay safe with the Daltons. They done their best over the whole war to stay out of everything and out of everybody's way. Besides, they're old people and surely they'll let them alone. John Lee ran his bad hand down the breech of the Spencer repeater, for though the hand and arm were withered the sense of touch remained keen and he admired the blued steel. He said, Isn't this one hell of a rifle?

Adair said, I'll go to the garrison first and ask after Pa, then we'll go to Daltons'.

All right. He paused. Take care of that old quilt. The Militia will take it from you.

All right. John Lee, I wish you wouldn't go. We need somebody to go home.

Home's gone.

The house ain't gone.

He had a grave and considering look on his face. He was a tall young male manned by great, silent, driving forces that worked in him like noiseless machinery. He had turned himself and these inchoate forces over to Colonel Reeves's Fifteenth Missouri Cavalry, CSA.

I like soldiering, he said. He rasped his palm on his rough homespun pants. If I live long enough to learn how. He paused again. I tell you what, it's exciting. Traveling around the country with Reeves's fellows. Hunting people. He paused. I shot a man for these shoes. The sun broke through, illuminating the light veils of snow. An explosion of crows in the treetops announced that more people were coming up the road. He stood in the stirrup and settled himself in the dragoon saddle. Though there's some of the men won't wear a dead man's shoes.

Savannah said, Now maybe somebody's wearing Pa's shoes.

Shut your mouth, said Adair. You just keep it up and keep it up.

Stop fighting, said John Lee. Look after one another. Family is all we got.

All right, said Little Mary.

Y'all take care, he said.

He put his spurs to his gray horse. He turned back in the saddle and watched them for a long time and then rode away at a gallop through the foreground snow, and into a path in the thick cane, trailing a cloud of horse breath and flying powder.

Sunday July 24, 1864:

Warm and pleasent in camp. In Camp al day. Enspection of armes by the Captain. Preaching at the schoolhouse. four of our bois from the Scout returned with 2 of the Mayfield girls prisonors. Rote a letter to My Sister and & Recieved on from her. The bois saw nothing of note.

—FROM *Found No Bushwhackers: The 1864 Diary of Sgt. James P. Mallery, Company A, Third Wisconsin Cavalry Stationed at Balltown, Missouri,* PUBLISHED BY THE VERNON COUNTY HISTORICAL SOCIETY, NEVADA, MISSOURI

March 29, 1865, Respectfully returned. The within named prisoners are hereby remanded to prison:

Col: I send you under guard the prisoners; Georgiana Taylor, Sarah L. Taylor, Virginia Taylor, Lydia Taylor, Mary Vaughn, Sarah Vaughn . . . Returned to Captain R.C. Allen the prisoner, John T. Taylor is in the Female Prison. [Probably a child.]

Signed, Albert G. Clark, Chief Examiner, Office Gratiot St. Mil. Prison, St. Louis, Mo.

—FROM *The Little Gods: Union Provost Marshals in Missouri, 1861–1865,* BY JOANNE CHILES EAKIN, TWO TRAILS PUBLISHING, INDEPENDENCE, MISSOURI, 1996

April 26, 1864: Tuesday a scrap of gossip from [the Federal prison for Confederates in] Rock Island was handed round; it seems that one of their prisoners, a portly young fellow in Confederate grey, was lately delivered of a fine boy.

—GRIFFIN FROST, *Camp and Prison Journal*

AFTER A WEEK THEY CAME TO THE IRON MOUNTAIN GARRISON. THEY had walked all the way up the Saint Francis River valley and into that range of mountains that were made of a dark stone the color of cast iron. The Union fort there was stockaded, and the gates were wide open like a mouth. The whole valley beneath Shepherd's Mountain and Pilot Knob had been cleared of trees for the iron furnaces. Loads of supplies were being brought in, teamsters stood on the loads and shouted at the girls to get out of the way. On Shepherd's Mountain they could see the ragged battalions of refugees and their tents of blankets and wagon sheets.

They walked through the confusion. The Union Army was rebuilding what Price had burnt down. Soldiers were making themselves shelters and sewing their own clothes. Some of them called out to the girls. There were Union Militia as well as Regular Army and U.S. State troops. Adair had never seen a gathering of people this large since the recruiting rallies in Doniphan at the beginning of the war. And none of these men were from families she knew, they were aliens with flat accents. A few light flakes of snow drifted from a low sky.

They passed an encampment of Iowans. Adair took off her daddy's hat and walked bareheaded. She was ashamed of the way she and her sisters looked.

Two Iowa soldiers were sitting together on kitchen chairs in front of their tent.

Another wildwood flower, one said. He made kissing noises.

These are the damndest people I ever seen, said the other.

Then why don't you go home? said Adair and walked on.

There were colored people living in tents and shanties at the far end of the breastworks, both escaped slaves and freemen. A tall colored man stood on a whiskey box and addressed the crowd. Adair saw that most of them were colored but white soldiers stood at the back with their arms crossed, listening. Adair and her sisters went close in order to hear what he was saying.

Live as free men! he shouted. But do not use your freedom as a pretext for evil but live as servants of God! So saith the prophet Isaiah!

The women stood holding children by the hands or upon their hips and the light flakes drifted onto their headrags. And the preacher, whose name was William Thurston, stood in the snow and the spraying mud and spoke to them about the gift of belonging to oneself.

The people that walked in darkness have seen a great light! They that dwell in the land of the shadow of death, upon them has a light shined! The crowd of colored people said Amen, Amen in a singing chorus. And from Deuteronomy, chapter thirty, verse three! Then the Lord thy God will turn thy captivity, and have compassion upon thee, and will return and gather thee from all the nations, whither the Lord thy God hath scattered thee! And if any of thine be driven out to the outermost parts of the heavens, from thence he will fetch thee forth! And the women turned to one another and then back, for their thoughts were on their mothers and fathers and other children sold into places they had no knowledge of.

Adair took out one of the silver shilling coins and bought three venison pies from a cook wagon that said SUTLER on a broad banner stretched across the front. The sutlers followed the armies and sold the troops various small articles and oysters and whiskey, and lent them money at high interest when the men had spent everything on drink and yet wanted more.

The sutler held up the old shilling between thumb and forefinger. I ain't seen one of these in a long time, the man said. You hill jacks come up with the damndest things. Mud and snow slush sprayed them from the wheels of a passing carriage with a Union officer in it.

Give me my change, said Adair. The sutler paused for a long time, for she was pleasing to look at with her black hair, her ebony black eyes, and her white skin. Her cheeks now very red from the cold. Adair had never been in such an industrious place of people. They were building and hammering and sawing. Men drilled with rifles and a sergeant chased alongside a column of men screaming at them.

What change you think I ought to give you? And still he stared. Her dress was dirty with the mud of the road and her shoes seemed like hooves they were so hard.

Give me a Spanish milled dollar and we'll call it even, she said. That coin is valuable.

He said, But a shilling is only worth a quarter dollar U.S.

Adair took the coin back and looked at it, and then returned it. Try and see how well it spends, she said. It was good enough for King George, wasn't it?

The sutler laughed at her. Well, go on then, he said, and handed her a Spanish milled dollar. He dragged his eyes away from her as if he were extracting something from a well. Adair took the pies before he changed his mind.

She was so nervous she only ate half of her own, and then put the other half, wrapped in brown paper, into the felt hat, her daddy's tavern hat, and then asked her way to the provost marshal's office. Her younger sisters trailed behind her, holding each other and their pies.

There were guards at the door in Federal blue uniforms. They wore oilskin capes that dripped, so that they were standing in the midst of their own puddles. Inside, an officer behind a counter. The rainy snow beat on the roof.

The guard said, Sir, there are more people here looking for relatives.

The officer was wearing a greatcoat with a buffalo collar and a sort of stovepipe hat.

There's a list hung up on the side of the building, he said. Of everybody in the refugee camp. They put up their names. He turned back to his papers. Or they get somebody to write it for them.

No sir, said Adair. She walked up to the counter. My father was arrested by the Militia a week ago. I want to know where he is at.

What'd he do? The officer tipped his stovepipe hat back. How come he got himself arrested? He had light eyes the color of tin. Behind him on the wall was a list of officers, and the name of the officer in charge was Lieutenant Colonel Miller.

Adair's voice was cracking and so she cleared her throat. She said, He didn't do anything. I want to know where you all took him.

Who was the officer in command?

Captain Tom Poth. And they took our horses and everything else they could lay their hands on.

Put it in writing, said the officer. What is his name? He took in her clothes and her face, a narrow stare.

My father's name is Judge Marquis Colley.

He got up and went to a box of pigeonholes that had been nailed to the wall and looked in several of the slots. He took out a paper.

Look here, he said. He turned and signaled to the guards at the door and they came and took her each by an arm.

You are accused of giving information to Rebel spies, and other things, the officer said. Adair's mouth dropped open and she turned and saw outside the people who had passed them on the Military Trace as she stood talking to John Lee. The man and the two women with the broken wagon. The Upshaws. They were standing in the snow flurries, staring in at the lighted windows of the provost marshal's building, and beside them their children pulled their cuffs down over their bare hands and kicked at the snow. Adair knew that they had denounced her.

She said, Let go of me. I don't want you holding on to me like that.

You are under arrest.

But I never did anything. Adair's voice was ragged, and her mouth was dry. She tried to jerk away from the soldiers who had hold of her arm, but this caused her to drop the tavern hat with the half a pie in it. One of the soldiers, a young man with a round pink face, let go of her arm and reached down to hand it back to her. Are you Lieutenant Colonel Miller?

Yes.

Well, sir, you are going to have to account for this. For arresting me. And everything you stole. You are going to have to account for this.

She tried to pull loose again but this time the guards had taken a harder grip on her arms.

Lieutenant Colonel Miller said, You are giving aid and comfort to the enemy and information as well.

No I didn't, she said. I'd like to know who said that. Adair was becoming reckless. Where's my father? And you have to account for our horses, you have to write down what you took.

The soldiers to either side of her held on to her, and looked from her to the lieutenant colonel.

This state is under martial law, said Miller. The Militia is here to enforce it.

Well, what is marshal's law? said Adair. You explain to me what marshal's law is.

The U.S. Constitution is suspended, Miller said. I am responsible for the security and peace of this region.

I don't know what you call peace, but you all beat up my father and took him away. I may be confused about the term.

Shut up, young woman, said Lieutenant Colonel Miller.

And you are *thieves*, you are thieves.

Shut up, said Miller.

Before they put her on the train to St. Louis she told Little Mary and Savannah to get to the Daltons, back down the Trace to the crossing of the Black River. She gave them the four silver shillings and the rest of her pie. The two girls held hands and stared, bereft, carrying the remnants of their bacon and cornmeal. Adair told them to go there and stay and be good and to help Mrs. Dalton in every way and to pray every night for this family. She said she would escape and come back to them, and send word to them that she was coming. They seemed very dubious about this, and beneath the doubt lay terror. They held each other and did not cry in front of the Union soldiers.

Then she was put into a truck car with three other women on a train north to St. Louis. Three guards sat in the pile of hay with them. Adair had never been on a train before, nor had the other women. They did not speak to one another for the soldiers would not allow it. The steam whistle shrieked so that Adair had to put her hands over her ears. The train began to move, jerking forward. They were all thrown sideways in concert, as if this aggregation of strangers had just become an accomplished dance team.

The wind and snow came in the open door of the truck car and as they went on the straw flew more thickly so that the women had to put their shawls across their faces. Adair held her tavern hat against her chest and wrapped her shawl over her head. The straw was peppered with fleas and manure and it was blowing up into her face. She watched out the open door as the forests tore past them at thirty miles an hour, through deep slashes in the hills that were still raw and red, and over trestles high above the Saint Francis River and the Meramec. The tunnel of limbs they sped through raked at the sides of the car, and steam drifted back.

Adair was silent with amazement. Things had evaporated so quickly she hardly had time to study on it. The other women in the car seemed to her very passive and resigned to being shipped somewhere like cows. Like creatures in bondage, and one of them glanced at Adair and then away again and her face was humble and whipped looking, and Adair wondered how the woman had got beaten down into that state, if it could happen to her as well. She put her fingertips across her mouth to guard herself against the flying dirty straw and the guard saw it, and offered her his canteen. She turned her back on him.

The train engine shrieked with its powerful whistle all through the mountains going north. At Overtop they paused while a second engine backed up to help pull the first one and its train of cars over the grade. The engineer came out and climbed up on the rails alongside the engine to blow the boiler down. He pulled a lanyard and the steam exploded outward along the track and drifted into the truck car. It froze to the pine boles in crystals.

By this time another upsurge of snow had come, a blizzard of snow, and Adair could see out the open doorway how the soldiers' blue coats grew shoulder bars of white. They stood guard while the locomotive engines poured out fire from their chimneys and sent red flashes muffling into the storm.

Adair watched it snow. She wiped tears from her face again, they seemed to flow of their own accord. The soldier who sat beside her wore the insignia of the U.S. Regular Army. He smelled of wet wool. He stared out at the retreating mountains and did not offer to help her again.

Then the train cleared Overtop and they lost the helper engine. They went on north through the tumbling hills, farther and farther north. The track followed the river valleys. The train clanked and jerked around the curves of the Meramec River while snow in drifting curtains swept slow stipples across the black water and the reeds stood up crowned in white. At a place called Jefferson Barracks alongside the Mississippi River Adair saw a great busyness in the train yard, wagons of provisions being unloaded and a troop of Union cavalry boarding their horses onto a cattle car.

The horses made a thundering noise, and she saw how deeply distressed they were, knowing nothing of where they were being sent, pressing up against one another in fear. They surged into the dark cave of the car because they were being whipped into it and could do nothing else. The great river was broad and cold and on the Illinois shore black winter trees turned red in the sunset light.

By this time it was nearly dark. Lights surrounded them, thicker and thicker, Adair had never seen so many gaslights and house lights and streetlights in her life. And so they came to the Pine Street Station in St. Louis.

6

In June, 1864, Major Jeremiah Hackett reported the arrest of a Mrs. Gibson and her daughter, caught while tearing down telegraph lines.

—from *Inside War*

A few days since, a party, several of whom were women, plundered the hospital at Ketesville robbing the wounded of their arms, clothing and money and the women taking the lead the latter whose presence in the hospitals should rather be to cheer the wounded than to terrify and rob them are now here prisoners along with several of the men.

—Diary of Henry Dysart, private in an Illinois unit in southeastern Missouri, quoted in *Inside War*

We would frequently see a squad of Union Militia start out after the Smiths [Confederate bushwhackers] and possibly the next day would hear that the Federals had dined at a farmhouse and in less than an hour the Smiths dined at the same house. The houses of these men were burned and their wives taken prisoner, but by threats of retaliation [that the Smiths would] burn the homes of Union men, forced the release of the women.

—Reminiscences of Mrs. C. C. Rainwater, from *1861 to 1865,*
Special Collections Library, Duke University

THE FIRST NIGHT THE GUARDS SHOVED HER INTO THE GENERAL WARD, A large room thirty feet by twenty-five. Adair kept hold of her carpet-sack and the quilt with both hands. In the dim light she saw other women shift and move in a sudden shrinkage of skirts. She heard sleet stuttering at the bars of the windows. In that wintry evening all the shutters were closed. The fireplace leaked a slow red light, and the bar shadows lined the opposite wall like thin soldiers or the wraiths of the prisoners gone before. Adair felt her hair slowly beginning to stand on end and her heart was wallowing and laboring in her chest and there was not enough air in the world. Her heart was crashing its two halves together like a boxer's fists.

A strong woman with big shoulders and a head of pasty brown hair put her hands around her mouth and called out,

Say thing! Thing and sing and bring! Say on and dog!

Thang, sang, brang, jeered another woman. Oan! Doag!

The only light in the dark January evening was from the fireplace. The women's figures were lit on one side only. Through the shutters, Adair could smell the latrines. It was like the Female Seminary of the netherworld. A ladies' academy in hell.

Adair went and sat by the fire on a barrel, tipped her hat back a little. They were all looking at it. Adair clenched her cold hands together and tried not to stare around her. They had been rained and sleeted upon all the way from the St. Louis and Iron Mountain Railroad terminal at Pine and River Streets. Now she could hardly keep her hands from shaking even though they were seized together.

What's your name? said the big woman. She bent down to pet a small terrier that danced around her skirt hems.

Adair looked around at all of them in the light of the fire.

My name is Adair Randolph Colley, she said. From southeastern Missouri. From Ripley County. And I am here because somebody said I was disloyal.

Well, *are* you disloyal? The big woman put her hands on her hips and stared.

Me? Of course not, said Adair.

Some of the women were staring at her with inflexible expressions.

It will be all right, said a sweet-faced young woman nearby her. Adair turned her head to the girl. She had light brown hair and a soiled dress of dark lavender. I am from Danville, Missouri, and I too was denounced. But we must get along here with people of all different persuasions, I suppose. My name is Rhoda Lee Cobb.

How do you do, Miss Cobb, said Adair.

I was imprisoned because of my opinions, said Rhoda Lee. Snatched from the Danville Female Seminary.

A woman with a crown of violently springing red hair coughed explosively three times into her hand and looked up again. Wiped her hand on her skirt. Beside her sat a woman whose face was heavily chalked and painted like a clown or perhaps an actress.

We have nothing to offer you, I fear, said Miss Cobb. We will be fed in the morning.

Who says she would get anything even if we did have something to offer her? asked the stout woman in brown check. She was chewing tobacco and turned and spat into the fire. Don't have any tobacco do you? She tried to stare Adair down.

I don't use it, said Adair. She seemed to be losing her anger, which had always sustained her, and now her voice was small.

You'll get used to things around here, said the woman. Her brown hair was pulled back so tightly and it was so dirty that it seemed she had a headful of wires, a telegraphic device. Then I'll bet you'll use it if you gets the chance.

The redheaded woman crossed her arms and stared at Adair, and her volcanic hair erupted in savage reds and oranges, backlit by the fire. You'll learn to get along. You got any money?

No, said Adair.

You got anybody sending you delicacies or dainties or comforters?

No, said Adair. Her word dropped into the well of stone silence.

Well what the hell *have* you got?

What I got in my hand here. Adair kept her carpet-sack in closed fists. Clothes. I guess I could try to write some relatives or something.

Out on Fourth Street, beyond their barred world of filth and stone, there was the sound of a fiddle and somebody dancing, thumping in heavy shoes. Then a scattering of applause.

The stout woman snorted. Her fists were on her hips. These here women might be whores and thieves and fortune-tellers and drunks but they are loyal.

And around her several women said yes, yes, in low voices. Adair did not look to see who had spoken.

My name is Cloris and I am the head prisoner here. We wash outside on Mondays. They feed us stew twicest a day and bread besides. Take that pallet over there. Throw your things down. Whatever it is you got.

Adair was not prepared to let go of anything she owned just at present. Her wet jacket smoked in the fire's thick heat. Her skirts were heavy with damp. We were pretty well all burnt out, she said. Adair still did not know whether it was smarter to appease these women for the present or fight them right off. She did not know what would work. She had never met people like this.

They was burnt out. The stout woman, Cloris, shook her head. Why, fancy that. Just burnt right out. Somebody come along and set they house on fire.

But the rain put it out.

Well, fancy that, said Cloris. She smirked a little but in reality did not know what to say to that. It seemed the work of a benign Providence, didn't it.

Adair said, God sent the rain and put it out, because the Union Militia who stole everything are bound for the devil's kingdom. She stared at Cloris. They are going to drown at the crossing of the Current River. You will be able to see their faces underwater.

See here! said Cloris. I believe that is disloyal!

Adair kept her chin in the air and turned her black eyes from one woman to another. See if it don't happen. She tried to look confident and evil, the sort of person no one wanted to cross.

Is she a-talking against the Union? This was from a very old lady wrapped in a striped blanket. She inhabited the far shadows against the wall. Is she a-talking against the Union?

How would we even know? said the redheaded woman. What goes on down there? They ain't nothing down there but iggerant savages.

And I'm one of them, said Adair. I dare any of you to lay a hand on me. She stood and waited.

Well, well! We bunk out on these straw pallets! said the actress. If that's what she was. Adair had never met an actress before, had never seen an entertainment upon the stage. The actress had bright red lips and cheeks, a white skin and her eyelids were sooty. Most of us are in here unjustly imprisoned. I was arrested myself on the charge of theft. I was hungry.

You just steal out of habit, said the redheaded woman.

We beat people who steal in here, said Cloris. Any information we get, we keep it to ourselves. If you get yourself a package of dainties you got to share some. That's the rules. She stepped two steps toward Adair and grinned. Her teeth were yellow as if she had slaked herself on limestone.

All right, said Adair.

So you just open up that carpet sack and show us what you got in there.

I don't think I will, said Adair.

Cloris stepped up to Adair so quick she could not react and struck Adair broadside across the cheekbones with a fist, yelling *There! there!* She hit her twice before Adair could even fall, fast as a copperhead.

Adair fell with her hands out and skidded on the floor, tearing skin from the heels of both hands. She heard her dress rip, the bodice tearing loose from the skirt.

Cloris regarded her own thick fist. That's from workin' in the Auxvasse silver diggins, she said.

Adair got back to her feet in an instant, her skirts swinging around her. She looked around for something to throw at the woman or hit her with.

Do you all just take this from this woman? Adair called to the rest of them. Her voice shook. Nobody moved. Adair's hat had fallen onto the floor and her hair was coming down. It spilled out in a confusion of black hanks, a mass of it all down her back. She knew if the stout woman could get those leathern hands into her hair, she would be in dire trouble. The woman would break her neck. Adair twisted her hair into a hank and jammed it into her collar.

The other women stood back. Rhoda Cobb retreated with her hand in front of her mouth and her mouth in an O. Adair reached then and pulled a heavy flaming stick from the fire.

Come on, then, she said. If you want anything I got, come and take it. Cloris laughed and looked around at the other women, who dutifully laughed too. Cloris stepped two steps to Adair's right, to the fire, as if she would back Adair into the shadows. Adair turned quickly and then realized the big woman was putting the fire behind herself to blind Adair with the light of it. The terrier barked like a mechanical thing.

Adair drew the heavy stick back like a baseball bat and took two steps forward and swung. She smashed it into the stout woman's uplifted arm and sparks flew from the flaming end and shattered over their skirts. When she struck it made a cracking sound on Cloris's forearm. Cloris shouted several syllables that were not in any language Adair knew and reached and took the burning end of the stick and tore it from Adair's grasp.

Stop! Stop! Rhoda Cobb took hold of Adair around the waist and began backing away with her, and two other women jumped in between them.

The stout woman stood holding her forearm with her burnt hand. Adair shrugged herself loose from the grip of the actress and the girl from Danville Academy.

I don't know how long I can stand listening to you tell me what to do, said Adair.

Rhoda put out both hands. Everybody better sit down before the matron comes, she said. I don't know if you all want something to eat tomorrow but I do.

Adair put her carpet-sack down on the pallet, which she saw was the thinnest one of all, and sat down on it. She was shaking with small, violent tremors of rage and fear. She sat very still and upright to try to contain herself. Slowly, like hens settling on their poles at night in the confinement of the fowl house, the women sank on their skirts and wrapped hands around their knees. The black-and-tan terrier leapt into Cloris's lap and stared at Adair.

There was a long silence and out in the city the great bell in the tower of the St. Louis Cathedral rang out ten.

Get that girl to sing something. Cloris waved a hand from her pallet by the fire. Or play that whistle she's got. She blew on her burnt palm. I'll settle things with you before long. Kisia, sing. The air inside the General Ward shook like a lazy jack from the tensions among them all.

Levina, the blonde actress, said, Kisia, honey, sing us something. She stroked Kisia's hair. My little niece here is just like my own child, and if we'd of had a chanct she would have sung on the stage.

The girl sat up from the pallet. Her face was pale as oatmeal, dotted with a few freckles, her hair braided with knotted yarns. Her face was light boned and drawn, her eyes deep-set and of some dark color. She began to sing. Her voice was clear and strong, with a wild, vital vibrato.

> *It was in old Wexford Town*
> *The judge come from afar*
> *A fair young lad with a tender heart*
> *Stood prisoner at the bar.*

Kisia sang four verses and then drifted off the last notes at the end. Then the girl lay down in her dusty homespun dress and she covered herself and her aunt with a woolen blanket.

Adair lay and watched the dying fire. She was sleepless and vigilant under her shawl and the extra dress. She lay against the wall as close to the windows as she could get despite the cold for she was shut in and trapped and thus her deepest fear had come about.

Adair drew the Log Cabin quilt out of its linen wrapping and examined it in the firelight, now that they were all asleep. She studied it with intense interest. The hearths were all velvets of varying reds. Carmine, scarlet, a garnet, a deep rose. Adair ran her dirtied fingers over the piecings in the vagrant light. There was a beautiful silk repeated over and over on the shadow side, which was dark brown with a figure in garnet that might have been the face of a clock. Adair spread her hand over one of the blocks as if over her home with its red velvet fire in the heart of her family, both living and dead.

7

*For northerners . . . the enemy was neither the plantation-owner nor his slaves
but poor southern white trash—"Pukes," as northerners liked to call them. . . .
Northern whites feared they too could be compelled back into a perceived impov-
erished barbarism, as they thought of the Pukes, away from the increasingly
mature prosperity and moral tidiness by which northern freemen justified their
individual existence and purpose of their society. Perhaps at some unacknowl-
edged level there was something enticing about a wilder, unstructured life.*

   *Louisa Lovejoy wrote: "Think of this, my sisters in New Hampshire; pure-
minded, intelligent ladies fleeing from fiends in human form whose brutal lust
is infinitely more to be dreaded than death itself." (Lovejoy to the Concord,
N.H.,* Independent Democrat *September 19, 1856, in "Letters of Louisa
Lovejoy, 1856–64") This beastly Puke attacked every civilized value. The
beast must die.*

—FROM *Inside War*

*Missouri is known as the "Show Me State" supposedly for the proudly skepti-
cal character of its natives. For some reason it is also known as the Puke State.*

—FROM *Don't Know Much About Geography*, BY KENNETH C. DAVIS,
AVON BOOKS, NEW YORK, 1992

THE FORTUNE-TELLER WAS NAMED MADAME ROSE. SHE SAT ON THE
floor beside the upside-down half hogshead, in the comforting shine of
the fire. She drew a pack of cards from her coat pocket.

She said, The cards care nothing for politics or the war of the Rebellion, nor General Lee nor General Meade. Only the war in the human heart. The forced marches of overweening emotions. The artillery of love. Piercings. Ambushes.

The fortune-teller laid the cards out on the barrel top. They were a strange deck, elaborate with stormy, extravagant figures. Great suns and moons and Egyptian priestesses, things Adair had seen in *Holland's Pictorial History of the World*.

And this one, the Burning Tower, speaks of the passions that come first, and after the Burning Tower comes War. Marching. The cards tell us of the Lakes of Fire that lie within us, and this one, a smooth pool, see here, the dog drinks up the water and the water of this pool will cause him to become something that is half a man. She sniffed against a running cold and regarded the card. She was oblivious to the General Ward. Walking. Got a dog's head upon his shoulders. He will weep and weep as he walks down toward Dougherty's Tavern. He's begging not to be made to drink anymore. And this is what crosses everybody, the Lovers, for they both join and disjoin again and again, and there is loss in the joining and pain in the separation. Life does not remain still, sometimes it is daft and makes no reason, but in every battle there are still moments. Her worn hands shifted the cards.

The matron opened the barred door with a clanging of her keys. She was accompanied by two soldiers. The guards sat the heavy kettle of stew inside the General Ward and then backed out. Adair watched as the matron counted the number of women prisoners and then took out a dirty piece of paper and pencil stub from her skirt pocket and wrote something. Rhoda Lee had told Adair that the matron's name was Buckley. The matron's dress was made of a loud plaid in red and yellow and brown.

Mrs. Buckley reached back and got a basket from a guard and set it inside too. Then she began to hand out tin bowls and spoons from yet another basket. She counted loudly as she handed them out. The matron was tall with knobby hands, and her fingers were covered with fawny rings.

One two three four, she counted. Adair crowded up close, beside Rhoda.

Oh Mrs. Buckley, she said in a firm voice. Mrs. Buckley, I want to send a letter to home.

Six seven eight nine ten eleven twelve.

Adair stood with ostentatious patience, her black hair sliding out of its braids and combs, now stiff as pasteboard with dirt. Her dress bagged at the waist where it had torn loose. She gripped the plaid shawl around her dress and jacket. I must send a letter, do you reckon that will be all right?

No, said Mrs. Buckley. You're not to be sending letters.

I ain't allowed letters? Adair stood and stared at her. I bet I am.

Adair, I'll tell you about the letters, let Mrs. Buckley do her job. Rhoda pulled at Adair's sleeve.

You're not allowed anything at all until they look into your case. Major Neumann is in charge of your case. This prison is run by the provost marshal, girl. Mrs. Buckley then wadded up the newspaper from the basket and threw it toward the fire. One of the prostitutes snatched at it. She took the printed sheet and began to smooth it out with great care.

You mean, the Missouri Union Militia?

Those scumbags! Mrs. Buckley laughed. The Militia! No sir, this prison is run by the *U.S. Army*. If you're goin to rant on about it, I'll have that jacket of yours. Mrs. Buckley handed out the last bowl. Then she reached and took hold of the edge of Adair's embroidered mandarin jacket between her fingers.

Get your hands off of me, said Adair.

Ssshhh, said Rhoda. Adair, be quiet.

Take your dirty hands off me, said Adair. Adair reached up and shoved the matron's hand away.

The tall matron looked at Adair.

Everyone else was silent.

Well, miss, I think you and I had better learn to get along with each other.

Adair paused. Good enough, I think so too, she said.

Shake on it?

All right, said Adair. She hesitated for a moment and then cautiously offered her hand. The tall woman in her bright plaid took it and crushed down with her considerable strength and Adair cried out. It seemed as though they were about to dance.

Let go, said Adair. She knew she should not cry or fight back but stand there and show that she could take it. Let go of my hand.

That's what it takes to be a matron around here, Mrs. Buckley said. Then she jerked backward with all her strength and threw Adair to the floor.

I am not unfair! Mrs. Buckley turned to the prison in general. I am not unhelpful to you dismal bitches! Am I?

No, no, said the women. The guards laughed, but quietly.

Adair got her legs underneath her, in her tangled skirts. She got up. Her head rang.

You just keep your drawers on, you little Rebel bitch, said Mrs. Buckley. You're going to be interrogated by the major before you get to write anything.

THAT NIGHT WHEN MOST OF THE OTHERS WERE ASLEEP SHE SAT UP IN HER blankets and took her piece of candle to the fire and lit it with a splinter. She looked in her little beaded bag for the tiny book of poems. She never read poems but there were blank pages in it. Then she tore out a flyleaf from *Friendship's Offering*, and took up her pencil, and wrote a letter to her sisters at Dalton's Store. It was very brief. She fell asleep with it in her hand.

8

As Missouri came under [Union] martial law, the Union military operated as the law enforcement agency during much of the war in most of the state, in effect superseding whatever civil legal structures remained in place. In such a position, the military had enormous discretionary power over civilians in the areas they controlled, unchecked by any truly effective appeals system.

—from *Inside War*

Prisoner Mary Pitman testifying against Mrs. William J. Dixon, wife of the keeper of the St. Charles Street Prison for Women:

"Forced Mrs. Carney, who was pregnant, to sew for the Dixon family and sleep in filthy rags. . . . on one occasion she demanded prisoner White's new comforter. . . . Dixon then locked White in her room on half rations and without toilet facilities. . . . Dixon only allowed her to clean herself and her room when the Union Colonel who employed the Dixons came for one of his inspections. Dixon also arranged evenings alone in the parlor for one prisoner, Miss Warren, and Captain Keyser, a defense lawyer. One evening I saw her lying in his arms."

—Investigation of the St. Charles Street Prison for Women, St. Louis, January 5, 1864, Two or More Name File, 2635, Record Group 393, NA, quoted in *Inside War*

Whu they were allowed out into the courtyard, Adair could hear the crowds in the streets with their tapestry of noises. People were flocking into the city in wagons, in streams of ragged folk, black and white, to get away from the incessant warring and burning in south-eastern Missouri. Southerners who finally realized the only safe place was to the north, among northern civilians. They were all becoming street people, peddlers, ditch diggers, people who had once had homes.

The winter air was still and unmoving, but warm air flowed out of the barred windows of the General Ward and stirred young Kisia's frail hair. The girl held Adair's hand in her own. I can come and go as I want, said Kisia. I am just here because my aunt was jailed for stealing and I ain't got nobody else to care for me.

Adair patted her hand and they walked on.

How were you disloyal? Kisia asked. Were you spying or cutting telegraph lines?

I killed a Yankee soldier, Adair said. I had a woman witch his horse and it threw him and broke his neck. He was a captain of artillery.

Oh you did not, said Rhoda Cobb. Her voice was prim and pinched. I warrant you never did any such thing, Adair. Witching is un-Christian.

Oh all right, then, said Adair. She joined the other women walking around the courtyard. Cloris strode along with the terrier at her feet. I shot him with a fowling piece. Rhoda hurried to walk beside her.

Now, Adair, you have to think better thoughts. About getting out of here. She leaned closer to whisper. My lawyer is *very* sympathetic. He is in the provost marshal's department.

What's that? Adair asked.

That's the part of the army that puts people in prison.

Adair looked up at the two guards sitting on the wall smoking, one of them had only one arm, but he was interested enough, grinning down at them out of his Federal blue. He was a hard grinner. The other was a child of about fourteen who was looking away. His mother probably told him not to look at or speak to the bad women.

Kisia and two other younger girls were running around the brick prison courtyard, among the barrels and crocks of soap. They were tagging one another.

Where is your family? asked Adair.

Scattered around, said Rhoda. And the darkies almost all run off and the fields are ruined. Five hundred acres of Missouri River bottomland in cotton and hemp and now it's all full of cockleburs. Mama just hides in that big brick house, her and her old darky woman. Rhoda bit her lip and stared at the cobblestones. Did you all have servants?

We never did, said Adair. We just let everthing go to ruin without worrying about it too much.

A young lady should have a personal servant. Life is so much better. Well, if we'd have known darkies was going to be so much trouble we'd have picked our own cotton. Rhoda put her hands over her face.

It would have done you good, said Adair. Builds character.

But it is so grand to have a maid. Somebody to do your hair and bring coffee to the bed in the morning.

Rhoda's voice took on a yearning tone. She took up the torn lace on the hem of her petticoat.

And do your sewing. I told Daddy I didn't want one born before 1850. We could have got a '51 if we'd have taken out a mortgage on Pompey and Juppy Easter at seven percent interest for only about eight hundred. And then if she didn't work out, if she sulked or one thing or another, she would have been good on resale. But Daddy said, Oh no, the war's a-coming, and any money put into darkies is money lost. Rhoda Lee looked at the line of women waiting to do their washing, standing in the steam of the barrels of boiling water. And here I am doing my own washing.

Who denounced you? Asked Adair.

Nobody did. I denounced myself. When Anderson burnt down Danville and the Seminary, the Union Militia came and took everyone that was walking around, including me. I told them right out, I stand for Dixie. Tears sparked in Rhoda's eyes. And that landed me here. I've been here three months without a trial. In the General Ward. And I do feel my soul has been cultivated here by suffering.

Adair said, Don't you have a plan to get loose?

Rhoda drew herself up, or together, as drawstrings clench a purse. The Union Army put me in here, and they can just take care of me. They owe it to me.

Well, if that's your idea of a good time, Rhoda, said Adair. I wouldn't differ with you for the world.

They have to be made to account for their treatment of people.

If I were to try to get over the wall, would you help me?

Rhode stiffened even more. She said, Adair, there are the right ways to go about things. There are still rules in the world. And one of these rules is that women must suffer our abusers without resistance. Ladies do not help themselves, Adair, we make appeals. We pray our complaints might be heard, but nothing more. Now the Mayberry girls bribed the guards with ten dollars in gold and went over the wall. I consider that very low-class. That is for white trash and the laboring classes. This is what the Yankees want to do to us. Destroy Southern womanhood.

Adair stood looking at the height of the wall. It was only about five and a half feet. But there were always guards on it. They seemed to use the top of the thick wall to sun themselves and smoke and talk. Did she have to have ten dollars in gold for each one of them? That they would turn their backs?

Well, Rhoda, I hope you can stay a lady and find somebody to abuse you.

I dwell on it often.

I bet.

Did you go to an academy?

Adair was still looking at the wall. She rested her chin on her fist, and said, I was in the Catholic one in Sainte Genevieve for six months. After my mother died. I wasn't a very good girl.

Rhoda laughed. They never taught us how to get along in a prison. They never imagined the United States Government would imprison ladies, I suppose. Just because of their opinions.

Adair said, I never told anybody my opinions.

Well then your family is Secesh.

I don't know if they are or not.

Well, you *should* know! Rhoda said. Of *course* you should know. General Sherman has gone down through Georgia and South Carolina and burnt everything in his path. Burnt, robbed, and stole all that lay in his way.

Good, said Adair. They been beatin up on us for solid four years, let those rich planters get their share of it, they started it.

Rhoda said, If you sign that awful confession and take the oath, there are all kinds of favors for you. She looked narrowly at Adair. There is another courtyard on the other side, for the matron. It's nice. Sign a confession and you can go there and sit and sew or fold her linens. You would like that, I suppose.

I don't think I'll sign anything. Outside the walls harness bells jangled and somebody's far thin voice shouted Merry Christmas! down the city streets. The newspaper boys screamed Nashville casualty lists! Savannah surrenders!

AT NOON THE MATRON AND A SINGLE GUARD BROUGHT IN A KETTLE OF ham hocks and navy beans. Adair held out her letter to the matron. She held the spanish milled dollar under her thumb. Please. My sisters don't know where I am or anything. It's addressed. The other women were holding out letters as well. They called out names and requests.

Mrs. Buckley read the address. Dalton's Store, Wayne County, she read. This is behind the lines. Down in Secesh territory.

The guard stared at Adair. His eyes watched from beneath the bill of his forage cap like the eyes of a stiff doll.

Well, where's the lines? asked Adair. Ma'am.

At Iron Mountain. Around there.

Well, said Adair.

Maybe I will. Or maybe I'll throw it in the street, said the matron.

Adair turned away before she found herself saying something that would get her in trouble. Now, she thought, I don't have a farthing of money.

Does anybody want to play some whist? The fortune-teller looked around, wiping her hands on her skirts.

Them cards are fallen to pieces, said the redheaded woman. She started coughing again, and coughed so long she bent her head and started to cry.

Whyncha read? It was one of the blonde whores. Look here. She got up and brought a sheet of newspaper over to Adair and stood in front of her. You can read, kentcha?

Adair said What? She sometimes could not understand their St. Louis accent.

Read this thing to us.

Go away, said Adair. She bent over her sewing. Rhoda was murmuring to herself in the corner; she had draped her shawl over her head and was praying into its fringes.

Yeah, said Cloris. She can read okay. Then the actress and the old lady began to say, Yes, yes. Let's have reading. Everyone ignored the redheaded woman, who was sobbing quietly and then fell to coughing again and said Oh Lord, Oh Lord.

Adair put down the green dress and stuck the needle into the fabric.

In the corner, the very old woman began to pray aloud. She said, Lord release me from this prison and from those in authority over us who hold us here.

Cloris got up and walked over to Adair. The brown-checked woman took hold of Adair's upper arm in such a grip that Adair knew there would be bruises. She gave her a shake.

Now, you read to us.

You let go of me or I'll kill your dog when you ain't looking, said Adair. She looked up at Cloris.

You touch my dog and I'll break your bones, said Cloris. She let go.

Yes, but it won't do you no good, said Adair. Because that dog's going to be drowned in the latrine.

God damn you, said Cloris. You wouldn't.

Yes I would, said Adair. You touch me again or anything I got, that dog will not live out the day.

Cloris turned suddenly and caught up the small terrier and stood with it before the fire. She glared at Adair over the dog's upright ears. She stalked over to one of the prostitutes to snatch the sheet of newspaper out of her hand. It was the sheet of newspaper that had lined the corn dodger basket, the one the prostitute had rescued from the fire. She had been hoarding it for days.

Cloris handed the terrier carefully to the redheaded woman and shoved the greasy newspaper at Adair and indicated a great many illustrations.

There, she said.

Adair held it between her hands and read the insistent phrases. She shrugged. I might as well, she said. It's too wet to plow.

Well gals, if she's goin to read, she ought to sit here by the fire, said Cloris, generously. Come on here and sit your Jeff Davis butt down here on this barrel.

But these here are advertisements, Adair said. She wrapped the quilt again and gathered her skirts, struggled to her feet off the pallet, and sat on the upended half hogshead by the fire. She took up the sheet of newspaper and turned so that the firelight fell on it. This whole page is just advertisements, she said.

That's what we like! cried one of the whores. We just love that stuff.

So Adair began to read.

Sterling's Ambrosia, she read. For the hair. This picture—she held up the steel engraving of a woman standing at a dressing table with a Niagara of hair falling down to the floor—is drawn and engraved from life. She turned so everyone could see it. They gazed at it critically. Levina the actress, her makeup faded now, crawled forward to look at it and then sat back, shaking her head.

Well would you look at it, said Cloris. She petted the terrier. Looka there, baby.

Adair read on in her precise, stern voice. Dr. Sterling's Ambrosia is a stimulating oily extract of roots, barks, and herbs. It will cure all diseases of the scalp, and itching of the head; entirely eradicates dandruff; prevents the hair from falling out, or turning prematurely gray, causing it to grow thick and long. Sold by druggists everywhere. Put up in a box containing two bottles. Price one dollar. Dr. H.H. Sterling, sole proprietor. Number sixteen Olive Street.

Oh let's dash out and buy some, said the redheaded woman. By God alls I need's my hair clean to the floor like that, shit fire, I could ride the omnibus naked down Market Street.

Musquito shield or guard. For the Army, Navy, Travelers, Sick or Wounded or anyone who is troubled with musquitoes, flies, or dust. National American Amusement Cards, colonel for king, goddess of liberty for queen, and major for jack.

The major looked at her out of his stiff armorial bearing, his mace upright.

Letter to "Dear Sister," From Eliza Draper, Danville, Missouri, November 12, 1864, an account of "Bloody" Bill Anderson's raid on Danville, Missouri, in which most of the town was burnt and sixteen civilians murdered. Bloody Bill Anderson advertised himself as a Confederate guerilla.

"[Several of the guerillas] came into the yard and said the Seminary should not be hurt . . . the minute they began to come to the gate the Rebel girls and a few of the Union girls went to the fence and stood talking to them all the time the town was burning. . . .

"The [Rebel] girls begged Anderson for buttons until he cut them all off. That coat was off one of the murdered [Union soldiers] at Centralia and the girls knew it and yet they begged for them. He was also carrying the scalp of one of the men he had killed in Centralia. . . . Mrs. Robinson and another girl and myself started out as soon as it was over, and I never heard such screams in my life as Mrs. Moore was giving, over her husband's body in a house as we passed along. . . . Of course I know more about the Seminary than any other place. I can't tell how the Rebels came in and which fired first."

Eliza Draper

—REPRINTED IN *Gateway Heritage,*

QUARTERLY OF THE MISSOURI HISTORICAL SOCIETY, VOL. 3, NO. 4, 1993

ADAIR COLLEY! THE SERGEANT BELLOWED. HE WAS SOBER AND IMPOR-tant with the nature of the magisterial duty he bore and the keys jangled in his hand. He was accompanied by two guards, as if it would take all three of them to drag her out of the General Ward. Here are the orders. He held out the papers that said he had escort duty for female prisoner Adair Colley. He stood at the bars and ran his eyes over the crowd of women.

They all turned to look at her.

Hey, you want us, fellows! You want us! The prostitutes snatched up their skirts to show the guards the tops of their black stockings, cruelly gartered into the whiteness of their flesh, and the hint of hair above.

Get that girl out of there, said the sergeant. The guards gestured at her to come quickly.

Adair gathered her skirts and stepped out of the barred door. The two privates stared at each other, then looked back into the great zoological cage of women. The sergeant slammed the barred door to. It rang like a church bell, the clash hummed all down the horizontal bars.

She went between them down the hall, refusing to be hurried, forcing them to either drag her by both arms or slow down as well. They slowed down. They went through another set of barred doors and then into a hall with the great doors to the outside at the far end. They came to the orderly room. Her mouth was very dry.

The sergeant bent forward and opened the door to the orderly room. Go on in, he said.

He shut the door behind her.

A man in Federal uniform was standing beside an oak desk, hatless. He wore a major's insignia, and he was of a tall height and very gaunt. His face was long and square-jawed. On his hand a gold signet ring. Deep circles under his hazel eyes.

Adair saw that his insignia was that of the regular Federal army. He was not the Militia. She was standing there like a construction of salt, and before total crystallization could overtake her she walked toward the sofa. It was upholstered in yellow damask.

Well, she said. Pretty day, ain't it? She smiled. How's the war going?

Miss Colley, he said. Sit down. I am Major William Neumann, of the judge advocate general's department. He stood and took her in, her face and hair and her dress. I am in charge of your case, so far. I repeat, sit down.

His voice was low, his accent was neither North nor South. It was an American accent but very odd. She sat on the sofa. Then he sat down as well. His officer's sword had been slung casually by its hangar on a hat rack, and as he turned to sit down his elbow knocked into it and it rattled in little metallic crashes on its chain. He took up his papers. She felt a tremor start up in her hands and she hid them in her skirt.

Miss Colley, you have been here for three weeks. He jiggled the papers. Imagine that.

He was saying something just to have something to say.

Time just flies by when a person is in good company, she said. Jolly evenings of improving readings around the fire.

The room was warm. She was surprised to feel how pleasant it was to be in a moderate-size room that was warm all over. She put her hands out to an ornate parlor stove with its leaves of shining chrome on the sides. There was a deep glow of coal through the isinglass window in the front. The floor was scarred with chair scraping, and the wall had a shelf of books about Indian languages and geographies of far places.

There were people and vehicles going by on the street outside. She could see that the storefronts were swagged with Christmas greens. Here inside was a table in front of the sofa with a lamp so far unlit. Behind the major was a map of the United States, in various colors. She was surprised there were not flames depicted on it, breaking out throughout the South like brushfires. Bullet holes. Sleet stung at the windows. Her heart slowed a little to a repetitive series of dull explosions.

I know you are uncomfortable there in the General Ward, he said. He paused and then began again. As if back onto an unalterable text. I know you are uncomfortable in the General Ward but this is how we process prisoners. At first they join the general prison population and then we conduct interviews and things may change for you or not change. He waited for her to say something.

Well, all right then, she said. What am I charged with? She leaned forward. She wished she were apprised like her father concerning the statutes of the State of Missouri.

He paused. He cleared his gravelly throat. He brought one paper out from under a pile of other papers. It was a printed form, and beneath it a large blank space that had been filled in with a minute hand.

I am not obligated even to tell you that, he said.

He sat and looked at her, at her deep Italianate eyes, the fineness of her pale face, and the pitch-black hair in a crown of braiding. Her narrow hands folded. The coloring of some prehistoric people of the British Isles that were there before the Saxons, perhaps even before the Celts, some ancient race of savages that had invented a terrible tale called Snow White. She was prison thin, and he saw her ears were pierced but she wore no earrings. He sat back and searched in a drawer for a pen that he did not need. He became firm again, lest he be seduced by appearances. Thus it was being assigned to the women prisoners. Temptation was ever before him.

He said, St. Louis, and in fact all of Missouri, is under martial law. Because of the extreme condition of guerilla warfare in this state. All right?

I see, she said. Then the state laws don't apply to anything at all?

He raised his head from the papers. His hazel eyes gazed at her solid as wooden buttons.

No.

No?

No, Miss Colley. He was impatient. Martial law applies.

What is marshal's law?

I don't see why you should concern yourself. He was irritated. What would you do about it if I handed you the statutes?

I'd sit here and read them. She brushed her hair out of her eyes. She was proud that it was clean, and that she had a clean dress and clean hands. The major probably took a bath twice a week in hot water.

You have no business reading them. You will merely get odd ideas and interpret them in peculiar ways. You will have a lawyer assigned to you to do that. He regarded her from under his thin eyebrows. Can you read?

Of course I can read. My father is a justice of the peace and he teaches the common school.

The major smiled. Read that, he said. He shoved a copy of *Godey's Ladies' Book* in front of her. They tell me this is suitable material for ladies.

Adair took it up. She said, Do I get treated better if I can quote some poetry? Should I have brought my watercolors?

Read.

She read, in a firm, clear voice,

"In the first place, the breathing of impure air tends inevitably to shorten life: the body loses its health and strength, the mind its vigor, and becomes feeble and desponding."

The major heard *In th fuss plaice, th breathin of impyuh aiy-yur* . . .

"People who breathe bad air day after day are always in a low, nervous state—they are, in fact, little more than half alive. A hundred years ago, the Lord Mayor of London, two judges and one alderman, all died from a fever which broke out at Newgate, owing to the dirt and want of fresh air." She looked up. Is there any chance you might take this here to heart or is it going right over your head?

He paused and for the first time he smiled a meager half smile. I have sent a copy to the matron, Mrs. Buckley, and have been told to mind my own business. I think they call her The Ironclad.

Well take it to somebody else, Adair said. Surely she ain't the last word in prisons around here.

I am doing my best, he said. Although I don't expect you to rise up and cheer.

Are you waiting for us all to die?

Young woman, I said I am doing my best. You are impertinent.

I'll pray for your soul, Major.

He turned his eyes down to his papers and cleared his throat. In regards to your case.

Why are you even talking to me about it? she asked. She kicked out her foot in impatience and made her hem jump with the toe of her stiff ankle-jack. If it's all marshal's law and I am a prisoner without recourse.

Listen to me, he said. Your treatment will improve if you cooperate.

How old are you? asked Adair. How'd you get into this kind of thing, you a major in the U.S. Army and tormenting women?

I am a soldier, he said. I do what I am assigned to do. He was furious. He bit his teeth together and pressed his fingertips on the paper. His fingertips were white. This is the kind of assignment given to those of us daft enough to have read law.

Well then, go on, she said. She turned to the window and saw a man on a gray horse going past. The horse had its chin tucked in and head tilted to one side as if it were searching for lost change in the gutters. She looked at the major again. I suppose you have to go on about it.

When I was first assigned here—

And where are you from, anyway?

Shut *up*! he said. If you continue I will send you back to the General Ward.

Adair looked down at her shoe toe. There was a long silence and the fire crackled in the stove.

He said, When I was first assigned here I found the situation confusing, as most areas of Missouri have both Union and Rebel adherents living sometimes side by side. You can imagine my relief when I was assigned to prisoners from the district of southeast Missouri. You are all Rebels down there. Solid South. Every man jack of you, and so there is no confusion whatever.

Well, said Adair. What a relief that must have been.

You can't know.

But there's about ten people gone over to the Union down there, she said. Is what I heard.

He went on as if he had not heard her. And we are occupying the southeastern counties by force of arms. But we cannot pacify the countryside, can we? Adair realized this was a speech that he gave to everyone. To all the women. He said, We dash out of Iron Mountain and Rolla, and burn things and then retreat to our garrisons. Then your people shoot at us from treetops and bushes. He ran his fingers through a drumroll on the desktop, his nails clattering on the oak like a startled horse. Then he stopped and picked up the pen. Our purpose there is to deny the guerillas sustenance, food, and clothing and whiskey. His voice was that of a lecture to the soldiers. All these things are produced by women. Apparently they are getting their horses from Illinois.

Think of that, she said. The Union Militia took my daddy and my horse both. Times are hard all around. Adair tapped her foot.

You really are insolent, Miss Colley, he said. He leaned back in his chair. He smiled at her. You are very good at it.

Well! Adair brightened somewhat. I never thought of it as a talent.

Do you think it will get you out of here?

Will anything?

Depends.

Well go on with what you were saying. I guess you got to say it.

He said, Ahem, as if it were a word. Missouri is under martial law, Union martial law, and the other side is not regular Confederate Army as far as we are concerned, but guerillas. They have no regular communication with the CSA staffs and are not part of the chain of command and they are not in regular communication with their superior officers in the CSA. So we maintain they are freelancers moving at will and freelancers are called guerillas. It is the rules of war. You see I have given this little lecture many times. He did not smile. You understand that captured guerillas are not accorded the same treatment as regular CSA troops.

She said, But, Major, I think Colonel Reeves has a commission from the Missouri State Guard and is charged with the defense of the state. We've been invaded by Buckeyes and Hoosiers and ice people from Illinois.

He said, Miss Colley, I believe it is wrong to argue the war with women. Since women are under our protection and cannot vote nor sit on juries. However. Reeves's Fifteenth Missouri Cavalry is, as far as we are concerned, a guerilla band, and they are outlaws, and criminals.

Well what do you know if they are criminals or not? said Adair. What about your own criminals? Her face tightened and her voice became heated.

He went on. And if they are caught they will be executed after a very hasty trial. With a drunken mob of Missouri Union Militia troops standing around outside screaming for the rope.

She said, The Militia don't give people trials.

He said, I know. He took a grip on the papers in front of him, as if to lay hold of the whole nasty business. I will admit we have had to court-martial at least fifteen men from those assigned to southeast Missouri for arson, theft, murder and one case of. . . . He paused. Arson, theft, and murder.

I would think that would be enough, said Adair. Surely to God you ain't waiting for them to start roasting babies before you do something about them.

He stared at her and said, The Union Militia is an embarrassment to the Union Army. We are trying to disband them. He fussed again with the forms before him. But they are Frank Blair's pets and Frank Blair is a powerful man. He tapped a forefinger on the papers. Blair organizes very popular parades and rallies here in St. Louis. They pass out pony kegs of beer and sing "Rally 'Round the Flag." It is all very patriotic and fervent. He cleared his throat. Men join up in droves.

I'm sure it's all to the good, Adair said. A way of admonishing the erring.

He bowed slightly. And are not we all erring in the sight of the

Lord? Pray for my soul, Miss Colley. He walked back to his desk and dredged up a report. But wait. There is more admonishing here. He looked down. Miss Colley, you are suspected of three things. He had a blank, careful expression on his face. He then turned again to the forms. First, with cutting telegraph lines. I am sure you know that in December of 1861 General Halleck declared that all those caught cutting Union telegraph lines were to be shot, women included. Secondly, you have been accused of harboring and feeding guerillas, and harboring can mean anything we want it to mean, including keeping guerilla money in a bank account under your name. This means we may confiscate your family's bank account on nothing more than suspicion, that order given by General Ulysses Grant. He who is even now trampling out the grapes of wrath in Virginia. Thirdly, you are accused of spying.

He put the papers down. Looked up at her without expression.

She said, Gracious. Adair nodded, as if she had just been told some interesting fact about the amazing volume of shipping in the St. Louis port. I've been a busy girl.

The spying part was supposed to be when you were brought here on the train.

It was flat dark, she said. It was the dead of night.

Adair thought, They have made up all these accusations. One of them ridiculous so it could be easily thrown aside and she would feel relieved and happy. She would confess to one thing but not another, they would become friends, she would begin to tell him things to please him.

Suddenly and without any preliminaries she felt panic and a kind of frantic surge of energy as if she were having a seizure. There was no way out. She had been shut up in a dark hole. She took in a long breath through her nose with her lips shut, as if breathing in secret.

Miss Colley. He was watching her, alert as a raptor. You have thought of something.

I thought . . . She paused. I thought of my father.

And where is he?

Captain Tom Poth and some militiamen took him away and he was very beat up and then I don't know.

She thrashed silently in the snare she found herself in. Her father might even now be dying of a fever, and his handsome big dark horse Highlander hitched to an artillery caisson and sprayed with flying metal. Her sisters sleeping on the floor of Dalton's Store and treated like redheaded stepchildren. Adair strove mightily within herself against the weird internal noises of alarm, as if she had just caught fire or were drowning.

He looked at her for a long moment and the parlor stove thumped and sucked air, radiant with dry heat.

Do I have your attention? he asked. Not unkindly.

Yes, she said. Adair knew if she kept on with these thoughts she would end by giving in. She read the titles of his books. There were large tomes by a man called Schoolcraft, *Lewis and Clark's Report on the Louisiana Purchase*, a *Report on the Flora and Fauna of Texas*.

He said, I can decide to turn any one of these accusations into actual, legal charges.

Well, don't wait for me to make up your mind for you. Her hands hardened together.

He paused. Then he said, You are quite brave.

I am? Adair was caught flat-footed.

Yes. He moved his chair to one side of the desk, and sat facing her, his hands clasped together between his thighs, bent forward to her. Miss Colley, the provost marshal's department seems bent on extracting confessions from women. I am one of the unlucky fellows sent to get them. I don't like this any more than you do. You must help me. You must plead guilty to one or the other and then write a confession.

She said, What am I confessing to? She looked at the forms. Do I get a choice, there?

Provisioning guerillas. That's the only way they can continue to operate.

Why is that?

Don't evade me, he said. When Captain Poth went down to oversee the November elections, he reports he found a number of uniforms and gray cloth in Doniphan. He drew out his handkerchief and blew his nose and put it away again. The uniforms were at a house belonging to the Colleys.

She stared at him. Well that's a flat lie, she said. We live fifteen miles from town!

Quiet down. He began to jiggle his foot. You all quiet down after a while. You start out all fiery and defiant and then you quiet down.

Adair said, That captain who wrote that was the one who came to our place. Took my father away. They beat him in the face with a wagon spoke. They broke his face bones. My father is a judge and a teacher and he wears spectacles.

The major regarded the floor between his thighs and interlaced his fingers. I am sorry for it. There was a long silence. What else did they do?

Set the house on fire. Took the horses. They smashed up everything, said Adair. Then she suspected his sympathy. Are you trying to get on my good side?

Do you have one?

When I'm not in prison I am very charming.

I am not interested in your charms. I am interested in some solid information.

Adair then opened her hands in her lap. She would try acting. She sighed and brushed a tendril of hair out of her face. Well, you had better give me some advice on what I am to do, I suppose. *Lord listen to me I am turning into Rhoda Cobb.*

Stop acting, he said.

Well, how could I know any of this? I am not a soldier!

You'll do.

My father is too old to go for a soldier. My brother has a withered arm and can barely plow!

Apparently your brother is with Reeves's Fifteenth. And are you not engaged to someone? His voice was slightly strained when he asked that question. Then he hurried on. I imagine you are.

My brother is not with Reeves, she said.

The major watched her.

And your intended?

I don't have one. She looked up at him. Last I heard. But they write anything they want on those reports, don't they? I am surprised they ain't give me six children and several husbands and a pair of bloomers. The standing water in her eyes spilled over. He had her fixed in his barbed black handwriting, the wrought-iron bonds of reports. Who writes all this?

Various people. He picked up his pen and laid it down again. Sign here. This guilty plea. Guilty to a vague charge of provisioning guerillas. Then you can be moved into a cell. I know perfectly well what is in the women's General Ward. I don't want you in there.

Adair raised her head. She said, Can you find out if my father is in any of these prisons up here?

Yes. Write down his name and the date when you last saw him, and where. And in return, Miss, I want you to write a full statement of all you know of Reeves's activities, Reeves or the Chiltons, or Colonel Berryman, the Freeman brothers. Names and mail routes, contacts with the CSA command, and so on. And a confession on your own account. Then perhaps release.

Adair bit her lower lip. Is that *all*? she asked. Anything else? Her voice began to quaver.

Buried treasure, he said. Indian herbal remedies,

Adair wept beautifully into her hands. Oh, Major, you can't know how it is in there. The latrines, and doing the washing with the guards looking on. She continued to cry in a light, dainty way.

He said, Miss Colley. Quit sniveling. It sounds very false. However hard you may find this, remember that the human beings that you people have held in bondage for a hundred and fifty years have been subjected to worse degradation than you can imagine. What you are suffering is nothing. Nothing.

She kept her hands over her face and was furious at how he managed to say all these things in practiced, smooth, complete sentences, and then remembered he had probably talked to a dozen women like herself. Had said all this a dozen times.

I never held a living soul in bondage!

But your society has. You see I have found the perfect, irrefutable answer to any complaint, he said. She heard him sit back with a creaking of the chair. Miss Colley, I am very sorry about all this. She kept on crying. I will do what I can for you. It is grievous to see a young woman like yourself in such conditions. She heard him rattle the accursed papers. Please think a little better of our cause. His voice was no longer officious. To preserve this country. To free an innocent people from bondage. He paused. I am attempting to drown you in guilt.

Adair was desperate to regain lost ground and so she began to cry once more. She began with a long snivel and then burst out in hiccupping sobs.

It's not fair, she said. It's not fair. She heard him walk toward her, his pocket change rattling and a few crashing noises as he passed his sword hung on the hat rack, he was simply a walking trade in scrap metal, noisy as a tinker. She looked through her fingers and saw his boot toes.

This is much more convincing, he said.

Adair wiped her face with the flat of her hands and straightened up.

Well, it ought to be. I am about to faint with all this arguing. Pretending to cry is not as easy as you think.

He opened the door. Sergeant, would you go and bring something to eat? Bring some coffee as well. Thank you.

Apparently a glass of something was ready to hand. Here, Miss Colley. Here.

No, she said. She smelled brandy. Get it away from me.

Very well then. His hand remained on her elbow, he was bending over to her.

Is she all right, sir? The sergeant was standing in the door. They always end up crying.

Yes, she is all right. Major Neumann turned and shut the door with a vigorous slam. She jumped. Miss Colley, listen. She turned up her face to him and saw that he had pulled his chair up before her with scraping noises and was bent over to her. He had a pleasant scent, of good soap and tobacco. Are we agreed? This is all I can do for you. I want you to write a confession to assisting guerillas, the one charge, and then I will do my best to see that it is taken lightly. After all, these are your own family.

Adair stopped crying. She looked over at the papers on his desk. Adair wanted to live. She was young and she had all her life ahead of her and she would live to go home.

A knock at the door. The sergeant came in with a tray and a disapproving stare. Adair reached for the tray almost before he had set it down. She sniffled and wiped her hands on the napkin. Tore a beignet into small pieces and ate the pieces one by one. The sergeant still stood at the door.

All right, Sergeant, said Major Neumann. You have some concern?

The sergeant said, I didn't spend fifteen years in the army to be a waiter.

All right, Sergeant.

To a secessionist gal.

Lady.

Sir.

At ease, Sergeant,

Sir. He saluted and left.

Adair drank a cup of hot coffee from a thick ironstone army mug and wiped her lips. Then she said,

Give me the pen. She got up and went to his desk, looked quickly at all the papers without appearing to.

It was a steel pen, and he dipped it into a glass ink bottle and handed it to her, and showed her where the line was, and she signed, and stood back.

He said, All right, then.

He bowed slightly. He took up the paper and blew on the ink. You will be put in one of the single cells on the second floor. He put the signed confession down. He turned to her stiffly. I am thirty-one, he said. From Havre de Grace, Maryland. I have been in the army for seven years at the insistence of my father. The result of a misspent youth. I hope you enjoy your new cell.

Thank you, she said. She turned for her shawl. She was thanking somebody for putting her in a cell in a great stone prison. I just appreciate it so much.

IO

Working with the Log Cabin quilt block, quilt makers added a domestic symbolism. . . . The block is built around a center square, usually about one to two inches wide; quilt makers refer to this square as the "chimney" or "hearth" and to the strips around it as "logs." The symbol of Log Cabin as home must have touched quilt makers deeply, for in all the lexicon of quilt making, only this block has names for its components.

Even the colors used in the quilt carried symbolic value. Quilt makers traditionally centered the block with red to reflect the fire on the hearth. Two variations were allowed—yellow centers to represent a lantern in the window, or, in a special variation, black in the center of a block. In this variation, known as Courthouse Steps, the black was thought to represent the Judge's robes as he entered the court.

*—*FROM *Gateway Heritage,*

VOL. 16, NO. 1, 1995

Union soldiers came through the Ponder homestead three times during the course of the war. . . . On one of these raids a soldier picked up one of Martha's quilts. Admiring the delicate handiwork, he said, "I think my wife would like this quilt." As he held on to one end of it, spirited Martha boldly gripped the other. "If you take it, you'll have to steal it." The soldier relinquished the quilt with an indignant retort, "I've never stolen anything in my life." After this, Martha gathered up the quilt and whatever precious, small valuables she could fit into a wooden trunk. She hid the trunk in a hollow tree near the house . . . the heirloom was salvaged and is in Woodrow's possession today.

—FROM *The Civil War in Ripley County, Missouri,* PUBLISHED BY THE
DONIPHAN PROSPECT-NEWS, DONIPHAN, MISSOURI, 1992

We have one eccentric genius in our number who I think deserves a sketch. We style him "Feminine Joe"; he is quite good-looking, medium size, has blue eyes and glossy black hair—which he curls; embroiders like a lady, and has a great fondness for teasing his fellow prisoners by catching them and hugging and kissing them, one in particular whom he calls "my Joe" and declares himself in love with; he torments him almost to death—if "my Joe" starts for a drink of water, the "feminine" is sure to follow; if he lies down, he is clasped in the loving arms; at table the "feminine" refuses to eat unless "my Joe" helps his plate. We all get provoked sometimes and read the offender a genuine scolding lecture but it is merely a waste of words. We are all fond of him and he is a noble generous fellow; but his feminine airs are often very provoking.

—GRIFFIN FROST, *Camp and Prison Journal*

THE WRITING PAPER LAY BROAD AND WHITE AS A COUNTERPANE. THE evening sounds of the city were beginning, men bringing around drays of wood for the evening fires, tired men and children from the factories riding home packed in wagons. Since Adair was now on the second floor she could see out the narrow window into the streets of St. Louis. Her window was so high in the wall she needed to stand on something to see out. So she stood on the writing table. At the edge of the great river she could see the steeple of St. Louis Cathedral and could hear the bell as it rang out the hours. Adair felt odd and light-headed, as if she had a fever.

Adair began to cough in small, surprising explosions and shut her teeth against it. The major wanted something that would get somebody imprisoned, or jailed, or run down in the pine forests of southeastern Missouri by a patrol of the Union Militia and shot. He wanted it in fair copy and signed. But it was not his fault or his doing. He was a soldier and he did what he was assigned to do, and so did millions of soldiers all over the world. She got up again and paced. Then took the quilt out of its linen wrapper for the pleasure of the brilliant colors and the feel of the velvet. The needlework was very fine and regular. Adair hated needlework and she could not imagine sitting and stitching the fine crow's-foot seams.

Writing was the same, the pinching of thoughts into marks on paper and trying to keep your cursive legible, trying to think of the next thing to say and then behind you on several sheets of paper you find you have left permanent tracks, a trail, upon which anybody could follow you. Stalking you through your deep woods of private thought.

Adair thought of Major Neumann and her talk with him and found herself wishing to talk to him more. Just the two of them in the warm room, talking and not writing. The two of them in that quiet room, and his voice. Because it was so good to have someone speaking to her and listening to her.

She carefully set the brass ink bottle and the quire of paper on her steel bunk with its shuck pallet, and then stepped onto the bunk and then up to the writing table. She gripped the limestone sill and looked out at the streets of St. Louis. If she managed to escape, which way would she go? She saw that the barrels had been moved away from the wall again. She counted all the guards she could see and there were six. The other six walked the halls of the prison or marched outside, along the sidewalk.

The sycamores around the old Presbyterian church held up their winter hands in the smoke of the thousands of coal fires and wood fires. She could now see the storefront signs, all the things the city had to offer. DAGUERREOTYPES, TURKEY CARPETS, INCORRUPTIBLE TEETH MADE TO ORDER.

Then in the distance Adair heard the loud laughter and abrasive shouting from Seventh and Morgan Streets where Dougherty's Tavern lit the dim day with its gas lamps. The Irish with their gins and porters mazing off into the urgent and smoky city streets. Christmas greens had appeared in drooping swags at every shop window.

There was a good snow beginning, with flakes large as doilies, softening the air and all the hostile sounds of the city, the wheels and train noises and steam whistle at the white lead factory. Then from down at Dougherty's Tavern she heard singing.

She saw Kisia standing at the corner beside the tavern, singing "The Holly and the Ivy," singing easily, negotiating the octave-wide shifts. The girl had on the actress's shawl, and a boy was with her, so she should not be alone on the street. He was holding out a tin bowl of some kind, and the girl's faultless unbreaking voice, alive with a shimmering vibrato, poured out into the winter air. Passersby slid coins clattering into the bowl. The street urchin, in a tall busted hat and striped muffler, danced with delight. He ran to hold the bowl out to passing vehicles. Kisia's pale Scots hair slid from under the shawl. It was frosted with snow. Her cheeks were bright red with the cold but she sang out over the rumble of iron-tired wheels and over the noise of draymen shouting at one another and the omnibuses clattering by. Adair began to cry because of the beauty of the melody.

So the engines of the city thundered into the Christmas season and Kisia stood on a street corner and sang old anthems of the solstice into the weave of the city's strife. Adair heard her song drift away into the noise. She heard paperboys screaming. This was the world of headlines. Of cities falling and burning. Of armies blundering toward one another at Petersburg and Nashville.

Then Adair saw the major come by on a dark bay horse with high white stockings. She stopped crying and wiped her eyes.

He stopped. His wide-brimmed hat was caked with snow and his collar was turned up. He bent down to talk to Kisia, and the girl ran up to him at the curb, put her small white hand on the stirrup of his military saddle. He waved her away with his gloved hand, and still she laughed and held to the metal curve of his stirrup. He reached down to remove her hand but still she would not let go. Adair's hands were nearly frozen with clinging to the bars of the window.

Adair heard music from a marching band and then the band itself came into the street. They appeared out of the snow in an undefined dark, striding mass that then distinguished itself into a drummer with a dull drum, its skin head loosened by the wet snow, and a flute and other shining metal instruments. Striding by on the street, going somewhere, a reception or a speech, playing as they went to stay warm. The flute player stopped playing a moment and held his hand over the silver mouthpiece to warm it and then began again, "The Bonny Light Horseman."

At last Kisia turned and grasped the boy by the hand and ran off after the band, turning once to wave at the major. Stuck her tongue out at him. The major sat his horse and looked after her, and then pressed his heels to the horse and rode on at a slow walk into the darkening scrim of the snowy evening. Adair suddenly saw how attractive the major was, and he was attractive, moreover, to other women. Any woman. Or girl.

The candle threw shadows upward, her great furred head loomed dark on the wall and up to the ceiling as if it would pour itself out and aloft into the darkening sky. The light in her high window faded. She got down and sat before the paper again. Picked up the pen and put it down once more. Because she knew she would see the major again soon she took the diamond-and-sapphire earbobs out of the soft soap in the blue mass tin, and cleaned them, and laid them ready to put in. She took her hairbrush and brushed the mandarin jacket until it was clean. She did the best she could with her hair without a looking glass.

Adair opened her beaded bag. It contained many sentimental relics, reminders of her former life. And there in the prison cell she opened it and found her mother's handwritten receipt for apple butter. Even though the handwriting was in some ways clumsy it was contained and ornate at the ends of words. It seemed as if her mother were utterly there and present in this very cell, as if she had never gone on before. As if her mother had just written it.

Adair sat and again and again tried to emulate her mother's hand. But her own handwriting was strong and definite, her mother's faintly unsure.

Wash and pare apples, (skin on).

Adair knew she must have written "and pare" by mistake or out of habit.

And slice into small bits. Cover with water and boil till soft.

Thus she had built her mother up out of these small remnants and had done so for years and now more than ever in the prison cell she must reconstruct her. Adair tried to copy her mother's hand, especially the *S* and the capital *T* but could not do it and so finally her pen began to move over the page.

And so she wrote. She wrote the first thing that came into her head. She wrote in tumbling artless sentences that rambled and stopped and jumped from thought to thought. She drove the pen across the paper, her fingers white and thin as pale horses. To construct a world of high romance and innocence, innocence above all, to show him who he held in this place and melt his heart and make him let her go, as the Huntsman had paused in the snowy woods of Grimm and said to Snow White, Run for your life.

Adair dipped her steel pen in the ink and began, *Once upon a Time*.

II

Artist Manuel DeFranca was St. Louis' most popular portrait painter during the mid-nineteenth century. His richly colored portraits adorned the walls of practically every upper-class parlor in the city. . . . DeFranca's success can . . . be attributed to his romanticized treatment of his subjects, a style employing nineteenth century standards of beauty. His portraits utilized rich colors, elaborate landscaped backgrounds, and an overall delicacy, traits that led to the artist's new reputation as a "lady's painter" . . . he died on August 22, 1865. [His monument] stands in Bellefontaine Cemetery in St. Louis.

— FROM *Gateway Heritage*, VOL. 16, NO. 1, 1995

SPECIAL REPORT E (SPY FOR THE [UNION] PROVOST MARSHAL'S DEPARTMENT, ST. LOUIS)

Dan Woods, Pat McKay & McLaughlin expressed themselves in the following manner, [on the corner of 14th & Spruce Sts.] "It was a damned good ball that killed General Lyon, the cowardly son-of-a-bitch" and other disgraceful and disloyal remarks. . . . They are on the police force at night. James Newell—witness. Duncan S. Carter. Loud in his denunciation of the Federal government—used very improper remarks regarding the "Provost Marshall," calling him a damned Scotch Highlander and questioning his right to close bars, &c., that he had purchased a good rifle and had a man to use it, in the Southern cause. . . . William Dutro—bricklayer, a tall, dark-complexioned man—living in the neighborhood of 17th and Biddle Streets, used the following expressions after hearing of the battle of Springfield, "Ah, another thousand of the damned Union sons-of-bitches have been made to bite the dust." . . . *Witnesses P. Goff, Capt. of Home Guards, cor. of 4th and Elm streets.*

—from *The Little Gods*

TWO DAYS LATER MAJOR WILLIAM NEUMANN RODE WEST ON LOCUST Street toward his boardinghouse at Twenty-first and Locust. He was nearly beyond the city's bounds. The streets were unpaved and rutted. It was six in the evening and already dark. They had nearly come to the shortest day of the year, December 21. This edge of the city was on higher ground; he could see down into the center of St. Louis. It was banked in coal smoke, the great church steeples rising out of it, and down in its heart was the dim glow of gas lamps as if they burnt at the heart of a cold foundry producing by alchemy the elements of war and progress.

In his saddlebags Major Neumann carried her confession. He would read it and he would then know something of her. Of who she was, where she came from, how she had come to be in that desolate prison. His tall bay horse walked down Locust in a reaching stride, and as they were nearing home the gelding lifted his head on his long neck and tossed his nose up and down as if nodding Yes Yes Yes.

He came to his boardinghouse. He dismounted in the gaslight and handed his reins to the giant Welshman who took care of the horses. His name was Christopher Columbus Jones and he would sleep nowhere but in a fodder box behind the boardinghouse. Not even if offered a bed.

Well ah, arrr, the Welshman said, and took the bay horse away.

Arrrr, said the major to his back.

The boardinghouse was pleasant and quiet. Heavy double chimneys at either end, verandas on both stories and the walls were plastered white. The major walked up the stairs with his leather portfolio in hand. He had a double suite of rooms and he paid a boy seven dollars a month out of his bachelor officer's allowance to keep the room clean and fetch hot water and take his clothes to the laundress. Army slang called the young and ragged valet a dog-robber, Neumann never knew where the word came from.

The fire had been laid and lit. He put the portfolio on the round lamp table. Opened the flap. He could see her handwriting and briefly in his imagination could see her head bent over the writing paper and her remarkable eyes. He reached for it. Then he decided to wait.

The twelve-paned windows looked out on the winter street, the diminishing houses and the gaslights. He listened to the click of gigs and rockaways being drawn past, on their way home, the crisp clip of the horses' hooves striking stones in the road. The dog-robber opened his door. Neumann stood holding his belt in his hands.

Coffee, said the major. And where is my bootjack?

Coming, said the boy. Within a short time a bootjack came flying into the room from the open door and then a pair of rolled fresh socks. Neumann picked them up. He stood on the bootjack with one foot and caught up the heel of his other boot in the crotch and felt great relief as it was drawn off. Then the right one. He stood them in front of the fire to dry. Pulled on the dry socks. He watched the flames burning yellow from new kindling, and tapped the gold signet ring on his left hand on his teeth so that it made clicking noises. His boots were wet through. Then the boy brought in a graniteware pot of coffee and an ironstone mug.

Take care of these boots, sir? The boy picked them up.

Yes, said the major. Don't be wearing them, either.

Sir! The child saluted. He was twelve years old and dying to join the army.

All right, Sarge, the major said.

He poured a cup of coffee and sat in front of the fire. Drank it. And then at last he drew the pages out of the portfolio and sat with them at the lamp table.

He read:

> Once upon a Time there was a farm in the Ozark Mountains. And
> there were a father and four chillren. Three were girls and one

was a boy. Their beloved mother had died of a fever in the spring
of 1855 when she seemed to evaporate out of human hands. She
was thin as smoke, as if her shadow had holes in it. She was laid to
rest on the Devil's Backbone never to be forgotten.

So they all went home afterwards. My sisters and I sat on the
veranda and cried until a storm drove us inside. We agreed to
meet in the barn loft for crying once a week but after a while we
forgot. Once we did but nobody could work up a cry and we
started playing wolves and chickens and Little Mary had to be the
chicken and Savannah shoved her out of the loft and broke her
collarbone. The hearts of children are hard naturally because of
their short memories. Everything they play with becomes true
and unquestionable such as an acorn cap for a Holy Grail, such is
the power of the untrained mind, and all our training of it is both
of advantage and not. I hope you will think on this, Major.

So we lived there summer and winter. Since my father could
not knit, our stockings wore out and then we tied up the holes
with string until Aunt Kelly came and made us new ones and said
we were like savages. My horse was named Whiskey, he came
from a trader near Cato Springs who traveled the country with all
manner of horses but my father chose him for me out of the entire
string because of the look in his eye which my father said was
noble.

We lived without telegraph lines. They are things that carry
evil gossip without your being able to see the gossiper and identify
them and take your revenge. They speak unseen somewhere afar
off. This spy voice is now ticking all over the Ozarks and ordering
the taking of women to prison and because of it fifteen Militia
shot Mrs. West in her doorway.

We had 1,200 acres all told. We had hay meadows, 2 cornfields,
forty acres in cotton, 25 sheep, pigs, silverware, clothes, a great
many law books for Missouri and also for the Texas Constitution
which interested my father, and other volumes with engraved and
colored illustrations. Also a beveled looking glass from Tennessee

recently smashed up by the crew of the MSM led by Captain Tom Poth who has red hair. Now this is the kind of thing people go to hell for. We did not look at ourselves again for a long time being on the road, so we presented ourselves to the commander at Iron Mountain and we were as uncouth as savages who never regard themselves. But are instead regarded.

He put his finger on his place and watched the fire. She had changed it all to a shining tale without stillbirths or floods, or parasites or deformed people. Her mother had not died screaming or crying but had faded away like ruined silk. There were no Confederates in this story. They were all perfectly innocent, set upon by lunatics in blue for no reason. And as far as Adair Colley knew there was no reason. What could she have known of the Constitutional issues or political clashes in far places? The major turned back to the script.

In the fall persimmins were plentiful as well as apples and I liked to put them in a bowl together because of their colors. We roasted the apples and had them with cream. These colors were also beautiful, the cream being a pale yellow and the apples carmine. You put maple sugar all over this, as much as you can get away with.

I dream of the provisions we had at that time and they seem like fare of great elegance but that is because of the dismal substances were are forced to eat in this place and of which I hope you will take note, Major. The bell of St. Louis Cathedral has just rung six o'clock with that old Catholic bell, which is suppertime in this prison. My father put the hams in salt to draw, for though he was poor at farming he loved to cook. I see him now with his hands frosted with the fine salt and his Tavern hat cocked on his head. I used to ride away up the Devil's Backbone when they killed a hog because it was not good for the horses to hear it or me either.

The heart of a pig is exactly like the heart of a human being if you have ever seen one, Major, and it was for this the huntsman killed a pig and presented the heart to the queen who said mirror mirror on the wall, so that Snow White could walk on through the snow with her shawl flying and herself on her way to a place like Iron Mountain. Now, think on this: Snow White laying still in her coffin with the piece of apple in her mouth as if dead, as it was depicted in our book of fairy tales. And did she not rise again when a prince came? I'll tell you who the prince was, it was the huntsman himself, who harries us away from the mirror, where we stand entranced with ourselves and mezmerized with what lies behind that mirror and the dark realms.

For we must not dwell on Death, as it is a mystery and it is something Unknown we leave to the Lord and his disposing for if we knew everything we would be too full of perfectly known things, and thus never rested nor content but driven with busyness and stuffed full. When I rode out in the early mornings in summertimes everything appeared to me, one after the other, in its own selfe without having to be known about beforehand, before you even get to it. In the order of the world is a deep pattern. You can't know it beforehand. If you did you would remain forever unsurprised and dwarfed and hardened. In the early mornings one after another we broke up the planes of water in the pools of Beaverdam with slow steps, horse and rider, and the trees appeared in their reflections like underwater spirits of themselves. Before these things a person is silent.

He held the paper tipped to the lantern light. And in her silences Adair Colley would spread out her old folk tales. What he was reading was a work of the imagination and a resolute determination not to live in the world as it was. Nobody brought the Rebel mail, nor were men hanged from white oak trees by either Militia or guerillas. No crows pecked out the eyes of men lying unburied. There were no latrines here or whores, and this information would capture no bushwhackers. It was a kind of music.

My father was too old to go for a soldier, and had poor eyesight from his law reading, and had always stayed out of local politics. My brother whom you accuse of being a soldier with Reeves's Fifteenth Cavalry CSA is on the contrary a cripple and could never carry a weapon atall, neither long gun nor pistol. They were putting J. B. Crean's millstone into place on September 10th, 1857, and there was a ten-cent piece laying on the lower stone and my brother John Lee said Here, I'll get it, and the stone rolled over his arm. The men in my family are thus useless for the ~~ingins~~ ~~injuns~~ enjins of war due to the law and a ten-cent piece.

This Rebellion against the lawful Order was ordained by Heaven, for the Lord must have planned and prepared for this as He does for all things and something this big surely did not catch Him by surprize but on the other hand there may be surprizes in Heaven as elsewhere.

The men alaying under the earth in gray have lain down their lives for some reason we may never know, just as the Lord knows all things, for some strange purpose He allowed this great conflict to take place on the earth and the people held in bondage to be unfettered and men of the South to be blinded even in their own doorways. And so everything is in an endless changing and disorder at present.

Only one thing I know, Major, and that is this War was sent by Heaven to free the slaves and preserve the Union. I have seen great armies of men with artillery and heard the canon in the hills. I have seen them come through my country in their thousands both in blue and gray and butternut and it was to the advantage of none. So the Lord has cast down his Rebel Angels. Did He not raise them up to Glory with a great congregation of flags and horse troops and music bands on that day of Secession? And yet the Rebel Angels are now cast down.

I remain,

Yours very truly,

Adair Randolph Colley

He sat with the pages a while watching his fire burn down the logs. Then he undressed and lay in his solitary bed and looked at the ceiling. He did not sleep well. He arose in the night and struck a match to the lamp wick and sat down and read her confession again and then put it away once more. Before the first light of dawn he dressed in his boots and his uniform, and went down the stairs to the kitchen. There the giant Welshman sat in front of the fire while the cook beat the biscuit dough with a wooden mallet as if it had been caught in doing something wicked.

Would you pull out my horse, Christopher? he said.

Awrahhhh.

He rode out into the dark streets and saw that the sky had cleared. Stars stood out in electrifying spangles, the Dipper and the Charioteer, riding over and over again their eternal routes across the heaven. He rode north at a slow walk, and his large bay gelding searched about for other horses and spoke in a low voice to the milkman's horse pulling a small two-wheeled cart. He had been told in Maryland when he was young that the Big Dipper was also seen as a milkman's cart called The Wain that turned on its route through the night hours and poured out its milk into the foam of stars. He had watched it swing through the night sky from the bow of a skipjack skimming across Chesapeake Bay, all canvas up and taut in the starry wind. He wished she were with him, riding alongside. The major felt diminished now despite his height because he was helpless to aid her. Shrunk by the problem he was up against. And the horse carried him on toward Florissant until the dawn came.

Neumann rode up to Bellefontaine Road, and into a great beech woods. He waited as the sun came up.

He put his gloved hand to his forehead in a nervous gesture of dismay, tapped on his forehead with his own knuckles. His fellow officers in other departments made jokes about his ladies. Six months ago at Benker's Tavern, he had told stories about the chilly Miss Rhoda Cobb, and hinted at the seductiveness of little Kisia. But after a while it came to him that they considered this assignment not quite honorable; this arrangement of papers and filing depositions, the interrogation of captive women. Then he had sent in repeated requests for transfer. To a fighting unit. But he was also determined to leave the judge advocate general's department with a successful record. Success in obtaining confessions that would break down Reeves's organization and with the credit accruing to himself. This credit standing him in good stead afterward when the surrender came.

He took off his broad-brimmed hat and sat on the horse and looked down the Bellefontaine Road, and tried to think what to do.

Then he turned back and rode toward the Ogley House, where the provost marshal's general staff abided in their confiscated mansion. Young women in bonnets hurried past on racketing clogs toward the big houses where they worked. Drays were now surging up Natural Bridge Plank Road with barrels of beer and cheese and fish and then came the bakers' carts. He would begin with the colonel, and try to push her case through as far as possible. And because he was trained in the law, he tried to think of their objections one by one, and how he could overcome them.

The colonel would say, Her male relatives are all known to have joined Confederate units.

He would say, Sir, I am not entirely sure of this, but at any rate, we cannot imprison the female relations of the entire Confederate Army.

Of course not, sir, merely the ones we can get our hands on. The ones who are keeping Colonel Reeves in the field.

Sir, she is eighteen years old and cannot possibly equip a regiment.

Major, the women of that section of the country are worse than the men. Martial law has been declared in this state.

Yes, sir, it certainly has, however the people of this sector have not been apprised of this as far as I know, and apparently her male relations are incapable of service in the army, one being too old and the other crippled.

Have you proof of this?

Only her word, sir. However, we seemed to be prepared to accept her word on other matters.

It is her loyalty that is in question, Major Neumann, not her harm-lessness. If she were to reveal something of what she knows of Con-federate operations in her area, it would prove her loyalty and then certainly she should be released. It is a dreadful thing to imprison women.

There have been several incidents, said the major. With the women.

We are aware of that. Charges are being brought.

What if she doesn't know anything?

This is impossible. Captain Poth has written that her father knows everyone in the area. Her brother was captured in Reeves's uniform and escaped.

I wonder about the trustworthiness of Poth's reports.

Major, what exactly is your interest in this matter?

Sir, my interest is that I would like to retire on full pay with a good record and have the girl released as well. How about that.

Major William Neumann rode looking at his horse's ears, as they twitched here and there picking up sounds, the sight of another horse. The perfect silver trunks of the beech trees passed him one by one and their shadows slipped over him like the bars of a prison.

12

In 1860 about one Missouri family in eight (as opposed to one in five in the lower south) held slaves, nearly three-fourths of those holding fewer than five, and only 38 holding more than fifty. . . . Ninety per cent of Missourians lived on farms or in villages of less than 2,000 people. With the exception of St. Louis, there were no cities in Missouri . . . statistically, the average Missourian was a Methodist from Kentucky who owned a 215-acre family farm, owned no slaves, and produced most of the family's subsistence.

—FROM *Inside War*

June 18, Saturday, 1864

At the Gratiot Street Prison in St. Louis, Mo., between the hours of 9 and 10 A.M., some prisoners exercising in the yard seized an axe from the kitchen and broke the lock on a gate leading into an alley. Some of the Rebel prisoners disarmed the guard from behind and several scattered in all directions. Troops from the 10th Kansas Infantry were sent after them and they were joined by other Union troops in the area. After a wild scramble over backyard fences, through sheds and outbuildings, and down alleys, two of the escapees were killed and three wounded. The remainder were captured and returned to prison.

—FROM *Civil War Prisons and Escapes*, BY ROBERT E. DENNEY,
STERLING PUBLISHING COMPANY, NEW YORK, 1993

Great Heavens, my blood boils—women in this hole of filth and blasphemy! I could scarcely believe it until I saw it with my own eyes, Mrs. Mitchell, who is here with a little daughter five or six years old. She is charged with smuggling goods through to the Confederacy.

. . . One old man named Murphy has been added to our room, imprisoned, he says, for selling miscegenation photographs.

—GRIFFIN FROST, *Camp and Prison Journal*

MISS COLLEY, HE SAID. HE SHUT THE DOOR BEHIND HER. I AM VERY pleased that you have professed loyalty to the Union in your writing.

Well, good. Adair sat down. She felt lighthearted. Just being in the same room with him. The cough rose in her chest and she subdued it.

He nodded. Placed all his fingertips together as if completing some kind of interior circuit.

And other than that, I don't have any information to give you about any one thing in particular.

He sat on the edge of his desk and looked at her. She had on a pair of sparkling earrings this time and an embroidered jacket. He crossed his arms across his chest.

He said, Do you have a mirror in your cell?

Oh, Major, how kind of you to ask, but I have a big hall looking glass, said Adair. And a dressing table and a clothes press and one of those things with pockets to put all my shoes in.

Can I not get a straight answer from you?

Adair said, I'm living in a filthy cell.

He lifted his hand. Well, then, here is my mirror, and I have brought you a brush. This is not proper, but we are not living in a proper world, here. He drew out his chair and placed it in front of the mirror near the stove. I have some reports to look at.

Adair took the brush from him and stood still for a moment without saying anything. Then she sat in front of the mirror with its beveled edges that caught the light in prismatic planes. She unpinned her hair and drew it out stroke after stroke, entranced with her reflection, in the warmth of the parlor stove. After a few minutes she began to hum a Scotch slow air and listened to the traffic outside the window, people talking as they went past. She separated her hair into two long hanks and then took one of the hanks and divided it into three strands. *Black, black, black is the color*, she sang to herself in a whisper.

He read his reports, and dipped his pen in the inkwell without looking up. He said, Miss Colley, what are you going to do with your life after you get out of here?

Oh I have dreamed of raising horses, she said. She couldn't imagine why she was confessing this to him. She braided one side and coiled the long braid. I guess I'm supposed to find somebody and get married. But I want to raise horses.

He shook sand on the ink and blew on it. And all that that implies, he said. Brood mares and a good stallion. I don't know if they allow ladies to do that, he said. You may have to get a dispensation from the Pope or something.

Adair braided the other hank, regarding herself carefully in the mirror, turned her head from one side to the other. She could see the major lining up two columns of names side by side and comparing them. Well, I'll just go to hell then, she said.

The major laughed. He opened a drawer and took out a cigar and cut the end of it off with a penknife. Lit it and blew smoke out of his nose. He went to open a window to let the smoke escape and threw the dead match out onto the sidewalk. A rush of cold city air and its coal smoke came in and he quickly shut it. He turned to watch her draw the braids around her head in a crown and lay down the brush.

He said, This is somewhat indelicate, Miss Colley. Ladies have no business with that kind of thing.

But it is so absorbing! It's magic. She stood up and walked to him, took one of his hands and lifted it, and the ring glinted. Ink stained, she said. You are an inky man.

How is it magic?

The mare and the stallion gallop away together in the fields. Then my sisters and I go inside the house. Then, you been waiting eleven months and then there they are. Adair went to the window to see all the traffic in the street and then turned to face him, leaned against the sill with her hands behind her. She tipped her head to one side. You wake up one morning and the mare is standing back in the trees. Looking out, so carefully. She won't move. Then you see little legs on her other side. The fog coming down off Courtois and Copperhead in long sheets, drifting clear over the meadow and there she is. This is how Dolly came to us. Adair turned and pressed her forefinger against her lower lip and stared out the window. They are made out of nothing. They come out of nowhere. Look there at that building going up. Now, you understand where all those buildings come from, but nobody understands how that young thing is made with eyes and everything. She sat in the chair again. Close to him.

They sat in companionable silence for a moment. Then he got up and cleared his throat, opened the stove door. Took up the tongs and placed several pieces of coal on the flames.

In some ways we understand but only in the most mechanical sense. We are a mechanical people.

Maybe *you* are, said Adair. Speak for yourself.

He smiled. And here you are in the city. Do you not want to be released, and then perhaps stay on here in St. Louis? The social events are endless.

Adair said, I don't care for them. What, dances? She laughed. Entertainments upon the stage? She lifted her fist to her closed mouth and coughed a small cough.

Ladies' clubs, he said. His eyes sparkled and he smiled at her. Charities and fawnings upon portrait painters.

Is this what you do? she asked. No wonder you want out of this cussed place.

No, he said. I've been to the theater but once. Major Neumann gave a small shrug. It was a lie, but a minor lie, for he wanted her to know that at heart the two of them were alike. He had been to the Holly Street theater many times.

Adair sat down and rested her cheek on her fist. Leaned her elbow on the chair arm. Of course I want to get released. I have never seen the like of the women in this place.

You must get out of here as soon as possible. The major cleared his throat. He troubled the glowing coals with the poker. I can't change things here. The solution is to get you out of here. He closed the stove door and turned the handle. When you are released, and you will be, have you ever thought about the western territories? To change the subject. The major indicated his books. Far away from cities. He sat down again close to her.

She said, I only heard about them. She got up and went over to take down one of his books. She ran the pages past her thumb. Is this where I can escape to, Major? She turned and smiled her brilliant smile. We had *Holland's Pictorial History of the World* and it had California in it. We have had people start for California from our county and when they make up a band of wagons and start out, the morning they go they always sing "Awake Awake Ye Drowsy Sleepers." She looked down at the book again. There was a page with hand-colored illustrations of Mandan Indians. Is this where I could escape to? You think I could keep my hair?

He could hardly keep himself from touching her. His desire was great. It was overwhelming. He saw her riding at a slow walk beside some reflective body of water, and the whippoorwill repeating itself in a cascade of liquid notes. It would be in a remote valley in the western lands, and the war far away. And there would be a trim small house beside the body of water and Adair in front of the fire combing out that long hair. In a nightgown. He wanted so to touch her.

He took her hand and said, Has the matron mistreated you?

Adair paused with her mouth open.

He said, Tell me.

Yes, she did, and I don't like to admit it. Adair slapped the book shut. If I were a free person I would have knocked both her eyes into one socket.

What happened?

I asked her when I could mail a letter and insisted on my rights. She said we ought to get along and offered her hand. And when I did she about broke it, and threw me across the floor.

His mouth made a thin line and he got up and went back to his desk and wrote something in pencil, but in truth he was only writing down a small list of purchases to be made for himself, *coffee*, *pen nibs*, *buttons*, because he found himself possessed by a boiling fury and he needed to calm himself and so he wrote it all out again. Writing calmed him.

Well, there, I have made a note of it.

Major, you are such a stick, said Adair. Whatever happens you have to write up a report.

Well, Miss Adair, sometimes it works. Do not turn up your pretty nose at reports. The provost marshal's department runs on paper. It is an engine fueled with paper. He paused and pressed down his collar. Am I such a stick? He smiled at her again.

No.

He reached out and drew his hand across her crown of braids. You look very nice indeed.

Thank you.

The clock on his shelf of books ate time, second after second, and the whistle sounded at the white lead factory.

It is time for you to go. He smiled. I'll tell you what. He went again to his desk and took out a deck of cards. It is Christmastime. We are not allowed to give Christmas presents to the prisoners. But let's you and I decide on who is to give who a gift. Leave it to chance. He fanned the deck and held it out. Take a card.

What for? Adair put out her hand and then hesitated. Explain this to me again.

Whoever draws the low card has to give the other one a Christmas gift.

I don't understand this, you are up to something. But she drew the ten of spades.

He nodded, and then drew one himself. It was the trey of hearts.

William Neumann smiled brightly. I owe you a Christmas gift, he said.

She looked up into his eyes. You have engineered this, she said. You cheated.

I did not. He picked up the cigar and drew on it. Now, I am afraid we must address this business of your confession, he said. This will not do, Miss Colley. Although I couldn't stop reading it. He held up the paper covered with her handwriting. Try again.

Adair looked again at her hands. She thought for a moment.

Then that's not a confession?

No. He was not smiling and stood very still. I must ask you again.

Against my own people?

I want you out of this prison.

What if I went insane? From time to time I feel that I'm not myself. Not the Adair Colley I used to know. At one time I was so sweet and gentle I couldn't pull a turnip out of the garden without weeping over the poor, dear thing. She put her hands together as if in prayer. You want something about my brother.

You must get out, he said. He reached out his hand and laid it in a light touch along her forearm. Women are dying here. He lifted his hand and touched her earlobe.

She turned her head away from his hand. But his touch felt very good to her.

Miss Adair. Write something.

I just did.

Information. Just some small thing.

Well then, she said. I'll keep on.

He smoked his cigar in a long draw. Then bent the glowing end off

in a coffee saucer and left it lying there. He got up and opened the door
for her. It's Christmas Eve, he said. I don't imagine Mrs. Buckley has
prepared anything special for her charges.

Boiled rats, said Adair. With little red ribbons on their tails.

He laughed.

Miss Adair.

Mr. William.

And here is the Christmas gift I owe you. He handed her a box
wrapped in red paper. Open it.

Oh my goodness! She tugged the paper loose eagerly. He noticed
how she handled it and slowly separated one bright, crisp fold from
another, cherishing the texture and the color of the paper. Inside were
taffies wrapped in more red paper, and a small book of poetry. Transla-
tions from the Italian. New mittens in indigo and red wool. She held
the package to herself. You did cheat.

I learned magic card tricks as a boy.

Then Adair put her forefinger on one of his chest buttons and said,
That's favoritism. Now you have to go and give everybody taffy.

Then it is favoritism. He bowed slightly as she went out the door.
You are in my thoughts.

DECEMBER PASSED INTO JANUARY AND ON JANUARY 9 SHE LOOKED OUT HER
cell window to see Rhoda walking down the street in a confused, shambling way, carrying a carpetbag. Her head down. Adair did not know
where she might be going in the confusion of the traffic but from what
she had heard of her parlor talks with the lawyer it might well be to hell
or a bordello.

At the washing that day Adair ran her yard-long hair through her
fists, mashing out soapsuds. She called over the steaming barrels to
Kisia.

What happened to Rhoda Lee?

I don't know, said Kisia. Aunt says I'm not supposed to know.

Madame Rose had her wet corset in her hands and pretended to play it as if it were a concertina, opening and shutting it with all its pink silk and stays. Oh, she got herself in the family way with her lawyer, she sang. Love, O love O careless love.

Is she gone home to her family?

Not her. Not her. She's gone a-follering and a-whining after him. Once I wore my apron high, now my apron strings won't tie.

Now I have two very pretty rebel girls on my hands as prisoners and what the devil to do with them I don't know, as I don't like to put them in the guard house. I expect I will have to take them into my room and let them sleep with me.

—Bazel F. Lazear to his wife, Harrisonville, Missouri, April 29, 1863, Bazel F. Lazear Collection, Joint Collection Missouri Historical Society, University of Missouri, quoted in *Inside War*

Union Correspondence
Headquarters District of Central Missouri
Warrensburg, Mo., September 10, 1864
To: Lt. Col. B. F. Lazear, Commanding Missouri Union Militia, Second Sub-District, Lexington, Mo.
Colonel: The commanding general is informed by Major-General Rosecrans that your troops are causing a reign of terror in LaFayette and Saline Counties and that it should receive your attention. He is also further informed that their officers are permitting them to rob the people of their property for their own benefit, to murder peaceable citizens, and commit other outrages upon the people while the pursuit of the bushwhackers is abandoned by loading the troops with plunder from the country. . . . He directs you will report fully in relation to these complaints.

Very respectfully, your obedient servant,
J. H. Steger, Assistant Adjutant-General
—OR, ch. liii, p. 145

AND AGAIN SHE WAS ESCORTED TO HIS OFFICE, HER THREE SHEETS OF confession in her hand, in which she had written about the blizzard of 1861.

Tell me about where you were before. Adair smiled brightly at the major and walked over to the map on the wall. You have had so many adventures.

Last time you told me I was a stick.

Well, only sometimes you're a stick. It's because of your being in this line of work. It's a line of paperwork, where it's nothing but words. She leaned to him and laid her hand on his arm.

Major Neumann laid his hand over her own and then there was a brisk knock at the door. They both jumped and Adair turned quickly and sat on the yellow sofa.

Major Neumann opened the door. The sergeant walked in with a tray of coffee and pastries, sat them down on the major's desk and gave them both a cool look.

Thank you, Sergeant.

Sir. He turned and marched out the door and shut it behind them.

The major stood for a minute with his back against the door. He expelled a long breath and then went to the desk. He poured coffee for them both.

Adair took the cup from him and smiled. She said, You were going to tell me about your exciting past life before that Hessian charged in here. I bet you were somewhere very interesting, before. She drank off the cup, set it down, and then went to the map.

Before? He smiled at her. She paused with her finger pointing at the map, circling.

Where? she said.

There, Kansas. Adair pinned her finger on the State of Kansas. Out of Kansas City, which was then called Westport. I was with a company of dragoons, Regular Army, for a while in Kansas. We were supposed to keep the Missourians and the Kansans from killing one another, but they were very clever about it. Killing one another, I mean. He leaned back in his chair. John Brown was very good. Jim Lane, the boys from Clay County, Missouri. We were not half as effective as they were. Adair could see he was too cheerful today to remain serious. You look much better today, Miss Adair. Is there anything you need?

She thought about it. I need phosphorous matches, she said. I can trade them, and I am an astute trader.

Low card wins, he said. He lifted a small bundle of phosphorous matches out of a drawer, and took out the cards as well and fanned them.

Now don't cheat, she said. And drew a jack. He laid the cards out on his desk and pulled one out; the ten of hearts. You could have arranged them any way you wanted before I came.

Not at all. And I keep coming up with hearts. That's rather significant, isn't it? He slid them together in a quick motion. You are looking better each day, he said.

Well, she said. I am thriving on German pastries. Have we eaten them all? Aren't there any more? Order some more. And more coffee.

Of course there are, he said. Of course. He went to the door and spoke to the sergeant outside and came back.

He pulled up his chair beside her. He reached to take her hand, and put his thumb and forefinger in a circle around her wrist. He said, You are very thin. I just want you to live. Live to go home.

She smiled at him and reached for an apple pastry.

But tell me about Kansas.

Well, while I was there, I met a man, his name was Schoolcraft, who was very interested in the Red Indians. He had written down enormous amounts of their language, a really thorough lexicon. He was with my unit briefly in Kansas, he had come to see the Poncas. Henry Schoolcraft. A brilliant man. He paused. I am interested in languages, I suppose because of my expertise in, in. . . . He paused. Well, in interrogation.

She laughed. So you will tie them up and make them confess all their words. She drew the end of a black braid under her nose and twisted it as if it were a mustache. And now I have you where I want you, my redskinned beauty!

Adair, please. He laughed.

Tell me your word for *dishpan*, for *throwing up*! For *twelve percent interest*!

I've decided not to tie them up, he said. Then he cleared his throat again and plunged on. And after the war I think I will put in a request to continue his work somewhere. For the Department of Ethnology. Schoolcraft has recently passed away, and of course with the war . . . with the war there's no time or money for writing down the words of Red Indians. He paused. But I think I would be good at it.

Of course you would! Anything that has to do with writing things down, you are top rail.

Stop. He laughed. I am not such a stick as you think. He then turned to regard the map of the United States, and its strange manner of drifting away into unscripted, unknown lands beyond Fort Leavenworth. He said, Adair, I find your companionship to be, to be . . . I value every hour I am with you. He stood as if to attention with his fingertips at the stripe of his uniform pants. Then he crossed his arms with slow resolution. Uncrossed them.

Adair thought of clean air and blue skies, all the war machines far away. All the burial grounds far away. She and the major standing at the window of a house looking out into a gathering storm of lightning. Long flat sheets of lightning over a land that had the aspect of an ocean of grass. The window would be in their bedroom. The bed covered with the Log Cabin quilt and fresh sheets beneath. She dusted crumbs from her hands. She had to go home first. Get out of here and go home and find her father and then she would think what to do.

Oh it sounds wonderful! she said. If I were released, the West is the first place I would go. And the savages sound so fascinating. Maybe they're more refined than the Shawnees. The Shawnees just brained everybody right away.

So I've heard. At last he turned and looked down at her. Adair, you must go.

I don't want to, she said. I want to be with you.

You must. Sit tonight and write something that will get you out of here.

He stood out in the hall and watched as the guard escorted her back into the prison.

THEN MRS. BUCKLEY CAME STALKING DOWN THE HALL LIKE A RAILROAD bridge on the loose and slapped a folded and torn piece of paper onto the crossbars of Adair's cell.

Well, here you are getting your mail delivered just like you was living in your own dwelling, she said. We are pampering secessionist spies.

Adair unfolded it and pieced it back together. It was from her sister Savannah.

Dearest Sister

I hope this letter comes to you without interference and Mary and I pray you are safe and will soon be out of wherever it is they have placed you there in St. Louis. We have asked again and again for father at Iron Mountain but we have got no results. Mary and I pray nightly for his safety and yours as well. We have attempted to send you a package. All this is coming through the U.S. Army mail from Iron Mountain to wherever it is you are in St. Louis or Alton. Mary and I have requested a pass to go over to Tennessee to stay with Grandma and Grandpa Colley at Sugar Tree and we will go with Lucinda Newnan and Aunt Kelly and we should be on the road for two weeks which is hard but the Daltons say that is the best place for us to go for the duration. We will go to Cape Girardeau and take a Union packet down to Dyersville and thence on to Sugar Tree if we can get a conveyance. They say it is all free of warring there. Mary and I have made up 15 yards of wool and good Virginia

*linen in madder and a dark yellow. Mrs. Dalton had 15 broaches of the
linen since 1861. She said we might as well make it up. We would send
you a dress of it but it is too nice for prison so we have cut it into a dress
for myself. I have met a man from Fredricktown, Missouri, of good family. We hope you will soon be released since we know you to be our good
and loving sister and free of all animosity toward the Union cause and
we know how you have always ardently opposed secession. Oh sister when
will this war be over? We are going to bring back lace goods from Tennessee for you. Mary and I will try one more package before we go and
hope it gets to you.*

*We will return when we can and believe us ever your loving and most
affectionate sisters,*

Savannah and Mary
Dalton's Store
Greenville Courthouse Wayne County Missouri

Adair read it over and over again and there in her sister's handwriting she saw that if she were to go home she would be alone in that
endeavor, but there was no help for it. It was very clear that the letter
was written with the censor in mind but it was easy to read between the
lines. If she could just see her home one more time. If she could find
her father. Then she would be free to think about a place where the war
had not come, where she and the major could start anew.

14

During the spring and summer of 1863, various Federal commanders insti-
tuted a policy of arresting women and teenage girls (sisters and cousins of the
men in Quantrill's band) who were suspected of aiding guerillas.... They
were confined ... in Kansas City, Missouri. On August 13, the looming,
three-story brick building at 1409 Grand Avenue in Kansas City that General Ewing was using as a prison for some of the southern girls who had been
arrested as spies ... collapsed. The females, none of whom was older than
twenty, had been confined on the second floor and as the building began to
shake and walls to split apart from one another, a guard scooped up two girls
and carried them outside. Nannie McCorkle leaped out a window. Thirteen-
year-old Martha Anderson tried to follow, but, according to accounts of survivors, she had annoyed the guards earlier that morning and to punish her
they had shackled a twelve-pound ball to her ankle. She went down in the
wreckage.

Soldiers and civilians rushed to the scene; however, a great cloud of dust
prevented the immediate extrication of the victims from the rubble.... As
soon as the dust dissipated sufficiently, the bystanders set to work digging
through the ruins. Groans and screams could be heard and one girl—thought
to be fifteen-year-old Josephine Anderson—kept begging for someone to take
the bricks off her head. After a while she fell silent. A large crowd gathered
and angrily listened to the shrieks and moans and watched the removal of the
bodies. A messenger was sent for Major Preston B. Plumb, Ewing's chief of
staff, and by the time he arrived on the scene the crowd's mood had become so

ugly he called out the headquarters' guard and ordered them to fix bayonets to
prevent a riot.

It is no longer possible to determine how many prisoners were being held on
the second floor—contemporary estimates range between nine and twenty-
seven—but . . . the toll among relatives of Quantrill's raiders was high.
Josephine Anderson (sister of "Bloody Bill") died before being freed, and
another Anderson sister, Mary, eighteen, was, in a phrase common in that
era, "crippled for life." The third Anderson sister, Martha, suffered two bro-
ken legs, injured her back, and her face was severely lacerated. Charity
McCorkle Kerr, John McCorkle's sister and Cole Younger's cousin, died. Also
killed were twin sisters of another member of the band, Mrs. Armenia Craw-
ford Selvey and Mrs. Susan Crawford Vandevere. Nothing is known about
the other girl who was fatally injured and who is identified only as Mrs. Wil-
son. Nearly all the survivors were badly hurt.

—FROM *The Devil Knows How to Ride: The True Story of William Clarke Quantrill*
and His Confederate Raiders, BY EDWARD E. LESLIE,
RANDOM HOUSE, NEW YORK, 1996

Mary Hall wrote to her sister, Venetia Colcord Page, who had been imprisoned
in Kansas City along with the sisters of Bill Anderson as an active guerilla
supporter, "Don't say one word before any. That will only make your case
worse. Remember you are a lady and act accordingly. The guards say they like
you and Miss Parrish. They say very hard things of the others. The officers
told me this."

—JACOB HALL FAMILY PAPERS, JACKSON COUNTY HISTORICAL SOCIETY,
INDEPENDENCE, MISSOURI, QUOTED IN *Inside War*

THERE WERE TWO COURTYARDS TO THE PRISON AND THE ONE ON THE
south side of the building was for the private use of the matron and
other prisoners who were favored. Prisoners who had perhaps betrayed
others. There in the windowless courtyard was silence and privacy for
a few hours.

She was sent there to fold the matron's sheets in the sunlight. She sat on a cast-iron bench and turned her face up to the blue sky overhead. The clear air would be good for her cough. She stood a moment and then shook out the bright white linens and snapped them and folded them into squares. They were in a fresh, light stack beside her. She stood up and between her hands sent a buoyant lawn sheet flying into the winter wind, billowing in ice white loops, and so frail was the material that the sunlight poured through it onto her pale face. She felt warmed. She sang, *Will they miss me at home, will they miss me?*

She turned in the wind and saw the major standing in the doorway.

You have a lovely voice, he said. He walked over to her and took the other end of the sheet.

Adair said, I could never get my brother to do this.

Yes, he said. They walked toward each other to put the corners together and their hands touched. He took her hands and the sheet corners in his own. She stood looking up at him with the flying whiteness between them. He bent down and kissed her. Adair felt as if she had been plunged into some sultry summer air. His mouth on hers was the most intimate contact she had ever felt. He kissed her on both cheeks and on the neck. He took her hands, held her head close to his chest.

Major, she said. She started to back away, but he held her tightly.

This is fraternizing with the prisoners, he said into her ear. I could be court-martialed for this.

She said nothing but stood close, in the heat of his body, looking up at him.

He said, If you were released, where would you go?

Home, she said. At first. Then I'd be looking to go west.

There is nothing at home, Adair, he said. In the southeast counties. Are you going to live in a cave? He looked into her eyes. I want you to stay here in St. Louis. I can arrange something. He clasped both her hands and the sheet corners in them.

Write up a release for me, she said. Sign that magic paper.

He dropped the sheet, and slid his hands under her shawl, feeling every bone in her spine and her ribs. He bent to kiss her softly on the neck again and again.

He said, You could remain at the home of an officer I know. An officer and his wife. I could arrange this. Until the war is over. He let go one hand and lifted his own to her cheek, his fingertips at her ear. Then we could go west. If you would consent to marry me. You would only be here in the city a year, maybe less. And I would give you all the horses in the world. Copperbottom horses, Virginia horses.

I won't live in this city.

You must give them something. Any kind of information. Anything. Then I could arrange a parole to Captain Gromann and his family.

All right, said Adair. Her black eyebrows were like two wings and her hair shone in the sunlight. He held her close, sheet and all. His hands moved up her back, into her hair. His mouth against her hair. He kissed her temple, her shut eyes. It was worth anything to hold her like this, anything, his career and even his freedom.

And so they stood in the winter air, and he pressed her head to his collarbones, and closed his eyes. And after a while he stood back and held her hands. Then he turned and left without saying anything and Adair still stood with the billowing sheet in her hands.

THAT EVENING SHE BEGAN TO WRITE DOWN A LONG STORY CONCERNING A secret organization called the Knights of the Golden Whiskey Jug.

It is well known that the Knights of the Golden Whiskey Jug foregather in the basement of the white-lead factory at night and get to plotting how to take over the St. Louis Army Command. They give one another names out of law journals. The main man is Tort, and then there is Derivative Suit, which is a man with a gotch eye, there is Subdivision A (1) with a thumb bit off, and Admissibility Jones, who can't keep his hands off a jug, a big man with huge feet named Prior Inconsistent Statement and old Burden of Proof, who is not much good in the organization because of his inability to keep his mouth shut and so if you all could get

hold of him you wouldn't even have to force him to confess anything, he would talk your ear off about the Knights of the Golden
Whiskey Jug and then go on to tell you in detail about his hernia,
his twin stepdaughters, how much money he owes at Hyssop's
Rest in Wilderness, and would offer opinions on electricity, the
Campbellites and Mesmerism. When he gets to going don't look
him in the eye or he'll back you to the wall with his theories on
paper money. They have a flag painted with one of those big fat
Greek women in bedsheets who is holding out a hand toward something like a Lamp of Learning or a Tree of Liberty or a Barrel of
Shoes. The meetings are chaired by Subdivision A (1) but he don't
know Robert's Rules of Order from Deuteronomy and so their
meetings fall to plain argying. Admissibility says anybody who can't
make money out of a good conspiracy is either drunk or crippled.
Their real names are Bluford Nighswonger, Epsy Bazer, Miles
Long, Eppaphronious Smitters, and Fenwicke C. Butterfield.

She touched her cracked lips and then blew on her fingertips. A slow
rain watered the world outside, and from time to time, far over on the
Illinois side of the Mississippi, long wires of lightning unreeled
through the sky with blazing, remote flashes.

MAJOR NEUMANN TURNED AS SHE WAS SHOWN INTO THE ORDERLY ROOM.

Adair. This isn't going to get anybody anywhere. Knights of the
Golden Whiskey Jug? How did you invent this?

Adair said, Well, I thought it was pretty good. She pressed her hand
to her cheek to feel if she was still hot and she was. I'm tired of trying,
Major.

I am tired of your not trying.

Well, we are both just wore out then, aren't we?

She stood up and he did too, and they were at odds with each other,
as if a door had slammed between them.

He turned to her. It was a cold look. Are you well?

Yes! she said. I am very well.

Major Neumann thought for a moment. How long have you been in this dismal place?

Let's see. . . . Adair tipped her head back to gaze at the ceiling. November twenty-third, December, January . . . She put her fingertip to her lips. Then she said, Two and a half months. Still she felt the cold air between them and said, Well, I didn't put myself here.

Do you not want out of here? He said. He seized up the papers. You think perhaps you care for me. Would you care for me if you were not here? And dependent on my good will?

Of course! Adair said. She was confused and shocked at this notion. She walked to him and took his hand. I could ask you about the same thing.

The major drew his hand away. He said, I have been thinking that if you were to merely come upon me, at a social gathering, you would possibly not even speak to me.

She started to deny it but then paused to think.

Because I am with the Yankee army.

Oh hush, she said. Because she couldn't think if this were true or not. I have met you. I do care for you.

He led her to sit in the chair and looked directly into her eyes. You have to write a genuine confession to something to get out of here. I have asked for another review board, again, to look at your case. But without a genuine confession I can only move people so far.

Adair regarded him with some caution.

Think of what you're asking, she said. Think, Major.

He ran the tips of his fingers across his forehead, tucking back short strands of hair.

He said, In early November, before you came, I applied for a transfer to a fighting unit. I decided I would rather be shelled than sit through this kind of thing anymore. He paused. I am subject to intense pressure from my superior officer. Today I had to endure a lecture that

I can't bear to sit through again. Mrs. Buckley has complained about us. You must give me names. Dates. Mail routes.

I can't, she said. And I won't. Mail routes! I can't even remember what day it is in this place. The noise is like somebody hitting me in the head all day long.

He gave her a narrow and searching look. Very well. He paused. I have asked for a search of our prison records for your father's name. They can't find anyone of that name.

But he could still be alive. He could have gone back home already.

I don't think so.

He could have got away to Texas.

Adair. He turned to take her shawl from the back of the chair and handed it to her. He put on his bang-up overcoat in Federal blue and walked to the door.

You and I will go across the street and have a small collation, he said.

Adair took the shawl. Is that a dance?

He smiled. No, that's a cotillion.

He put his head out the door and looked down the hall.

Here I am fraternizing with a lady prisoner, he said. I don't see Mrs. Buckley.

Fraternize away, said Adair. She was delighted and, despite her small persistent cough and now the fever, felt suddenly possessed of energy and a kind of brightness. Don't let me stop you.

Sergeant, said Major Neumann.

I can guess, said the sergeant. And finally he smiled. He shifted his wad of tobacco. Go on. The Ironclad ain't around.

They walked quickly out into the hall and then through the doors. Adair discovered she was walking out the prison door with her hand clasped in the major's elbow. They were actually walking down the street. Adair tilted her head and closed her eyes as the light of heaven poured down on her. She held out her hand to it, the palm upward.

Hold tight, he said. He put his hand over hers and they went at a fast walk across the street. Slush flew up from the wheels of a wagon. A mail deliveryman strode past with a leather sack over his shoulders, glancing at the addresses on a sheaf of letters in his hand. Chimney pipes thrust out of windows high overhead, but a bright prairie wind from Illinois scoured away the smoke. In the door of a barbershop Adair saw a black man in a fine gray coat putting his barber scissors into a jar of alcohol. There were many mirrors. A giant hat stood high up on a pole on top of a building. The hat was two stories tall.

She held his hand and stopped in the middle of the sidewalk on the other side. A boy came running down the street in a set of knickers and a hank of hempen rope around his neck, he had no hat nor shoes. Down a block, under a half-finished building, two men were alternating strokes with eight-pound hammers, pecking at a square of stone, above them a block-and-tackle rigging. In a glass-fronted store with large panes, Adair saw ladies' shoes all in a row and herself wavering past. In the crowds of people she saw what must be wealthy women in hoops the size of hot-air balloons holding them down desperately as little urchins jammed up against them to see the hoops fly up behind.

Then they were inside a restaurant and he sat her down across from him at a table with a white cloth. Adair picked up one of the bottles of sauce from the middle of the table, put it back down again. The salt and pepper were in small bottles with metal caps, and the caps had holes in them to shake out the contents. Giant silver coffee urns spouted steam; in one of them she saw herself very long and narrow.

Miss Adair, he said. I have long admired you from afar. Waiter!

I would think so, said Adair. She settled her shawl around her shoulders. She leaned over and brushed a light dusting of ash from his sleeve just for the joy of touching him.

The waiter came. He ordered the fricassee and bottles of charged water, and after they would have the pie. Adair sat and listened as he ordered up all the food he wanted.

If we were both free, he said. Of our present entanglements. Let me think how to put this. He touched her elbow.

The way you put it is one of those forms for release.

He ignored this. Drummed his fingers on the white tablecloth. He said, Have you been proposed to before?

Adair leaned toward the major and said in a low voice, Yes, but he was a ladies' man. He was surrounded by immense droves of wild women.

In Ripley County?

We are fairly wild down there.

Am I standing in line?

Adair opened her black eyes wide and stared around the restaurant. Do you see a line here? She turned back. And the food came. Adair ate with little conviction. She didn't seem to need victuals, the light skimming fever that inhabited her, and the presence of the major, seemed to be all she needed.

Do eat, Adair, he said. You are diminishing to nothing.

I am trying. She wrapped her hands around the enormous coffee mug.

You make me feel like deserting, he said. Or joining the Russian Navy. One or the other. He put his hand palm up on the table, and Adair placed her hand in his. She knew that she loved him. She looked into his eyes and there saw regret.

What? she said, alarmed.

I am being transferred to Alabama. General Canby's troops.

When? She stared at him.

I am almost ready to say let us leave now. As we are. Walk to the landing and get on the first boat.

Why not? Adair smiled at him. She felt her freedom only inches away.

I misspent my youth already. He watched the people at the other tables for a moment, and then turned to her again. I will come back for you when the war is over. I will find you either here or in Ripley County. I will find your home.

But Adair didn't hear him. Two tables away a waiter shouted toward the kitchen for a dish called copper pennies.

But you were to get my release . . . !

I can't. I want you to go over the wall, he said. He held her hand tightly. Can you do it?

Adair looked up at him in surprise. Over the wall, she said. Yes I can. I have to catch it at a time when the supply barrels are up against the wall. Then Rhoda said you have to bribe the guards.

He gripped his cup. Take these. With the other hand he slid across the table two gold double eagles, worth twenty-five dollars each.

My God, said Adair. She put her hand over them and slid them down and into her lap, and then put them in her waist purse.

Don't let the matron get them.

All right. Adair wondered if any of the jittery urban people around the restaurant might be thieves, might have seen her put the money in her waist purse. She had fifty dollars in gold on her person.

And then you're going to have to get aboard a southbound boat. You have to have a pass, and you'll be stopped everywhere. You'll be searched before you get on the boat and afterward. He lit one of his malodorous cigars and waved out the match. Here. He slid a pass across to her. Put it somewhere else besides that waist purse. Put these things in two different places. He drew on the cigar and blew out smoke. So you won't lose both at the same time if it comes to that.

Adair looked down at the pass. Read the printed form and her name written in below it and his name as the authorizing officer. Her mouth was open.

Neumann reached across the table and put one knuckle under her chin and shut her mouth.

Don't look so surprised. Or grateful. I don't know how far that's going to get you.

Adair tucked the paper into her sleeve and looked at him. He leaned back and smoked.

So you are off into the streets, girl.

Adair said, When will you go? Her voice was high and alarmed.

He leaned his forehead on his fist and waited without interest as the food was delivered. The waiter dodged around tables with the pies and more coffee. Two men bumped past them. One was drunk and the other was holding on to him in handfuls of his brown coat.

In three days.

Adair put down the pastry and her fork clattered.

Three days!

I will come for you, Adair, he said. When the war is over. But I must go where I am sent. I have to. Otherwise I would be a deserter, and they have taken to shooting deserters. He watched her. Not to speak of the disgrace.

You could have got my release any time you wanted, she said. She said it loudly, and the drunk man and his companion at the next table looked over at them. But I didn't tell you where to catch my brother so you're off to the battlefield. And I can just run through the city like a rat.

I asked to be transferred months before you came, he said. I told you but you didn't hear me. You hear what you want.

As far as I know you could have somebody else waiting in a dog-house at the edge of the city. She began to cry and then bit her lip. You could be *married*. With twin babies and a mother-in-law.

If you think that then give me my gold pieces back.

Not on your life!

I am not married, nor do I have some mistress languishing in a love nest in the stews of St. Louis. I meant everything I have said to you.

Adair thought she saw hurt in the lines of his face and was glad.

Oh. And think how you're going to miss all your ladies. Adair's eyes sparkled with tears and malice. Maybe you'll be transferred to some women's prison down in N'Orleans, same thing different city. Go on. I'm glad.

And it's quite possible that you have a beau as well, he said. That you are promised to another. What do we really know of each other.

He's dead, said Adair. They're all dead. Cal and the Parmalee boys and Speece Newnan and all of them.

He almost said *I'm glad* but he stopped himself. He said, Don't think about those things. Think about starting all over again.

You're a stick, she said. The only thing that means anything to you is paper. If I were some kind of a legal brief you'd be running off with me to California right now.

He held on to her hand. Listen to me, make sense. When I am discharged I want to go to the West. I want you to come with me. California, Texas, whatever. You wrote of your home, opened your heart, it was very brave. He kept a death grip on her hand. It hurt. She tried to pull away but he would not let her go. Even if you glossed over.

It was all lies, she said. I made it all up. We live in a cave and Mama makes whiskey and Daddy balls the jack.

Don't use that language. No matter how hurt you are.

Adair blinked. What does balling the jack mean? She got her hand away from him.

I don't know, he said. He leaned to her across the table as if across a widening chasm between them. She was on the far side and farther away every minute. He reached for her. He opened up his heart and the secret places he had held in reserve. Adair, be my companion. You are the woman I want. Be my companion. Away from both sides. Where men haven't killed one another in the thousands. No political slogans or women in prisons. I want a place up a valley somewhere. A person could build their own house anew. Their house and their life.

I'd rather go back to my filthy cell now, she said. They are loading the shit barrels and I don't want to miss it. I hope you get run over by a caisson. Maybe your boat will blow up.

She stood up.

Stop, he said.

I hope you get squashed.

Adair. Listen.

But she had turned and was walking toward the door of the restaurant, back to the prison cell, and he could do no more than follow.

June 9—Yesterday four citizens were brought in from Callaway County; three were physicians and one a lawyer—Jeff Jones—they are suspicioned of being connected with the Knights of the Golden Circle.

—GRIFFIN FROST, *Camp and Prison Journal*

Interrogation of Mary Vaughn, [whose son was a member of Quantrill's gang] and her daughter-in-law Nancy Jane Vaughn, and her daughter Susan, which took place in the Gratiot Street Prison in St. Louis, spring of 1865:

"I never willingly furnished the rebels anything last year except my own sons and son-in-law who belonged to Price's army, whom I willingly fed when at my house. . . . I have tried hard to act as a loyal woman. I have reported my son and two others to Union authorities, and have often seen guerillas eating at the home of my daughter-in-law Nancy Jane Vaughn."

In turn, before her death of cholera in prison, Nancy Jane Vaughn turned on her neighbors, naming nine young men of her neighborhood who had become bushwhackers, and stating that two neighbor women were "bad rebels."

Susan Vaughn then turned on Nancy Jane and reported that bushwhackers had been visiting Nancy Jane's house.

—QUOTED IN *Inside War*

March 12, 1865: One of the lady prisoners, Mrs. Reynolds, is very sick—has been insensible for three days; her friends, especially her cousin Miss Maggie Oliver, seems greatly distressed about her.

March 19: about five o'clock this evening Capt. Gibbs came in and announced the death of Mrs. Reynolds.

—GRIFFIN FROST, *Camp and Prison Journal*

THE MAJOR STOOD BEFORE THE COMMISSION IN THE OPERATIONS ROOM at headquarters in the Ogley House. It was a commission of inquiry. The day was warm for late February and the windows stood open.

It was a panel of seven officers. The flags of the United States and the state of Missouri stood each to one side, the national flag on the right. The long windows looked out on the graceful trimmed shrubbery of the Ogley House. Whose owners were in jail in Alton for disloyalty. The staff officers of headquarters for the provost marshal had scarred the polished floors with their boot heels, and used the library shelves for piles of papers and forms and tins of tobacco and lost articles, single gauntlets and a lonely dress spur without its mate.

Major, said the chairman. He was a colonel. He did not want to be there. Major, we have spoken and taken depositions from a great number of people here, and there seems to be quite a few accusations made as to the conduct of the personnel of the prison, mainly Mrs. Buckley. She has attacked prisoners, stolen prisoners' parcels, stopped letters. This, for instance, is an exhibit. It would have probably done the prisoner some good to have read it. She could have contemplated the rigors of war.

He indicated a stained torn letter. The seal had been hastily ripped open so that the bottom half of the letter was torn nearly across. It was water stained and illegible. It was addressed to Adair Randolph Colley, from Savannah Colley, Sugar Tree Creek, Tennessee.

In addition, said the colonel, this Buckley woman has been accused of arranging improper and licentious meetings for some of the officers acting as lawyers for these women.

The major bent his head slightly.

He said, I understand, sir. The breeze came through the open window and surrounded him and went on. He heard faintly the great iron bell of St. Louis Cathedral ringing the hour of two. Had I known it I would have stopped it, but I was told these things were not my responsibility. Mrs. Buckley goes to her patron in the political sphere.

We know about that. The judge advocate general's department moves rather slowly. And you know that there has already been Captain Wentworth's court-martial on that matter. With a young woman from Danville. Rhoda Cobb. And you know he has been dishonorably discharged.

Yes, sir, I know.

The colonel lifted his eyebrows and peered down at the papers without lowering his head; he was trying to see the print without putting on his spectacles.

Mrs. Buckley has a powerful supporter in Frank Blair, however. He blew out air through his mustaches. She is a political appointee.

Yes sir, Major Neumann said. It seems to be prevalent.

The colonel turned to the panel ranged beside him. Lieutenant Brawley?

Well, sir, the major has done this report on the inadvisability of continuing to arrest disloyal women. Brawley grinned in a loopy way as if all reports on disloyal women were hilarious.

The colonel turned back to Neumann. We appreciate your report. It is true that it is a thing that can lead to corruption, and we can see that it has. I don't care for it either but here we are and we must do our duty. I will forward the report. At last he reached for his glasses and put them on, drawing the wire earpieces carefully over each ear. Now, this information about a secret conspiracy from this Miss Colley is scarcely credible.

The colonel picked up a page with Adair's handwriting on it. He held it by the corner, between two fingers.

I thought it actually might be true, sir.

I think not. Knights of the Golden Whiskey Jug, wasn't it?

The other officers on the panel laughed. Lieutenant Brawley nearly choked. He rolled up his eyes. He bit the end of his pen. He said, Sir, it is unlikely that it is anything but stoneware.

And you have applied for a transfer to a fighting unit. That was four months ago. Which has finally been granted. I understand the pressures and unpleasantries this assignment has brought on you. It cannot have been easy.

No, sir.

Very well. And Lieutenant Brawley has also been reassigned.

Brawley ducked into his collar as if there were incoming shells even now.

The two of you are both going to Mobile.

Neumann bowed slightly.

Thank you, sir.

ADAIR FELT SO HURT THAT SHE SEEMED TO BE DAMAGED INSIDE. SHE HATED herself for writing all those things, it was all sentimental and gushing. She had left out the women's miscarriages and the animals born deformed, the drunks and floods and the crawling mold overtaking the dried fruit in an expanding gray mush. She had left out Sam Billingslea's legs sticking out from under a hundred-foot white oak that had jumped the butt and crushed him, his face blank as the earl of hell. Her brother shooting a man for a pair of shoes. She stared at the floor of her cell for a long time. The floor was dirty with trodden straw and so she left it that way. All the stupid things she had written would come back to shame her like nasty, boisterous clowns.

She put the paper and pen and ink bottle outside her cell bars in the hallway floor, and soon one of the women trustees came and took it away and the table too.

Adair got up and took the pass from her sleeve. She put it in the pocket of the green camisette and sewed the pocket shut.

She lay down again and felt the fever beating like a hot engine in her face. She could not stop coughing and coughed until her ribs felt broken.

Adair woke up in the middle of the night, and found she was being shouted at by other women in the cells down the hall.

Sometime after that the matron came and brought to her a tin pitcher of water and a tin cup and Adair sat up and drank almost all of the water in the pitcher. It was muddy Mississippi River water. They kept trying to keep the blankets up around her. Then there were several people in her cell talking and she wished they would go away. She saw Kisia wrapping her waist purse by its strings around her wrist. Then she found herself being stuffed into some kind of a wrapper over her chemise and wavering down the hallway. Two people were helping her down the stairs, into another room.

Kisia was saying, You all are going to just let her die.

I am not unkind! shouted the matron. I am not unmindful of those who are unwell!

Then she was in the sickroom. Adair sat up in bed and said, Don't let the matron get my Log Cabin quilt.

I'll look after it, Miss Adair, said Kisia.

Adair said, Promise me you will not let them take me to the city hospital.

Then she turned on one side before Kisia could say anything and lay looking at the wallpaper. What time of day is it? she asked. Her teeth chattered of their own accord.

Adair, it is the latest watch of the night, said Kisia. Better eat this.

Adair lifted the tin spoon to her lips but that was as far as she got. Without warning she seemed to be blooming into a very large red flower that was made of blown glass. She dropped the spoon. She felt she was being annealed in a glass furnace. Her hair slid and pooled on her shoulders. She felt no need of either food or sleep. Now the heavy blankets were a trouble to her. It was like being flattened in a cotton press. She shoved them down and away.

I want some water, please, she said. Adair took the cup of brownish water that was handed to her and drank it off and then another and another. She lay back and drifted.

Another time came when the major opened the door. Before him stalked Mrs. Buckley, who pulled the blankets and sheet up to Adair's shoulders and went to stand picket at the open doorway.

She has been given the very best of medicines! cried the matron. She has not been unattended!

The major took up a chair and sat it beside the bed. He wavered in and out of focus, but there was no mistaking the touch of his hand and the glint of his hair in the lamplight which gave it reddish tones. His round hazel eyes and his intense gaze.

I love you, she said. But I am in such terrible trouble.

Major William Neumann took her hand in both of his.

Your hands are hot.

I have to get home.

He sat and said nothing and seemed to be waiting for her to continue. She closed her eyes. The major said, Adair?

That's me, she said. I think. What do you think?

Have you seen a doctor? He reached out, felt of her forehead and her cheeks with his other hand. You have an excessive temperature.

And also, I dreamed the fire tongs came walking up the stairs. To us girls' room. They were coming for me.

Mrs. Buckley said from the doorway, That must have been when she was screaming. I asked that watch be kept on her *day* and *night*!

Where? said the major. He held on to Adair's hand and turned to look at the matron. When was she screaming?

In her cell, said Mrs. Buckley. It took her a while to get this sick. We can't just run people down here whenever they have a little sniffle!

Call Dr. Stilman, he said.

When our boys are dying in Mobile without doctors or hospitals, said Mrs. Buckley. I'm to run get the best for this little secessionist gal.

The major stood up and Adair saw him smile at the matron. He said, Mrs. Buckley, we have a sick girl on our hands. Let's you and I try to forget our differences and get along for once.

Well, Major, glad to see you can accommodate a little. Mrs. Buckley nodded and took a comb out of her thick hair and combed back a side wave and stuck the comb in again. Time you learned to be more accommodating.

Shake on it? Major Neumann held out his hand, and his broad-brimmed hat was in the other. Mrs. Buckley's smile was thin, but she held out her hand, and Major Neumann took it. He crushed down with all his strength and the tall woman cried out and tried to pull loose but she could not. Neumann took a long step backward, and with a strong jerk threw her to the floor.

Mrs. Buckley shouted and struck the stone floor with the heels of her hands. She struggled to get up in a welter of plaid skirts, caught her skirt hem under her knee and ripped loose some of it from the bodice. The glass and pitcher on the nightstand chimed and spouted drops.

Major Neumann dropped his hat and bent down and lifted Mrs. Buckley by the collar of her dress.

I will hurt you very badly if she's not taken care of. He pressed two thumbs into her neck. I will draw my revolver and blow you through.

I am going for the doctor, said the matron. To protect me. If that's how you're going to do a person. Let go of me.

Neumann didn't say anything but turned her and shoved her toward the door. She went out the door and shut it quickly behind her.

He stood for a moment watching the door to see that she was well gone and then came and sat down beside Adair again. Adair's throat was aflame and she needed to swallow and then could not. She began to choke. The major poured a cup of beige water from the pitcher, and sat on the bed. He put his hand behind her head and lifted her upright, held her against his chest. She took the tin cup in both hands and drank all of it down. Strands of her hair caught on his sleeve buttons and he gently drew them loose. He held her in the crook of his arm.

You look like a mezzotint, he said. He held her burning hand.

I'll have nothing to do with those foreigners, she whispered.

That mezzotint *The Lady of Shalott*.

The one where she's wallowing around in that tiny boat?

The very one. He stroked her hair away from her face. Get well. Get over the wall. Then show the guard one of those twenty-five-dollar gold pieces in your hand, and then say there is something down the street that needs his attention. She could smell the freshness of his snowy coat and the good strong male smell of his skin. Drops sparkled on his shoulder bars. He kissed her lightly on the cheek and then eased her down onto the bed again. He sat back. That would get me a court-martial. He regarded her. You've worn me down. Just go home. I'll find you.

She fell asleep suddenly, into a profound and quenching sleep. When she woke up again he was there, and another man as well. A man in a long black coat. The doctor asked the major to leave. With the matron standing by, the doctor began to thump on her narrow breast-bone. He lifted her lids and looked into her eyes. He made her sit up and listened with his instrument and its chill, coin-size head, to her breathing.

I have no idea, he said. Maybe consumption. I hear rales.

Adair saw them evaporate out the door into the square of light. The major stood beside her once again. He held her hand and shook it slightly to get her attention.

I want a promise, he said.

What?

That you won't run off and marry some hillbilly until after you see me again. Then if I am missing a leg or something you can marry any hillbilly you want.

I don't know, she said. I might die. My mother died of a fever too.

That is all I am asking. Promise.

All right.

She focused on his face. He took the signet ring from his left ring finger and held it between his thumb and forefinger.

Can you see this?

Yes. It's your ring.

I'm leaving it with you as a fee, that I mean what I say.

They'll steal it.

He unbuttoned her nightgown to her waist. Spread it apart. Inside the printed flannel her body lay as white as bone, her nipples, like her

lips, bright red with fever. He drew up the ribbons that tied her drawers, untied them, and threaded the ring onto the ribbon and tied the
ends again.

Then when you are dressed, keep it tied to your stays.

He drew his hand down over her body with fingers spread and then
buttoned her nightgown again. Slowly, button by button.

All right.

To leave you like this is the worst thing that has ever happened to
me, he said. I do not believe the war could be any worse.

Where are you going?

I told you. Alabama.

All right, Major. She was whispering. She had round red spots on
her cheeks.

Call me William. I want to hear you say it before I get my head shot
off. Or you could call me Major Stick.

She gripped his hand. William, she said.

Adair.

Then he bent to pick up a valise or portfolio or some carryall from
the floor and then he was gone.

16

Entries in 1860:

Joseph Yezach, [A Bohemian lad] garroted accidentally by a machinery; at work at the rope factory in New Bremen with loose hemp coils around his neck [as is customary with factory boys] the hemp caught the shaft of a wheel and it strangled him.

Man killed on the track of the North Missouri Railroad at Bellefontaine Rd.

Dead on the floor of a bar-room

Fell from the West wall of the Southern Hotel at Elm and Walnut, 2nd block south of the courthouse, near Cathedral.

Run over by an ice wagon

Overdose of laudanum, Ellen Clark, since found to be one Deborah White, of Peoria Illinois

P. Dexter Tiffany, suicide, slit wrists; a millionaire

Louis Drucker, an Indian doctor, disappeared from a levee boat at Carondelet, found later below Quarantine, near the magazine, had on his person papers, snuff box, letters in a spectacle case

Thomas Wilkerson, a Scotchman, a machinist employed in Hannibal Missouri, in the machine shop, fell from the steamer Louisville

Jean Baptiste Augier, a member of the Farienne Society of Cheltenham, Mo., a native of Bargemont, near Draguinan, Dept. of Varennes, France: suicide by drowning whilst laboring under brain excitement caused by congestive chills and socialistic ideas.

Coroner Louis-William Boisliniere

—St. Louis County coroner's records, Northcott, Missouri, 1997

At the hub of development in the 1850s was St. Louis, one of the fastest grow-ing industrial cities in the Union. St. Louis more than doubled in population in the 1850s to 166,773 persons of whom 60 per cent were foreign born, the highest percentage of foreign-born in any American city. This included 39,000 Irish and nearly 60,000 Germans.

—FROM *Inside War*

There were others who did not . . . survive the suffering which they experienced [as refugees]. On November 21, 1864, four children from Georgia died at the Chattanooga Railroad depot [in Nashville] from "cold, hunger and exposure."

—FROM *Reluctant Partners, Nashville and the Union,* BY WALTER T. DURHAM,

TENNESSEE HISTORICAL SOCIETY, NASHVILLE, N.D.

S HE WOULD GO OVER THE WALL TODAY, WHEN THEY WENT OUT TO THE washing. As in Acts 5:18–20, when the angel of the lord came and opened the door of the prison, and told the apostles to come out and go and preach to all of the people the words of this life. What life? Adair wondered. What life did that mean?

She sat in the sun, trying to stitch the Log Cabin quilt back together. It had nearly come apart. She told herself she was not ill. She told her-self a little fever burnt out the bad humors and was good for a person from time to time. That when she was over the wall she would begin to get well in the fresh country air.

It was not until late afternoon that the wagon came in with its sup-plies of hardtack and pork, sacks of white beans and cornmeal. Adair watched them unload the barrels and stack the empty ones in the mid-dle, away from the wall. Kisia and a young mulatto girl were playing some kind of dice game with the ham bones.

Kisia, roll one of those barrels against the wall, behind the washing. The blonde girl put down the ham bone dice. I am going over the wall in the next fifteen minutes.

Kisia stuck out her lower lip and looked at Adair very doubtfully, her pale, tangling hair corkscrewing in the breeze.

You are in no condition, she said.

Go on.

So Kisia rolled one of the empty hardtack barrels against the street wall of the courtyard, behind the washing lines of dresses and petticoats and stockings. She jumped up on it, her ragged skirts flying. She called to a young mulatto girl.

Kisia shouted, You are the Moorish Battalion and I am the Queen of the Barrels! The mulatto girl laughed and grabbed her by the ankles to pull her down.

A guard watched from his position on the wall on the other side of the gates.

Get that barrel away from the wall, he said.

Soons I pull her down! said the mulatto girl.

Get in there and get your washing done! the matron shouted at Adair. She stood looking at her with her hands on her hips. So Adair stood up and carried the green camisette and her shawl with her behind the lines of washing and shoved it into the pot of boiling, soapy water. There was no help for it. She would have to leave the green dress behind, but Adair knew she had to go now. If she were going to go. But it didn't matter. When she was in the sickroom somebody had stolen her diamond-and-sapphire earbobs, and the mandarin jacket, but what were they as compared to her life?

Adair rolled the quilt tightly. She was sweating. She looked at the dress in the boiling water and realized she had left the pass in the pocket and it would now be paper mush and the ink washed away. Oh my God what have I done? She grabbed at a sleeve but the water was too hot and the pocket was sewn shut, and she knew the paper was boiled to nothing. There was no help for it.

Kisia, she said. Go start a fight with somebody.

The child jumped down and ran to her. She took one of Adair's hands in both of hers. She said,

Good-bye, Miss Adair. I love you.

And I love you too, Kisia. The Lord keep you.

The two girls ran under the lines of washing. Then darted away among the stacks of barrels being unloaded. Adair stood up to go over the wall and was suddenly overwhelmed with fright. A crash of panic went through her. Suddenly Adair felt as if she were going to die in the next moment.

She shut her hands tight and waited for the feeling to pass. But it began to build inside her. As if her interior was something like a nautilus shell, building and building a terrible pearl of overwhelming dread. They would shoot her. She was going to be extinguished. She was going to be lowered into a grave and the earth shut over her. Electricity of some kind ran in waves through her, and everything, every object, seemed very distant and false.

The matron's big dress was hanging on a long pole. Adair turned her face up to it, and it seemed like an angel in the wind, as if it were going to open the doors of the prison for her. The dress cracked its silks in the wind and opened its arms and said, *I will devour thine enemies!*

Adair looked up at the great flying dress. It ballooned up on another gust of wind, a wild and buffeting angel, and held out its arms and said, *Come with me now!*

Suddenly there was a great noise of screaming and shouting from the lower windows that gave into the General Ward. Adair heard Kisia shouting You will not, Cloris! I will pull ever hair out of your head! Everyone in the courtyard began to run toward the door into the ward. Even the guards jumped down from the wall and began to walk across the courtyard, and then in the door.

Adair stepped behind the clothesline and pulled off her dress and drew Mrs. Buckley's petticoats over her head. She tied them with the drawstrings. Then she pulled Mrs. Buckley's big dress over her head and jerked it down straight. It was a glossy, brass-colored silk twill with a navy blue figure in it, and there must have been eleven yards in the skirt alone. She took up her waist purse from the heaps of folded material that was her old plaid dress. Then the plaid dress and the quilt and its wrapping.

Adair stood up on the barrel and glanced right and then left. The outside guards were all down in the street buying some old wormy last year's apples from a cart. Except for one. It was the man with one arm. The grinner. He stood on the street, looking up at Adair on the wall with a somewhat amazed expression. A great swirl of the limestone dust rose into the air and surrounded her.

Cloris's terrier had jumped up on the barrel and was barking at her with its red mouth open as wide as a bat's mouth. Adair reached down and grabbed it by the lower jaw and threw it over the wall and into the street. She was possessed of a kind of lunatic strength. The terrier ran wildly between carriage wheels, heading down the street, and was never seen again.

Adair said, Let the found be found and the lost stay lost. She swung over the wall and dropped to the sidewalk.

The guard came up to her. Looking at her with curiosity as if wondering what she was going to do. He was perhaps in his forties, grizzled and his Federal uniform somewhat shabby.

I thought you were the matron or I'd have pulled you off that wall, he said.

Adair slipped one of the double eagles out of her waist purse, and held it in the flat of her palm and showed it to him.

There is something down the street that needs your attention, she said. Her hand was shaking violently.

He stared down at the double eagle for what seemed an eternity while her freedom leaked away drop by drop. Then finally he nodded.

Well, I had better go see about it, he said. He took the gold coin from her palm with his only hand. He grinned. Good luck, girl.

She went off walking down the street without a hat or anything she owned except her waist purse and the ungainly wad of quilt and dress under her left arm. It was all back in the cell. It didn't matter. She strode off and her skirt hems dragged along behind her like dogs.

There were no shouts or shots or whistles. She clutched her skirts with her right hand. It was shaking. She was walking, miraculously, down the streets of St. Louis. She was afire with a kind of feverish panic.

It was so sudden that for a moment Adair did not exactly know how she got where she was.

She held her head high and kept walking. Adair felt as if she were running away from her own execution. She did not hear anyone shouting or calling her name or calling anything. It was now sunset, and clouds with precise, hard edges skated across the early-spring city sky looking as if they were infused with some sort of aerial foxfire, gleaming on the edges like white silk.

She stepped up on a white limestone curb and kept on. Still no one shouted. She held herself as stiffly as if she were carrying a glass of water full to the brim. She was about to spill. She went on down St. Charles Street. Adair wondered which way was south. Her heart was racing and despite its terrible smashing she thought she might be drifting several inches off the ground and this was a dangerous feeling. She walked past a cast-iron horse head with a ring in its mouth and touched it, for iron was of the earth and it grounded you. She was a silent, drifting bolt of lightning. She might come apart at any moment. A peculiar ragged man with a great wen on his forehead came past her, nodding, screaming *Ratbane!!* Adair held up the bundle of cloth like a shield and dodged to one side and kept on.

A troop of Wisconsin infantry came past, shining with banners and buckles, taking up the entire street width and making incoming vehicles from Sixth and Fifth Streets pull up. They stormed past in files with their flag, which was blue and had a man chopping wood on it. They smelled of woodsmoke and tobacco. They were gone on past within a minute like a brief, moving vision of triumph and order, and she crossed the street as the last rank went by.

As she walked along, a miraculous thing happened and that was she began to recover herself. It was as if she was gathering herself up. She felt like she had gone to pieces and was now back together. She kept her calm and continued to walk.

She should get on one of the omnibuses. She pressed aside, into the wall of a furriers' shop, as one came bashing down the street with a jangle of trace chains and hooves and people calling to one another. But she only had the gold coin, and how could she pay a penny fare with a twenty-five-dollar gold piece? The omnibus went on, slicing the mud with yellow wheels and rolling on its rounded and curvilinear body. It said *Arsenal* on the front. Adair didn't know if the arsenal was a place she wanted to go, but all she could think of to do was to get on a street near the levee so she could get her directions from the river, and then turn south and keep walking south.

She came upon a daguerreotypist's shop. In the window were portraits of famous people. She stood in the doorway and pretended great interest in the pictures and her heart was pounding. Behind her she heard several men running, shouting, coming down St. Charles Street. She didn't need to look, she knew it would be men in blue with the insignia of the provost marshal's department.

She opened the door and walked into the shop. A man with a lean, dark face asked her what she wished. He smiled at her. But there she was without a bonnet or purse or market basket. She seemed to have just stepped out of her own bedroom.

Why, I wish to have a portrait made, she said.

I see. He nodded. He was confused as to what sort of person she might be.

I just live around the street there, she gestured vaguely, and her hand was shaking as she did so, so she hid it in the folds of her skirt again. And I had a few minutes and I thought I would step in here real quick to see about getting a likeness made.

All right, I am happy to oblige.

Adair smiled at him as she listened to the men running by outside. The daguerreotypist listened too but he didn't say anything. She did not turn her head but she counted as they went past. It was hard to talk and count as well so she paused. Seven eight nine. There were twelve guards altogether. The daguerreotypist looked out at the running soldiers and then back at her. Ten eleven twelve.

Now there were no more noises from the street other than ordinary street noises.

Thank you! she said. She smiled her white smile at him. She turned and gathered up as much of the front of her skirts as she well could. The daguerreotypist paused for a moment with a confused frown. She was breathing too hard. She could not quiet herself. Adair smiled again and she could feel her mouth was very dry and her lips were shaking.

For what? he said. You haven't seen the studio yet.

Well, I'd better be on my way! she said with false brightness. I was just taking these things to the washerwoman.

Why, are you not interested in a likeness?

Adair took in a breath as if to speak and then held it for she couldn't think of what to say. Then she said, I think I felt an earthquake! She looked around in alarm.

The daguerreotypist held himself in a long pause. He was speechless.

She said, Better stand in a doorway!

An earthquake? What? He held both hands out to his sides, alarmed, and then placed one hand on the vitrine of the showcase to feel for vibrations and it looked as if he were prepared to go outside and see if anything were falling.

So she turned quickly and went out the door and back into the street.

St. Charles Street went straight down toward the levee. Here and there were small frame houses jammed in between tall three- and four-story commercial buildings. They were the remnants of the older city. Inside these ancient houses old ladies looked out, wearing coal-shovel bonnets with long sun flaps over the shoulders. Adair thought, Maybe they are Dutch women, or Irish. She strode on, taking long steps, flying down the brick sidewalks under awnings, around stacks of casks and piles of siding. Her fever beat like a foundry hammer in the veins of her face. She was alone and had no bonnet on her head and men in uniforms were hunting for her.

Young woman! an old lady called to her in good English. Your dress is too big and you are running too fast!

My aunt is about to have a baby and I am going for the midwife, said Adair, and kept on. She didn't even know where she was going. There didn't seem to be any particular place to go. She turned right on Third Street. She could hear the noise and commotion of the levee, and she could glimpse it through the buildings at Chestnut. She could see the steamers. Their sterns were all turned downstream. So now she knew which way south was. She kept on down Third Street.

At last she came to the old French houses around St. Louis Cathedral, and sat down on the steps of the cathedral and put herself in the hands of God. Any God, even a Catholic one. The stone-paved street was full of traffic, people on foot and coal carts bringing coal from the Gravois coal diggings and dropping bituminous chips up and down the street at random, a milk cart tugged along by a ponderous red-and-white ox, a light surrey with a lady in it. Adair put her head in her hands. An omnibus pulled by two thin horses came by and the driver yelled out, Kennet Shot Tower! over and over. Biddle Street Levee and Kennet Shot Tower! Adair sat on the steps of the cathedral and told herself over and over, I am in the hands of God.

A woman in a very old-fashioned dress with the waist high up around the armpits and a narrow skirt came up the steps. She wore a broken straw bonnet and wooden clogs on her feet.

Are you well, then, kulleen? she said.

Adair looked up, trying to breathe normally. I can't understand you, Adair said. She began to cough again and shut her mouth against it and the cough exploded out her nose.

Are ye well?

Yes, I am well. Don't you speak any English?

I'm Irish, said the woman.

Well go on, said Adair. Just go on. She put her fist to her mouth and coughed violently.

The woman went on into the church. Startling bongs came from overhead as the great bells rang for mass. More people began coming up the steps and so Adair got up again and picked up the front of her skirts and went down the steps to the street. She went to one side of the enormous cathedral and found a doorway and sat in it. It was the door to the old sacristy. She had put herself in the hands of God and she liked the feeling and wanted to stay in it but shreds of dirty coal smoke began to drift along overhead now with the evening fires and Adair felt that it looked spectral and dangerous. Soon it would be night and she didn't know where she would go.

She got to her feet and left the doorway and walked back into the darkening March streets.

There was the rail station at Pine Street, where she might get on a train of cars of the St. Louis and Iron Mountain railroad that would take her down to southeast Missouri. But she dare not approach anyone now, at night, to ask for information. They would think she was a prostitute. That anyone would take her for a prostitute made her start crying. She strode along, down a street of brick buildings and walled-in interior yards, wiping tears from her cheeks. A lamp-lighter came down the street cursing in German. He put his ladder against a lamppost, and the first rung stove through when he stepped on it. He cursed again with frantic rage. He stomped on the second rung and climbed up, opened the glass and turned the key and put his punk to the valve and a thin bluish light leapt out through the glass.

She kept on walking south, feeling the increasing danger of the night. If only she had a market basket to carry, or some sort of grip and a bonnet. It looked as if she had stolen the bundle in her arms and had run off with it directly. Even a scarf over her hair would do. Then she would look normal. Then she would appear to be a young woman who had a family here in the city, and a home, and people who loved her and cared about her. Who was hurrying home from errands. A place with a door that shut and locked and a mirror and a fireplace and people who would say, Well *there* you are! We were worried about you! And she would drink deep of whatever boiled on the fire.

Now she was in a neighborhood of jumbled houses, some of old stone and some of frame and some of brick, brand-new. The crossways were lit by gas lamps. Each house had a number painted on it somewhere, over the door or to one side. It was as if they were drawers in a thread shop, or slots for letters in a type case. Adair realized it was so strangers could find the houses.

She walked past a tavern, one of the little old houses with twelve-paned windows and a puffing chimney stack at each end and a low door. A sign over the door said it was the WILLIAM TELL TAVERN AND FAMILY GROCERY. Men were laughing and smoking inside.

Good evening, sweetheart! A man called from inside.

Adair grasped up as much of the great volumes of skirt as she could in one hand and ran fleet-footed down the street, past Myrtle and Elm and Almond. She dodged past late-homing carts driven by boys riding splay-legged who spoke to her in low tones and made kissing noises. Three black children walked up Third Street barefooted in raveling clothes of fustian. They held one another's hands and looked at the paving and went past her.

She slowed at Poplar Street to a walk again. She looked down Poplar to the levee. Down there the great steam-driven boats bumped one another with knocking sounds, and men carrying torches moved in crowds, with all the loading and unloading and repair work. She heard the long groans of six-inch hemp ropes straining to hold the paddle wheelers against the current, tied to massive iron rings. She thought, I will turn down to the levee and steal something or find something. Just a market basket, an old basket, and I will look more normal.

But some soldiers were coming up from the levee. One of them paused beneath the pale gas lamp and began a jig. The others stood back for a moment and watched this display and then started clapping time and singing.

Adair stood back against the wall of a small wooden house jammed in between two brick tenements to avoid them. The shutters of the lit-

tle house were open to the night and the coal smoke, and halfway up
the wall the boards had been spattered with mud and gravel from passing vehicles. The house was so old that she could see the marks of the
broadaxe on the window framings. Adair leaned back and pressed herself as flat as she could between the two open windows.

17

In addition to St. Louis as a trading center for stolen goods, Kansas provided a relatively secure place for resale. Illinois [especially Quincy], Iowa [especially Keokuk], and Kansas City were the other usual market places. Kansas Union Private W. W. Moses, for example, wrote his sister in 1862 that he had "Jayhawked some silver cupps and sent them to Illinois."

— FROM *Inside War*

Black marketing of stolen goods such as clothing, jewelry, and home furnishings reached an impressive scale. Brigadier General Benjamin Loan in Jefferson City [Missouri] in 1862 offered a clear analysis of illicit commerce. Either "good society" or economic double-agents "claiming to be Government contractors and with provost marshal's passes in their pockets would contact guerillas directly, purchase their stolen goods, warehouse them, and transport them, generally by riverboat to St. Louis, reselling them through merchants who either were secessionists or did not ask probing questions. Loan was particularly incensed that in the end government contractors repurchased Union horses stolen elsewhere in Missouri.

— FROM *Inside War*

INSIDE A LITTLE OLD MAN AND A LITTLE OLD LADY WERE HAVING AN argument.

Adair stood and sought for a clear breath and listened. The argument was about what the little old lady should be buried in. Adair breathed through her nose slowly to keep back her cough. Around the corner and down the street the soldier-dancer beat out time with his government shoes and his audience sang a song from the theater. It was "The Girls of Gravois Mills."

The old woman said, I done went and bought it and it cost me a quarter dollar so I don't want to hear you crying Hark from the Tomb about it! Lillie Sheehan made it!

She made it, did she? the old man shouted. Hark from the Tomb is what you'll be doing if you are buried in that floozy's hat. Lilac. With green ribbons and plaster fruit. Think how you'll look a-layin in your coffin in that. I won't be seen in the church with you.

Adair wondered what kind of an awful thing the hat was, if he was carrying on so about it.

Well, I won't care, Mr. Casebolt, I won't care. Just stay to home then.

You ain't wearing that hat at your funeral. That's all she wrote.

Adair heard stomping steps across the creaky floor and then a thump. He had stalked across the room and thrown himself into a chair. Then there were raking sounds as he took out his outrage on the fire. Adair saw even bigger puffs of smoke coming from the chimney overhead and some ashes rained down on her. Coal smoke from the soft St. Louis coal lay heavy and serpentine.

Oh I don't care one way or another. What use is it a-argyin with you? I'll just cast it out, then, will *that* satisfy you, Mr. Casebolt?

Adair flattened herself even more against the muddy wall of the house and the hat came flying out the window. It struck the brick sidewalk with a rattle of plaster cherries. Adair stared at it for a second and thought, Lord, I wouldn't be buried in that thing either. But Adair knew that Jesus had given her a hat so that she could walk the streets of this alien place in disguise, and also that it wouldn't be long before the old lady changed her mind and came looking for it. After all she had paid Lillie Sheehan a quarter dollar for it.

A dray came by, driven by a tall black teamster, full of coal sacks, and she watched the wheels straddle the hat and pass over it without harm. Adair ran out and pounced on it and carried the hat away, turning the corner onto Poplar as she put it on her head. Behind her she could hear them still yelling at each other.

The hat was made of hard lilac-colored straw and had a smart little brim in front and a cockade of cherries and guinea feathers. She tied the ribbons under her chin and forged past the dancing soldier and his audience. She needed something more: a basket, a grip, a ticket to somewhere. Reserves of strength that she did not know she had had opened up to her. But she was spending these reserves at a great rate.

The soldier stopped his clog dance and called out, Good evening, Miss, are you lost?

She ignored him. She had risen on the social scale now that she had a hat, and ladies don't talk to strange men.

She kept on. The air was still and in its cool untroubled sea the moths massed around the pale lamps. The sun fell below the city skyline, and the shadows of the great mercantile buildings that lined the entire riverfront were cast far out onto the river and over the steamboats.

She walked out from Poplar Street onto the granite stones of the levee. It was a seething confusion of crowds and moving lights. Men and vehicles crossed one another in every direction, their faces appearing and disappearing in the lamps and torches. The steamboats were loaded and unloaded in a tide of black dockmen, free and unfree, carrying America's tonnage on their backs. Adair could find some kind of a basket or grip down here somewhere, even one that had been cast aside, even a busted one. She walked into the swarming torchlit dark, and the incessant crashing noise.

She stood for a minute to look at the great flues erupting in sparks. There were bars of red light from the boilers, and the interior lamps and candles now being lit in the passengers' rooms. The levee was frantic and opulent with war and the needs of war. Adair had come only to steal a basket.

She walked down the long cliff face of mercantile houses. They said it stretched from Convent Street to the wood yards at Bremen. For miles men and animals carried war materials and firewood and coal and passengers and preserved foods and fruit and furniture and glass panes packed in straw, copper wire for the telegraph lines and cotton bales and chemicals and shoes back and forth. Toted them in handbarrows and on dollies, in buckboards and two-wheeled drays. From far down toward the south levee Adair heard somebody playing on a concertina "Hard Times Come Again No More." A tall black stevedore turned in the light of a torch and slowly placed on his head a new cap saying The LaSalle.

Adair lowered her head and pushed through the blundering dark shapes. Accountants and clerks called for the unloaders to Stop, stop, I have not yet enumerated these goods yet sir, and the men with carts appeared in the pale illumination of the warehouse doorways as if bringing some offerings into the ken of the beings of light, up out of the dark and the dark of the river and the dark of the war.

Adair moved down toward the packet landings, and to the glassy flat plane of the Mississippi beyond. The runneling lights streamed in unstable streaks far out over the black and oily surface, as if the city would print news of itself endlessly. Across on the Illinois shore a few lights stood out at the eastern railroad terminals and among the black sticks of the March woods in the American Bottoms.

A block down she saw a great sign made of planks and lit by cressets, KEOKUK PACKET. The planks were white and the letters bright red, and a knothole had fallen out of the O of *Keokuk*. Sparks cascaded out of the flue as the Keokuk boat came in. People stood around under the sign ready to entrust their lives to the nighttime water in their urgency to be in Keokuk.

Adair walked forward with an expectant look on her face. They would think she was meeting someone. The massive tent of Mrs. Buckley's dress shifted around as if she were appearing in her own personal circus, and her lilac hat felt top-heavy. She pressed in with the other excited nighttime people. The stern-wheeler bumped in and in its wake a long train of roiled and frothing water. Coiled ropes were cast into the air and uncoiled themselves hurtling through the torchlight down toward the dockmen.

She stood directly behind a woman and her husband. She was a plump woman in a cream-colored dress that had a black dot in it, and many black ruffles. The woman looked around her for someone to hand the grip to and then looked toward her husband. He was paying their fare in coins.

I am ten cents short, said the man. Dorcas, give me ten cents if you have it.

What? Dorcas started to put the bag down and leaned toward him. Adair stepped up closer behind her and reached, but the woman did not put it down. Dorcas looked around her. It is so noisy.

I said, give me ten cents if you have it.

Dorcas finally put the grip down and Adair said to herself she would wait until the man turned to pay the fare. With intense concentration the woman dredged up her coin purse from the chain at her waist. She was clearly afflicted with bad eyesight. So Adair reached again.

A few minutes later she was hurrying down the levee, among the crowds. She carried the stolen grip like a load of sin. Thief! Thief! The high, repetitive birdlike cry made her heart clack frantically like a sticky, fibrillating valve.

Adair could never have imagined herself alone on a great levee like this and stealing somebody's luggage. I guess you can get used to just about anything, she thought. And this is wartime anyway. Soldiers went past her at a trot casting about for the thief and here she was carrying the thing. She pushed on through the crowd. She wished to be in the dark where she was not so easily seen and where no doubt other thieves held their jubilees in corner taverns and empty lots.

She walked more confidently now up Plum Street on the gentle rise away from the river. Adair did not know how many miles it was to Ripley County but the only way to get there was to start walking. Her longing to be away from the noise of the city and the war was the most intense thing she had ever felt in her life.

She had to stop someplace now, where there was a light, and see what it was she had stolen. She had nearly spent the strength that had come to her. But she could go on a ways yet.

She had come so far south in the city that the streets were now unpaved. Sometimes there was an empty lot between houses walled off with a plank fence, and a board door in the fence. At one of these she stopped. Small casks were stacked around outside the door like fat men and smelling richly of cheese. Inside the plank wall there would be a place to hide. From the second story of the brick tenement, gaslight poured down from a window into the courtyard. If she could get in there quietly, she could inspect the contents of the grip in the hard, acidic light.

Adair took one of her hair combs from out of her hair to slip it through the crack and lift the latch. The board door was plastered with torn and flapping advertisements for Dan Rice, the World-Reknowned Clown, and her sleeve rasped against the paper and it sounded as loud as a gunshot. The metal latch rattled. She lifted up her pale face to look at the second-story window, but no one came to peer out.

She went in and shut the latch behind her in theftlike silence. With all her skirts close around her she walked silently among cheese casks to sit in the slat of whey-colored light from above. If she made a noise again the people up in the second story would look out and they would know very well what she was doing. Gloating over her stolen articles.

Her plaster cherries rattled slightly. She pressed the brass swinging clasp and opened the grip wide to the light. She lifted out a pair of drawers with tatting on the legs. Clean underwear! She found spectacles in a hard leather case, and then there was a daguerreotype of somebody dead in a coffin, a man. She put that on the ground and would leave it there. But the frame was good. She left it anyway. There was a little velvet sack with a silver-backed hairbrush and some steel hairpins, a pair of backless slippers, a light silk petticoat wadded tight, cotton stockings, a canvas sack containing cornstarch and a cotton one full of raw cotton bolls for applying the cornstarch. She felt of a paper package of long things. She carefully unrolled the paper.

She heard voices overhead but they were just talking to each other. The voices of two men. Four tallow candles and a bundle of matches fell into her hands. This was so they wouldn't have to pay for candles on the boat north to Keokuk. Her father had done the same thing when they went up the river to Ste. Genevieve from New Madrid. The steamboat people charged you the earth for everything they gave you, even that common brown soap. Then Adair found four folded handkerchiefs, one fancy linen with openwork and the other three cotton. There was a small sewing kit in a roll of plaid flannel with three needles and six colors of thread.

She ran her hand along the bottom lining. It was heavy canvas. There was nothing else in there. Adair felt much better. She took a deep relieved breath and leaned back against the brick wall. She felt armed. Now she needed some kind of permit they issued to you to go where you wanted to go. There would be people in St. Louis who forged those sorts of passes all the time.

Above her she heard the two men in earnest discussion about whether to go to work in Belcher's sugar refinery or not. That the tubular boiler had exploded not four years ago and was it worth the wages. One of them came to the window to reach out and closed the shutters against the increasing damp of the night and so she sat still. Overhead the shutters banged to and shed flakes of old paint and rust. They fell onto her lilac straw hat with tiny rattles.

Adair got up and moved out and away from the cheese barrels, slow and smooth like a nocturnal animal. She wished she had a nail bar or crowbar for she would have had the lid off of one of the cheese casks in a moment, but she did not. They were as closed to her as they were to the rats.

She opened the creaking board door in the plank wall, and rasped past the posters of Dan Rice with his lines of circus horses. She walked on down Third and wondered how she could safely pass the night.

Maybe walking, but that was dangerous. She went on, trudging heavily. This was all something that just had to be got through. It wasn't permanent, being a thief and alone and being stuck in this awful hell of coal smoke and brick.

After a while she came to a wagon yard and slipped in. She spent the night half-sitting in a pile of hay with the quilt around her shoulders and the stolen grip in her lap.

18

Confederate Correspondence

Camp Emmet McDonald, April 4, 1863

Maj. E. G. Williams, Assistant Adjutant-General

Major: Captain Timothy Reeves reported this morning that he had informa-tion of 200 cavalry on the march to burn Bollinger's Mills and destroy the records of Doniphan. He asked for reinforcements. I wrote him that his force was sufficient to defend the mill, and ordered him to do it. This Mill has the capacity for grinding for 5,000 men, and is the only one between the Eleven Point and the Current, south of Doniphan.

Colton Greene, Colonel, Commanding Brigade

—OR, CH. XXXIV, P. 813

William L. Russell, who served as combination county clerk and circuit clerk and recorder, heard rumors of a Union order to occupy Doniphan. . . . He took all of Ripley County's record books and hid them in a cave along the east side of the Current River just south of town for safekeeping. The cave had a small opening, just big enough to accommodate a youth or a very slim person, lying on his back, to ease the records inside. . . . In 1867, G. H. Hucherson, county clerk, retrieved the records and returned them to Doniphan. Few records from Ripley County exist from the period 1863 to 1867.

—FROM *The History of Ripley County*, CHAPBOOK, PUBLISHED BY
THE DONIPHAN PROSPECT-NEWS, DONIPHAN, MISSOURI, 1992

THE NEXT MORNING BEFORE FIRST LIGHT ADAIR TOOK UP HER CARPET sack and set out. She would not feel she had escaped until she had passed the city's bounds. She walked through the limestone dust of the streets, and paused by a cart where hot sweet potatoes were sold, looking at them. After a minute the man who owned the cart handed her four hot sweet potatoes in a brown paper wrapper and shook his head when she said she could not pay. He didn't speak English. It sounded to her that his words were Irish, but she wasn't sure.

She dodged into a doorway to get out of the way of a drove of horses coming past, urged along by men in wide hats and weathered coats. They were being taken to market somewhere. She looked through the crowd of nervous horses as they trotted by, searching for Whiskey or Highlander, Dolly or Gimcrack but the dust was thick and they were moving too fast.

The train station was a great wooden hall with many large doors in it and a crowd of people going in and out. Adair stood for a moment to see how it was that people went about buying a ticket. She was afraid of the crowds.

She stood in line behind a man with a long back. He wore a striped coat that hung on him as if on a peg. Adair stood quietly listening as he spoke with the man selling tickets. The ticket seller hid within a sort of booth and peered out at the world from behind brass bars. He had a large beard with stripes of gray coming from the corners of his mouth. To one side was a dish of fried potatoes. It was his breakfast.

Where's your pass? he said to the thin man.

Here, sir. The man laid a folded paper on the counter.

The ticket seller unfolded it, held it to the light. I been seeing nothing but counterfeits lately, he said. Adair stood off to one side so she could watch the thin man being humiliated. Soon it would be her turn.

Well, that isn't a counterfeit, said the thin man. What in hell is wrong with it?

The ticket man handed the pass back.

Well, it's got fried potato grease on it now, he jeered. Too bad. Where do you want to go?

The thin man bought a ticket to Gray's Summit. He bought it angrily, throwing down a Boatman's Bank note for fifty cents. Outside Adair could hear the roaring boilers of the engine.

She came up to the window. The hot sweet potatoes felt warm in their brown paper. The ticket man glared out of his brass bars.

How much is a ticket to Iron Mountain? she said.

Seventy-five cents. Where's your pass?

Adair stood resolutely and looked up into his face. His eyes were beset with wrinkles and pouches.

I don't have one. Why do I need one?

The ticket man bent forward. To get to Iron Mountain, that's why you need one.

Well, where do I get one? Adair bent forward too. I have just got to have one.

The provost marshal's office at the Customs House, he said. He looked past her. Next!

Well, sell me a ticket now and then I'll go get one, so I don't have to stand in a line again. I am traveling alone. It cain't be helped. I don't care for standing in line. Please?

He chewed on his mustache a moment.

No, he said. If you want to get somewhere, start walking.

ADAIR BEGAN TO WALK SOUTH ON THE CARONDELET ROAD. THREE MILES south of the city she passed an old stone house on the river bluffs, and a group of quarrymen living there called out to her. She walked on. She carried her stolen grip and walked slowly and rested frequently. Her lips and palms were hot with the persistent fever and she could feel the heat of it in her mouth.

Soon there were more and more spaces between the houses and then the houses sat in the midst of a few acres. Wagons passed her by and offered her a ride.

No, she said. I am just going down the road a ways.

Now it was quiet. The lethal noises of the city fell behind her block by block and then lot by lot and then field by field. Before long, the road turned away from the river and into the Meramec River bottoms. She stopped by a farmhouse beyond Dutch Bottoms to ask for a drink from the well. A woman came out and drew up a bucket of water, looking with concern into her face.

Adair tipped the gourd back and drank deeply of the clear water. It was the first clear water she had had to drink in a long time. She drank so much and so fast that she got the hiccups. The woman made her sit down and take a spoonful of molasses with a dash of black pepper on it. Adair breathed deeply with her mouth closed, her nostrils flared. At last the hiccups stopped and she thanked the woman and went on. She was now on the Military Road, or the Nachitoches Trace as it was called, and also called the Wire Road. The telegraph lines were all up and still standing.

In the middle of the Wire Road Adair stopped and began to turn around and around until her skirt hems flew out in a circle, her arms loaded with the centrifugal force of her carpet sack in one hand and the bundle in the other.

Hard times, hard times, come again no more
Many times you have lingered around my cabin door, oh!
Hard times come again no more!

That night she slept in an old stagehouse. It was made of stone and the roof was half gone but for one room. It had been long abandoned because of the railroad. She said her prayers for her family. She prayed that a large stone from some of the construction in St. Louis would fall on Mrs. Buckley and crush her like a toad and her legs would be sticking out one side and her head on the other and her face would be as dead as the earl of hell.

Although it was early March and yet cold at night she slept there well enough. She lay on the linen cover and the quilt, and put the Sutherland plaid wool dress over herself and slept very heavily.

The morning following she had a difficult time awakening. She coughed until the iron taste of blood came to her mouth and then she lay back carefully until it stopped. After a while she took up one of the handkerchiefs and wiped her mouth and hands. She ate one of the sweet potatoes and then spread out the Log Cabin quilt to repair it and spent several hours at it with needle and thread. All the edge binding was now sewn back. It was not such a long task.

She turned the twelve-inch hem on the brass-colored silk twill that she had stolen, that had waved its angel arms at her, and cut strips from it. She began to replace the disintegrated silk organza with them. Several times she heard a troop of teamsters and perhaps soldiers go by but she scrunched down in the corner and didn't look out.

Always in the distance she could hear the sound of the St. Louis and Iron Mountain Railroad engines, their long wailing. Like the beginning note sounded by a choirmaster for a phantom choir that never sang.

The next morning she did not cough so much, or at least there was no blood. She combed her hair and rebraided it. The ankle-jacks had entirely busted out, and the soles were coming loose from the uppers. She sat and stitched them together again with the sewing thread and she knew they would not hold much longer. The Military Road was broad and well traveled.

Lord! she called out in a strenuous voice. What do you want? She walked on down the road. What do you want that I might live? That I might find my family all well and then go with the major to the western places?

At the town of DeSoto she saw the United States flag flying over the post office. She walked into the small brick bank and asked the man behind the counter if he could change the twenty-five-dollar gold piece. She had spent all her silver dollars looking after her little sisters and now had only this gold piece that their father had left to them. She lifted her round black eyes to the clerk.

Well, of course, Miss, said the clerk. Of course.

The clerk gave her twenty-five U.S. silver dollars and a small canvas sack to carry them in. So she crossed over the town creek on a wooden bridge with her long heavy hems dragging. She went into a general merchandise store to see what they had.

There was a good stock of things come from St. Louis. She bought a warm jacket. It was a bright red Zouave jacket with black cuffs. Some soldier's jacket abandoned for regulation blue. Although it was somewhat too big Adair liked it very much and was pleased with it. She bought hard crackers, dried beef, and a wheel of cheese. She chose some Lucifer matches and a small steel saucepan. She paid too much for the saucepan, but it was very good and she had never seen a steel one before. This was all she would buy, for the rest of her money had to last her, as far as she knew, for the rest of her life.

She drank a pint of milk sitting in the store. While she drank it she heard the noise of a troop of men marching, their step and the concerted clash of their equipage. It was a squad of Union mounted infantry and at the front an officer on a yellow horse. The clerk went to the window to look at them.

Adair stayed in the store. The one street of the town was filled to the brim with the noise of fifty horses clattering through and the windowpanes in the stores reflected them piecemeal. The soldiers fell out of formation and tied their horses. One stood guard and the others walked off to go and sit on the raised boardwalks or drink at the town well. One dropped the bucket and cranked it up for the others to fill their canteens or bottles. The windlass made a shrieking scree-aw scree-aw sound.

The officer came into the store. Adair sat on a barrel with her carpet sack and bundle at her feet and drank her milk. He regarded her for long seconds in her bright red jacket and her lilac straw hat and her green brocade bedroom slippers.

We're missing a man, said the officer.

Well, said the clerk.

Some of the men come to drink at Mosier's Grocery and they all came back to barracks but one.

The clerk said, Mosier's Grocery is half a mile on down the road.

I know it, said the officer. But people drink there that come from all over.

Well, I never seen a lone soldier or heard anything about it, said the clerk. He was nervous. I never even seen anybody go past. But I live back on the old Blackwell Ferry Road.

All right, said the officer. Hildebrand is running loose all over this part of the country and you know it and I know it. He's stealing horses and shooting Federals.

Well, I don't know, I live back there on the Blackwell Ferry Road and never see much of anything of an evening. The clerk lined up several boxes of biscuit powder and wiped his hands on his wool pants.

Young woman, said the officer. Are you from this town here?

Adair said, No, sir. I have a commission with the Lord.

He paused. Well, are you staying here?

I'm going down to the St. Francis to see my sister. I come from Carondelet.

Do you have a pass to travel?

No, sir. We got word she had twins and I just started out directly to help her. They wouldn't let me on the train. Adair looked into her milk bottle and swirled the milk around. So I don't know, I just started.

Well, get a pass here before long. Get one at Iron Mountain.

All right.

You just fill out the application. Can you read and write?

Yes, sir.

Well, get it done.

He turned out the door and left and Adair and the clerk watched him go. He crossed the street to the blacksmith shop.

The clerk said, You got to have a pass just to go from one town to another. Ain't that something?

Here's your bottle. Adair handed him the bottle and two cents. I'll just sit here till they go.

You make yourself at home, said the clerk. So Adair sat in the warm sunlight coming in the window until she saw the Union troops had all left.

Then she stood in the road and yelled after them,

Y'all come back soon. Don't be a stranger!

[Missouri Union Militia] troops frequently upset the security of the civilians they were supposed to be protecting. Federal officers themselves often reported being driven frantic by the mob-like activities of the troops ostensibly under their command. The Lieutenant Colonel who had just taken command at the [Union] garrison of Warsaw [Missouri] in August 1863, wrote his commander that "our soldiery" had committed "six murders within the last ten or twelve days. . . . There is a feeling of insecurity universally prevailing with the peaceable citizens . . . all in this place that can get conveyances express an intention of leaving. There is no discipline whatever exercised over the soldiers here, which, added to the indiscriminate sale of liquor, renders the soldiers fiends rather than soldiers. The best citizens here have been menaced with death by the soldiers."

—Lieutenant Colonel T. A. Switzler to Brigadier General E. B. Brown,
Warsaw, Missouri, August 11, 1863, OR, quoted in *Inside War*

In 1863 . . . I was to go to Maryland [from Warsaw, Missouri] and visit relatives until peace was restored . . . because of threats to burn the house over my mother's head if I remained inasmuch as my husband was in the Rebel army. In 1864, while in Maryland, I received word that Major Rainwater had been dangerously wounded at Ditch Bayou and wished me to come to him. . . . [After arriving in St. Louis] the plan was to go by boat, be transferred to the gunboat patrolling between Helena, Arkansas, and Vicksburg, and get the Captain to put us ashore at Columbus Arkansas. . . . There was a detective on the boat whose duty was to search all baggage for contraband goods, such as

Confederate gray cloth, letters, gold coins &c. . . . We had all gray cloth in make-believe underskirts. . . . To our dismay we passed the patrol gunboat in a fog at night. . . . About dusk the Captain and his Lieutenant came up to see how we were getting along. . . . almost immediately we heard the report of a gun and then another. . . . in a moment the firing seemed general and we thought the Confederates had made a dash sure enough. Our own Captain, Miss Miller, was equal to the emergency. Her order was, come help bar the door and now girls drop on the floor and be out of range of the bullets.

—Reminiscences of Mrs. C. C. Rainwater

In Camp before Spanish Fort. Mobile Ala., April 7th, 1865

We heard pretty good news yesterday, that Sherman had possession of Charleston. I think we will soon have the bottom knocked out of the Confederacy we are pouring it on them thick and fast and I hope we will continue to do so, till they have not a place left to lay their heads and call their own. I forgot in my last to tell you what a time for oysters we have had over in Cedar Point on the west side of the bay a man could roll up his breeches and walk in and get as many as he wanted I got some vinegar in my canteen and sat down to a pile with my screwdriver and opened and eat till I could eat no more. We are laying close siege to the works the mortar battery right by us is firing on them throwing 120 pound shells and I tell you it shakes the ground when one of them fires.

*—*LETTER FROM F. F. AUDSLEY, COMPANY A, FORTY-FOURTH INFANTRY MISSOURI VOLUNTEERS (UNION), TO HIS WIFE, WESTERN HISTORICAL MANUSCRIPT COLLECTION, UNIVERSITY OF MISSOURI, COLUMBIA, MISSOURI

T HE *LADY JANE* WAS A SIDE-WHEELER OF NINETY FEET AND SHE HAD lost the railing on her Texas deck to Rebel artillery and was punctured here and there with bullet holes. One of the more experienced officers on board the *Lady Jane* advised Major Neumann not to hang on the rail to watch the scenery go by. Rebel sharpshooters sat out there in those swamps. They especially liked the glitter of officers' insignia.

So William Neumann stood between the great side wheel and the passenger accommodations on the second deck, looking forward. He stood in the wind and watched the broad Mississippi and its uncut swamplands sliding past, the state of Mississippi on one side and Arkansas on the other. His orders were to report to Colonel Benjamin Hayes of the First Indiana Heavy Artillery at Mobile. He turned his back to the wind to light his cigar.

He would bring her with him when he struck out, after the war. They were alike, the two of them; almost alike. Neumann enjoyed being among society more than he had admitted to her, and it was because he saw himself walking into some gathering with her on his arm. How they would stand at the double doors of their home and greet the guests, and the guests would all linger to look at her because she was so beautiful and so lively. They would walk out under cotton-wood trees of great height to the whitewashed stables. And afterward they would talk about the people who had come and the dancing. In their own bedroom. When that mass of black hair fell down her back and it would be like silk in his hands.

About one in the afternoon the *Lady Jane* slid past Greenville, Mis-sissippi, with its wood yard and the planked-over log cabins on a low shore. A man in a blouse-sleeved shirt was asleep on the woodpile with his pipe unlit in his hand. Major Neumann stood on the Arkansas side of the steamer; the swamplands glided by and the sun's reflection gal-loped along after them, glinting through the duckweed and the cypresses. The trees would make the best lumber on earth, fine grained and perfectly straight, as much as sixty feet without a knot in them. He thought how he would see to the construction of a house of that lum-ber for himself and Adair. Neumann watched while the fifteen-foot blades of the side wheel roared over his head, flinging flat sheets of water, and crashed into the river, smiting it.

He wished he had acquired a daguerreotype of her. Or a tintype or some sort of mechanical reproduction of her face. Then he would not have to puzzle over his memories, of exactly how she had appeared.

At two in the afternoon a minié ball came directly between the blades of the side wheel and struck him with a ripping sound he later remembered hearing even above the noise of the machinery. It felt as if he had been struck in the face with a poker. Blood jumped in ropes down his tunic. It was splashing on his hands, running out of him, staining everything red. Lieutenant Brawley came running at him with wide eyes.

Neumann pulled his revolver so fast he didn't remember doing it, and stood at the rail with it at arm's length looking for a target and his hand was stained with blood. He saw a puff of ochre gunpowder smoke rising above a tall cypress in the swamps on the Arkansas side.

There he is!

Sir, get away! Brawley yelled at him. He's reloading!

The hard watery wind off the Mississippi tore into his eyes and the shifting brilliant planes dazzled him but he held to the rail and tried to take aim. Another ball came past and below men were yelling *Sharpshooter! Sharpshooter!*

Neumann fired all five shots in quick succession out of rage, though he had no chance of hitting anything. One was a misfire but the other four clipped a limb from a cypress and sent the new green needles spraying. Neumann stood watching intently, he was seized by the fierce craving to see a man fall out of one of the cypresses, to see him tumble out with his long rifle crashing through limbs before him. Thick smoke from his revolver barrel drifted away in lengthening streams, and the side-wheeler slid downstream on its flat, keelless bottom.

He looked down at his uniform coat and saw streams of blood staining it, running off and spattering the deck. Where am I hit? Where am I hit? I've been hit.

Come on, sir, down to sick bay!

Brawley pulled out a cotton handkerchief and shoved it against the major's right cheek. Brawley pressed hard and the side wheel churned on, bearing them downstream, past whatever cypress remote in those swamps that had been the perch of the Rebel sharpshooter.

Here, let me have it, said Neumann. He snatched the handkerchief out of Brawley's hand. Damn that son of a bitch, damn that son of a bitch.

He proceeded to walk calmly down the vibrating deck and into the passenger compartments, laying out behind him a train of blood like a powder fuse. He walked down the stairs to the first deck. There some of the troops looked up at him from where they lay sprawled on the decks.

Knock any teeth out? said an infantryman of the Eighth Iowa. I'd rather lose a finger than get any teeth knocked out.

At ease! yelled the lieutenant. He walked behind the major to watch and see if he would faint or not. The men stuck their heads out of the cargo doors where they had been bunked in. At ease!

Two men were busily cleaning their rifles, sawing up and down industriously with the ramrods.

Did you get him, sir?

No. I just knocked his teeth out. Neumann had to say this around the bubbling blood in his mouth. He had to lean and spit.

I don't see no teeth in that, the infantryman said.

I don't expect he got him, said a sergeant. Usually you can hear them splash. They go eeeeeeee whumph.

Neumann lay down on the cot in sick bay and turned to one side as the doctor began threading his needle. He stared resolutely at the white-painted wainscoting. His thoughts were nothing but a long furious stream of swearing. The curved needle penetrated the skin of his cheek and his guts coiled inside him as he felt the thread being drawn through.

That night he sat in his bunk in passenger accommodation no. 10, fighting against the pain. His face was swollen like a full moon and his skin strained at the stitches. Lieutenant Brawley read the New Orleans newspaper by the light of a candle. There was a ping and Brawley looked up.

There was one, he said.

I think they're shooting at your candlelight, said Neumann.

Let 'em shoot, sir, said Brawley. What they're using is those old smoothbores. That ball can't penetrate nothing.

Did pretty well on me, said Neumann. His whole head throbbed, and it beat out a rhythm with the blades.

I mean these bulkheads. The lieutenant looked up from his newspaper. Now, if it had hit you in the skull, you see, you'd never have felt it. Brawley laughed in a sort of snorting chortle.

Goddamn, Neumann said. Just think. There was another ping, and a thunking sound. They both looked up. The old conical .54 caliber ball had bit into the bulkhead and stopped. He thought, One could well come through the window. But neither of them had his head hanging out the window so he supposed it was all right. The side wheel walked across the waters of the Mississippi with smashing steps, drawing them down into the sugar country.

THE NIGHT BEFORE THE BOMBARDMENT OF THE DEFENSES OF MOBILE, Major Neumann had absentmindedly pulled out all the stitches of his face wound. His face was permanently distorted where the ball had chipped a cheekbone but he didn't think about it, he was possessed with the nervousness men had before a battle, a kind of vivid, jittering dread.

The Federal baggage train had bogged down in the sandy road coming up from Fish River, and the wagoneers were trying to jack the wheels out of the sand with new-cut pine poles. Neumann rode full tilt between the pines to one side of the jammed-up Federal wagons, looking for the First Indiana Artillery, his orders in his tunic pocket. The road alongside Mobile Bay snaked among the saw palmettos and the pines, a highway of red sand into which wheels sank and men straggled ankle deep. Enormous horseflies feasted on them at leisure.

A. J. Smith's men were volunteer troops from Iowa and Indiana. Veterans of Chattanooga and the march through Georgia. They called themselves Smith's Gorillas and had learned to pray and eat and reload on the run and they were good at arson. The men had started burning houses and barns and sheds and fence rails at Fish River, as soon as the gangplanks were down. They marched through the sandy pine forests from one small village to another, from Fairhope to Montrose, and more often than not they took what was available.

Neumann and Lieutenant Brawley came upon Company A of the Eighth Iowa Infantry rooting around in the sheds of a small farm among the pines. They called out to the dusty veterans in their blue faded tunics to keep moving on. The men dodged him. They had chickens tied to their haversacks and bunches of sugarcane in their hands.

Wait till we get within range of their guns! Neumann shouted. Then you'll think about something else!

Go on, Major. A bearded and weathered corporal walked and ate a slab of the sludge called candy that came from the last boiling of the cane. I didn't have my breakfast.

There's killing going to go on today, said Brawley. As if he had experienced much.

I hope you find time to do some fighting, Corporal, said Neumann. As well as eating.

I'll see what I can do, sir.

They slogged on through the sea grape and wait-a-minute vines. In the villages alongside Mobile Bay, hidden back in the thin forests, Neumann saw a people that seemed to him to be Red Indians. They stood in the doorways of huts thatched with palm leaf and moved very slowly out of the way as Smith's Gorillas set the huts afire. They dressed themselves in dusty fustian with bright woven sashes and their bangs cut straight across their foreheads. They were a people of ancient lineage who cared little about modern war or soldiers of any stripe. As if they had retired from the world and from all desire for real estate or love of possessions. They sat on the ground beside their hammocks and watched their huts burn and the rats bolt out of the burning thatch.

The corporal came upon a basket of dried peaches and began to devour them with one hand while carrying his Springfield in the other.

Neumann rode past and said, If you men would stop having yourselves a party!

One of the Iowa men yelled at him, Sir! The corporal's eeeatin' agaiiiiin!! You better stop him! Once he gets started he eats everthing, live chickens and everthing!

Neumann shut his mouth and looked straight ahead.

We'll keep you informed whenever he's eatin' again! The private that yelled this at Neumann nodded eagerly with a bright sarcastic smile.

Thank you, Private, said Neumann and rode ahead.

The lines of men in blue forged on at route step. The veterans had tied rags or socks over the firing mechanisms of their rifles to protect them from the sand, and as they swung along in they sang.

They marched past large plantations, and the slaves abandoned their tools in the sugar fields, among the new shoots of cotton, their hands scarred with the cuts of cane leaves, burned with the sugar-boiling. So cruelly marked by their enslavement and yet they came singing. Four women with their arms across one another's shoulders, dancing a jumping line dance. Calling to the men in a kind of song, and the men came before them calling out the response. Neumann could not understand the words, but it lifted his heart. The former slaves followed the army in the hundreds, shouting and waving.

Then they came within range of the Confederate guns at Spanish Fort. Neumann heard a heavy crump. The groups of slaves from the fields turned and ran into the line of trees, and the women's dresses flew like sheets before the wind, like quilts on a line, and they carried their children against them as they ran.

A fountain of sand and palm leaves and pine branches blew skyward and it then rained down on the blue-clad troops with rattling noises, then two other hits nearby. So began their bombardment. And behind the screen of their artillery the Confederates put out one last line of troops.

The Confederate infantry fired one volley from the pines, and then Neumann saw a solid wall of running men in butternut, the flash of ramrods in the air as they reloaded. They came running out of their own thick banks of smoke. They appeared out of the palmetto and pine like dismal ragged spirits, screaming, and their torn clothing fluttered. Neumann drew his revolver and suddenly found himself staggering forward on foot and his horse thrashing on the ground behind him. Apparently his horse had been shot out from under him and he had landed on his feet or maybe scrambled up.

A man was coming at him under the umbrella of a wide-brimmed hat the size of a dinner table, and for a shirt he was wearing a woman's dress bodice frothing with dirty lace and ribbons and he was barefoot. He held a six-shot revolver in one hand, and he was looking for a target. Neumann stood and held his own revolver straight out and fired. The ball hit the man in the right shoulder and he shot backward as if jerked by an invisible rope. The man came to his bare feet again like a cat. Then Neumann found himself among men in blue who were running, running past him and over him, nearly knocking him down. The Union forces were running forward over their own dead and wounded. They were racing toward the Confederates in a wild charge.

Stop! he screamed. Stop and form up!

Hoooooo, they yelled at him. A peculiar sound, as if a million men were blowing across the necks of bottles. A shell exploded nearby and Neumann smelled blood and turpentine but he did not stop to see what had been hit, because the men of the Eighth Iowa had not been prepared for this last Confederate charge and their ammunition was still on the baggage wagons, they had only four more volleys. He caught a loose horse and managed to get on it as it circled and circled in a wild panic. He shoved his foot in the stirrup and swung up even while he was being thrown outward by the centrifugal force of the horse's spinning.

The Union quartermasters were bringing up the baggage train in a frantic charge and the rest of the men coming up were forced to scramble over them, split up and run around. The big six-ton freight wagons needed a wide crossing to get turned onto the Spanish Fort road, but the road was narrow, three were jammed in the pines, sunk to the hubs in sand. Several had turned so tightly that they had overset and their teamsters were scrambling to cut the mules loose. The mob of bluecoats were running around and through the jammed wagons. They stopped to load and fire and load and fire again, and Neumann counted three good volleys that fogged the crossing in cordite smoke.

Neumann put his horse in a gallop and the long, feathery bunches of needles on the loblolly pines lashed him in the face. Artillery boomed behind him, the peculiar wowing sound of a Parrott shell. A lieutenant colonel rode directly across his path.

Get those men to form up! They are bunching up!

Sir! shouted Neumann. Permission to help clear these wagons! He knew the men were not bunching up. Smith's Gorillas were too experienced to pack up. A shell went by overhead as if it were a train on some solitary journey, determined to arrive on time, perhaps in Atlanta, for it tore past on a flat trajectory, removing limbs and treetops as it went. Branches fell on them and the smell of cordite came in clouds from behind them.

Abandon them! yelled the lieutenant colonel. Just abandon the damn things!

Neumann kept on. The horse under him probably had not rested in five days. Its gallop was uneven and stumbling. Men streamed past, keeping a distance from one another, stopping to kneel and reload, and then they went on. Smoke drifted among the pines in thin, trailing veils. The five-foot wheels of the wagons ground through the sand on their iron tires with a crisp sizzle.

Two baggage wagons had locked wheels, and the teamsters were screaming at each other and shoving at the wheels while sweat poured down their faces. Neumann hauled up on his horse and at that time heard the low and ugly sound of a Whitworth mortar, the whoo-der whoo-der noise it made as it carved its way through the dense air, coming straight down on them from overhead. Major Neumann put both arms over his head. His horse squatted in terror.

The mortar struck a commissary wagon and Neumann was sprayed with flour and blood. He felt as if he were somebody else, that he was living outside his own body and wondered for one millisecond if he were dead, had been beheaded. Two mules were down, one of them missing its forelegs, and the stumps churned in the air and hosed the men alongside with blood. The sides of the wagon were scattered in fragments among the trees and the trace chains were embedded in a pine at the side of the road. A mule hoof was sticking out of a burst barrel of flour.

Cut loose and leave it! Neumann could hear himself screaming, so he couldn't possibly be dead. In fact he was immensely alive. He jumped off his horse and drew his sword and began to cut what mules were left alive out of their harnesses. When he laid his left hand on his scabbard to draw out the sword with his right, he discovered he was missing the little finger and the ring finger on his left hand, ragged white leaders sticking out of the stumps. He took off his neck cloth and tied the hand in a tight bind, then got his sword out and went back to cutting the mules loose.

Another shell came whooing overhead, a struggling mule kicked one of the teamsters in the face and knocked out all the upper teeth on one side of his mouth, so that when he jumped to his feet again Neumann thought the man had been hit with a shell fragment. The teamster spat blood and teeth onto his blue uniform coat and did not seem to notice it. Together Neumann and the teamsters wrenched and tore at the harness and then the mules were loose and the teamsters jumped on their backs to ride them back down the road out of range. Horses would stand through a bombardment, but mules would bolt, and so they had to be taken back. His coat was covered with flour and his ripped hand spewed blood out of the neck cloth.

Neumann galloped to the next jam and the next. The wagons were turned every which way. Their wagon tongues were thrust into the Alabama sand, the mules kicking at the wagon tongues or their drivers or whatever they could reach. Neumann put his sword on the inside of the harness, ran it between mule and leather and then cut it through in one stroke.

Lieutenant Brawly came up at a gallop and called to Neumann,

The First Indiana's guns are going into line up ahead! And Carlin's guns are still on the transports!

What the hell are they doing there? Neumann yelled. He had the almost overwhelming desire to knock the young lieutenant off his horse. Go back and tell him we are clearing the road for him! They are shelling the hell out of us!

Yes sir! Ain't this something? Brawley grinned. They've got Texas and Missouri troops in that fort, ain't going to be easy to get them pried loose.

Go on, Brawley.

Neumann watched him go and then got on the commandeered horse. The road between Fish River and Spanish Fort was littered with Confederate caps and rifles and shoes, he saw powder horns and the bits of paper that served for wadding. The contents of Union baggage wagons were spewed over the trees on both sides. Somewhere in all that mess lay his fingers.

THEY BIVOUACKED BEHIND A SLIGHT RISE OF GROUND, WITHIN THE SANDY pine forest east of Spanish Fort. The quartermasters were still attempting to sort out the stores of the baggage train.

At the surgeon's tent he bent his head down to his knees while the surgeon held his hand and whacked loose the ends of the leaders and drew the skin over the stumps with dirty thread. He heard men screaming in the tents beyond and before long he was screaming like the rest until the surgeon jerked the last thread tight and tied it off.

Are you going to pass out? the surgeon asked.

No, no, just wrap it up, said Neumann. His voice was hoarse from the screaming and the cordite smoke. Suddenly he felt his mouth fill with water and he fought back the vomit.

Looks like you got hit before.

Don't remind me.

There may be some metal fragments in here.

Just leave it, said Neumann. I got to get out of here. He walked away from the tents to find Brawley. As he walked he shed flakes of flour and blood over his boots.

He walked through the pines and both hands shook slightly as if they were jig dancing to some private music of their own and he could not stop them. He felt elated and alive in a peculiar and contingent way. He kept thinking of a body he had seen earlier, draped over the walls of Spanish Fort, missing its entire left side, so blood soaked he could not have said whether it were Union or Confederate or a butchered hog or a strung-out bag of rags.

He found the fire near the beach where he and Brawley had unloaded their saddles and bedrolls. He felt the tension thrash through him, felt it beat its way through every muscle in his abdomen and his shoulders and then drain out of him. He ducked his head twice, to pull at the muscles at the back of his neck. He pulled his saddle blanket over his face and listened late into the night as the men of the Eighth Iowa waded into the waters of the bay for oysters, breaking them loose with their bayonets, calling out to one another how good they were.

Neumann went over all that had happened to him since daylight, his horse shot from under him and Smith's Gorillas, who had put him neatly in his place, baggage wagon jammed up and then the shelling, his hand half torn away. The day came back in a series of detailed images with himself moving through them. He had done his duty, he had not run nor cowered, there was a stronghold within him that would not give way. For this he felt a profound relief, a sense of gratitude. He watched the coals of the fire for a while and then finally fell asleep.

On April 8, very early in the morning, Neumann rode up to the First Indiana Heavy Artillery, where its line of cannon was being brought up to the east of Spanish Fort. Twenty-two Parrott rifled guns were being brought into line with their caissons and limber chests, drawn by teams of heavy bay horses. The mouths of the cannon looked backward from the caissons and as the teams drew up their equipage they swung in a circle so that the cannons faced the fort. Then a crewmember pulled the pin to release the team from the caisson. As soon as they heard the pin clatter loose the horses charged forward of their own accord without waiting for the driver's signal and galloped away in the jangling music of their harnesses, out of range of Confederate fire.

Neumann found the nearest battery captain standing beside his gun and crew.

Where may I find Colonel Hayes? he said. I have orders to report to him. Neumann stepped down from his horse with his bandaged hand close to his chest.

Up ahead, said the captain. Welcome to the First. But stay and watch, sir. Watch me take out the head-log on that embrasure yonder.

All the cannon were in line now and the battery captains called out their orders. *Load!* they shouted. *Rammer! Ready! Gun number one fire!* And almost simultaneously the shouts *Fire! Fire! Fire!* went all down the line.

All twenty-two guns cut loose. Neumann and the captain stood in the obscuring smoke, their hands over their ears. And the tubes of the cannons shouted for joy in a flattening roar and the earth jumped beneath their feet. Neumann's horse tore the reins from his right hand and galloped back to the artillery horses and stood trembling.

Spanish Fort burnt under the cloudless sky, and the men who served the guns fed them on gunpowder and iron. Standing columns of smoke poured upward. Sprays of debris rose in the air, he saw timbers turning end over end and with them pieces of stone and human bodies and barrels and wagon spokes. Lord God, he said. The detonations shook the ground beneath his feet and fewer and fewer of the Confederate pieces replied.

Neumann found Colonel Hayes at his headquarters in a Sibley tent, standing with a sheaf of papers in his hand, watching the bombardment, and his face had a deep lustrous glow as the cannons spoke again and again.

Sir, said Neumann. Major Neumann reporting, sir. Here are my orders.

Very well, Major, very well. Organize some kind of an escort to get the rest of our ammunition up here as fast as possible. Is it unloaded? Ha ha! The colonel laughed. There, there, that was Captain Shaw's piece, he could take out a bird on the wing.

By nighttime Spanish Fort's defenses were knocked in, the head-logs over the Confederate batteries blown out and most of their guns silenced. The gun bays were spilled outward in avalanches of red brick, and inside the shattered interior the remaining Confederate troops hunkered behind any cover they could find. Across the bay Neumann could see the lights of Mobile, and there was a dim glow to the north of the city where the Confederate troops were burning the stores of cotton. A thin moon came up over the glowing rubble, and the Gulf of Mexico shifted its planes like gelatin under the glittering fields of stars.

Neumann lay beside his campfire and his nerves seemed to sing along the lines of his body, from the noise of the guns and the artillery duels between the two forces that had gone on for nearly a week. They sang a pleasing music. His hand was throbbing in the exact rhythm of his heartbeat. He wadded his saddle blanket under his head and reflected that if he lived he could get to like it. Especially when his side was winning. Brawley tore apart a paper package on the other side of the fire. It was a package of red peppers labeled HOT DEVIL MONKEY.

Where do they get these names? asked Brawley.

Damned if I know, said Neumann. He looked at his hand. The stumps were still leaking blood through the bandages and it hurt very much.

Are you still going to be able to play piano? Brawley dropped a pepper into their kettle with a great show of caution.

No, said Neumann. I couldn't have before, either. He thought, if he had not given Adair the signet ring it would have been blown off and lost in the flour somewhere. This had some good meaning. The smoke lay low on the ground and in the distance Neumann heard some men singing, *Hail Columbia, happy land, If I don't burn you I'll be damned.*

Overhead a fireball shot up from one of the Confederate Coehorn mortars, a fireball made of wadded raw cotton and turpentine. It arched sparkling through the nighttime air. It lit up the Federal entrenchments, and then the shallow crack of Enfield rifles came from the burning defenses of Spanish Fort. The Confederate sharpshooters were determined to keep them awake all night.

From another campfire in the distance, Neumann heard a long singsong cry, *Oh Major, the corporal's eeeetin' again!*

Neumann laughed. He might as well eat while he could. He heard the noise of the batteries starting up again, this time against Fort Alexandria and after that it would be the city. The men smashing into the dramshops.

He listened to the incessant thundering. It sounded good. He felt a long burning up his left arm.

John Smith T was born John Smith in 1770 in Essex County, Virginia, to a
family richer in Revolutionary War heroes than it was in land and slaves. . . .
Although he briefly went to William and Mary College . . . John soon [went]
west, where he immersed himself in a variety of money-making schemes. . . .
It was during this period that he added the 'T' to his name. . . . Along with
his new name, Smith T gained a reputation as a dead shot: a man with a hair
trigger and a temper to match. . . . He began to buy up many arpents of land
in the lead and iron-mining district of southeastern Missouri in 1806.

—FROM *Gateway Heritage*, VOL. 14, NO. 2, 1993

UNION CORRESPONDENCE
Headquarters District of Southeastern Missouri
Pilot Knob, Mo., October 25, 1863
Capt. W. T. Leeper, Patterson:
On Tues. evening, the 27th instant, 150 well-appointed troops will arrive at
Greenville from Cape Girardeau. You will join them with all the men you can
spare from post duty and during their stay in that region, give old Tim [Reeves]
and his rascally gang such a hunt and extermination as they never yet had.

You will summon all the wives of the bushwhackers you can reach to come to
Doniphan, and give them plainly to understand that either their husbands
must come in and surrender themselves voluntarily and stop their villainous
conduct, or their houses, stock, and &c. will be given to the flames, and the
families all sent down the Mississippi River to be imprisoned at Napoleon,

*Ark. . . . be firm, but discreet. I shall look for some good work in the lower
counties during the next twenty days.*

Clinton B. Fisk, Brigadier-General

—OR, CH. XXXIV, P. 678

*Dave Maberry had come home from the Rebel army and stayed at home and
round about home. He was standing in his yard when the Federals came. They
arrested him and took him with them. They dashed on and caught Akins.
They went on down the valley and crossing the river at House's ford, they saw
Frank Wheeler . . . he ran across the field going north and had reached the
top of the field when they caught him. He had two pistols with him but a bullet from the enemy had shattered his right wrist so he could not use the
weapons. He cursed them until they shot him in the mouth with his own pistol. Next the leader signaled some of his men to shoot Akins. Mr. Akins, divin-
ing their intentions, ran into some woods and got about two hundred yards
when they shot and disabled him. They placed him on his feet and tied him fast
to a tree and tortured him by shooting him sixteen times, making slight
wounds in his flesh. Bud House, then about fifteen years old, stood in his yard
nearly a mile away and heard him scream many times.*

—J. J. CHILTON, FROM THE *Current Local*, FEBRUARY 3, 1932, REPRINTED IN
The Civil War in Carter and Shannon County

ADAIR RODE IN A WAGON TO THE TOWN OF VALLES MINES. SHE GOT OUT
and had to sit down for a long time on a bench beside the town well.
Then she began to walk again. On the single street of this town was a
sign over the door of a frame house: STEAM DOCTOR.

Adair gathered her skirts in her hands to go up the steps and opened
the door. A small bell jingled. Inside a gray-haired man in a black coat
glanced up. He had been reading in a heavy leather-bound book.
When he saw her he took off his delicate spectacles and stood.

Good morning, Madame, he said. Or Miss.

Adair laid down her burdens. She drew the collar of the bright red

Zouave jacket up around her neck and took off her hat because it was bothering her.

Miss, she said. Miss Adair Colley.

The office smelled of medicines and soap. Perhaps up there on the shelves, in one of those bottles, was something that could help her. On the wall was an engraving of the St. Louis waterfront seen from the Illinois shore, and a man whose muscles and organs were all exposed. All his parts were numbered. Leaf shadows played on the plaster wall and there was the sound of somebody clipping a lawn outside.

Well, said Adair. I would like to consult with you concerning my cough.

The doctor nodded. He regarded her. Her cheeks blossomed with the roses of fever and she was very thin. She was pretty, but consumption would take whoever it could get, the pretty and the plain, the old and the young.

He put out a chair for her. Sit down, he said.

Adair sat down facing him and he turned his chair away from his desk and bent forward and looked at her.

How much do you cough? he asked.

Well, it is getting better. Adair said this in a positive tone and nodded to him.

Whenever you exert yourself, said the doctor.

Yes. And when people make me mad. Ordering me around. Then I have bad dreams and I cough.

Are you coughing blood?

Adair looked at her hands. They were dirty and the nails were worn. Once or twice a spot as big as the ball of your thumb.

Lying won't do you any good, my dear. He leaned back in his chair.

Well, a little more, said Adair. Every morning.

He nodded. There is no need for me to examine you. Except. He reached out and laid his hand on her forehead. His hand was cool and dry and it felt good to Adair. As if someone cared for her. You are running a small fever all the time.

Yes sir, she said. It never seems to really go away.

Is there any person who can care for you? Relieve you of work?

Adair said, I am going home and I expect my sisters will soon be home. We are all scattered because of the war.

Yes, yes. He tapped his spectacles against his teeth. So many are. He crossed his hands in his lap. Well, some people have survived consumption.

He had said the word. Adair put her left hand to her mouth and then back in her lap again.

I'm listening to you, she said.

Some people have survived it and in a manner of speaking come to an agreement with it. Let us say a standoff. Lived to a moderately old age with it.

He could plainly see the young woman's ardent wish to be one of those persons, for she looked up to him with an anxious hope and her eyes were round and black as jet. Her hair was still healthy and it shone like rock oil. She was thin but the physician could see in her a certain vitality and a will to go on.

How do they survive it? she asked. Her hands were hidden in the red sleeves of the jacket and only her fingertips appeared beyond the cuffs.

The doctor said, Good food and rest and maintaining a calm mind. Nervousness draws a person down. It consumes your vital energy. This disease of consumption, if it were to have a mind, thinks of human beings as food. It is a predator. You must have nothing else drawing on your strength, and allow the inner electricity of the body to rearrange itself for this interior affray. You must maintain temperate habits of mind and body. You don't use tobacco do you?

No, sir.

Not in any form?

No, I don't.

Well. He turned and looked through his desk drawers. Let's see. He brought out a small round tin. Are you sleeping well at night?

Very well.

Traveling and all. We generally don't sleep well unless we are in our own beds, but with this war a-raging here as it is sometimes even our own beds are not sufficient. The guerilla Hildebrand has been shooting people in their own beds so there you are. He opened the tin and looked in it, and then shut it again.

I sleep just fine, said Adair. She took the tin from him.

Now, I am what they call a botanical steam doctor, the elderly man said. In that I refuse to use all the old drugs. Like blue mass and calomel and sugar of lead. I do not practice bleeding, which the old-style doctors do, much to the detriment of the patient. They use harsh and violent purgatives and other compounds. You will hear much disparagement of steam doctors. He leaned forward. But the only manner of surviving this is to husband your strength.

What's in this tin? asked Adair.

Stop talking and listen. He caught his thumbs in a pair of striped braces under his coat. I can see you are alone in your traveling. As are many women these days. Fathers and brothers gone to war or killed or imprisoned. Widowed ladies. Where are your menfolk?

Well, said Adair. She took a breath to speak and she heard the rattling of thick rales in her chest. She lifted a palm to begin a new story as to where all her menfolk were but he said, Never mind it. It does not do to ask. But I will draw up a dietary regimen for you, and in that tin is a powder made from infusions of the red willow bark, of the genus *Salix*, which has been given the chemical name of salicylic acid. This makes it more acceptable to the patient, where in reality it is merely an old Indian recipe.

Then I could make my own when this runs out, said Adair.

He put on his delicate spectacles and took up a pen. Don't talk so much, young woman. Your task in the next year or so is to get better. I am describing here a dietary regimen for you. He wrote. Beef broth frequently. Avoid cooked vegetables but take them fresh. Sassafras tea is very good for the blood. Liver. Avoid beef itself for it demands too much of the digestive system. A great deal of liver. Preferably that of young venison or neats but take whatever you can get.

Adair nodded. She had no idea how she would get liver.

Two or three eggs a day, raw, beaten up in a glass of milk. Buy fresh eggs as you travel and cover each egg with a thin film of butter and they will keep indefinitely, even in the hottest weather.

I never heard of that, said Adair.

That is why people consult steam doctors. He blew on the ink and then handed her the sheet of paper. Take a pinch of that powder in a glass of water for your fever. Now you have plenty of fresh air. But on another matter, somewhat delicate. He cleared his throat. Take the sun as much as you can on the greatest part of your person that you feel comfortable with.

Take the sun?

Remove as much clothing as you feel comfortable with, he said. And take the sun.

Adair folded the paper and nodded.

Cold baths.

All right.

Avoid all excitement. Keep a Christian outlook on daily events. Do not become exercised about anything, but command your feelings.

All right.

He looked at her in a long pause. Then he said, And if you find yourself getting weaker, and more blood appearing, I would make sure you turn your thoughts to your Eternal Home.

My Eternal Home, said Adair.

Yes. With a delicate gesture he pinched up the cloth of his trousers at the knee and then crossed his legs. I would have the important things in order.

All right, said Adair, and looked at the floor. Then she reached for her carpet sack.

That will be a dollar, said the doctor.

She bought eggs and butter from a farmhouse on down the Military Road. The woman tried to sell her duck eggs and then offered the heavy and freckled guinea eggs, but at last Adair left with ten chicken eggs. She stopped to cover them with butter and put them in a wad of grass inside the steel saucepan, and the pan inside the carpet sack, and then walked on. She felt better. She was doing something to save herself.

Lord! Lord! she called out as she walked. Look on me and I'll tell you a story! She then told God a story about a horse called Whiskey with his shoes turned backward against trackers, a horse who appeared head and shoulders and all in a pan of water when he was called by candlelight, his black eyes looking with keen intent out of the black fan of his forelock and she stepped into the plane of water and the golden dun horse took her directly to her father. Or maybe it wasn't God, maybe the major was the image in her mind.

People who passed her on the Military Road gazed with interest and some pity on the good-looking young woman walking southward, loaded down with her carpet sack and bundle. Her red coat that was too big for her with its black military cuffs covering her hands. Two women pulled up in a light gig. They had a full-grown hog on the floor between them. They wanted to know where she was bound to. It looked as if it were about to rain.

Adair said, I have the consumption and the steam doctor in Valles Mines says I must eat eggs and get a lot of fresh air and rest. I can't rest until I am home.

Where's that?

Near Doniphan, in Ripley County.

Well, I understand that, said the young woman driving. I hope you last till you get there.

The other said, We would carry you on down the road a ways but we can't because of this hog. The hog made a deep, compact grunt as if it knew it had been referred to. You would do well to get you some kind of animal to pack that load of truck even if it is only a jackass.

There are none about, said Adair. Because of the war, I suspect.

Are your menfolk off fighting? Which side?

They are all dead, said Adair.

Well, you be careful. There's nothing going on around here but horse stealing, said the younger woman. That scoundrel Hildebrand and his men are thieving horses from the Federals and holding them here and there, and then running them to market in St. Louis. They don't care who gets in front of them, either, they'll run right over you.

The other woman said, I'd keep on going through Rouenne if I were you.

I'll be careful, said Adair, and went on.

ADAIR CAME WALKING, TIRED AND COUGHING HEAVILY, DOWN THE SINGLE street of Rouenne at about noon. She looked upon the few small French-style houses with great discouragement. They were built of stone with thick walls, a high, steep roof and long verandas. Beyond them, at a far bend of the road, she could see a two-story frame house in the American style, with tall windows and peeling paint. The March sky was full of eastbound clouds in running streams. She was suspended on a light fever once again. This was disheartening. She walked down to the bend in the road, and then sat down on the stone curb in front of the grand old house. How many miles on to her home? She sat in the sun and drew back the long cuffs of the red jacket so she could count on her fingers.

She must stay on the Military Road, and cross the St. Francis at Greenville. Then the Military Crossing of the Black River, after that it was Cane Creek and then Ten-Mile Creek. Adair put her forefinger to her head, between her eyebrows, as if it would help her think. How many miles was it between all those crossings? More than a hundred.

A woman came out of the house and regarded her.

Well now, there you are, all on your lonesome, said the woman. Lorn and lonesome.

Yes I am, said Adair. I am walking home. I thought I would sit and rest here for a minute.

This March weather can go bad any hour, said the woman. You'd better come on in. She had a print dress and a large scoop-shovel bonnet on her head. She opened the door and gestured inside with an imperious motion.

I don't think I want to, said Adair. This stone wall has gathered heat for my benefit.

You don't look well, said the woman. I don't want you a-sitting out here.

The house was very silent. Adair came into the hallway and looked around her. It was a big house and echoed to their steps because there was almost no furniture nor rugs. Adair put down the carpet sack and bundle and smoothed back her hair.

Come in the kitchen and have some buttermilk and cornbread, said the woman, and so Adair followed her. Adair did not like the feel of the place, as it seemed very empty and devoid of life. There were old silhouettes on the walls, cut from black paper, framed in ovals.

I'm Lila Spencer, said the woman. This here was my grandfather's house.

How do you do, said Adair. I'm Adair Colley, lately of Egypt.

Adair sat at the kitchen table and ate the cornbread with butter on it, and drank the buttermilk. She did not take off the red jacket. It had a mandarin collar that stood up around her face and made her feel armored against the world. The March sun came through the tall windows in twenty-four squares and the kitchen smelled of old ashes and a cold fireplace.

There ain't nobody here but me and my daughter, the woman said. She took off her bonnet and sat across from Adair. He's gone off with Van Dorn's men two years ago and I ain't seen him since.

Adair nodded. You're better off.

I think you ought to get to bed, said the woman. She was a thin woman and had a receding chin. She reached out to Adair's face and touched her cheek. I think you'd best spend a week in bed before you go on anywheres.

Maybe I ought, said Adair. She felt so weak she put her head in both hands. But I got to get home.

What for? Where you going? The woman bent forward, looking at her intently.

Adair saw that the grain of the wood tabletop appeared to her in marvelous clarity. A knot that seemed to be an eye staring up out of the wood, some strange being trapped in the tabletop and staring out.

I am going down to Ripley County, she said. That's where my home is. She tried to think of why she would have been in St. Louis. I went up to St. Louis to see if I could get my brother out of Alton. He was captured at Shiloh.

Huh! said the woman. I bet that's a lie.

Well! said Adair. I don't know why I'd tell any lie. She thought, No wonder her husband run off to fight with Van Dorn.

You been up there chasing a man.

Adair reached down for her carpet sack. I think I'll just go on. She was not supposed to become exercised about mean, vulgar people but to command her feelings so her inner electricity could assail the predator Consumption.

The woman stood up and came around to Adair's side of the table and picked up the carpet sack and hoisted it.

You are far too sick to go on. You come on with me. Adair followed the woman into the pantry and watched her as she pulled sheets from a shelf, and a down quilt in an embroidered covering. Then into a drawing-room on one side of the great hall. The woman made up an ancient chaise longue into a bed. Directly Adair sat down on it she felt as if she were falling asleep. She took off the lilac straw hat.

I bet he was a Yankee soldier, wasn't he? Lila Spencer beat up a pillow and put it in place. She almost seemed to be talking to herself so little reference did she give to anything Adair said. And he come and just won your heart and then went on to St. Louis.

No, ma'am, she said. I went to find my brother at Alton and that's all I went to do.

Adair took off the red jacket. She struggled out of her dress and the corset and retied the signet ring securely to the stays. She kicked off the ankle-jacks. Then she fell asleep. It was a sleep so deep as to seem drugged. It was like a coma. Every corner of her consciousness was extinguished in her body and mind's effort to heal itself, to set things to rights in some deep interior affray.

She partly awoke late some time that evening. She heard noises from the other houses in the small town just up the road, people cutting wood for the evening fire, and a churn thumping in its barrel. The sound of two people out on the road in front of the great house speaking in French. She heard the ringing of an anvil.

There were voices and the noise of clattering dishes in the kitchen. She heard a fire crackling. Lila Spencer and her daughter were talking. Adair listened. She couldn't do much else but listen. From what Adair could gather from their conversation, the woman's husband was not with the Confederate general Van Dorn at all, but a plain bushwhacker with Hildebrand, and there was a price on his head and another woman in his arms.

They came into the room to look in on her, and then sat down.

Adair tried to look as if she had just woke up and had heard nothing of their talk. She nodded sleepily as they told her that this ancient house was the construction of a man named John Smith T, who had added the *T* to his name to distinguish himself from the hundreds of other John Smiths. That was his cutout there on the wall. He came from Virginia and claimed land from the French government in 1806, and started up the silver diggins here in this country, near DeSoto and Valles Mines and Bonne Terre.

Adair drifted in and out of their talking. She managed to nod as if all were normal. Days seemed to go by. She sat up and then fell asleep again over soup. Once she woke up in the night and stayed awake for a long time. As she lay there she saw a cart going slowly down the road with a lantern hung from the back. Bars of light following behind as if tied to the tailgate.

O, for a beaker full of the warm south, said the girl. Adair opened her eyes and sat up with the blankets around her to look at the young woman. She sat on a chair beside Adair with a hand gin and turned the crank. Cottonseeds rattled into the tray. Instead of this cold March weather here in this forsaken district. And then the girl whispered to Adair, *My father is with Hildebrand, robbing and killing, and he's run off with another woman.*

Adair lay back down and went to sleep again.

21

About this time [when Lefors was five or six years old, at the family farm just south of Fort Smith Arkansas] a squad of Yankees came to our house and hitched a team of fine mules to a large wagon and loaded it with grain and feedstuffs, then hitched up another span of good mules to a smaller wagon and loaded it with all the provisions they could find in the house. They even taken the bedding off the beds and taken all the best of the women's clothing to give to the Yankee women, and turned over the cupboard and stomped the dishes. One soldier grabbed my sister Dollie and tried to Kiss her but she jerked back and slapped him a hard blow in the face. He then started for her in great anger but one, I suppose the officer in charge of the soldiers, said to let that girl alone. He did so. Dollie was about 17 years old.

My father and brothers were in the Southern Army, brother Perry was about 16 and brother Bill was about 15 years old. In 1863 a squad of Yankees captured my brother Perry and was holding him along with some other men of the Southern Army for exchange. Perry heard the Yankees planning to come to our house to kill my Father who was then about 55 years old and a neighbor, old man Bunch, who was about 70 years old. Perry managed to escape that night and walked and run some 15 miles, and come by Mr. Bunch's and told him what he had overheard. But Mr. Bunch said they would not do that to an old man like him. . . .

I remember they saddled a small black pony for my father and helped him on it, as he was crippled from the rheumatism, and they left, my brother on foot. They made it to some southern army. I think it was General Price's army. Soon after daylight the next morning a squad of Yankees came to our

house to kill my Father, as they came by Mr. Bunch's and shot him to death.
My father told Mother before he left to load up what she could in a small,
rather old wagon, and she with us children to go south and try to make it to
Texas.

—*Autobiography of Rufe Lefors*, BY RUFE LEFORS, UNIVERSITY OF TEXAS PRESS,

AUSTIN, TEXAS, 1986

THEN IT WAS EARLY MORNING. THE YOUNG WOMAN WAS SITTING ON THE
single chair and looking at Adair. In her hands she held a sheet of
paper. It was a playbill, and she had written on the back of it.

She saw that Adair was awake and sat up straight.

Would you like to hear some of my compositions? said the young
woman. There are so few people here I can share them with. Everybody around here is French and they are very common people. People
of a low class.

Adair brought herself upright in the chaise longue, and the sheets
tangled around her legs. You are going to read me some of your compositions?

Poetry, said the young woman. My name is Rosalie. She nodded as if
to encourage Adair to agree with her.

Adair wiped her hands across her face, pulled her long hair to the
back of her neck. She began to cough but lay back again still and quiet.
It went away.

Well, I guess, she said. I sure don't want to be like all those low people. Read on.

Adair felt she had slept out her fever. She had emerged on the other
side of it. There did not appear to be a fire in the entire house. The
drawing room fireplace was utterly empty of ashes and its cream-
colored stones were swept clean.

The young woman cleared her throat. The playbill advertised a
monologue by the famous comedian Philadelphia Jones, with an
engraving of his face. It was from several years ago. Clearly paper was
scarce here as elsewhere.

The girl held the paper straight up so that Adair was looking at the grinning face of Philadelphia Jones. She read in a strenuous voice.

> *My heart has ached, and panted so at dawn*
> *O Aurora, in Thy simple gown of lawn*
> *My senses dulled as if of Morpheus' potion I had drawn*
> *When on Thee! I think, Thou cruel soldier of my heart.*
> *When we last did kiss and then did part*
> *And me didst Thou pierce to the soul with that dart*
> *Of love. Here is leaden-eyed despair, I cannot lift*
> *My lustrous eyes but remain alone and miffed*
> *When on Thee I think, lain in some cruel field. . . .*

Rosalie paused, staring at the paper, and then let her hand fall lightly to her lap.

Field, she said. She gazed out the window. *Field, smield, dealed, peeled, reeled* . . . She bit her lip. I don't have a rhyme for it.

Adair said, Y'all don't have anything hot to drink, do you?

Oh! The girl leapt to her feet. Let me bring you something! Stay there!

Before long she was back. Rosalie pulled up an ammunition box from the corner, an empty one, and set a tray on it beside the couch. There was food on china plates and hot sassafras tea.

And really, *field* is a diphthong, said the girl. And then anything that rhymes with it makes a feminine rhyme. I don't want a feminine rhyme here. Feminine rhymes are for limericks and they are of course comical. Rosalie turned over the playbill. Like old Philadelphia Jones, here. She then looked at Adair with intent, sad eyes. I *know* your heart is torn for him. Mine as well. A different him. My father . . . The girl paused. Then she whispered, Gone with another.

I thought you said he was with Hildebrand, said Adair. She ate the cornbread and curds. She swirled the cup of red tea. She drank it all.

The girl whispered, No! With Van Dorn. Then she laughed in a nervous trill and tossed her head. I just said that other to be *dramatic*. I am naturally dramatic.

Well, I don't know what to say. Crushed as I am by the dreadnought called fever.

There is aught to be said! Rosalie got to her feet. I have to go do something about the wood. She paused, and took a small anxious breath. Were you raised in the country?

Yes, said Adair. There are hardly any towns down there to be raised in.

Then you know about firewood and everything, Rosalie said. You know. Rosalie looked down. You had such *good* sturdy shoes.

Adair gazed down at the sorry pair of ankle-jacks, their tongues sticking up out of the lacing as if they were panting their last. The thick soles and square toes grinned at them like nosy redneck jokesters.

My mother and I just . . . Rosalie waved her hands in little circles on the ends of her wrists. Well, all our servants run off. She turned and gazed out the tall windows. And these people around here, they won't work and they're too lazy to steal.

I don't know a *thing* about the wood either, Adair said. She flopped both hands down with the palms up in a helpless gesture.

Where are you going to, all by yourself? Rosalie asked. And ill?

Well, I have bouts of dementia, said Adair. Sometimes I come to myself and I am ten or fifteen miles from where I thought I was.

Rosalie considered this.

Well, where were you?

I don't know. Adair put her finger to her lips. Was it anywhere near here?

I have no idea, said Rosalie. Were you not going to Iron Mountain?

It seems to me that I was, Adair said. But what do I know?

She got up slowly and pulled the matron's big dress over her head and then turned and without another word walked to the kitchen. Rosalie came behind her. She sat on a kitchen chair and watched while Adair made herself more sassafras tea and then drank it all.

My mother and I are going to town, said Rosalie. Now she was hesitant and uneasy. To see if there is anybody to hire to work around here.

Well, go on, said Adair. I reckon I'll be here. I don't think I'll have another seizure.

So, well, make yourself at home, said Rosalie.

I will, said Adair. Though I think my true home is in the Forbidden Realms.

Rosalie hurried out the door.

ADAIR WALKED SLOWLY TO THE BACK DOOR.

Out in the field behind the house Adair saw a herd of horses grazing on what little grass there was. They had so many horses out there on so few acres that they had eaten off the grass, even the newly grown spring grass. Adair knew that they had all been stolen, probably from the Union, and were being held there until they could be driven to market. She watched while Rosalie, the daughter, walked out into the field and put a halter on a lineback dun gelding that had tiger stripes on his legs.

Adair held her breath.

The women hitched up the horse to their small wagon.

He was ganted and thin and there were open sores under the sliding and ill-fitting harness. His hooves seemed to be too heavy for him to lift. His black tail hung thick almost to the ground and his body was an unusual taffeta of pale gold and gray. When Lila and Rosalie dropped the harness clumsily on his back he flung his head around as if he would bite them, and then dropped his head and stared with furious boredom at the ground.

It was Whiskey.

Well, we are off to town! Lila Spencer called out. Next time you will be well enough to come along!

Adair waved, but she could not take her eyes off the dun. The sun sparkled in that deep blue part of his eye and he suddenly turned his head and stared at her. Adair felt the pressure of tears behind her eyes so she smiled at them. She watched the dun horse struggle forward in his harness. The girl Rosalie bit her lip and hit him hard and repeatedly with a coach whip. Whiskey resigned himself, and strove nobly forward against the heavy weight of the wagon, struggling to do what was asked of him. The wagon began to move. Every pale gold hair on him sparkled in the March sunlight, and tufts of his winter hair were coming out. He looked like a couch that was losing its stuffing. Dust rose up in puffs when the girl struck him.

Stop hitting him! thought Adair. That's my horse! She watched, both hands over her mouth, as they pulled out onto the road. Tears were streaming down over her hands.

22

Yet as primitive as Civil War medical conditions were, the majority of amputees were probably saved by the saw. According to fairly well-kept Union records, of some twenty-nine thousand amputations performed, a little more than seven thousand resulted in death. Operations performed within forty-eight hours of a wound were twice as likely to be successful as those performed after that length of time. Union medical records—the Civil War was the first bureaucratic war, and very good records exist, at least on the Union side—show that amputation was far from a death sentence, depending on what was amputated.

—FROM *Don't Know Much About the Civil War*, BY KENNETH C. DAVIS,
WILLIAM MORROW, NEW YORK, 1996

MAJOR WILLIAM NEUMANN ENTERED THE COLONEL'S QUARTERS AT seven in the morning. He held his bandaged left hand against his chest to keep it from bumping into anything. The colonel of the First Indiana Heavy Artillery had taken up his quarters in one of Mobile's old Creole homes on De Tonti Square. The early light was brilliant on the whitewashed walls. They were the color of salt. It was the time of day for the adjutant to read the morning reports, for orders of the day to be issued. The tall windows, which reached from the floor nearly to the ceiling, filled themselves with a soft sea-light.

Well, Major, did I not ask you to report to the surgeon?

Yes, sir, you did, said Neumann. And I haven't gone.

Well? Colonel Hayes looked up. Well?

It was healing up and then apparently there was a piece of spherical case still in it.

And?

I'm afraid he'll say it's gangrenous, sir.

And he'll take it off. Well, it's going to have to go off, Major Neumann, if that's what he says and this time I am ordering you to the surgeon's. That's an *order*.

William Neumann leaned on his stick. Sir, would you write out my furlough then? If you'd write it out now. I don't know if I will be walking back here to get it from you afterward. Nursing my bloody stump.

Yes, I certainly will. Colonel Hayes pulled out a form and dipped his steel pen in an inkwell. I know this is hard but you're alive.

Yes, sir. It is hard.

And the surgeon has ether. It has just come in. He is there in the cotton warehouse on Water Street. It's like a regular hospital.

He walked slowly from the Creole house on Tensaw Street toward the bay. The streets of Mobile were filled with the soldiers of the Union Army. With men of the Eighth Iowa and they saluted him as he went past them. They had stopped yelling *Major the corporal's eeeetin agaiiiin!* He was sorry they had.

At the bay tall iron cranes stood silent, their hooks for lifting cotton bales dangling in the blue middle air. Egrets stalked through the shallow water at the slant of the brick levee. Men sat on boxes in the sun in front of the cotton warehouse being used for a hospital, their stumps wrapped in white cloths. Hair sticking up like spiky furniture dusters. They had been utterly changed in their demeanor and outlook, from one side of the bone saw to the other.

Neumann found himself stripped of his uniform jacket and lying on a long wooden table. He was in what used to be the office of the cotton warehouse. His arm was as round and hot as a stovepipe. The stubs of the missing fingers were healing well but somewhere in his hand a fragment of shrapnel radiated infection and rot. An attendant leaned against the wall and slowly picked dried blood out of his fingernails. The attendant wore an apron that was stiff with blood.

He'll be here in a minute, the attendant said. I know it's hard.

There were shelves of accounting books and a sentimental engraving of a plantation scene. The Big House, the happy white children in pantalettes and velvet bows. The blithe colored cook cheerfully offering a plate of dainties. And out in the cotton fields, the merry Negroes laughing under the lash. Neumann could smell the ether.

On another table, the bone saws and things for pulling bullets out of flesh, and probes, and the clamps for shutting off spurting arteries. His arm throbbed, and every red streak that shot down from the imbedded metal fragment in his hand was a line of fire. His thoughts were not thoughts but a series of pictures, colored engravings. Of trying to drive a wagon into the west with one arm. Of greeting Adair once more and her eyes going to the pinned-up sleeve. Of trying to handle a team with a wooden arm. Of getting in bed with Adair without his clothes.

The surgeon was outside arguing with someone. The argument was about the disposal of remains. You can't go throwing legs and arms in the bay, the surgeon said.

Just a minute, said the attendant. I got to go help Dr. Wheatly.

Sounds like he needs it, said Neumann. I'll just lay here and suffer.

When the attendant was gone out the door and Neumann could hear that the argument was well in progress, and the soldiers sent to dispose of remains were stoutly defending themselves, Neumann got up.

He pulled on his blue wool uniform jacket and pulling on the left sleeve was a matter of enduring pain so intense he nearly blacked out. All from a tiny sliver of spherical case. He took up his signed furlough papers in his right hand and put on his forage cap. He turned and walked out the door into an alleyway. His entire right arm was a column of pain.

He kept on. He did not hurry. Down Water Street, under the scattering flocks of gulls, and then on to where the Eighth Iowa was bivouacked in a place where they made pottery. A potter's field. He found his and Brawley's tent in a stand of pines, and pulled out his haversack and his Spencer rifle and his blankets with one hand. The railroad was not practical; the Mobile and Ohio had no rolling stock left and Wilson's raids had torn up hundreds of miles of track.

It would have to be on a steamer carrying wounded to New Orleans or St. Louis. The colonel had signed the furlough and there was no one to stop him, and so he turned with his haversack over one shoulder and the rifle over the other and started toward the bay. He walked very slowly. He passed the Cotton Exchange where the Stars and Stripes cracked in the sea wind from its flagpole. He walked into the files of wounded both on their own feet and being carried on litters, onto the steamer *Alabama Star*. As he walked up the gangplank, he saw a man's leg floating in the water with the shoe still on it.

When are we leaving? he asked one of the attendants.

In an hour, sir, the man said. If you are able, go and help them get the litters into the passenger compartments. Sir.

I'm able, said Neumann. And we're docking in New Orleans?

Well, I guess we are. The attendant was chewing tobacco and leaned over the rail to spit. You're on the right boat, all right.

I didn't want to end up in Pensacola.

Neither do people from Pensacola, sir.

By sunset the steamer was beyond Mobile Bay and into the Gulf itself. They cleared Point aux Chenes and were churning slowly past Pascagoula, the low-lying sandy coast marked here and there by faint lights.

Put that hand in cold water, said the attendant.

Neumann was sitting on deck in a canvas chair with his left arm laid across his stomach. He was sweating.

How am I going to do that? said Neumann. I am open to ideas.

They's a hose and a stop-cock they use to clean the decks, the man said. Come on down, sir, and I'll have it on and pumping and you run that cold salt water over it for as many hours as you can stand.

So former Major Neumann sat with his left arm hanging over the gunwale on the starboard side of the *Alabama Star*, and drank whiskey, and poured cold salt water over it for twelve hours straight.

23

Saw several pretty women, secesh, bewitching. Good circumstances, no men.

—Diary of Corporal Seth Kelley, in northern Arkansas,
"The Diary of Seth Kelley," Kansas History, quoted in *Inside War*

One of the unexploded shells at Pilot Knob on Iron Mountain, Missouri, a few days ago, came into the possession of a party of four children, one of whom attempted to extract the fuze by driving it out with a hammer. He exploded the shell in his efforts, killing himself and two of his playmates instantly and mortally wounding the other.

—St. Louis Republican, October 25, 1864

Johnny Payne, Daniel Payne, Geo. Young, Newt Baker and William Panel camped in a canebrake in Rapeeds Bottom a few miles above Doniphan in Ripley County and, unfortunately, slept until after daylight. A band under local leadership (i.e., a Union scouting party led by a local person of Federal sympathies) slipped up and shot four of them as they lay asleep. Johnny Payne was shot seven times in the top of his head, possibly by a charge of heavy shot discharged from a shotgun. Daniel Payne was also shot in the top of his head. Young and Baker were laying dead close to where the Payne boys were lying, so if they waked, they had no chance to get away. William Panel was killed on a low bluff a short distance from camp, indicating he had attempted to escape when disabled by the enemy's fire. So far as the writer knows, there were no charges against the boys except that they were keeping out of the way of the enemy to avoid being killed or sent to prison.

"Nigger" Ol, a colored man quite old, who had been arrested several times or rather imposed upon, harassed, made to furnish meals and food for horses and do other things for both parties, and was reported by both parties to both parties by enemies on both sides, was also a victim of the same gang that killed the five reported above.

—J. J. CHILTON, IN THE *Current Local*, DECEMBER 24, 1931,
REPRINTED IN *The Civil War in Carter and Shannon County*

ADAIR PAUSED BEFORE A LOOKING GLASS WHOSE BACKING WAS DISINTE-grating, and combed her hair and then took it up and braided it. She looked out the window but she could not see Lila or her daughter. Whiskey was grazing in the pasture beneath the mountain, and although he was thin and ribby, his long tail lashed in a beautiful black slurry of hair. He searched with great determination for every edible blade of grass. Some of the other horses seemed to have given up and stood with lowered necks as if their heads had become an insupportable weight, staring dully at the dusty ground, but Whiskey ranged the pasture and chewed up whatever he came to. Adair knew this was danger-ous. In his hunger he could graze on datura or jimsonweed.

She went out and saw that they had rigged a brass bell over the gatepost, with a string that led to the drawbar. When she started to draw the bar, the bell clanged. She left it alone. She gathered her skirts and stepped up over the gate. Then Adair held out her hand to the horse and he lifted his head with a jerk, his eyes fixed on her. He tossed his head so that his black mane flew, and then came toward her directly in a quick, sure step. He pushed his head against her and made sounds deep in his throat. He smelled of her hair, blowing his hot breath all over the top of her head like warm water. Adair searched the horse all over for cuts, stood a long time with him, wiped his sticky eyes, pulled tangles from his mane, leaned against him, cried until her nose began to run snot and then stopped herself. They would come back and find her bawling over a horse they thought was theirs to steal and sell. She went back in.

At the window she pressed her fingertips to her lips in a worried gesture, leaned her nose against the cold glass and watched the horse wandering in his grazing. Whiskey had clearly become the boss horse of the pasture, for if he saw another horse had found something to eat, he walked over directly and took it away from him. Whiskey was strong, he was beloved, and he was on her side. He would be her companion. That was what the major had said. *Be my companion.* Adair had never been in love before, and the love she felt for Will Neumann flew like a flag, stainless and new. She could almost reach out and hold his hand. Send the clean sheets flying out from between her own hands for him to catch across the distance between them, wherever he might be on the other side.

She saw Lila Spencer had come in to make up the fire in the kitchen fireplace.

Field, said Rosalie. She chucked the pieces of wood into the fireplace. I suppose I could do with a slant rhyme. But then, there is *annealed.* Or *wield.* There! *Wield!* She dusted off her hands and hurried from the room.

When are you leaving? asked Lila Spencer. She looked at Adair with narrowed eyes.

In a couple of days, said Adair. As soon as my spirit guide tells me.

Rosalie rushed back in, the playbill in her hand. She said, When on Thee I think, lain in some cruel field, whose pale hand once the sword did wield, and myself alone in trembling weakness drooped, recalling how once past my house you *trooped!*

Ain't that pretty? Lila said, Now, we are going to walk up to Will Walker's place. A mile up the road. We're going to get him to come mark out a garden. The older woman beat ashes from her hands and jammed shavings under the wood and lit it with a Lucifer match. Since Adair ain't going to be any help.

Be sure to put in some of that old shoepeg corn, said Adair. That's the best kind.

You can stay till it's ripe, said Rosalie. And help shuck it.

I never shucked an ear of corn in my life, said Adair.

Will Walker can be trusted, said Lila. We can't have just anybody around this place since my husband is known to have gone with Van Dorn.

I thought you said he was with Hildebrand, said Adair.

I never said that! Lila flashed a furious look at Adair. Them horses out there are legal come by, if that's what you're thinking. The Federals get them all wore out and then sell them, and we buy them and get them fat and rested and sell them again, that's what they're out there for.

Well, I wouldn't know, said Adair. I'm scared of horses. They're just so big.

And you're supposed to be a country gal. They both put on their bonnets and went out.

Adair watched them leave.

Lord! Lord! she said. She kicked the door several times. Give me walking power! Give me stealing power! She danced on the kitchen floor and sang "Gypsy Davey" when she was sure they were out of earshot and then took all the cornbread and meal she could find out to the gate for Whiskey. He ate everything she held in her hands. He would need his strength. He stood chewing for a while and then tossed his head and trotted back to the other horses.

Then she went back in. Her footsteps clattered in the empty house. Adair walked around looking for whatever she could take with her. She felt very lighthearted, and she took this happenstance of coming upon Whiskey as an omen that maybe her life would take a turn for the better now. She would take the down quilt and its cover. She found slotted spoons of silver and lacquered caskets of buttons, women's purses of gold thread, quilts of flowered appliqué. The articles were in baskets or wooden ammunition boxes or just lying on the floor. This is what it looked like when people came home with stolen loot. So Adair took what she wanted of it.

She took a silver fork and spoon and a small silver dish that appeared to be meant for candy. Both articles had the engraved initials *WB* on them. Behind a door she saw a man's coat hanging on a hook. She held it to her nose. It still smelled strongly of woodsmoke. It could not have been hanging there long. It had not been but a few days since a man had been standing by a campfire in this coat, with his two hands clasped in front of him, and once in a while moving to get out of the smoke, and talking in a low voice to other men warming themselves at the same campfire, where they made up their ammunition and plans and drew diagrams in the dirt with sticks.

Over the mantelpiece in the drawing room were books, good ones with leather bindings. Books of poetry with other people's names written in them. Delilah Forister, Shiela Dunleavy, A. C. Pearson. She flipped through the pages; it was very emotional poetry so she didn't take any of the books.

Adair found a new pair of women's shoes in saddle-colored leather. They were the newest kind that had a right and left foot. They nearly fit. Adair smiled and admired them. They laced up on the inside of the ankle so that the foot seemed smooth and elegant. She hid them under the drawing room couch where she slept. She found in the pantry several yards of folded canvas ducking and shoved that under the couch too, feeling pleased and excited over her riches.

Adair walked out to the stone washhouse. She took two large bars of fine soap that had chamomile pressed into it when it was set. It smelled very good.

She walked around behind the washhouse to look for the best way out to the road when she left with Whiskey. Grapevines tangled over the path. They had grown up here in such profusion because of the wash water thrown out over the years, and their new, tiny leaves made a speckled light on the path.

The path passed under a heavy arm of grapevine. There she saw a sunken area as large as a grave. The rain last night had consolidated what had been loose soil and now it was sunken in the middle.

A human hand was sticking up out of the sunken dirt.

Adair cried, What? She halted in midstep and her stomach turned. She stood as still as if she had been suddenly fired in pottery.

She stared at it. To see if it were not a doll's hand or an old leather glove left out in the rain. It held itself still.

She saw the rags of the sleeve cuff of a Federal uniform. The hand was gray and wrinkled and it was crawling with flies. Adair stood fixed, she could not seem to stop looking at it. It was reaching up out of its unquiet grave. Toward the air.

Down the road she heard a woman's voice calling *Pelagie? Pelagie?*

The flies fought with one another and sparkled with their green backs over the fingers and the knuckles. Adair backed away and then turned quickly and ran back to the house. Her hair crept up her neck.

She stopped in the kitchen. She looked back out the window toward the washhouse again, as if the dead would arise and come shambling in the sunlight toward the kitchen door. She turned and ran to the drawing room. She stumbled and nearly fell. She wiped her palms on her skirt. It was some Federal soldier who didn't want to give up his horse and look where it got him.

Rosalie and her mother came down the road talking together. The gate clattered. Adair tried to think if she had left tracks behind the washhouse. It was too late to go back again and see.

Lila began supper, stirring up the fire and setting on a kettle. Lila smiled at Adair with a deadly and intense smile. It was a smile made of nettles and spines. Her eyes stayed open and glassy when she smiled.

Well, old William wants fifty cents to lay out a garden. There is so little cash these days.

Hardly any at all, said Adair. Maybe they had gone through her things when she was sleeping out the fever and knew she had the silver dollars. She fervently wished for night to come, in case she had left tracks by the washhouse. The sun hung suspended at the edge of the mountain and it seemed like it would hang there an entire day more, as when Joshua said, Sun, stand thou still upon Gibeon, so it could shine down on all the dead soldiers. Adair smiled quickly at Lila and walked to the fireplace and then tried to think why she had done so. She took the poker and stirred the coals.

Lila began to hammer at a piece of steak with the meat mallet. We need your help around here, girl. You've been eating our rations and not doing a thing.

Then hand over that meat mallet, said Adair. Lila went on striking and striking. Adair stood up. I can pound that steak as well as you.

There's shovel work to be done, said Lila. This rain has settled things.

Hush, mother, said Rosalie. Just hush up.

Give me that meat mallet then, said Adair. And you go do the shovel work. She put her hand out for the mallet and smiled. Lila frowned.

Just sit down for now, said Lila. You ain't well. She drove the knife with a fine, expert cut into salt pork. She looked sideways at Adair. Things have to be done that you evidently can't imagine.

That night thunder strode up out of the west, marching toward Rouenne, and its echoes rolled over and over through the hills. Then it began to rain again. It came in flat sheets shivering down the glass panes, and the pecan trees outside bowed over. The house shook. Adair knew that the thunder was making iron. Lightning and thunder collided with the granite hills of the mining country and it made iron. She listened to the hammer of the storm strike the hills as if they were anvils. They all sat out on the veranda and watched the storm pass. After an hour it rumbled off to the southeast.

Sometimes people went by on the road but no one looked up at the house or hailed them. Rosalie read in a small thin book of poems for a while until the light failed. Then they went inside and lit three candles. Each of them sat in a chair in the drawing room to do their needlework. Adair sat on the couch with her candle on an upended ammunition box. She sat on the end where the shoes and the other things had been shoved under, so her skirts falling to the floor would hide them better. Her hands were sweaty and the needle slipped from between her fingers repeatedly. She tried to wipe her palms on her skirt without the two women seeing her.

She took out the Log Cabin and began to piece in strips she had cut from the brass-colored silk twill, to replace the disintegrated silk organza. She waited. Soon they would become sleepy. Soon, soon.

That's a Sutherland plaid, isn't it? Lila gestured toward Adair's worn dress.

Is it? said Adair. I forgot which clan we were. They would give over and go upstairs to sleep and she would walk out the window and down the road and take Whiskey with her.

But they sewed on, and chatted, bright-eyed and nocturnal.

Adair forced herself to yawn, for yawning was contagious, and soon they would yawn too, and be sleepy and stupid. She was pretending to yawn but soon enough they were real ones.

That was a good quilt, said Lila, and yawned. Well, excuse me.

Is it all silk and velvet? said Rosalie. What happened to it?

Adair said, Well, a neighbor woman wanted to do my mother a favor and washed it in boiling water and thrashed it with a washing dolly. And it just come apart.

Why, I would have thrashed that neighbor woman! said Lila.

It's a Sunshine and Shadow, isn't it? asked Rosalie. Adair said it was, but then Lila kept on about the neighbor woman. She was working herself up into an indignant fit and so would be wider awake than before. Outside somewhere in that dark and starving pasture Whiskey was grazing desperately on whatever he could get. Ragweed. Leaves and sticks. Adair would leave with him this very night if only these murdering owl-women would go to sleep. The hand reached up into the back of her mind as if seeking a way in and Adair bent to her work and thought of her horse, and how she would save him, and the power he would convey to her, the power of flight and distance.

It was then ten minutes after ten. She yawned again like a jar mouth.

I've thrashed people, said Lila. I took after that Pelagie Benet with that meat mallet, her trying to take something that wasn't hers.

Let's talk about something else, said Rosalie. Something else than thrashing.

Lila snorted. She said, I suppose that is an old family quilt, Adair.

Adair wiped her eyes and said, Yes, it is. There's a lot of stories in it. Then it occurred to her she could put them to sleep with stories the way you did children. Long, dull stories.

Mother was never a hand with quilts, said Rosalie.

No, no, I am just left to do all the shovel work around here, said Lila. Well, shut up, Mother.

Don't tell me to shut up, Rosalie May.

Adair said, Now this piece was from Tolliver Jackson's wedding dress and they said she was a deaf-mute and never spoke a word in her entire life. She ran her thin fingers over the dark rose velvet hearth. Deaf as a cow skull. She blatted sometimes. Like a sheep. When she was excited. And out in the pasture by the road all the sheep would look up and stop chewing. It wasn't a human sound. It was a kind of a call of the wild. I never heard it myself but they said it would raise the hair on your neck especially if she was up in the dark and wandering around the house.

Rosalie should have been born a deaf-mute, said Lila. We'd have all been better off.

Adair said, *But!* there were those who said as a baby she could tell most conversation wasn't worth the trouble it took to learn how to talk or listen either. Adair lowered her voice, kept her voice low so that they had to strain to hear her. And you know, one time her father my great-great uncle who was a justice of the peace, he was Nathaniel Crownover Colley . . . let's see, but she married James Harvey Jackson, that's right.

Of the Waxhaw Jacksons? Lila asked. She yawned and wiped her eyes. Adair glanced over quickly at the women. They were nearly bald eyed with boredom and fallen into various states of hypnosis. Lila yawned so hard she sniggered.

No, ma'am, no relation to the president. James Harvey Jackson always said he fought in the Revolution because he bit off a Tory's finger in a political brawl in front of the Mecklenburg mailhouse but myself, I don't think that counts.

Adair leaned closer to her candle. She peered at her stitches.

Now he hired a professor to come down from Transylvania College, whose name was, his name was . . . Adair let a long pause drift into the room.

The women waited impatiently, stabbing the cloth with their winking needles. Rosalie wiped her eyes.

His name was Cromwell Backhouse, Professor Cromwell Backhouse, or it could have been Cromwell Chesholme. Or both. Maybe he had two heads and a name for each one. And a hat for each one.

Adair drew out her thread and with it a long considering silence.

No, it was Backhouse. He was supposed to come and talk to Tolliver concerning things of interest. Adair stopped and yawned and then both of the other women yawned. Notions and theories. The motions of the stars and other celestial spheres, and the pressure of water per square inch.

Rosalie's head dropped on her sternum and then snapped upright again. She yawned and squinted at her embroidery.

But she didn't respond to any of it at all. She fell asleep lying on the dog. It was one of those big old yellow hounds that don't care if you lie on them. And she would get tired like that and just lay down and go to sleep and just sink away into sleep because she couldn't hear anything, not a sound, she lived in a world of peace and quiet where she could just lay down and go to sleep anytime day or night.

Suddenly both women yawned at the same time. Adair leaned close to one of the garnet pieces. The ones with the clocks on them were very pretty but they had curled up.

She used to go to sleep in the sunshine on the porch and then once she fell asleep in the hay wagon when it was coming back from the fields and it was rocking back and forth so gently and she would get the deepest sleep of anybody, and she fell asleep once in the middle of a militia parade and slept the entire afternoon while everybody else was arguing about the war, and she would also sleep for hours when they took the horses to be shod and the anvil ringing and men telling stories, there she was dozing very peacefully in spite of the swearing and dirty talk, nothing bothered her while she slept and slept and slept.

She heard Lila yawn again and say in a low voice, *Oh Lord.*

Rosalie closed her eyes and then opened them very wide and stared at the towel she was hemming. Lila's head had fallen on the chair back. Then she opened her eyes and threw her head forward to try to bring herself upright and awake. Laid back again.

Adair was silent for a long moment and the candlelight shone along her needle. She began to cough, and so she put her fist to her mouth and choked it back.

She would sleep there at Sugar Tree while the men were sitting outside in the yard telling stories, and I remember that my daddy was with them and the hens were pecking around their feet and it was summertime. There was this hen that got hold of a grasshopper that was as big as your entire thumb and the hen was shaking her head and trying to swallow it but the grasshopper was a-crawling back out with all six legs like it was rowing up the Ohio. And Tolliver was asleep on the dog. . . .

Rosalie's head was on the chair arm. She was sound asleep. Adair spoke more and more slowly. Asle-e-e-e-p on the dog and the d-o-g was asl-e-e-e-p too, and a-snoring, with its big old lips flubbering in and out. . . . Lila's head dropped forward.

Adair paused. The silence of the house was broken only by the whippoorwills singing in the outer darkness and the clock snicking out the seconds as if it were cutting them off from an endless strand of seconds with a sharp, invisible knife.

Adair was silent for a long time. Suddenly Lila jerked all over and sat up and said,

My goodness it's late. Mother and daughter struggled up out of their sleep and stood looking around themselves like dazed chickens.

Well, good night, said Rosalie.

Adair laid her wet and sweaty hands flat in her lap, the needle and thread laid across them. She said good night and watched them carrying their candles in hand to the stairway and thump upstairs. Their shadows streamed downstairs behind them. She listened to the beds creak. She sat for a long time in the beauty of the secret and private darkness.

24

CONFEDERATE CORRESPONDENCE
Camp Martin, On Cherokee Bay, June 13, 1863
To: Brigadier-General Marmaduke From: Captain Timothy Reeves

I wish to say to General Price that there are distilleries on the borders of Arkansas and Missouri that are consuming all the corn through this country (they pay $4 per bushel), taking the forage from our horses, and leaving the soldiers' families in a state of suffering, unless they pay $4 per bushel for corn for their subsistence. They sell their whiskey for $20 per gallon, making about $60 out of a bushel of corn. It is the wish of the majority of the people that there be put a stop to it, which we submit for his consideration.

There are several applications by Missourians to become members of my command. My company being full, I cannot take them without permission to raise another company. You will please let me know what I shall do in regard to it.

Yours, respectfully, T. Reeves, Captain, Commanding
—OR, CH. XXXIV, P. 867

Captain Lucien Farris and a large band of the Rebel faith, paid us a visit in November or early December of 1864. They came past Mr. Moore's and on down to our home and pitched camp by a twelve acre field of yellow corn and yellow pumpkins. They used the pumpkins, cut in half, as bread trays and the corn to feed their animals. They selected two fat heifers belonging to Robert Taylor and butchered them. They stayed three days and as there were 400 of

them and 400 horses to feed, you can imagine our corn crop was missing many
bushels at harvest time but it was a friendly visit you know.

—J. J. CHILTON, FROM THE *Current Local*, DECEMBER 31, 1931,
REPRINTED IN *The Civil War in Carter and Shannon County*

AT MIDNIGHT FURNITURE SHAPES STRANGELY HUMAN AND HUMBLE
stood around like wooden servants abandoned. Adair got up and pulled
on the plaid dress. Mrs. Buckley's dress was stuffed into the carpet sack
and so were the shoes that laced up the side. Also a length of hempen
rope. In the silence she heard her own breathing, the searing crackle of
her lungs.

The window stood open to the spring air. It was March 25. She drew
on her red jacket, and took her carpet sack in one hand and her hat in
the other. She stepped out of the drawing room window, and dropped.
She walked across the north lawn to the rails of the pasture. The scent
of honeysuckle was sweet and very lulling. She walked silently on the
new grass.

Adair felt a cutting chill breeze spring up at her back. It would carry
her scent downwind to the lineback dun horse. She stood still and
waited. Whiskey lifted his head in a startled motion and opened his
nostrils to the wind. Then he pricked up his ears and turned and
looked at her standing at the rails. He nodded several times and lashed
his tail and then he came striding over to her, shushing through the
ragweed.

He walked slowly, his strength very low, but still with that inner
vitality and intelligence, the alert curiosity. He stepped forward on his
good straight legs, and no matter how thin he was he still carried his
head well on his arched neck. She stood watching him come. He came
finally to the rails. Adair stroked away the long fan of his forelock and
pressed her forehead to his. Her lungs sang and whistled. She drew out
the butcher knife she had stolen from the kitchen and tried to cut the
string but she saw that it was smooth wire. The bell trembled overhead
but did not ring. Then Whiskey shoved at the gate with his nose, impa-

tient, and the bell jingled. Adair grabbed his head and pushed him away, and quit trying to get the gate open.

She put the carpet sack and her heavy bundle over the rails, and then silently slid over herself. She put the rope on Whiskey's neck and led him away from the gate, along the rail fence behind the washhouse and there she slowly lifted down the top rail without dropping it. Then the second one.

Come on, she said. She tugged at the rope. A wind started up and the brass bell began to ring. Come on, Whiskey, she said. You got to come on.

Whiskey stared hard at the bottom rail as if he might have lost some of his eyesight, and then bent to sniff at it. She pulled again. He sat back on his haunches, and she knew he was going to jump it so she stood aside and he lifted himself and sailed over it. For a moment he was in the night sky and outlined against Capricorn, his mane a black wave. He plunged ahead of Adair, into the grapevine thicket and pulled her after him. She hung onto her baggage, and Whiskey stepped into the grave with one hoof and it went in up over his ankle, and Adair felt her feet sink and her skirts catch on something, then she was pulled behind again as Whiskey kicked himself loose and gained the road.

Adair took up her carpet sack and bundle, and then she and Whiskey hurried southward on down the road in the starlight. The roadside fields soon gave way to thick forest. Her skirts blew out around her ankles, and she kept her hand on his neck. He turned his head as he walked and pressed his nose against her again and took in her scent. Then he strode along willingly, but sometimes he would drop his head low and she knew he was not his former self. They went on all night under the stars and she felt no need of sleep because of her vigilance and her fear of the Spencers.

Adair jumped onto his bare back at a low place, and held her baggage in front of her and pushed him into a trot. He struck out and looked around himself with a deep interest. His smooth trot was the same as always, long and reaching. She thought it was possible that they covered a good ten or fifteen miles before first light. Whiskey's spine was like a rafter but with her skirts packed up under her she could sit him well enough. He nodded his head up and down in a fit of nodding as if very pleased with himself and with her and with being on the road home, or on the road to anywhere. He was a traveling kind of horse.

At dawn they came to a trail that went off to the left. The road went down to a bottomland, where hackberry trees made a grove of shade and under them grew acres of the short oat grass that horses love. Among the hackberry she found an abandoned log hunting cabin and tarried in it for a day. Adair turned him loose in the oat grass, and he grazed very hungrily, as if he would not leave a blade of grass standing. He ripped up fifteen bites before he even stopped to chew.

Adair hung her red Zouave jacket out in the sun. She combed her hair with the silver-backed brush, looking at herself in the hand mirror. Well, at least she didn't kill anybody for it. She sat down and put on the new ladies' shoes. They came up above her ankle and laced up on the inside. They would not slide and her feet could heal. She went repeatedly to the slanted doorframe to look at her horse, at the way the sun shone on his taffeta, changeable coat turning pale gold and then silver-gray in the shadows, the burnished black stripe down his spine. A great joy seemed to possess him as he walked as a free being in the rich grass.

The sun came through one of the empty windows and glistened on the cobwebs strung across the opening. Adair looked at it carefully, bending forward with her hands upon her thighs. She searched for his initials, *W* and *N*, and when she didn't she pulled several strands loose to make it look as if there were a *W* and an *N*. William Neumann. Then she watched at the doorway to see if the Spencer women had come after her.

Then that night she lay down and dreamed a terrible dream that she remembered in infinite detail and in which she was being hanged for cutting telegraph lines. She woke up exhausted.

And so they went on down the road south, moving toward Iron Mountain. Traveling at evenings and early mornings only, through the heavily forested county. Over the next few days Whiskey began to gain strength, for Adair found every lush creek bottom on the way south and paused there to let him graze. She stood off the trail at least twice, when she had heard Union patrols in the distance. She got Whiskey upwind of them, so he would not call out to their horses.

The third time they nearly surprised her coming around a bend and the officer calling out "By twos, at a trot!" The only way clear of them was up a steep bank, but Whiskey dug in his toes and clawed his way up the bank, bucked himself upward the last five yards and over the top, thrashing his tail in the joy of it all. They rode into a pine thicket, and Adair jumped down and clamped his nostrils shut, so that when he did call out to the Union horses he made a peculiar buzzing noise and was startled at himself. Adair stood very quietly and listened. Whiskey was the sort of strong and lively animal an officer would like to take from her and ride him into battle. Well they will do a good job getting him away from me ever again, she thought. She waited until they were well gone and their commands and hoofbeats faded into the hills. Then after a half hour she went on.

Often during the night she heard the remote barking of dogs at house places far off the Trace, up distant mountain valleys and on hillsides. A light could be seen a long way off. But lights were rare in the dusk, and in the early mornings they started before dawn but there was no smell of woodsmoke from breakfast fires anywhere about them.

The road stayed mostly in the bottomlands, and when it forced itself upward over a ridge the stony roadbed made Whiskey pick his way carefully, his hooves slipping among the granite rocks. When they regained the bottomlands again the road became easier and once again floored in sand and gravel. It was hard going but Adair thought of her home with the lights in the windows, and being up in the girls' room by herself with everybody else downstairs and herself dreaming in silent privacy, watching the lightning crawl up Copperhead. A house they themselves owned and were beholden to no one, were not beggars asking a place in somebody else's kitchen.

She had to go around the Union garrison at Iron Mountain, so Adair took a road that went off to the west; the sign said it would arrive at Mungar's Mills. After a mile or so of the clattering rocky bed, it did as it promised. In a good flat valley, alongside a graveled river, a mill-house stood asleep in the sun. The mill's eighteen-foot undershot wheel made a regular thundering sound as the blades struck the water in the race. Houses beside it were all abandoned. There were no worn footpaths going from house to house, or smoke from the chimneys, or bedding being aired, nor cats in the windows. Three or four were burnt and only the chimneys standing. Adair crossed below the dam, riding through the spray. An elderly man sat on the steps in front and stared at her as she rode up.

What river is this? she asked.

North Fork of the Black. He nodded. Yes, ma'am, that's the North Fork of the Black River.

I'm going around Iron Mountain, she said. How do I get around from here?

The man sat back and stared at her. His beard came down to the middle of his chest, and his hands were stained and feeble.

Well, if I was you, with that good-looking horse, I'd stay away from the Yankees too, he said.

Well, that's what I am doing, said Adair.

Reeves or Coleman will take him from you too, any road.

I know it.

Where do you want to go to afterward?

Down to Doniphan Courthouse.

Well. The miller nodded to nobody in particular. Do you want to buy any corn? I have a sack of cracked corn. Red and blue. Country corn. The mill wheel revolved, spilling its slats of water.

I'll take it, said Adair.

He lifted himself slowly and went into the millhouse, and came back out packing a twenty-five-pound sack of cracked corn.

Just stay on this road here, and it will take you to Centerville. You'll be a good twenty miles southwest of the Union hole-up. Then on south on the Van Buren road, but them patrols go raiding down that road all the time. Stay on to the west of it. I'd go through the Irish Wilderness and then around. They raid down from Patterson all the time.

I know it. Thank you, said Adair. She handed him two silver dollars.

Have you heard aught of the war? he asked. He stood with his hand on Whiskey's shoulder, patting him. Whiskey was looking at the mill wheel with great curiosity, his ears cocked up straight. We heard Lee was boxed up on ever side there in Virginia.

No, sir, I ain't heard anything, she said. But it can't go on much longer.

Well, you could stay here, he said. It's hard getting up in the morning and nobody here.

I better keep on.

At nighttimes them houses look like they were talking to one another. Yersty a door fell in at Wellams' house. Hinges rotted and it just fell in and laid there.

It looks pretty lonesome.

I have not fared well without my daughter. Her and the baby is buried in the floor of that house there. He turned toward a house place nearby and gestured at it. I was going to burn it down over their grave and leave the chimney for a headstone. She just screamed two-three days. Daddy! Daddy! But I couldn't do nothing about it. The baby wouldn't come.

I am sorry to hear it.

You could stay on here a while.

Well, sir, I'm sorry, but I got to be a witness in court in Oklahoma Territory.

She put the sack on behind her and then went on. She rode with her skirts tucked up under her and her stockinged legs hanging down each side. She leaned down often to pat Whiskey and stroke his neck. He strode along now with his old springing step, his tail lashing, looking about himself with interest at the the world. Several times he went forward at a trot and danced about in the road when she held him in. The leaves were already as large as a squirrel's ear. Just beyond the mill and the houses, Adair made camp beside the ford of a little creek, under a sycamore whose shattering bark lay in rolls like paper at its feet and so it was easy to start a fire. The sycamore leaves were always the last to come out and the immense white limbs stood out lucent against the blue sky. She fed Whiskey handsful of the cracked corn and then boiled three eggs in the steel saucepan.

The next day Adair woke up to a clean sky and the sound of Whiskey devouring the new bluestem grass nearby. She sat up in her blankets. Whiskey dropped down to his side and rolled over and wallowed on his back, his feet swimming in the morning air. He jumped up and snorted and shook himself. The forests of the Ozarks had never been cut, so the yellow pine and oaks were sometimes fifteen feet around at the base. They stood far apart from one another without underbrush, and it was good traveling then, through the greening world. At the seeps and springs, there were banks of violets and fern, sweet williams and miniature wild irises whose flowers were no bigger than a person's thumb and two fingertips held together. Wild pansies looked up with lion faces, the shadows of the new leaves were faint as the shadows of an eclipse.

At the next ridge south of Mungar's was an open prairie of grasses of several acres. It was what the people called a barrens. Adair could see for a long way. The hills poured out southward, one after another. The wind tore at her hair and she felt herself lifting like a kite. She stood for a long time to listen for the sound of a mill wheel or a church bell, or foundry or circle saw squaring logs, the ringing of an anvil.

The hills were silent. She stood listening for a long space of time. There was only the long wind singing off the top of the receding ridges and their heavy forests.

It seemed all the people were gone. Soon there would be some other world and some other people to take their place. The grasses on the little barren seethed in the wind with their new seed-heads, and the wind was chill, and so they went on as the road drove downhill toward the main fork of the Black River.

The seventh day of slow traveling found them up and moving by dawn. It was very cold that morning, for it was yet early in April and she wore the Zouave jacket and the down quilt over her shoulders on top of it. They followed the road as it swung along a steep hillside in an oak forest. They were southwest of Iron Mountain, and she had no idea what was the name of the road.

Then Adair smelled smoke drifting up the trail toward her. It eased long through the tree trunks. She and Whiskey stopped in the road.

Whiskey threw his head up and stared, he began to dance around in the road. She heard a galloping horse. Adair turned Whiskey into the pines alongside, behind a screen of vines. It was a loose horse. The horse caught scent of Whiskey and turned in and came to stand beside them and touch noses with the dun gelding, and Whiskey flattened his ears to the mare to show her her position in the world. She wore a halter and a broken rope, so Adair leaned down and caught it up and went back to the road. She saw that the mare's tracks turned off onto a side trail and so she took it. Then heard below her the noises of a camp.

Early in the Civil War, Timothy Reeves became the Captain of a hundred Rebel soldiers, and whether his army was at any time attached to any Rebel army the writer does not know, but in the last two years of the war he was a serious menace to the Federal scouts in southeast Missouri. In one instance in St. Francois County, he discovered Captain William Leeper and party who were doing scout duty in that territory, and started chasing him. While the Federals were running down a hill towards the St. Francois River, it is reported that one of Captain Leeper's men said, "There is a ford to the right!" The Captain replied, "Any place is a ford in a case like this," so their horses leaped off a bluff some twelve feet high, into as many feet of water, and escaped, as Captain Reeves stopped at the bluff.

Mr. Reeves kept his company together and took care of them until the end of the war. He was cunning and his men so resistant that the Federal scouts got so they would rather hunt for him than to find him.

—J. J. Chilton, from the *Current Local*, November 12, 1931,
reprinted in *The Civil War in Carter and Shannon County*

Union Correspondence
Patterson, Mo., December 19, 1863
General Fisk;
My scouts came in from Doniphan. They report that Reeves has got a colonel's commission and is conscripting every man between the ages of eighteen and forty-five years and has ordered all to report to him for duty and when they all

get together he will have 1,000 men. Can this old scoundrel not be taken in or run out of the country? He is said to be about Doniphan.

W. T. Leeper, Captain, Commanding Post

—OR, CH. XXXIV, P. 745

I remember an old man named Freshour. He was old and deaf and as he was walking along, the Yankees came up behind him and hollered at him to stop. Of course he did not hear them and they shot him in the back and killed him. My mother and some more ladies had to dig a grave and bury him, for my father and two brothers who had been home on a furlough had already gone back to the Southern Army. . . . On this same raid they went into the home of two of my uncles and took them out and hung them to their own gatepost. They were both big men and were my mother's brothers. My mother was there and saw it all and as long as she lived she never got over the shock. And they called that a civil war. It was the cruelest war we ever had.

—E. J. WALKER, QUOTED IN *Oldtimers*, BY FLORENCE FENLEY, THE HORNBY PRESS,
UVALDE, TEXAS, 1936. WALKER WAS BORN IN NORTHERN ARKANSAS IN 1856,
SON OF A METHODIST MINISTER.

WELL, YOU HAVE DONE CAUGHT MAGGIE.

An old man with one eye sat in front of a fire, tending a blackened coffeepot. Beside the elderly man, in a mess of tattered blankets, sat Greasy John.

Adair Colley! he said. He struggled up and picked up his old bowler hat and put it on. He then swept it off. You're the best thing I have seen since 1802.

Greasy John! Adair smiled at him. Well, or whatever your last name is.

He wiped his hands on his pants and offered her one, and she shook it. Last name's Grissom, he said. You are as pretty as you ever were. He put both hands on his hips. And ain't that your horse Whiskey?

Adair patted the horse's neck. Whiskey looked at the string of other horses back in the trees and called out and was answered immediately. She dared not let him go; he would trot to the strange herd and forthwith begin to make himself officer in charge. She threw his lead-rope over a low limb nearby and returned.

Yes sir, that's him. She tipped her head to one side to look at Greasy John. You are the first person I have seen that I know. First person in a long time. She slid off and shook out her skirts. She stood beside her horse. It was a broad valley and the grove of trees stood in it like an island, their dawn shadows standing long across the stretches of grass. The old man took the red mare, Maggie, and tied her back with the others. The horses were all slashing their tails against the flies. He came back. His eyehole was crusted with blood, and fluid from it slowly leaked down his cheek. He wiped at it.

John there is my old cousin, said the elderly man. We are all old cousins now, all us first cousins. I'm Asa Smitters. He placed a skillet on the fire and began to cut up jelled cornmeal mush from an earthenware pot. He dropped it into the greasy skillet to fry. Smoke roiled around him in the blue air. We're related on our mothers' side. Greers, from Hickman County, Tennessee.

Adair looked around at the camp; the smoke puffed up into the oak limbs high overhead and she saw gravestones all around beneath the trees. They were new, and some of them said MCCLOSKEY. A stone jar of lard sat on one of the gravestones and a saddle was set over another. On one sat the head of a razorback boar and the blood and fluids leaked down the lettering of a headstone and stained the figure of a woman mourning by a weeping willow and over all this sorrow the boar's head grinned with its roach of bristles between flop ears. The flies danced around it.

Now, where have you been, Miss Colley? asked Greasy John. Come and join us here at our spring arbor. He bent down and picked up a blanket, shook it out, and folded it. He laid it down again, and indicated with a sweep of his hand that it was to be her seat. He lay back among his own sorry-looking pile of blankets. The last I seen of you was you and them sisters of yours refugeed upon the Military Road. Carryin' skillets and wearing peculiar hats. His bald head shone in the spring sunlight. His dusty bowler lay in the dirt beside him. A jaunty turkey feather was stuck in the band.

I am just coming from St. Louis, Adair said. I was held in prison and I escaped. I got clean away. She fanned away the smoke. I run right through the city afoot. Wait till I get my plunder. She went to Whiskey and took up her carpet sack and came back. Adair felt very anxious. Greasy John might know something of her family. She didn't want to ask for fear of what she would hear.

Asa Smitters got up and searched around in a wooden ammunition box. He found a galvanized tin cup. He blew in it and then filled it with coffee and offered it to Adair.

A young girl like you traveling the roads alone. This is what the war has done to this world. He shook his head. Here, this is the only tin cup we got. We been drinking out of cow horns like savages. He began to spin a cord out of massed strands of horsehair. Hildebrand and his boys shot my eye out at Dent's Station. Just to be shooting something.

Oh, I am sorry, said Adair.

Well, I still got one anyhow.

Where did you all get coffee? She lifted the cup to her nose and sniffed. Is this real coffee? She pulled the red jacket collar tight around her neck for it was cold at that hour of the morning.

Prison! said Greasy John. Surely you did not confess in an attempt to get a wagon ride to the garrison at Iron Mountain.

That coffee is from the Yankee commissary, Asa said. It is pure Rio, charmed to offer it. He sat down and once again took up his horsehair work. He was spinning them together between his fingers into a long strand. He squinted at the strand and bent closely to see it with his one eye. I guess I'm lucky I ain't dead.

Adair sat down and her skirts spread out around her. She was wearing the big dress. Smoke from the fire drifted around into her face and she took off her hat to wave it away. She drank the coffee. It was real and strong. She had almost lost her taste for it.

I am on my way back home to Ripley County. The frying mush made crisp noises and smelled of bacon. Adair thought of how good it would taste with honey and butter. What county is this?

You are in Reynolds, my dear. The early wind made tufts of his hair stand up over his bald head. They looked like horns. And now tell us what happened.

Well, some people on the road took a dislike to me and went and told the Yankees I was a spy or something, said Adair. People named Upshaw. Or Upshears. No, it was Upshaw. She glared down into the cup. And I got sent up to St. Louis to a stone building of a prison and I tell you it was like being shut up in a butter churn.

My Lord, my Lord, said Greasy John.

Well, I made my way over the wall and headed home. I come down the Iron Mountain road, the one that goes alongside the railroad. She glanced up at the two elderly men with an anxious look. If a family was all scattered, don't you reckon they would all make their way back to the home place if they were alive? I was shut up in prison while I should have been trying to find my father. The wind turned the woodsmoke into her face again, and this time Adair began to cough. It felt so explosive that she got up and walked around the fire until she conquered it and then sat down. It had exhausted her but if she sat still for a while she would recover.

Asa Smitters and Greasy John looked at each other in the drifting smoke.

You are not well at all, said Asa.

Yes I am, said Adair. It is a catarrh.

Doesn't sound like the catarrh to me.

Well, it is too. This is what catarrh sounds like. It comes and goes, sometimes I don't cough at all for a long time. I think it's that smoke. She fanned at it with her hat but the wind shifted again.

Greasy John said, A young girl held in a vile dungeon and long in city pent. He shook his head. He then smacked his hand on top of his bald head and killed there some sort of biting insect. He put on the bowler hat with the turkey feather. Is there no end to their disregard of the laws of nature?

Depends which nature you are talking about, said Asa.

And you are on your way home, fleeing the dreaded constabulary. He suddenly sat up and looked back up the Trace. He was alarmed. They ain't in pursuit are they?

No, said Adair. I think they were glad to get rid of me. She hesitated, and then asked, Where is all my family at? John? Do you know aught of them?

Well. Where are they at. He sat down in his blankets again and scrounged around for his pipe, filled it and lit it with a stick from the fire. Your brother is with Reeves and has not been killed or wounded as far as I have heard. I think Reeves sent him down to Texas for more horses.

How do you know? Adair asked. She clutched her hands together inside the sleeves of the red jacket. That he hasn't been killed or wounded?

The Federals have taken to publishing the names of prisoners or arrestees in their paper out of Bloomfield, the *Stars and Stripes*. See here. He worked up a cloud of smoke from the pipe. He shoved a newspaper at her. And as I am addicted to reading, I discover all sorts of things in it. I read your father's name November last, arrested for disloyalty. But nothing since. Now, your two sisters were at Dalton's Store at Christmas anyhow. I went there for the festivities. Wartime Christmases are always very festive. A ball of sorts was held. Young soldiers falling in love with your sisters, gallant boys in gray or some approximation of gray. A lot of Virginia reeling and schottisching. Knocking down the biscuit powder.

Adair smiled. Then the anxious look came back to her face. You ain't lying? she asked. You ain't just making that up to ease my mind?

I saw them with these bleary, whiskey-dimmed eyes, he said. But they have gone over to Tennessee with some family.

I know it, said Adair. I got a letter in prison. With my cousins and my aunt. I guess it's better in Tennessee. She poked a stick at the fire. We're beat, ain't we?

Yes, we're beat. Greasy John worked hard at his pipe and got up big clouds of smoke from it. He said, John Lee won't come in to surrender. The Militia shot down seven men come home from surrendering in Virginia with Federal passes in their pockets, a week ago, not too far from here.

Adair crossed her ankles under her skirts and reached down to take hold of them. Her shawl ends lifted in the breeze. She appeared like a Hindu woman or a girl of the Bedouin tribes of the Holy Land.

Or he might go up to St. Louis looking for you if he ain't got word you are home.

Well, said Adair. I left a message there at the prison for him with a girl.

We're going into the stage business after everybody surrenders, said Greasy John. Now John Lee might want to get in on something like this, if he did come back from Texas.

He'd be crazy to come back from Texas, said Adair.

Well, we're going around buying horses. Or stealing them, whatever.

Adair nodded. It was what she had wanted to do herself at one time. To deal in horses in some way. But that time was long gone.

Well, you rest up, said Greasy John. Smoke roiled up around his head. It was a cool blue dawn and the smell of the fire, the frying mush and coffee hung heavy in the grove and drifted over the gravestones. And you will not guess what horse my old cousin Asa Smitters has got in that string.

Adair looked up from her coffee.

Who?

Why, Dolly. Greasy John nodded. And I thought we were going to get away with her. But here you are.

No! She laughed. She got up and ran out in a great thrashing of skirts past the McCloskey gravestones, and she went down the string one by one. Yo! Yo! she called to them, touching their rumps.

Until she came to the gray mare. Oh my Dolly! This startled the gray mare, and she pulled back on her halter rope and stood thrashing her head back and forth. Then she saw it was Adair. Slowly her ears came up and she put her muzzle in Adair's hand.

The pale gray mare walked forward and turned her head back so that she caught Adair in the curve of her throat. Her eyes were dark and surrounded by gray shadings. Adair knew every mark on her, and the old wheel-tire scar on her ankle, her long tail like a broach of silk thread.

Then Adair leaned her face against Dolly's neck for a long time until the mare became impatient. Adair then stroked her neck and looked her all over, and found her to be in good flesh and unscarred. Her hooves were in good shape even though unshod, but Dolly had always had good feet, hard as cannonballs.

Well this is hard to believe, said Adair. Dolly flashed her eyes at the horse next to her and flattened her ears. You are as spoiled as you ever were.

Ain't you going to eat? asked Asa Smitters. He was looking at Greasy John. Looks like it's a family reunion is going on here.

I'd rather drink, said Greasy John. He felt around in his blankets and came out with a large, dark-brown glass medicine bottle. He tipped it up. He wiped his mouth. The Yankees are going to make us get licenses to sell this ambrosia after the war.

Adair came back, smiling, with a great swinging of skirts and sat down again on the horse blanket in front of the fire.

It's her, she said. It is her. What are you doing with them? Where are you going? You ain't taking them to Reeves are you? Not Dolly. You ain't doing nothing with my sister's horse but giving her back to me.

Well now, said Asa. I don't know. He stared into the fire. The flames were nearly invisible now that the sun was well up. Fox squirrels sat in the oaks limbs above and insulted them at length with insistent clattering. Asa looked over the tossing uncut new grass that gave way to the morning wind in a series of waves. He was a man that was always checking things. Alert. That's how he came to be an old man. He said, She was running loose with busted reins in Cane Creek Fields. No saddle. The bits was stamped CSA at the bit guard.

Adair glanced from one to the other. They were in smoky-smelling clothes, for they had been on the road a good while. Tattered check shirts and worn boots.

You don't know what? Adair reached into her carpet sack and took out her silver fork with the initials *WB*. She edged a slice of the fried mush out of the skillet and onto the small silver candy dish and ate it. You better not be thinking about going anywhere with Dolly.

I was, said Asa.

I will pay you for her. I have some Federal silver dollars and I will pay you for her. For your trouble. She pulls back and busts her reins all the time, that's how come she was running loose along Cane Creek. She bites the other horses, my sister let her get away with anything and she's spoiled rotten. You don't want her.

Greasy John had taken up a fallen oak stick to shift the coals and bring more smoke against the insects.

He said, I can make you a deal on the mare and also I can get you a sidesaddle.

Adair said, I'll give you twelve dollars in silver for both.

Greasy John said, Now, Asa is at some risk to go get that sidesaddle.

Adair hesitated. Twelve is all, she said.

Asa gazed around at the meadow with his one eye, and his empty leaking eye, and at the string of horses tied among the gravestones. Now I was at some risk to get that mare, too. I could of been shot at.

Well, what, then? asked Adair.

Fourteen.

Adair placed her feet together sole to sole under the skirts and petticoats. Twelve and a half. And draw me a map so I can stay off the Military Trace. So I can get home again and not be robbed of them again.

There is an older trace, said Greasy John. And a map of it would be some trouble to puzzle out and then reproduce on paper.

And that will cost you fifty cents, said Asa. So, thirteen for everything.

Where did you get the paper? Adair finished her coffee.

Greasy John dragged his saddlebags to himself and opened one pocket and brought out a sheaf of five-by-four sheets of printed forms.

I'm using the back of these, he said. They are Union telegraph forms.

Asa said, There's a cutoff down here about twenty rod that goes back fifteen miles to the Military. The telegraph poles come down on it. So the Militia can get their news and so they can tell where everybody's at. Send orders. What we do is, we cut it and then repair it with these horsehair strands so they can't tell where it's cut. You can hear them soldiers cussing all the way to St. Louis.

Greasy John said, And I found these here forms out on the Military laying in a heap, I guess they fell off a wagon or something. When they were looking to repair that line.

You should hear them cuss, said Asa.

All right, said Adair.

And we will throw in some smoked ham from that boar pig there. He was young and tender. We ate all the fresh and smoked the rest of him. You look like you need building up.

Greasy John then took the turkey feather from his hatband and looked at it carefully. Then he lay back on his blankets so he could get at his penknife in his pants pockets. He sat up and cut the quill at a slant against his thumb. Then he opened a much smaller and narrower blade and dug the fiber out from inside the quill.

Asa, hand me that ink.

Asa found a ladies' perfume bottle full of a purplish homemade ink in the ammunition box.

Now this is the oldest trace of all, said Greasy John. He began to lay in a line of ink. It has been deserted since the Mexican War of 1846. It is older than the Nachitoches and the Military. It is as old as the Shawnee. It is called the Atchafalaya Road, or Stanger's Steep. John ran a dotted line toward the crossing of the Black River to the west. The road of bandits and lost tribes. It was made in the beginning of the world. It is a trace that has its own mind.

He wiped the nib on a leaf of flannel mullein and dipped it again.

It was on this route that chief Benge of the exiled Cherokee struck off from the main body and toiled with what remained of his people west to the Indian Nations. Benge was driven from his own land in Georgia but also from his own people, for they say he had an ungovernable temper and took delight in causing fear and terror in his own clan and killed men for the joy of it. For sport. We have seen his like in this war several times over.

Greasy John searched over the map. Adair stood at one shoulder and Asa looked over the other. Gnats danced over the wet ink.

I can hardly see anymore, said Asa.

Wait just a moment, then, Asa, said Adair, for it occurred to her that among the articles she had found in the stolen St. Louis carpet sack were a pair of spectacles. She squatted down in front of the opened grip and fished around and came out with the pair of lady's eyeglasses.

Asa was delighted. He had to bend them nearly out of shape to get them on but he did it. Well, I'll be, he said. He peered at his own hands and the strand of horsehair with his one eye and his other dark hole of an eye. Well, I'll be. See, I could black out that other glass so people wouldn't have to look at my bad eye.

Well, then, I will only charge you a dollar for them, said Adair.

Then the price for Dolly and the saddle and the map will be thirteen dollars.

Done, said Adair. She put out her hand and Asa took her hand in his and smiled down at her.

You are a brave and charming girl, he said.

Greasy John said, From the crossing of the middle fork of the Black at Centerville, Stanger's Steep will go south directly for a way. It will be marked with old rut marks, and it will have been worn deep in the

earth. Here and there will be the remains of an old cabin where somebody overwintered and grew a crop of corn before going on. He drew
in a small cabin.

Now I can see that just as clear, said Asa.

John said, Stanger's Steep was the route of bandits and road agents
and those too poor to pay the Spanish toll at the Sabine River when the
Spanish had that country. But then Texas freed itself of those despotic
governments and the route has fallen into disfavor. It goes by dangerous ways.

Greasy John took up a second telegraph blank and turned it over,
numbered it 2 at the top and went on.

Now between the Black and the Current Rivers, Stanger's Steep
wanders without much direction in this part of the world. It goes to
water in the valleys and then it stops on the high barrens and there it
will wait for you to take your rest, there where the wind is good and
blows away the gnats and the mosquitoes and the horseflies. Make your
fire in the valleys out of sight. When you are ready to go on in the
mornings, the road will go on as well.

She'll cross the Current at House's Ford, said Asa. Don't linger so,
John.

She's paying fifty cents for this, Asa, he said.

Well, you are not drawing up a legal brief.

I know it. I am filling in this bare sketch with word pictures to make
it fifty cents worth.

I'd say it was getting up past a dollar. He went on spinning his horsehair strand. It's wonderful how I can see this now.

Greasy John drew in Stanger's Steep as it wavered between one
drainage basin and another, through the uncut forests that clothed the
mountainsides in kelly green and the deep greens of pine. Over heights
of land. Above the heads of Hominy Creek and Sweetwater Creek. He
told her not to lose her horses or her supplies for the land was bare of
sustenance and those people who remained in the counties were at the
edge of starvation.

He said the Steep would take her through a place called the Irish

Wilderness and back in there men in butternut, Freeman's men, drifted like feral things, men who had not known what it is to sit content before their own hearths in three long years. The Irish Wilderness was cut deeply with dark narrow valleys, the ridges only thinly clad in soil.

Greasy John said, And here are a set of old charcoal kilns just before the crossing of the Current at House's Ford. You will not want to miss these interesting ruins.

Now as you go along the Pike Creek Valley for a good many miles take care not to take the deer trails off on one side toward the creek. Stay on the Steep. No shortcuts. For on all those deer trails, the Huddlestons have been setting up deer snares since the beginning of the war. So as not to shoot off arms and be located by the Militia. There is a snare on every deer trail down there, and if you don't want to expire hanging by one leg in the air, stay on the trace.

He dipped his quill. Thence down to the town of Wilderness—aptly named!—and straight west to cross the Current once last time at Racetrack Hollow. Thence it is two miles to the headwaters of the Little Black, and that will take you home directly. Greasy John blew on the paper. It is winding and devious but you will stay out of the hands of the Militia. John turned to look at Adair. He handed her the papers and said, Have a care of it. Stanger's Steep sometimes captures those who travel on it, and they never leave it, but travel on forever.

Adair looked back at him. Her expression was dubious. You are a storyteller, she said.

Have a care, said Greasy John.

Asa picked up a wooly worm. I can see ever hair, he said.

26

In the year 1863 there were 3,000 Federal Soldiers moved from Pilot Knob (Iron Mountain) to Van Buren where they encamped. . . . And in order to keep in touch with all the movements of the war, they put up a telegraph line from Pilot Knob to within five or six miles of Van Buren and in some way the builders were menaced until they quit building. Others tried to finish it, but without success.

Finally Mr. Crow said he would finish and operate the line. So he went to work on the line just above the Shade Chilton home. James Maberry and Martin McLemurray seemed to be the hindering cause of the failure to complete the line to Van Buren. The insulators were nailed to trees along the . . . (military) road over which the soldiers had moved to Van Buren. Mr. Crow started his work and set a long ladder against a tree and went to the top of it and was nailing an insulator to the tree when a shot was fired from nearby and Mr. Crow dropped from the ladder and was taken to the Shade Chilton farm and buried. The grave was as completely hidden as possible.

The soldiers soon moved away from Van Buren. The citizens took the wire down and found many uses for it. My father got enough of it to trellis fifty grapevines and we used it in place of hickory withes and papaw bark around the farm and feed lots, much as we use baling wire now.

—J. J. CHILTON, FROM THE *Current Local*, SEPTEMBER 13, 1933,
REPRINTED IN *The Civil War in Carter and Shannon County*

December 27, 1864; Miss Smith, the lady, or rather child, that cut the telegraph, informed me she was captured with the hatchet in her hand, and after

*her trial, they told her she was sentenced to be hung, but they would release her
if she would tell who told her to cut the wire. She told them she would rather
be hung than tell. While she was in prison in Rolla, they treated her very
badly—gave her nothing to lie on for six weeks except the bare rock floor.*

—GRIFFIN FROST, *Camp and Prison Journal*

UNION CORRESPONDENCE
Patterson, Mo., Feb. 1, 1864
Brig. Gen. C. B. Fisk, Commanding District of St. Louis
*Sir: The guerillas have made their appearance again in squads from 2 to 15
in number. Yesterday a gang was between here and Iron Mountain. My men
are after them. General, I have watched them long and I become more than
ever convinced that many of the people between here and Arkansas will have
to be either killed or moved out of the state. Our good, loyal friend Mrs. Byrne
has been a regular spy since the commencement of the war. . . . General, if
Mrs. Byrne was a man and guilty of the crimes that she is, she would not live
twenty-four hours.*

W. T. Leeper, Captain, Commanding Post

—OR, CH. XLVI, P. 213

ADAIR SPENT THE NEXT MORNING PREPARING FOR HER JOURNEY; SHE
and Greasy John cut the ham into pieces and fried them, then tied
them into four separate bundles. They gave her ten pounds of bolted
cornmeal and half that of flour, a tin of saleratus to raise the cornbread,
a hard, sticky package of dried apples and a cloth sack of salt. He threw
in a roll of hempen rope for picket lines. At evening time, Asa saddled
a brown mule and rode off down the Military. Before long he came
back with a bridle and a sidesaddle.

It was considerable of a saddle. The leather was glove leather on the
fender and the seat was of a velvet flocking, the single stirrup of good
heavy steel.

We got things stored in a cave, said Asa.

Adair sat it on Whiskey's back to see if it needed padding but it fit him well. Adair had determined never to be caught riding astride. It was something that hillbilly women did. Adair knew now that she must never appear to the Union soldiers as a woman of low degree. They felt that all women of the hills were women of low social class, and a southern woman who seemed poor and ignorant and who could be labeled white trash had no rights that any Union soldier was bound to respect.

Now, I have a pair of saddlebags for you, said Greasy John. He rooted around in their pile of camp gear and came up with a small set of saddlebags that was stamped with *OM*, which he explained meant Overland Mail.

We'll steal from anybody, said Greasy John. In a war there is always just so much *stuff* laying around.

I want to get my hands on that copper wire from that telegraph line, said Asa. But I ain't got any way to get it to St. Louis to sell it right now. And I am too old and at the end of my days. I remember when Thomas Jefferson was president.

ADAIR SLEPT AMONG THE GRAVESTONES. SHE LAY DOWN BETWEEN MRS. Minerva McCloskey and four of her children who had died in infancy, with only natural stones to mark their resting places and the initials carved on each one. Like a hen and chickens made of stones. She folded the down quilt and then lay on it under her blankets and the wrapper in her chemise, her face to the stars. The boar's head sat on the gravestone that it seemed to have appropriated to itself in lieu of a body, out of its razorback roach watching the night through, it's mouth open and greedy for darkness.

Adair listened to the slow approaching footsteps of one of the horses. It was Dolly. She had got her halter rope loose and came to stand over Adair and smell of her, and of the quilt, and the carpet sack, as if to ascertain where she had been and what had happened to her. Adair turned and looked up into her muzzle and eyes and felt very tired. But she got up and wrapped her arms around the big bony horse head, and then retied her and then went to sleep.

Her dreams now took her to some home place that she knew even though she had never been there before. There was a house in a valley with a light in the window and at first she was afraid to approach it but there was singing inside. It was beautiful and holy singing, and she stood outside and tried to make out the melody but it was only a long chord of harmony that went on and on and never changed, never finally devolved into a melody.

IN THE PALE, SMOKY MORNING OLD ASA SMITTERS TOOK HOLD OF ADAIR'S reins.

Listen and I will tell you something about getting horses across water.

Adair said, Whiskey will take any river I put him at.

Sometimes even the most courageous horse will hesitate. Listen to me.

Adair became silent and listened.

I was raised on the Georgia borders with the Choctaw and I learned their language and I minded their ancient tales. I was there when the treaty was signed at Dancing Rabbit Creek with Gordon Lincecum and Pitchlynn, when he was translating, so you don't have to think I'm a crazy old man.

I don't, Mr. Smitters, she said. I am minding you.

Greasy John shook his head. The young are so easily deceived.

They say there is a long cat that lives under the water of the rivers. She is called the Underwater Panther, and she loves horsemeat when she can get it. And that this is why most of your common horses never want to cross water. But if one goes in and they see that the Underwater Panther ain't eat him, the rest will go. You just get one horse in the water and the rest will come, but do it quick, because if you hesitate too long, they think you've seen the Old Lady and you'll lose them all.

I'll get them across, said Adair

Between here and Van Buren the grass is good. But listen now. Push them hard through the Irish Wilderness. There ain't much to eat there, and you will lose them of a night when they go a-wandering in search of grass, so do not tarry but push on to the town of Wilderness, through Pike Creek and Big Barren Creek as fast as you can.

All right.

Greasy John handed her the *Stars and Stripes*. Something to read so you don't forget your alphabet.

She rode away with the newspaper clutched in her hand.

27

Houston, (Southeast) Missouri, November 17, 1863:

To: Captain Murphy, Commanding Post, Houston Mo.

Sir: In compliance with Special Orders No. 43 . . . I started on scout . . . Missouri State Militia, in the direction of Spring Valley . . . visited the residences of Benjamin Carter and Wilson Farrow . . . Burned Carter's house. . . . Found fresh trail of horses, followed them to Jack's Fork to the residence of Miles Stephens and brother Jack Stephens, whom I was satisfied were bushwhackers. Burned the house . . . Proceeded down Jack's Fork 10 miles having marched 30 miles that day. Camped at Widow McCormick's. Had positive evidence that the widow had kept a general rendezvous for Freeman's and Coleman's guerillas. On the morning of the 6th, burned the buildings. Learned from the widow's son that on the previous evening James Mahan had got him to give news of our approach. Sent back and took Mahan prisoner. . . . Prisoner Mahan attempted to escape and was shot. On the morning of the 9th . . . discovered about 20 of the enemy on the bluff above us; fired a few shots at them when they fell back . . . they had all fled into the rocky ravines and hills where it was impossible to pursue. . . . Had gone about one mile and met three men, who started to escape on seeing us. Killed two of them, whom I ascertained from papers found on their persons to be William Chandler . . . and a man named Hackley, who had in his pocket a discharge from Company F, Mitchell's Regiment, Rebel army. . . . Two miles further on we captured William Story on a United States horse. . . . He attempted to escape and was killed. . . . (next day) Marched five miles and captured William Hulsey, James Hulsey, William McCuan and Samuel Jones at the house of James Harris. . . . The first three, viz, the Hulseys and McCuan, were killed. Jones, on account of his extreme youth and apparent innocence, I brought in a prisoner. Five miles farther at the house of John Nicholson, a known Rebel . . . we captured the said John Nicholson, Robert Richards, and Jessie Story, all of whom we killed. . . . All arrived here this evening, all in good health, having been out six days, marched 145 miles, killed 10 men, returned one prisoner, burned 23 houses, recaptured nine horses, and took six contraband horses and mules. All of which is respectfully submitted, John W. Boyd, First Lieutenant, company I, 6th Provisional Regiment, Commanding Scout.

—OR, CH. LXXX, P. 492

Boyd had been one of the few people from Shannon County to enter Federal service . . . before the war, he had known many of the men he killed.

—FROM *A History of the 15th Missouri Cavalry Regiment, CSA*

A DAIR RANDOLPH COLLEY STARTED OUT ON STANGER'S STEEP ON THE eighth of April, 1865. She tapped Whiskey into a smart trot and crossed the shallow water of the little creek and Dolly came behind. They rode up the faint marks of the old trace where thousands of sojourners walking and riding both had crossed it and before them the buffalo far back in time. She joined the stream of humanity that had gone down that road, just one more story in a stream of narratives both likely and unlikely that were being told somewhere even now, by someone, in a far place.

As she came into the valley of the Black River, she rode out of the forest and into long fields of grass. She passed between High Top and Taum Sauk mountains in this pleasant valley. The stands of big bluestem grass were as high as her shoulders where she sat on Whiskey, and by noon she could hear the booming of the shut-ins where the Black River battered its way through a canyon of granite.

It was chilly, and she could see her breath. She kept the red jacket buttoned up tight and the big sleeves rolled down to her knuckles. That night she tethered Dolly and Whiskey to the limb of a white oak on the slopes of Lee Mountain, with an oak forest thick around her.

She made no fire that first night. She ate her food cold and then sat in the quiet evening listening to the insects and the whippoorwills and the absence of human endeavor.

There was a vanishing quality now to the light and the portions of the day. The day vanished into evening, one valley into a forested highland, the evening vanished into the dusk and from there seamlessly into the night and the stars also were imperceptibly quenched as the daylight grew. The bloodroot flowers opened themselves and the old leaves drifted down from the oaks, pushed off by the new ones. In St. Louis there had been such violent sharp edges to time and light and occurrences.

In the days that followed she grazed her horses as often as she could, for here and there the great forests seemed to open of their own accord to form a prairie of grasses an acre or two acres in size, and in these prairies the bobwhites and yellowhammers flushed up from the grass at their feet. She let them go all night and in the mornings would find them coming toward her where she slept, with that alert and nervous air unridden horses always have at dawn. They are remembering some far time when predators came for them at first light. So they came toward her with the strange and painful air of fallen angels, treading carefully and slowly as if the earth were foreign soil. Their manes and tails moving in the dawn wind. Sometimes Whiskey would stop and lift his muzzle to drink in the wind and the messages it might be carrying, his ears cocked stiff and his eyes very alert, curious, interested.

The Steep led not from town to town but from water to grass to salt licks. And because human beings had ceased to inhabit the country, the bottomland trees were now inhabited by flocks of the tiny, red-beaked Cumberland parakeets that had not been seen for years. The mountains now occupied by black bear and panther and feral pigs.

Two days after she started, Adair saw, in one of the small open glades, what seemed to be a man in a fur suit wrestling with something that lay on the ground. It was a sow bear. Her twin cubs boxed each other in play and squalled and strove with each other. The wind was behind her, so Adair knew Whiskey would not get their scent. She swung her plaid shawl around her head and said,

Bear, bear, Indian hair, go on home, your dinner's done.

Adair saw that the sow bear had been tearing up the body of a man and she was so shocked she felt faint at first. He was strung all up and down the open glade, the arm and part of the torso torn loose, a checkered shirt ripped from the ribs, the skull with the hair nearly worn off it rolled into a stand of limestone where it took on the color of the rock except for the patches of deep auburn hair. The sow bear shook her head to loose one of the legs from the spine and it seemed half a man kicked and danced in her jaws.

She turned Whiskey before he and Dolly could get the scent of the bear, and galloped down the road a quarter of a mile with her dress flying. At a creek crossing, they came upon a one-room cabin sitting upon sandstone sills. It was in a stand of walnut trees and the earth was beaten bare at the doorsill. A woman stood at the doorway and watched Adair and her horses. She wore a dark brown dress that came only to her shins and she was barefoot. Then after a moment a yellow-pale child came and stood at her skirt. It was so thin it seemed to be constructed of bones and its face was very old. It wore a rag with a hole cut for its head. The woman's feet were broad and coated with horn and she was thin as a shovel. Adair and the woman stared at each other for long moments.

The woman said, You got ary thing to eat?

Adair said, Yes, and reached into Dolly's pack for a package of the ham and threw it to her. Whiskey twisted and danced impatiently, he seemed to have caught wind of the bear. Dolly stood staring around her, snorting.

The woman sat down directly on the ground and opened the burlap and began to eat the ham with both hands. The eggshell-colored child sat down in front of her and watched her eat without saying anything.

He's going to die anyhow, the woman said. A man child will die before a girl will.

Give him some, said Adair.

The boy carefully pinched a piece of the ham steak and took it apart in his insect fingers, as if food was no longer of any interest to him. He stared at the red, dry meat. He bit into it with great care. Then bit again. The woman sat steadily eating.

There's a body over there a ways, said Adair.

I know it. It's Basil. I ain't got no way of burying him.

A bear is at him.

I cain't help it.

Adair said, You better leave. Why don't you and that boy go up to Iron Mountain?

It was only last week Basil died, the woman said. We were going to last them out till the war was over. We thought we heard them coming and he reached for his pistol and he kindly had it hung on the wall by a ribbon around the trigger guard, and he grabbed that ribbon and it went off. It hit him just behind the jaw and came out the top of his head.

She handed a piece about the size of a buckeye to the boy. Leave us what you got, she said. We might make it if we walked.

I can't, said Adair. I am heading to the Little Black and this is all I got to get me there.

The woman stood up and went into the cabin and Adair could see that she took up a large wooden hayfork and dug into the dirt floor. There was nothing in the cabin in the way of furnishings but blankets on the earth and some few dishes of horn and clay. The woman came back out again with a tow sack and slowly unwrapped a silver cup. She took up her skirt hem and wiped the cup and its elaborate decorations clean of dirt.

I'll give you this, she said. Just give me the rest of that pig meat.

I can't eat that, said Adair. Ain't you got his pistol? You could have shot you that bear.

I can't make myself do it, the woman said. To eat of her. She's been eating at Basil. And I don't have no powder. Do you have powder?

No.

Well, I have put up a snare and we are waiting for something to get into it. I figured I could kill it with a rock if something got into it.

The boy began to sing in a low voice. He whisper-sang to himself. He sang of Barbara Allen and how Lord Bailey turned his face unto the wall though she was only a girl of the castle town and he commenced a-crying, Hard-hearted Barbara Allen. Then hard-hearted Barbara did say, Young man, I think you're dying.

You could take him with you, said the woman. Our names is Hightower. Mine was Presley before. He'll work. He's a good little worker.

I hope you get something in that snare, said Adair. I got to go on.

THAT NIGHT SHE LAY IN A DREAM OF PERFECT CLARITY AS IF SHE WERE broad awake and in it her father came to her dressed in his black broadcloth judge's suit, and his white neckcloth and without a hat. It was not that he came to her so much as he appeared there in a place that was no place, but behind him a pleasant background of valley and mountain with wildflowers growing. He stood utterly still and unmoving, and indeed it was not him but a portrait of him, formal and resolute.

In this portrait he wore a pleasant expression and looked off into the distance. Adair knew that he was dead, and he had sent her this remembrance of him as a keepsake forever, and that in whatever place of filth and misery he had been kept, and in whatever wounded condition, he was now beyond all earthly cares, and in her dream she cried extravagantly and without cease all the while the portrait remained luminous in every detail. In the morning when she awoke she told herself that it was a dream only, that still he might live somewhere.

AS THEY TRAVELED SHE FELT THE MONTH OF APRIL GOING PAST THEM AS IF it were a slow-moving stream. The leaves came fully out except those of the sycamore, a tree that released its leaves reluctantly and slowly. The sassafras held up small mittens of green like elves' hands and she stopped to take up the roots for tea. On the banks of creeks and springs the buckeye was blossoming in rich pink candelabras. Adair often made her camp by midafternoon, and piled her carpet sack and bedding together, and turned the sidesaddle up on its fork to relieve Whiskey of the pressures of it. Then she sat bareback and astride on Dolly as the horses grazed, her skirts billowed up around her thin legs and knees, wearing the red jacket and the shawl around her neck, not to be caught afoot if the soldiers or outlaws came upon them.

And once in a while, during the day, Adair would hear a long holler-ing through the hills. A man's holler, calling out long, long. Yo! and whoever it was would stretch the Yo out until it was a mile long and an octave lower. These calls would echo among the bluffs so that the source of them was confounded, and no one ever seemed to answer. Disembodied voices on Stanger's Steep.

Sometimes she walked alongside Whiskey and Dolly in the grassy valleys. The horses drifted along either side of her, grazing. Their lips moved without sound and it seemed they were talking to the earth in a long, complex conversation. On the high barrens of the ridges, the wind tore at her hair and sent her shawl and strands of her black hair streaming behind her. The horses walked beside in protection. They spread the wings of their souls on either side of her. They drank of the air, and Adair walked lightly along with them.

She made her camp one warm evening in a valley where the high bluffs on one side leaned over a fast stream, and in the bluff was the dark eye of a cave. She tied both Dolly and Whiskey to picket ropes.

She put aside the lilac straw hat. The cherries had been torn off long ago. There was a freshening breeze, and so she decided to walk by herself to the next ridge and look for signs of human beings, for evidence that the world before her and the trace she was traveling on was not entirely deserted.

At the first dimming of the light the tree frogs began to sing in a loud choir of crude noise. They seemed to lure her on down the trace.

By dark she was on the next ridge. She looked out at the hills sweeping south, one ridge after another. The thin rind of the new moon blazed with light so that the old moon's dead heart shone with a deep chocolate glow. Then below her she saw a gleam of light and over the rushing noise of the wind she heard something that sounded like a human voice singing.

She walked a ways closer and before long she found herself halfway down the ridge. Through the trunks of the white oaks shone the light of a fire. A man sat in front of it playing a fiddle there on the old trace for himself alone. Adair tucked her hands in the long sleeves of the Zouave jacket and leaned forward anxiously, trying to make him out. He wore a battered felt hat and a long red beard.

He seemed to pause in thought, staring at the fire, and then played in sequence "The Eighth of January" and "The Hunters of Kentucky" and "Soldier's Joy."

Adair had not heard this old mountain music for a long time and she was very much moved by the songs. In these forlorn melodies she seemed to hear all the stories of the people of these hills and other hills, and the mountains to the east in Tennessee and the Carolinas, where they had come from. They were a bordering people come across the sea from Scotland and Ireland and the north outlands of England, to cross the Atlantic with nothing in their possession but five silver shillings and the clothes they wore. In those melodies she heard the crowded ports of the New World, their strivings and conflicts. And how they moved along in the wilderness of the Carolinas, refusing to work for any but themselves, a people who made their own whiskey and pulled their own teeth and were unconquerable in a fight and for this they had paid a great price. The road to hell was paved with the bones of men who did not know when to quit fighting. Like the Wild Geese of Ireland they were used and spent like coins by one army after another.

And the red-bearded fellow played on into the night until the fire died down and the tip of his bow leapt and shone, weaving out the patterns in the mind. Patterns of beauty, without weight or substance, called up out of the deep structures. Handed on to others through starvation and wars, from one border to another, over the border of one life to the one to follow.

When he played "Killiecrankie" he suddenly stopped. His face and beard were lit with the low firelight. He stood up with his fiddle in one hand and the bow in the other, and sang,

> *If you had seen what I had seen, you would not be so cantie-o*
> *If you had seen what I have seen in the hills of Killiecrankie-o*

Adair listened and would have listened all night. The songs were like an intoxicating drink in their high romance, their extravagance, the ballads of the border people in their poverty and their bitter, violent pride. Tales of revenge and murder and lost loves, lost heroes and war.

At last he played himself out and Adair slipped silently back up the Steep to her camp.

SHE AND HER HORSES CAME TO THE MAIN FORK OF THE BLACK RIVER, FIVE miles from Centerville. The Steep seemed to lead into the water there, but Adair did not like the look of it. She went on farther up the river, where it ran fast and the current would have swept away the deeps and bogs. Another half mile, around a protruding bluff, she found a cairn of stones on the bank and guessed that this was the ford, and so it was. There was a clear hard bottom with a fast current. She turned Whiskey to the water and he did not pause but galloped in.

The sheets of water flew up around them and soaked her red jacket and she laughed. Whiskey charged into the deep but it came only to his chest, so in the middle he stopped and Dolly stopped and they drank deeply, and they were all pleased with themselves.

Then they rode on toward the Current.

Adair made a fireless camp that evening on the barrens of a high ridge, and turned the horses loose to graze. There she had a long view of the country ahead of her. The heavy forests were confining, and she wanted to see the sky and the stars. The redbud trees had lost their blossoms and were leafed out now. The dogwood still flowered in sprays of white. A thunderhead stood hard-edged as stone on the western horizon and the shadows of turkey buzzards slid over her. She made herself comfortable on the down quilt, and in the last light sat down to read the *Stars and Stripes*.

The wind took her hair in long tendrils as if combing it. She bent to the rattling sheets. It was dated March 30. There was news about North Carolina; a battle at Bentonville and then more descriptions of the burning of Columbia. Then there was an article about a Lieutenant Davis who took a scout down into the swamp country beside the Mississippi and killed a Confederate named Lieutenant Reed. Hildebrand was chased by a patrol of Militia to Dent's Station on the Iron Mountain Railroad. The Seventh Kansas Volunteers found more Confederates below Bloomington in the swamps and killed most of them. There were no names of the men they killed.

Then she found news of the siege of Spanish Fort and gripped the paper tight. It was Canby's men, and General A. J. Smith. He was there somewhere, with Canby or Smith. They had come up from Fish River and were bombarding the fort. She found the casualty lists and went down to the Ns with a shaking finger. Naves Neal Nelson Newbury Nice Nolan Norris Norse Northfield Nottingham Nugent. He was not among the casualties.

Adair lay back on her down comforter. Not far away Whiskey cropped the grass with ripping noises. She watched the sunset clouds slide past in thin, almost transparent swirls. After a while she fell asleep and did not think about the major any more that night.

THE NEXT MORNING SHE WAS HALF A MILE OFF STANGER'S STEEP IN A VAL-ley that her map said was named Tinker Hollow. The creek that ran through it was called Hominy Creek and it was of a good size with gravelly shoals and banks. In the wide valley there was a stand of hack-berry trees, and beneath them a thick growth of the oat grass that the horses loved above all else. There was no underbrush and the air beneath the hackberry trees seemed as green as underwater. Adair put her hand upon her other arm. She felt very thin. Insubstantial. She had begun to breathe in a shallow manner so that she would not cough and sometimes this worked, but it left her tired.

So Adair turned the horses into the grass and laid out her canvas and her shelter half on the warm sands. She lay at the bend of the creek where there were stands of sycamore saplings with small new leaves, and a stand of cane to screen her from the wind. The cane was ragged, with its winter leaves striped white by winter freezes. The new leaves were still very small. The cane and the sycamores kept the wind from her and the sun was hot.

Adair remembered the steam doctor's instruction to take cold baths and lay unclothed in the sun. She sat up to listen carefully but she heard no one or any sound of hooves. She then took off her dress and shoes and stockings. She untied the signet ring from her drawers, wrapped one of the ribbons from her stays around and around the ring, and then forced it on her finger so as not to lose it in the water. She stepped into Hominy Creek along a shoal of gravel until it came up to her waist. The water was very clear and so cold it seemed it had shut around her like a hand but she ducked under. Overhead banks of cumulus built up with icy bright edges and the sunlight came through the canopy of sycamore and elm in dots and dashes on the water. She burst up gasping, and strove through the dense water to the bank again.

She took up all her clothes and washed them, and herself and her long hair with the good soap. She wadded up her hair in a mass of suds and then ducked under the water, the suds drifting in white islands down-current.

She lay down shivering on the red gravel. It was good to lie in the open air as if the world were at peace and no danger anywhere. In a patch of sunlight she was warmed finally and so she lay and day-dreamed. About the time they met in the matron's courtyard with the fresh sheets flying and how he had put his arms around her and kissed her. The touch of his lips so intimate. She had breathed in his breath and felt his heart beneath the woolen coat. When he had opened her nightgown. She thought of the open stretches in the map of the West where they might have walked through the gates that shut them in and gone on to another world.

Adair drew out her long black hair through her fingers to dry it. Overhead a great blue heron honked, sailing like an airborne cross. Adair looked up at it. They weave not, neither do they spin. It was the world of people that had set them apart one from the other. Not this one here.

She clasped her knees and worried about it. Down the small creek valley sudden flights of small birds sprang up out of the grass meadows, and Adair saw a red-tailed hawk casting in a straight, lethal flight, flushing them up. Then with marriage she would be caught up with eternal work indoors, with carding wool and washing babies' diapers and a truck garden and chickens and canning and the eternal weaving and spinning. She could probably not manage it even if she were to live.

She jumped up from the canvas. She did not want to die and leave this world for something called an Eternal Home. She began to cough from the exertion. Her enemy lay inside her. She walked among the sycamore saplings standing apart from one another on the gravel shoals, switching at them with a cane. She prayed briefly that the Lord would let her live, and had not her own mother prayed the same thing?

She held out her arms and looked at them. She had not gained anything, but she told herself, neither have I lost. Lord, why would you take me to die? She put both hands to her eyes and the tears streamed through them. Lord, I'd rather you didn't pay any attention to me one way or the other if you don't mind.

Her toes gripped in the gravel as she rinsed soap out of her clothes and she became deeply chilled. Then she lay in the sun in her chemise and then in a fit of daring took that off too and lay naked in the sun. The steam doctor said it would be healing and so indeed after a number of hours she felt very well. Then she went in the water again and made herself endure it, naked but for her hair falling over her shoulders. She was in the water half of the day. The cold water made her fever go down and she felt very sleepy and very good.

SHE STAYED TWO DAYS ON THIS CREEK. SHE LAY IN THE COLD WATER FOR A long time and then on her canvas in the sun on the gravel bank. Her hands and nails became very clean. She washed her hair twice each day. She lay in the sun and worked on the quilt and saw it was becoming whole again.

Well, I should not marry, but live at home, and I will have my sisters for company, she thought, but then she knew they would be meeting new fellows in Tennessee. Her cousin Lucinda was right, they would be married, because they expected to be; because they counted forty white horses and counted nine stars on nine nights and made a wish, because they sought to read his initials in apple parings and in cobwebs and sprinkled salt on the fire. Because they had little clocks ticking away inside them that told them it was time to have children and the numerals on these internal timepieces were coins to be spent on domestic affections.

She closed her eyes and fell asleep. In a dream Adair's mother appeared to her on the far bank of the stream, wearing her blue-gray London Smoke silk, of the style of the 1840s, turning toward her with a pleased smile. Sarah Colley smiled at Adair over the stream's clean waters, come from a far land, and dry leaves fell through her and a bee wavered among her transparent skirts.

A thunderstorm grumbled at the edge of the world in the far west, and her mother said, *Have you fed Dolly?* Adair wanted to make some excuse but she fell even more deeply asleep and did not awaken until she heard the distant sound of men's voices and horses walking. At that time she was dreaming again that she was walking down a valley road in the twilight, and there were the cut stumps of Osage orange trees, and that someone was coming behind her with a message concerning her death.

She woke up as suddenly as glass smashes. There were men and horses coming down the trail among the hackberry trees. Crows were scattering across the sky, black check marks, with their chipping and alarmed voices. Where were her own horses? They had gone farther up the bends of the creek and she prayed they were upwind of these sudden horses. Adair reached up quickly and pulled down the big silk twill from a sycamore sapling and crawled into a tangle of driftwood.

The grind of hooves on gravel grew louder and they were talking, their talk was loud and desperate.

She tried to put the dress on. She pulled it over her head but she could not find the neckhole once she was inside all the yardage of it. Then finally she stayed still because the weeds grown among the driftwood would thrash around and there was no wind. They were coming very close by. She was trapped inside the giant silk twill skirts of the dress. Finally she saw light and held the neckhole around her face and at last saw them passing by, heard the ceramic rattle of shod hooves on gravel. They were crossing upstream about ten rods.

They would want her horses if they had not already got them. Adair could see horse legs and none of them were hers. She lay with her face out of the neckhole of the dress and watched calmly between two old tree trunks of the driftwood. She saw them start into Hominy Creek. Between the men in butternut homespun was a young Union Militia fellow with his hands tied behind his back. His hair was long and blond and tied behind his head with a wrapping of buckskin. He was wallowing in the saddle. On his face was a look of terror as she had never seen and his face was bruised on both sides. His nostrils were rimmed with blood.

He was repeating over and over, Fellows, they just went and forced me to join up. What can I offer you fellows? Boys, there's money in this for you.

The entire troop then churned into the stream and Adair was surprised to see how deep it was farther up. The water came up to the young Union soldier's calves and his horse, like his fate, strove onward to its appointed end.

On the far side Adair heard them struggling with one another and then Dolly came bolting out of the patch of cane stalks and into the creek so that Adair had to struggle up with the dress half on and catch the gray mare by the neck-rope and hold on to her. Then Adair pulled the dress the rest of the way on and lay hid and heard at a distance the young man's high screams. How he pleaded for his life and how he promised all sorts of things and denied others.

How come you to kill old Asa Smitters? A man shouted. How come you to shoot that old man?

He was cutting the telegraph lines, we get to shoot people who cut telegraph lines, the prisoner said. It sounded as if he was trying to get his captors to see it from his point of view. He was so old he was near dead anyhow.

How come you to shoot him in the head you son of a bitch?

He wasn't no good to anybody, the young Union soldier said. He was just an old man.

She put her hands over her ears and stood up. Then at least two long guns went off and there was a long, high shrieking that went on and on. He was only half dead and thrashing around in the brush and the cane with a peculiar, repeated yelping at a high pitch, and Adair heard Reeves's men laughing.

Jesus look at him, he looks like a jumping jack.

The yelps were louder and wilder, and Dolly stood with her eyes rimmed in white and God alone knew where Whiskey was, and still it went on.

Just kill him, just kill him, Adair thought. She backed Dolly into the cane again and saw the young soldier flip backward over the bank of the stream and lie there in the shallows with both arms and both legs doubling up and then jerking straight out over and over and his head nodding like a Lazy Tom, yelping with every nod. Then a man came to the bank of the stream and fired a final pistol shot. Two more came and they dragged him from the water by one arm and one leg and then they went on.

Adair stood with Dolly in the cane for nearly an hour.

Toward late afternoon Whiskey came cautiously to the edge of the water, looking for her or for whatever had caused the noise and the screaming, turning his head here and there and he was very jumpy. Adair gathered up her traps and put the bridle on him and stood while he drank. As she crossed the creek she saw a piece of the soldier's skull with the hair still on it. A triangular chip.

That evening she camped again without a fire on the high barrens so she could see in every direction and watched late into the night.

28

Union Correspondence

Patterson, March 13, 1864

To: Brig. Genl. C. B. Fisk, Commanding District of St. Louis:

Sir: General, we are beset here with more Rebels than we can manage. I know our situation. I see it all. I can destroy them if you will give me the means . . . let me have Captain McElroy and his company and I will put down jayhawking and treason in this country or I will make it one desolate waste where no white or black man can stay.

   W. T. Leeper, Captain, Commanding Third Missouri State Militia Cavalry

                                —OR, ch. xlvi, p. 588

Confederate Correspondence

Headquarters Shelby's Division

Camp Twelve Miles from Patterson, Mo., September 21, 1864

Col. L. A. MacLean, Assistant Adjutant-General:

Colonel: I am this far on the way and am encamped at Captain Leeper's, U.S. Army, a notorious robber, house-burner and marauder, where I found plenty of forage and beef. The scout I sent out night before last after the Federals that burnt Doniphan, overtook them the next morning, attacked and routed them, losing six men killed and wounded. Federal loss unknown. Killed some Union guerillas today . . . the country passed over has been rough and sterile in the extreme.

    Very respectfully, Jo. O. Shelby, Brigadier-General, Commanding Division

                                  —OR, ch. liii, p. 948

In no other part of Missouri was the loss of property and life more devastating
than in Southeast Missouri. . . . the story of the Patterson family who lived four
miles south of Marble Hill is a vivid reminder of the savagery of the war. Here,
along what was once the main trail to Zalma, William Patterson, a Confeder-
ate officer, his wife and their four young children were murdered, and their bod-
ies, weighted with rocks and thrown into the deep spring on their farm. The
family's house was burned and it was several weeks before the bodies were found.
— A Guide to Civil War Activities in the Southeast Missouri Region,
BROCHURE DISTRIBUTED BY THE SOUTHEAST MISSOURI REGIONAL PLANNING AND
ECONOMIC DEVELOPMENT COMMISSION, N.D.

THE NEXT MORNING ADAIR DID NOT PAUSE TO MAKE A FIRE OR BREAK-
FAST but started out with the horses directly. They went down the wandering trace, downhill, into forests of pine and oak mixed, and here and
there at the edges of one of the inexplicable open glades, flowering
chestnuts.

At noon of that day the world was overwhelmed with flights of wood
doves that came in the millions and weighted down the limbs of the
trees calling to one another with such a noise that it almost deafened
her. The silky rustle of uncounted wings made it sound as if the woods
were afire. All around her their droppings cracked on the leaves on the
ground, and once she heard a limb breaking from the weight of a hundred doves who had fluttered down to crowd onto it. It was a storm of
doves, the sunlight became dim as it would dim in an eclipse and she
rode hard to get away from them. She rode ten miles at a trot before
they were clear of them. She and the horses both walked into a wide
pool of water in a stream and washed themselves clean.

ADAIR AND HER HORSES APPROACHED THE CROSSING OF THE CURRENT
River near the place where Jack's Fork came in, called House's Ford.
She waited until it was late evening and then rode to the edge of the
river.

It was a deep river, and dangerous for all the trees it had taken down, rolling their great revolving wheels of roots along the bottoms. The spring rains had taken the bank of the ford away, and it was now a ten-foot bluff on this side, but low on the other. The bottom was clear and appeared to be hard.

Adair would cross now and go on in the night. She would travel in the dark until she was well beyond this crossing, for both armies used it frequently. It was just at sunset. Flights of mourning doves and wild pigeons wheeled in the darkening air.

Dolly went to the sloping bank and stared into the water and its insubstantial reflections.

Adair sat on Whiskey and looked at the broad river and knew this was going to take some doing. It was deep and fast. Dolly snorted angrily for she knew she was going to be asked to cross it, and knew it was unnecessary, for there was very good grass on this side of the river.

They all stood on the bank of red sand; the far shore was a low sandy beach. Great sycamores stood in the bottoms and made shadows on the glittering water. In between the trees she could see Stanger's Steep going on.

It was dangerous to cross a river sidesaddle and so she took the saddle from Whiskey and put it on Dolly, for the gray mare to carry across. Adair took off the big brass-colored twill dress and stuffed it in her carpet sack, and made sure the carpet sack and pack and all were secure on the sidesaddle. She would cross in her chemise, for the great yards of skirts would tangle and drown her for sure. She tied her shoes round her neck. She got up on Whiskey by jumping across his back on her stomach and then righting herself.

Whiskey, go on, she said. If you go Dolly will go.

The gray mare with her black eyes stood at the ten-foot-high bluff. She hesitated. She saw no reason to plunge into this mysterious water. The tops of the sycamores and oaks on the other side were still tipped red with the last light and so were reflected on the fast black water. To

Dolly it seemed that these were evil illuminations below the surface. Where the Underwater Panther housed herself and in slow watery strokes trod the currents.

Adair broke off a stick of cane. She took hold of Dolly's lead-rope and rode Whiskey to the edge and pulled hard. Whiskey was eager to get into the river but Adair did not want to leave Dolly hesitating on the bank. The chemise rode up to her thighs and its insubstantial lawn was no more than a dirty gray film over her body and it was tearing in several places, so worn it was. She smashed the cane crop down on Dolly's haunches and yelled

Go on!

Dolly wavered back and forth, back and forth, and so Adair struck Whiskey with the cane. Whiskey sat back on his hocks and slid down halfway, bringing down with him an avalanche of dirt and rocks. Then sprang into the dark water in a long leap. This snatched Dolly's lead rope out of her hand with a skinning rip.

It seemed they were in the air for long moments. They fell through the air of dusk and sank into the water. It was so cold Adair cried out and then went under.

It was very dark under the water. Whiskey was surging upward so violently that his mane was torn out of her hands and she was swept away. Adair fought for the surface. She burst out into the air and saw she was being flung downstream faster than she thought. She clawed at the water as if it were a ladder or a stair but it dissolved beneath her and she went under again. She was swept onto Dolly, and the gray mare's thrashing front hoof struck Adair in the forearm with such force Adair thought she felt it break but then she had hold of the sidesaddle and clung to it with both arms. The shoes were swept from around her neck and went down the current and were forever lost.

Dolly fought toward the far bank as if she were some great engine, steadily, mechanically. Fountains of water marked her passage and at a slant she roared up out of the shallow water, onto the low sandy beach, and stood. Adair let go of the saddle and dropped down on the sand.

Dolly shook herself so that she seemed surrounded by a fine mist. Then Whiskey came trotting up.

Adair was gasping for air. She pulled on her wet stockings. They were all on the other side and alive. The trees of the bottoms were swagged with grapevines and darkness was developing in their shadows. Then Dolly lifted her head and saw Stanger's Steep going on in the last of the day's light, and began to trot down it, into the tunnel where the trees overhung the ancient trace.

Wait! said Adair. But Dolly did not like being on this dark shore, so near to the dominion of the Underwater Panther, and the night growing blind and sinister all around them. She trotted down the old trace at a good speed to get past the heavy woods of the bottoms and into some upland before full midnight was on them.

Whiskey fell in behind her and Adair ran between them, her chemise sticking to her wet and cold, but she could not stop them. The horses pulled on past her and were now independent of her, for their needs were their own and none of hers. At last she stopped running and walked. She walked and listened to their diminishing hoofbeats. Dolly gone with the grip and everything she possessed on her back. They were gone into the wilderness of Shannon County and she was in nothing but her chemise and her stockings. She could hear them far down the road begin to gallop, then they were gone entirely.

ADAIR WALKED FOR SEVERAL MILES BECAUSE SHE COULD DO NOTHING ELSE. Soon enough the road came up out of the bottoms and climbed switchbacking to a ridge and there the night wind blew through her threadbare chemise with a severe bite. Stars stood out in their millions.

Well, I have cut quite a figure as a lady of high degree here in the world, haven't I? But in some way it was amazing that here she was nearly naked and afoot in the night in the most remote wilderness of the Ozark mountains and wondered if ever such a thing had happened before. She was perishing of the cold. The wind seemed to come down from the great cold spaces of the stars themselves. She kept on walking.

Soon the moon came up and this caused several startled songbirds to whistle. A mockingbird ran through its warbling and erratic music. The three-quarter moon shone through the trees slantways as it rose, as if a giant lantern had been lit somewhere in the woods. White boulders and stands of limestone shone among the oaks and she was as pale as they. Another mile along she saw a house in a small clearing beside the road. There was no smell of woodsmoke, nor of horse manure, nor yet any dogs arising to bark, nor any noise or light.

Adair stood in the faint trace of Stanger's Steep within the moon shade of a massive white oak and regarded the house. It was of log but sided over, the windows shuttered, the morning glory and trumpet vine thick over the front veranda. Because of this she thought surely it was deserted. Adair held herself tight for the relief of warmth she got from her own arms. Whippoorwills started up suddenly and so close she jumped. They began their demented, repetitive song and would go on all night.

She sat down on the bark fragments and acorns under the white oak listening to the sounds of the night. She sat with her knees drawn up and her arms clutched over her breasts. She would have to go on hunting them tomorrow, surely they would stop at the first good stand of grass and graze for the day.

Back in the woods raccoons began to argue among themselves, they were swearing and cursing at one another in loud voices. Then she heard wolves, but they seemed to be several mountains away. It made her hair stand on end. Adair prayed that they would stay several mountains away. Their voices carried such great distances so as to silence everything else. Adair listened. They were the lords of the night and all speech of animals fell silent when they sang. Their crazed sopranos made all creatures hold their lives close and in silence. The raccoons stopped in midsentence.

Adair stared at the house; she wanted to go in. She wanted to sleep under a roof for a night or two nights. She decided not to. She could not sleep for the chill, but her head dropped forward on her knees and she began to dream of her cousin Lucinda Newnan, that she came visiting from Tennessee but there was a snowstorm, and the kindling was wet, and they could not get the fire started. Adair said that they should burn the tablecloth and Lucinda said that was the stupidest idea she had ever heard. Adair said, Shut the door, it's wide open, and look at the snow coming in. Lucinda said, I will go outside and see if there is not some shavings in the barn, and Adair heard her footsteps crunching in the dry grass.

She was indeed hearing footsteps shushing in the grass. And so feral and wary had Adair become that she woke immediately and did not lift her head for the white flash her face would make in the night. Only very slowly and just enough to peek over her forearms.

A man had come out of the house. He was walking in the weed-grown yard. The moon shone on him and he was entirely naked. He looked around himself in every direction and in one hand he held a large revolver. The man's body was as pale as a mushroom. He took his private parts in one hand and began to piss and did so for a long time. His eyes roved from the forest behind the house to the road to the weedy grasses of the clearing. One side to the other and back again.

He must have heard her horses go by. He would be very alert. A soldier of either side or a refugee or a spy. Adair waiting, sitting unmoving in a state of simple and uncomplicated terror for him to see her. His body was long and thin, he was clean-shaven as an egg, a V of tan at his neck like a bib. Adair could not stop looking at his naked body. His sex was hidden in its dark frame of hair, his thighs were long and lashed with whipcord muscles.

He finished and stood a few moments longer, watching. The moon showed the broken rail fence as plain as at sunrise. Adair eased her face down again to give him no more to look at than the vague white of her chemise, which might well be taken as a stand of limestone. She heard his dry footsteps again, whispering back into the house and inside, across the floor. There was a flash of light from between the shutters; it glowed out of their missing slats.

Oh Lord he is going to sit up all night in there, Adair thought. She sat perfectly still in her own near nakedness for as long a time as she could. Lord help me out of this, she thought. There is no one else here on earth to do so. I can expect aid from no quarter but from Thee. Curse this man. Make him deaf. Make him fall over dead.

At last the moon slid behind the trees on the other side, sinking with its astonished face into the shifting leaves. And the light inside the abandoned cabin went out.

Adair stood up very slowly. Her joints hurt her, unbending from her clutch of arms and legs. She must walk down the middle of the road, as she would make too much noise beneath the oaks. The worst of it was that if he caught her here in her chemise, it was ragged and gray and something to be ashamed of.

She came to the edge of the road and its soft dirt and began to run on tiptoe at top speed. She ran along the edge of the road with her knees flashing and her chemise flying out behind her in pale waves. She spurted into the long aisle of trees on the far side of the clearing where Stanger's Steep went on its way. She ran along the road as it bent sideways along the side of the mountains, her hair flying out of her braids.

She heard someone running behind her.

Adair couldn't go on as long as he could. She was tired out already and she turned to see him running toward her, the shirtless top half of him very pale and the bottom half nearly invisible in dark blue uniform pants.

He came up to her in the dark like a spirit and grabbed her by the hair.

Were those your horses? he said.

What horses? said Adair. Let me go!

They turned around and around in the dark as she fought to get loose of him. But he was very strong and shifted his grip to her arm where Dolly had kicked her and she cried out in pain.

Let me go, she said. I haven't done nothing.

You've spied out my cabin, he said. And there's likely more of Freeman's boys somewhere behind you. He started off down the road in the moonlight in the direction that Dolly and Whiskey had gone with her arm in one hand and the revolver in the other.

Look there, he said. What's that?

Ahead of them in the road was a black bulk. Bright things lay all around it. She stopped. It appeared to be a hunched troll squatted in the road and sorting among his collected trash.

It was her carpet sack and the bundle of bedding. Dolly had bucked it off. He held his revolver on her and said, Go pick it up.

Adair collected her silver dish, which she could see glinting faintly, and her tin cup. Then she started to pick up the carpet sack.

Leave that alone, he said. You could have a sidearm in there.

All right, Adair said, and held it upside down and shook it, and grabbed at the things that fell out. She got down and snatched up the green brocade slippers and the matron's big dress and her silver brush and shawl and the candy dish. She raked the Zouave jacket toward her.

I said leave it alone!

Adair put on the bedroom slippers and pulled the dress over her head.

Don't you tell me I can't get dressed, she said.

He picked up the tow sack. Is there corn in there? he said. She saw in the moon's light that he was medium tall and his eyes were hard. He watched her and untied his uniform shirt from around his waist and put it on.

Yes, she said. Corn. She was breathing in heavy gasps.

Stand on that bluff of rock and shake that bag of corn, he said. He buttoned his shirt.

On ahead of them the Steep led to a shelf of rock where they could see out over the valley as if placed there by a kind Providence for travelers to sit upon and look out over the nighttime valley, even now silting up with shadow as the moon extinguished itself. She looked out over the valley ahead of her and thought it must be Pike Creek Valley from what Greasy John had drawn on the backs of the telegraph forms.

No, she said.

He didn't say anything, but bent and jerked open the carpet sack and spilled the rest of her things on the ground.

Just so there ain't no sidearm in there, he said. Now, go on. Shake that bag of corn.

No. Shoot me. Sue me in court.

He took Adair by the arm and went to stand on the shelf of rock and shook the bag of corn.

Come boys! he called. Come boys!

Before long Whiskey and Dolly came trotting up the trail. Dolly was a pale bulk but Whiskey was nearly invisible in the dark. They came and nosed at the bag.

The man took them both by the halter rope and the reins and laughed.

Good. I ain't got no use for that saddle, he said. Pull it off.

Adair unbuckled the cinch and pulled off the sidesaddle.

Don't take my horses, she said.

My mama didn't raise no idiots, he said. You been out slipping around in the dark, spying out my camps, and your horses got away from you. You got some patrol close behind.

Well, what are you doing up here by yourself?

You ain't asking the questions. He took Whiskey's reins and Dolly by the halter rope, and led them to a tree. He tied Dolly on a low limb. I got my horse stolen two days ago, Reeves jumped me and Billy Simes and took Billy off and shot him somewhere. Now these are just what I need.

Ain't the war over? asked Adair. You can't take my horses if the war is over.

Not here it ain't, he said. Not for a long time.

Suddenly Dolly reared back on her tie rope, bracing her front legs and jerking wildly.

Stop that, you bitch, said the man, and kicked Dolly on the hindquarters. She bolted forward, turned to face the man with her round dark eyes and her ears cocked. I said cut that shit out. He approached her and she pulled back on the halter rope again, fighting hard to break it. He said, I hate a horse that pulls back. He walked up to her and kicked her hard in the chest, and then Dolly reared up and pawed the air. She stood out pale in the night with her big horse belly exposed to them, striking with her front feet.

The man shot her in the head. His revolver bucked in his hand and flame poured out of the muzzle. Adair screamed in a long diminishing tremolo that repeated itself from hill to hill. Dolly jerked rigid, her legs stiff as pipes and trembling wildly. Then the gray mare went down very slowly, a large hole high up on her jaw. She lay down as if performing a trick she had never done before. Blood dripped from her mouth. She lay down on the leaves with her head still held up by the halter rope. Her eyes closed very slowly, inch by inch. Whiskey stood strained back on his reins, thrashing his head.

Oh don't kill my horse! said Adair. Oh look how you've hurt her!

I done killed her. He walked to Whiskey. Now what is this one going to do?

Nothing, said Adair. He won't do anything. She went to Whiskey and patted him. Be good, she said. Be good now. Dolly still hung by her head and the blood was dripping from her mouth. Whiskey stood and his skin trembled all over his body in waves.

Then you come on, you ain't running off to go tell Reeves's fellows where I am. He pulled Whiskey's reins free and walked along leading the dun horse, and had her in the other hand. If you do anything I will kill this horse too. He's your pet, ain't he?

Adair said, I just traded for him a couple of days ago. He don't mean anything to me but I got to get home. Give him to me, and she reached for him.

He knocked her hand down. I bet you're a Snider. I bet you'll high-tail it back to the Sniders' and bring them all a-running, he said.

They walked on.

No, I wouldn't, said Adair. Just give me my horse.

He's your pet all right. The man let go her arm. I'm going on to Pike Creek and I'll get a saddle there from the Upshaws. They're Union. They'll give me a saddle. So you just come along, Miss, and if you run I'll shoot this horse dead. You can stay at the Upshaws until they can take you in.

Take me in where? said Adair.

Under arrest.

I was just running down the road! Adair said. I lost my horses!

The man walked on. Now, you can prove you're innocent before the provost marshal. His voice became less harsh. She still could not see his features. They went on down the trail, a broad road into the valley before them. There were no house lights in all the dark stretches of the hills but it was late in the night.

Let me put on my jacket, she said. She looked back at Dolly, who hung by her halter, splattered with dark blotches over her pale neck and head, and who was very still except for the slight fluttering of her mane in the night breeze.

Well, go on. I guess you're cold.

Adair put on the Zouave jacket and held it around her. They walked on into the night where the whippoorwill sang its one repetitive song over and over. Whiskey blew hard and stared around him. He thrashed his head from side to side against the bit.

Stop it, you son of a bitch, said the man.

He don't mean nothing, said Adair. He's just scared.

The man laughed. He's your pet all right.

Adair strode long steps to keep up with the man. They went on down the hill and came to a branch and crossed through it in noisy splashes. It was not deep, but Whiskey sat back on his hindquarters and made a roaring snort like a stag, his nostrils open to red holes. He gathered himself as if he would jump the water or sail into the air.

It's all right, Whiskey, said Adair. She put her hand on his shoulder.

Go on, go on. And the dun horse stepped through the water in high steps as if it contaminated him. He was cautious of everything now. All around them the dry grasses from last summer stood tall, the color of bronze.

Well now, this is companionable, ain't it? the man said. Do you have any favorite subject of conversation?

I don't know, said Adair. She tried to sound light. What about you?

Did you ever hypnotize a chicken?

Well, now that you mention it, I did, she said, in a gay voice. It's just funny one time.

You can hypnotize a man before you shoot him, the man said. You put that gun barrel in his face and bear down on him and stare him in the eye and it's like he's kind of fainted away but his eyes are open.

Well isn't that something, said Adair. That's really interesting. She hurried along beside the man and Whiskey trying to see where they were going in the dark.

It is something, he said. You hear people talk about it. He cleared his throat and spat. That scare you?

Well, no, said Adair. I guess that's what it's like being a soldier. She laughed, in a ragged trailing noise.

Yes it is. I'm tired of being a soldier. A man should relax. Have some fun. Adair didn't say anything so he said, Don't you like relaxing and having fun?

Well, sure, said Adair. Her voice was high and thin. They went on along the road with the big bluestem grass nearly touching overhead and through the waving seed heads the low moon flashed and glittered.

What kind of music do you like?

Oh, I like the modern waltzes, said Adair. And some of the old tunes like "Soldier's Joy."

I like that jigging music, the man said. But you need a good fiddler. You don't need such a good fiddler for the waltzes. They can kind of shin through because they're slow and easy to play.

I never thought of it like that, said Adair.

Are you lagging behind? Come on. Walk up.

Wait, she said, I can't hardly go on.

Yes you can, he said. I enjoy your company. You just keep walking and talking.

Let me walk on the other side and hold on to his mane. She trudged along in the bedroom slippers holding to Whiskey's mane. The Steep was leading them through the open valley of Pike Creek and the big bluestem stood very tall in the moonlight on both sides with the pale rutted track going on.

Where does this come out? said the man. I thought it was taking us to Upshaws'.

Well, they call it the Arkansas road, said Adair. It comes out in north Arkansas, I guess, and it goes on to Little Rock and then to Mexico or somewhere.

I ain't going to Mexico, girl, I am going to get me a saddle.

Well, Upshaws' track is down here a ways.

Where does it go before it gets to Arkansas? He stopped and in the dim tall grass struck a match and lit a pipe. The match shone on the grass stems and his ordinary-looking face and then he threw it down and stepped on it.

Well, it goes on to Wilderness.

He laughed. This here is all a wilderness.

No, I mean the town of Wilderness. That place where Hyssop's Rest is at. The tavern. Adair coughed and leaned and spit into the road.

What's the matter with you?

I don't know. I got a cottonseed down my throat.

Well, quit making so much noise.

Adair took up her skirts in both hands and kept walking.

The tavern. I know that place. But I got to get to Upshaws' first.

It's just a little ways.

You show me. Show me when we get there. His revolver occasionally took up a flash of moonlight that ran liquid down the barrel. He said, Hyssop's Rest has got to be a good fifteen miles from here. He smoked and paced on into the seething grasses and said, When I get me a saddle from old man Upshaw then I'll ride and you can ride behind. When we get to Hyssop's we can have a drink.

All right, said Adair.

Do you take a drink when it's offered?

Once in a while.

Well, this is one of those onces. He laughed. Jessie Hyssop. She cooks for the Rebs one night and us fellows the next.

They went on through the broad valley of grass where no trees grew because of the floods that came down out of the mountains from time to time and swept everything before them except for the pliable grass that bent before everything and then came up again to respond amiably to any wind that came and outlasted everything except the willows, which also bent. Even now to the southwest came the rumble of thunder or it could have been artillery.

Off to the right in the creek bottom several hen turkeys burst out in a squalling nighttime argument and were then quiet again.

What was that? He stopped and snatched back on Whiskey's reins to keep the horse from walking over him. Some of your friends signaling one another? He knocked out his pipe and stepped on the coal.

Adair knew he meant Colonel Reeves's men, or Freeman's men. Sounds like hen turkeys to me, she said. The high grass sang around them in a whisper of coming rain, the seed heads tipped uneasily to the northeast over their heads. The thunder sounded again afar off, behind it a glimmer of lightning.

If I don't look out here I'm going to get myself shot, he said. How do I know this is the Arkansas road? We might have turned off.

I'm following you, said Adair. And you have my horse.

If you run I'll shoot him.

Before long they came to a place where a deer trail turned off into the grass, and Adair peered at it and thought it might be the place marked on Greasy John's telegraph forms where the deer snares were.

What's that? the man said. He paused and wavered at the entrance to the deer trail. The narrow trail was a black slit full of darkness in the wall of grass. I got to get out of this goddamned grass.

No, just go on, she said. She made herself sound urgent. Anxious. Go on! On down this road is where we want to go.

Well, I bet that is the path to Upshaws', he said.

No it ain't! Go on ahead. She backed away.

He turned and came back to her and stood over her. I can shoot this horse in a second, he said. He put one hand around her throat and closed it.

He's no good to you dead, Adair said, and she coughed, and her throat convulsed under his hand. This road crosses Pike Creek just down here, and the Upshaws' track is on the other side. He dropped his hand. He was so afraid she could smell him sweating. She could see his Militia insignia and knew it was coming light now.

You're lying like a shithouse rat, he said. He took Whiskey and turned off into the dark passageway in the grass. I got to get out of this grass, you can't see nothing. He pushed on into the big bluestem, ungrazed these four years of war. He said, You don't want the Upshaws to see your face, do you?

This here is a deer trail, said Adair.

Shut up. You said not to come this way so this is the way we're going.

They came to a place where the tall bluestem gave way to the shorter oat grass, and Adair could hear the creek running. The deer trail was now plain, and it ran straight to the sandy bank of Pike Creek under sycamores. She thought she saw the taut cord of a snare but the moon had gone down and now all the world was gray. Whiskey danced to the side.

Go to the left, she said. Don't take the trail over the bank. Go to the left.

What are you holding back for? he said. He put the revolver barrel against Whiskey's neck.

Well, I am tired of arguing with you, said Adair. You keep asking me the way to Upshaws' and I am telling you. She raised her voice. Just shoot him! Go on!

Which way? He put the revolver barrel toward her.

Go off to the left! There's a big broad clear space to cross in! She was shouting, she couldn't help herself, her nerves were gone, everything was out of sequence, there was no safety anywhere, not even in the hot dark.

Be damned if I will, he said, and turned, and walked down the deer trail under the sycamore saplings and straight into the snare.

With a slithering whine the snare came off its circle of stakes and the soldier seemed to vault feet first up into the night like a circus performer, his one leg clasped by the ankle. Whiskey's reins were ripped from his hand and the dun horse ran backward, snorting. The man leaped and flew, his arms beating the air. You bitch! You bitch! In the dim light of coming dawn he grabbed wildly, upside down, and the limber sycamore that held the snare line beat about among its more sober fellows like a live thing.

I'll kill you! he screamed. He poured out two wild shots and the muzzle flashes came first from one place and then from another.

Whiskey ran backward. He ran over Adair and knocked her down. She scrambled out away from his hooves and then caught his reins. The man seemed to be a flying demon hurling around in the middle air, up by one leg like the Hanged Man in Madame Rose's Tarot cards. Things were falling out of his pockets in shining trajectories—coins and a watch and his penknife.

Adair threw herself up and across Whiskey's back and turned him down the deer trail before she even righted herself. As they went through the narrow slit in the high grass the revolver went off again.

A ball tore through the grass stems and struck the dun horse. He suddenly jumped into the air with his back arched, went sideways as if the ball had thrown him off his footing, but he came down with his rear end under him and went smashing on through the jungle of grass with an erratic crabwise gait. Adair in her oversize dress ballooned along with him. She buried her hands in his mane and felt him falter under her again and again but he remained upright and moving. Far behind she heard the man screaming but he did not fire again and at last the road crossed Pike Creek on a bed of timbers. She slid off Whiskey's side and led him to water.

A long stream of blood spread out in a fan from a bullet hole just above his stifle, where his hind leg joined his gut, and she put her hand against the pumping hole. It looked as though he were gutshot but it might have lodged in the muscle. Then he would have a chance.

He stood nodding his head up and down, and then made a low throaty noise and turned and pressed his forehead flat against her.

Don't you want some water? said Adair. She patted him and stroked him. Come to water. Come to water.

Whiskey walked limping through the sand down to the creek and dipped his muzzle into the water. He drank, and lifted his head again, and the drops made expanding circles in red fire as the sun rose and shone through the sycamores.

When he drank as much as he wanted, Adair drank too, and then she took up his reins and led him on down the Steep, watching like something gone wild at every movement of the leaves, every sound.

29

Union Correspondence

Headquarters, Department of the Missouri

Saint Louis, June 20, 1865

[To:] Major General G. M. Dodge, Commanding Department of
the Missouri

General: I have the honor to report that the expedition which left here on the 20th of May for north Arkansas to parole [accept the surrender of] the command of Brig. General M. Jeff Thompson returned this day. . . . General Thompson met us in the most friendly manner and acted very honorably. The only person that presented himself that we declined to parole was Colonel Tim. Reeves, Fifteenth Missouri Cavalry. He is the officer that ordered the shooting of Major Wilson and six of his men in the fall of 1864, after they had surrendered.

Very respectfully, your obedient servant, C. W. Davis,
Lieutenant Colonel and Assistant Provost-Marshal
—OR, CH. LX, P. 237

Colonel Reeves then led the regiment, those that wished to go, to Jacksonport and surrendered. Union officers were taken aback that 829 officers and 8,782 enlisted men surrendered. . . . Colonel Reeves was the only one that was denied parole. He was held for the murder of Major James Wilson, was taken to St. Louis, but was eventually released and returned to his pre-war occupation as a Baptist preacher.

—FROM *A History of the 15th Missouri Cavalry, CSA*

THE BLOOD DRIED ON HIS HINDQUARTERS, AND OFTEN ADAIR STOPPED to let him eat if he would. Sometimes he stood without grazing, his head bowed as if to some invisible deity and then Adair wrapped her arms around his head and he was content to stand that way for a while. His wound sealed itself with dried blood and pus. There was a swelling as big as her two hands. Once he lay down with a groan, dropping slowly behind and then the forequarters, and she had a hard time getting him to his feet again.

Come on darlin', come on. Get up, come on. And he heaved his head forward and struggled to his feet and they went on.

After two days she heard from a distance the sound of a church bell tolling. From the north, toward Van Buren. It was shortly after noon. The bell clanged its wordless news out into the morning air. It tolled for a long time in a double clang. Perhaps thirty times or more.

THAT DAY ADAIR CAME TO THE LITTLE TOWN CALLED WILDERNESS, WHICH lay at Slayton Ford of White's Creek. It lay ahead of her in a small clearing in the pines. So Adair rode into a town for the first time in two weeks.

There were but five log cabins there and a gristmill on White's Creek, and a long, low tavern made of logs and sealed over with boards of yellow pine. The signboard over the tavern said BEDS, FOOD AND WHISKEY. HYSSOP'S REST. A pole thrust out of the eaves with a lantern hung on it, and at the end of the pole a torn glove pointed toward the west in a ragged, imperative gesture. The little settlement stood low and smoky in the aisles of pine. Thunder was prowling once again at the edge of the western horizon.

Look at you! said Jessie Hyssop. She was standing in the doorway of the tavern. As she came out several reddish orange hens came trundling up and began to peck at her feet. Adair Colley. I thought I might never see you again.

She was as tall and strong as she ever was, with her thick head of medium-brown hair uncovered. She was big in the hips and thighs and had bare feet and had been barefoot all her life from the way they were shaped. Look like you come far, Adair.

I have, said Adair.

And you look sick, Jessie said. Your path has been stormy.

Jessie came out and stood to look at Whiskey. He stood with his left hind leg cocked up, and a stream of pus and clear matter glistened fan-wise down his stifle and on down his tiger-striped leg to his hoof. The flies of Hyssop's Rest came and chattered over the wound and were delighted with it. Adair waved them away.

Somebody shot him, she said. Adair stood under Whiskey's neck and stroked him and felt his warm breath down her back. He might be gut-shot, she said. But he is eating and drinking.

Who shot him?

A Union Militia fellow. He was trying to take him away from me. He shot my other horse and killed her. Then he ran into a deer snare down on Pike Creek.

I never heard you say that. She prodded at the swelling. Where have you been, Adair?

In St. Louis. After I saw you. They sent me up there on the train with all those women they arrested.

They let you go? Jessie turned to look as two of her feist dogs came up to worry the hens.

I never told them nothing, said Adair. I escaped. I put myself into the telegraph line letter by letter and come out at Iron Mountain and was reassembled.

Jesse smiled but didn't say anything. The rain was coming now.

I never told nothing on anybody.

I never said you did. You said that twice now. How long have you been on the road?

Well, I don't know. Maybe three weeks.

President Lincoln has been shot.

Adair stood and stared at her. No! That is hard to believe.

It's true.

Who shot him?

Some crazy man from Virginia. They are going to come down hard on us now. Jessie stepped out of the doorway. Go on in and see if you can find you something to eat. You look poor. I will see if Medical Dick can tend to this horse. Where's your traps?

I lost them. When that militiaman tried to get Whiskey.

You aren't saying much, are you?

There's hardly anything left to say, said Adair. I just ran out of things to say.

ADAIR PICKED UP HER SKIRTS AND WALKED INSIDE THE TAVERN AND STOOD until she could see in the dim interior. There were shelves on the far wall: wooden boxes of biscuit powder, several writing slates, two bottles of pickled vegetables corked and sealed with paraffin, and a stone jar of something. Jerky was strung from the rafters. Bunches of turkey quills stood up like bouquets. They also had three doorknobs for sale and a can of pepper.

Adair walked around the tables and chairs and stood at the counter looking at the maker's labels on the pickles and the can of pepper. They seemed to her very beautiful. The colors were so strong and pure. Great tall women in Greek bedsheets stood in front of rising suns and fields of vegetables. A Turkish pasha smiled from the pepper can.

In the kitchen she found food cooking in the fireplace, crisping itself in a skillet and a kettle, as if it had all set about cooking itself or had been witched into doing so. She sat down and ate. She heard the remote rumbling of thunder and before long the anvil-headed cloud had come toward Wilderness and shut up the sky. The pines bent and whistled in the wind.

Come on out, said Jessie. Come to the barn and help with this horse.

Then the lightning came in sheets and there were no intervals between the flash and the thunder. Adair's horse stood in the log barn with his head down. The chickens hid under the millhouse, darting into a hole beneath the log sills at a place they clearly much frequented.

Medical Dick waited for them in the log barn with a sack full of instruments, which he drew out one by one. A tiny pair of shears for cutting skin and a long bent probe and a rubber bottle.

Well, here's the storm, he said. Adair stood to one side of him. You ain't the fainting kind, are you? Medical Dick wore a hat made of fraying wheat straw that was longer in the back than the front. His beard was striped black and white like a bobcat. He was barefoot. He stuck the curved probe into his leather belt.

Well, it depends, said Adair.

Hold him. Medical Dick took out the shears and put the lower jaw into the bullet hole and sliced through the skin. Whiskey groaned and fell back on his halter rope.

Jessie, said Adair. Don't you know how to cure a wound like this without cutting on him? Her voice was rising. I thought you were a horse witch!

Fresh blood poured out.

I'm a marriage and baby witch, said Jessie. And I make whiskey and I run a tavern.

Why do you have to cut him? said Adair.

Don't be a titty-baby, said Medical Dick. Hold that horse. He took his probe out of his belt and thrust it into the slashed hole. He jammed the probe here and there with great vigor into the muscle and a gout of pus poured out over the probe and over his hand. It dripped into the straw. Whiskey lifted his rear leg high and his hoof trembled the way a human hand would tremble under great pain and weakness.

I feel it, he said. But it's been in there a while and scar tissue is starting to grow around it. He went on jamming the probe into the muscle. I said hang on to that horse.

Adair sat down.

They don't feel pain the way you and I do, said Jessie.

Medical Dick laid the probe down into the straw and took up a pair of long-nosed pincers. He pushed these into the wound and drew out long strings of white tissue.

That there is scar, he said. Grown up around it. He stared at the strings and then threw them down on the floor and drew out more. Adair heard a light click. The ball came out caught in the pincers, trailing red strands. Rain hammered down on the roof and leaked onto the hay above, made a beaded curtain at the window.

There it is, he said. A thirty-two caliber. Anybody want it for a souvenir?

Throw it away, said Adair.

Medical Dick went to a water bucket and filled the rubber bottle with water. He squirted the water up into the wound so that fresh red blood poured out, and bits of flesh and pus. Whiskey's neck was wet with sweat and still he held his trembling leg in the air. The pale gold and gray taffeta colors of his coat seemed dull and lifeless.

He's poor, said the man. Carrying a ball like that will draw you down.

I'll give you fifty pounds of corn if you'll help me out here, said Jessie. At the tavern. While he rests up. You can eat all you like and take on some flesh yourself.

I'll do it, said Adair. Can I feed him now? Before I do the work?

He wants water, said Medical Dick, and Whiskey drank the entire bucket that Adair brought to him, and then half of another. She washed the blood and pus from his leg with a tow sack and stroked his neck and left a pile of corn in front of him. Then finally went back to the tavern to see what work Jessie wanted done.

A GROUP OF SOLDIERS CAME OUT OF THE PINES. THEY WERE A GOOD MANY, fifty or more. Many of them were barefoot and all were stained to the knees with the red dirt of the trace. They wore butternut homespun with hand-embroidered insignia. Some were missing an eye or a hand. There were men with old wounds carrying nothing but a blanket over their shoulders and sometimes sections of rifles. A stock or a barrel or a flintlock mechanism.

They came all the rest of that day, in the rain. Sometimes five or ten in a group. Their beards burst out from under their hats like hair cascades. Sometimes a pair of men possessed a mule or a Chickashaw pony and one of them rode, and some part of the rider would be thick with bandages made of rags, often the rags were wrapped over a stump.

To save her slippers and stockings Adair went barefoot in the tavern to carry food out to those who could afford it and they asked her who she was and what had brought her here. Adair told them of her father but no one had heard anything of him.

More came. Then a group of Union officers going down to oversee the surrender in Jacksonport, Arkansas, rode out of the pines to come to Hyssop's Rest. Adair would not go out to serve them but stayed in the kitchen to tend the fire and bring water. To cut up the hindquarters of pork and beat up the biscuits. She would not sleep in the tavern, either, not in any place, not in the kitchen or the woodshed but went to the barn instead with a wool U.S. Army blanket taken from Jessie's stores and slept in the barn loft over Whiskey's stall. Listened to him grind up the corn in his great molars, got up often to look and see if he were down or still standing on all four feet. For more than a week he stood with his leg drawn up and moved with great difficulty.

Still the men came. They slept in the mill loft or came to sit on their heels in front of the tavern. Many sat under the eaves and watched the rain come down, and some came in and looked at the shelves and said nothing, for they had nothing to spend. They listened to the June rain.

They talked in low voices among themselves and then there was laughter, for they were telling stories. They were making their past lives now into tales, and they were exchanging the tales so they could go and tell not only their own, but also others', and somehow this would make a sort of thin, fragile text or texture that might give way and might not, might hold, might be raveled out and be gone forever.

An old man and an old woman came in to sit uneasily at one of the tables, looking around themselves. They also stared for a long time as the sun came in the open door and drew a luminous band across the things for sale on the shelves, the bright images and maker's labels.

The old man was bald on the crown, and a mane of snow white hair poured down from all around the edges of the bald spot. His tiny old wife sat across from him and stared out of the cave of her coal-shovel bonnet.

They come down here and went to killin' and burnin' to liberate the niggers, the old man said. He held his hat in his lap. He said it to Hyssop's Rest and the mill on Slayton Ford and the town of Wilderness in general. They come down here warrin' and shootin' for four years to liberate fifteen niggers.

More like seventy or so, said the old lady. Better watch what you say or you'll get us in trouble.

They could have bought ever one of them darkies with the money they used up on Parrott shells, said the old man. Or horseshoes. Bought 'em and set 'em free and give 'em silk dresses and a carriage each one. With the money they used up on hardtack. If that isn't the ignorantest damn thing I ever heard of in my life. Fifteen niggers.

Seventy, said the old lady.

If I ever see a nigger again in my life I am going to shoot him. There ought not to be no niggers down here ever again. The sons of bitches draw fire.

Mason, said his wife. Why don't you hesh.

ADAIR LIFTED THE BAGS OF BEANS AND BUSHELS OF TURNIPS. SHE WAS bloodied to the elbows cutting up meat and she walked barefoot in the big kitchen upon discarded turnip tops and spoiled cornbread batter. She cut off the ragged hems of her dress so that the hem came to the middle of her shins and under it she wore a pair of men's long-handled underwear that wadded up and hid her ankles. In the evenings she walked up White's Creek to a pool and washed her hair and her clothes and sat in silence for a long time.

AFTER A WEEK JESSIE SAT DOWN WITH HER IN THE BARN WHERE HER BED was, up in the hayloft.

You have no business getting married, Adair, if in fact you have a fellow in mind, she said. I have heard you coughing in the mornings.

Well, how do you know if I have a fellow in mind or not? asked Adair.

I looked in a pan of water, said Jessie. With the new moon over my left shoulder and all things become clear to me. Now, consumption does not allow of those hopes. I am a marriage and a baby witch, and I have been forced to give this advice before now to young women with consumption. Take Ada Blair for example. She died with her first baby and the baby died too, and it came about that she somehow gave the consumption to her husband and then he up and died.

I know it, said Adair. She began to cry. Well, stop it, she said to herself, and felt around in the hay to see if one of the chickens had laid nearby.

Jessie said, the work is too hard unless you marry a rich man with servants, and there ain't none left around here. Washing and the bread and weaving and scrubbing floors with sand. It's all you can do to help me out here. And you get to quit of an evening. If you're married you can't quit of an evening. You will be up all night with a baby or sewing and repairing things that are broke.

Adair dredged up two brown-speckled eggs out of a nest under a timber. She said, I could do it. There's some people that have lived with consumption.

They'd have to have an awful good husband.

Maybe I could find one.

Well, you can stay here and do what you're able. You can live here. You can read and write and do sums, and you could help me with the accounts.

No, I am going on home here in a little while, as soon as Whiskey can travel. I can't figure very well, and all the people all the time, I would end by becoming a lunatic.

OVER THE NEXT WEEK THE MEN KEPT COMING. IN THE MORNINGS THEY would get up from outside the tavern or wherever they had slept. Forty or fifty or more. They were shouldering their burdens with the ease of long habit. They began to walk off down the roads, each one to take his own way home.

Then one day the men paused in their departure, for up the trail had come a kind of hallooing, that long call that was meant to carry from mountain to mountain.

Colonel Reeves! they called. Reeves! The call echoed from bluffs and from the newly spread plates of green oak leaves, it came up the trail from man to man.

Colonel Reeves!

A party of horsemen bearing a flag came into view. At their head a tall man with a rifle in a scabbard and eyes that shone like bone china. Colonel Reeves rode past on a buttermilk dun, a worn horse with a shock of black mane, at the head of a contingent of officers. They carried, unfurled and lifting slightly in the spring breeze, their State Guard flag, a faded blue silk, and in the middle of it in a battered gold color, the state seal and the growling bears of Missouri. The men lined the road. There was a long silence as Reeves and his officers came down the trail and through Wilderness, past the tavern. As he went past the men's hats came off, one after the other like a line of birds taking flight. They stood holding their rifles or their cut hickory walking sticks, their hats in their hands.

Colonel, they said.

Colonel Reeves gazed out from under his hat brim. It was a cavalry officer's hat pinned up to one side. One boot was kicked out of the stirrup and his uniform was worn through the leather patches at the elbows, the leather hung in little fluttering banners.

Men. Good day, men. God bless you all.

He nodded to each man and looked each man in the eye and then they rode on and the strange flag disappeared into the descending hillside of yellow pine, riding slowly out of the official history of the world.

THE UNION OFFICERS SAT IN THE TAVERN'S SHADE AT WOODEN TABLES and smoked and watched the last ragged soldiers go by. A young officer seemed to be something of a scholar with eyeglasses and a book of reports in which he wrote industriously. He became curious about Adair, even as she hid from them in the kitchen and the barn. The thin girl with remarkable black eyes and her hair so carefully braided in a crown and the rest of her ragged.

She sat in the kitchen reading *Harper's Weekly* with her bare feet up on the table. She was reading about the hanging of the conspirators in Washington. The ones who killed Lincoln. She examined the engraving of the hanging bodies and saw they had tied Mrs. Surratt's skirts around her feet. So that as she strangled she would not kick and show her legs.

Miss? Excuse me.

Adair laid down the *Harper's* and put her feet on the floor. She stood up.

What? she said. What do you want?

I would like to talk to you. He smiled. His eyeglasses shone and his blue uniform was neatly brushed. The smoke of the kitchen fireplace leaked into the air.

Well, I don't want to talk to you, she said.

About rare coins, he said. He followed her out the door. I have heard that many people down here have hoarded coins. I am a coin collector. For instance old shillings.

For instance old shillings, Adair said, and broke into a run for the barn.

And I wanted to get acquainted with you!

She ran up the ladder to the loft. He stood below.

I didn't mean to frighten you! he called.

In the loft, Adair took up her tow sack with the silver dish and brush, candle ends and a rusted ladle and hardtack and her bedroom slippers, her jacket and shawl. She grabbed her blankets and Whiskey's bridle. She hurried ankle deep through the sifting hay and the stripes of sunlight that poured through the cracks. She came down the ladder and did not care if he could see up her skirts. He wanted to ask her about the Union militiaman hanging by one leg in a deer snare. And then she would be in prison again until she was led out to the noose and had her skirts tied around her ankles.

The young officer in blue stood back with his hands at his sides, long, thin hands and his hair brown and curling. His eyebrows were wrinkled up in the middle.

This is very distressing, he said. I can't imagine what I've said to cause this commotion.

What? said Adair. I'm deaf. I can't hear good. She put the bit in Whiskey's mouth and the crownpiece over his ears.

Miss! he shouted. *I would be glad to lend you a later edition of Harper's!! I have the latest one!!*

I don't believe I will! Adair shouted back. *I already ate!*

She led Whiskey out of the barn at a run and led him to the tavern steps. She jumped on his glossy back astride, barefoot. Several of the Union officers got up from their tables and Jessie came out of the kitchen.

Adair kicked Whiskey and he went trotting out of Wilderness, his limp gone at the thought of being on the road again, through a flock of chickens, down to the ford. The mill wheel covered the noise of the shouting behind her. She splashed past several women washing their dishes and Whiskey stepped on a tin plate and crushed it into the gravel.

Around the first bend they settled into a walk and Adair rode on to the crossing of the Current, and then to Beaverdam Creek. It was a good clear day and the way lay open before her.

"Glorious cause." "Lives sacrificed on the country's altar." "Hearts bleeding for the country's welfare." Some modern readers of these (Civil War soldiers') letters may feel they are drowning in bathos. We do not speak or write like that anymore. World War I, as Ernest Hemingway and Paul Fussell have noted, made such words as glory, honor, courage, sacrifice, valor *and* sacred *vaguely embarrassing if not mock-heroic. But these soldiers, at some level at least, meant what they said about sacrificing their lives for their country.*

Our cynicism about the genuineness of such sentiments is more our problem than theirs, a cultural/temporal barrier we must transcend if we are to understand why they fought. And how smugly can we sneer at their expressions of a willingness to die for their beliefs when we know they did precisely that?

—FROM *For Cause and Comrades: Why Men Fought in the Civil War*,
BY JAMES M. MCPHERSON, OXFORD UNIVERSITY PRESS, NEW YORK, 1997

THE FERRYMAN HAD A PET RACCOON ON A CHAIN, AND THE CHAIN HAD bells on it, so the creature was tortured both day and night with the sound of its own movements. The raccoon stared at Will Neumann briefly out of its mask, its demented small eyes, and then went back to fingering through its tail for fleas.

Will Neumann stood down off his bay horse and walked down the

earthen slope to the ferry landing. They stood there on the Kentucky
shore, and behind them a cornfield's long leaves hacked gently at the
July air. He had turned the sign over on its swinging pivot bar, from
NOBODY HERE to the other side: COME AND GET ME. And after a while
the ferryman on the Missouri shore put down his pipe and began to
crank the ferryboat across on its cable.

Neumann led the bay onto the planking. The big horse came reluctantly, with timorous steps, as if expecting the decking to give way any
moment. Neumann tied him to the railing. He reached up and read-
justed the haversack tied behind the saddle, the enormous striped
umbrella he had acquired in a rainstorm in Natchez, and the saddlebags. The long-nosed revolver in its pommel holster. Neumann's nails
were black with campfire ashes, and so was the bandage on his left
hand.

Where you coming from? the ferryman asked. He had tied a ban-
danna over his long light brown hair, close down over his eyes. His
beard jumped when he talked. He wore trousers of reddish homespun,
high in the waist, with a broad waistband, held up by one gallus. His
riverman's shirt had bloused sleeves and he was barefoot. The ferryman
shoved off with a pole and grasped the cable. The sun flashed up from
the sliding flat plates of brown water in wavering planes across his face.
His big, prehensile toes gripped at the boards.

I'm coming from Mobile, said Neumann.

You're a Yankee officer, said the ferryman. Discharged.

Yes.

What are you coming down here for?

The ferryman stared out over the water. Neumann stood with his
legs apart and his back to the rail, one elbow on the railing and the
other with a thumb hooked into his front pocket. It was noisy now with
the wind and the water splashing. The ferryman pulled heartily on the
cable crank. Neumann declined to help him. It was too close to the
water and Neumann knew the ferryman could tip him into the river in
a moment.

I'm looking for somebody.

Now they's the Union over there, said the ferryman. On the far side. Just your kind of people. He jerked his chin toward the ferry landing on the Missouri side where a group of Union soldiers sat and smoked and watched the ferry cross.

All right, said Neumann. They may or may not be my kind of people.

I killed as many of you sons of bitches as I could, the ferryman said. They's just so damn many of you.

We breed like rabbits, said Neumann. Who were you with?

Seventh Missouri, CSA, said the ferryman. Then we got so shot up they put me in with a bunch of Texans. Terry's Eighth Texas.

Neumann braced his feet and rode on the taupe silk sheets of the Mississippi. He watched the ferryman's hard hands on the cable crank and saw no weapon about the man. The world was in truth made of jackstraws. The world was very combustible, the human body was partible in ways heretofore unimagined. What held the civilized world together was the thinnest tissue of nothing but human will. Civilization was not in the natural order but was some sort of willed invention held taut like a fabric or a sail against the chaos of the winds. And why we had invented it, or how we knew to invent it, was beyond him.

Neumann had seen some truth that was completely out of his power to put into words. But he had come away knowing that even though the world of civilization was made of straw and lantern slides, he must live in it as if it were solid. Even when the heat of the lantern itself burnt away the illusions and a black hole appeared in the middle of the slide.

He looked upriver at the immense road of water that flowed from the heart of the nation, down from St. Louis and the northern cities, carrying in its bloodstream the silt and alluvial sands from the Missouri River, which poured out the rich gifts of the plains.

The baking wind tore at his hat and he held it by the brim with one hand. It relieved him to look at it, for the great river was like a long tale, of both great joy and great woe. And it seemed to be a story road that a person could take, and it would take him to some place where he could free his mind. Men had striven against one another to control the unreeling river-road, battling at New Madrid and Island Number Ten, at Baton Rouge and Vicksburg, in the heat of the summer and the humid, choking air of the malarial swamps. But the river carried away men and guns and the garbage of war, covering it over, washing itself clean again as if they had never been. Neumann turned his face toward Missouri.

From the approaching shore he heard strains of music. At this crossing, the west shore was the low side, a swamp, except for the small rise where the Union soldiers were encamped. He heard a fiddle, a pennywhistle. He could see the group of Union men sitting around the ferry landing. The ferry creaked as it slid on the glassy surface of the river. His horse shifted and rebalanced himself, and the far shore drew nearer and nearer.

He saw the smoke of a breakfast fire in the early-morning dimness. The smoke slid in evaporating planes into the uncut forest and wetlands around. The fiddler was playing "Caragan Goalach," slow and sad. The pennywhistle punctuated its long lament with bright trills, and Neumann could hear one of the soldiers in blue singing with it, singing in the Irish tongue.

THEY APPROACHED WITH A SMOOTH, DREAMLIKE MOTION ACROSS THE water. The odd Celtic melody lifted his spirits, and just as they docked he could see the men wore Union Militia badges.

The bay horse bolted down the gangway planks for solid land in a brief thunder, and then stood nodding at other horses tied back in the trees. The fiddler spat and turned to see who had arrived, and a redheaded captain stood up.

They came walking toward him through clouds of mosquitoes. The bearded fiddler called out,

And what delight he takes in his umbrella! His hand is on fire and the cooling rains have not put it out yea though it rain forty days and forty nights.

He ain't right in the head, said the boy sitting at the fire. The boy was hatless, in a blue uniform coat. He put the pennywhistle to his lips and blew spit out of it.

Who are you? The captain stared at Neumann. Got your discharge papers? Furlough?

Who are you? asked Neumann. The war's over.

I am Captain Tom Poth of the Union Militia.

Neumann stared for a long moment at Captain Tom Poth. The other men, in decayed blue uniforms, stood around the fire with tin cups in their hands. Their insignia were frayed, their weapons muddied. Then he remembered the man's name. He and his men had burnt down the Colley farm and had taken the judge, had sent Adair and her sisters wandering down the roads of the world.

Neumann knew there was nothing at this point that he could reasonably do. He turned to the captain. The ground they stood on was squelching.

Why do you want to know? he asked.

These southeast counties are under military rule, said Poth. Martial law. I've got the right and the duty to call to account ever wanderer and sojourner that comes passing into here. He squinted at Neumann and lit a cigar. The Constitution is suspended down here for a couple of years until we get things squared away.

It is, said Neumann. That's an interesting state of affairs.

And I am empowered to ask for your papers, sir, and I'll have them now.

Neumann reached into his saddlebags and drew out a leather folder, took out his furlough and handed it to the captain.

You are this Major William Neumann?

One and the same, said Neumann. Shortly to be discharged.

That so. The captain puffed on the cigar and then said, You a Baptist? and held out another cigar.

No, said Neumann. I'll smoke the damn thing. He took the cigar and put it in his pocket. Where'd you get this tobacco?

The captain ignored Neumann and turned to the men around the fire and said, He ain't no Rebel. He doesn't talk like one.

Neumann said, What if I were?

I don't guess you'd get through that swamp, the captain said. There was four men yesterday who didn't make it. Wasn't there, boys? A merry band of Rebels coming home to make trouble, but they will make trouble no more.

The men at the fire turned back to regard the flames with long, interested stares, and were silent.

What are you carrying in that saddlebag? And the haversack? Is that government property?

It's my property, said Neumann. He turned his back to Poth and threw the stirrup over the seat with his right hand, took up the billets and began to tighten the saddle girth as best he could one-handed.

I could look in them if I wanted, said Poth. We're under martial law here. We can look in anything and go in anybody's house.

But you don't want to, said Neumann. Do you?

What's in them?

Look out, Captain, he'll beat you over the head with that umbrella, said one of the soldiers at the fire. The fiddler started in on "Soldier's Joy." A young corporal complained, I can't sing that. They ain't no words to that.

The fiddler said, Yes there is, they are round ones though, like the bitter fruit of the Osage orange and they come to me when I am in the mountains and have no noise of my own.

The fiddler ain't right in the head, the boy said to Neumann.

Neumann mounted up.

I ain't give you permission to go, Poth said. State your destination.

Don't fool with me, said Neumann. He pressed his boot heels to the horse and they started down the sloshing trail into the wetlands.

It had been a hot, dry summer and the Great East Swamp was not as wet as it was at other times, and here and there dry ground stood up out of the water. Back in among the boles of the great trees the occasional white face of a swamp flower shone, big as a cabbage, in standing pools. From across the river the raccoon chittered in a long, lonesome trill, calling out to others of his kind, and was answered from somewhere in the trees of the Missouri side. Neumann listened. The thought occurred to him that the calls could be men signaling one another in the dim shades. It could be anything.

His horse wavered on into the hundreds of square miles of wetland, into the nation of mosquitoes and rare, damp flowers. The boles of the immense trees standing away like the arches of a cathedral. Neumann was sweaty and dirty, his horse's hooves sucked holes in the mud and water. He leaned forward on the split pommel of the saddle. He took out his penknife and cut the end from the cigar. He lit it with a phosphorus match, dropped the smoking match into the water. He puffed on the cigar and waved it to keep the mosquitoes away. He made himself use his injured hand in spite of the pain.

He went on for another mile or so. Enough to smoke half the cigar. Neumann rode the bay up to the bole of a water oak and pressed the glowing ash from the end of the cigar, to save it. Then he rode on for a while, leaning forward over the horse's shoulders to try and see what it was they were stepping into.

He put the cigar butt in his jacket pocket.

All morning he threaded his way through the swamplands, guessing where the high ground lay beneath several inches of water. They splashed on through and listened to the sounds of bitterns laughing, something unseen hurrying away. Neumann lifted his hat from his head and ran his clawed fingers through his hair. His left hand throbbed.

Then he pulled up the bay horse to listen.

For the last half hour he had heard a distant steady splashing, drawing closer and closer.

Neumann took out the half cigar and lit up the cigar stub again, squirting out fumes, tipping his head back.

He turned, and through the trees he saw Captain Tom Poth come riding. Neumann reached behind himself and worried the umbrella loose from its ties. He laid it across his lap.

Poth came up to Neumann, weaving through the dark water on a jittery, nervous sorrel horse. He was smiling. There was a long roll of rope tied to a saddle ring behind the cantle and he was carrying in one hand, loose in his lap, a government issue revolver. Hanging from his belt was a pair of manacles. They jingled. His face wavered through the shadows of the vast trees, grinning.

I'm empowered to look in them saddlebags, he said.

Don't they pay you people? said Neumann. That you have to make your living by robbing? The damp air closed around Neumann's chest like a vise and he wondered if he should shoot Poth's horse now. Do something now. He was so close to finding Adair and was so weary of dead men.

He said, I'm tired of the war, Captain Poth. Let's see if we can come to some kind of an agreement here.

Tom Poth had taken off his coat in the heat, and had tied it in a bundle behind the saddle. He was wearing a nonregulation checkered shirt of green and blue linen homespun. His hands were hairy with red hairs and his nails were black. His face was freckled and running with sweat. The sorrel he was riding jittered and stamped, afraid of the swamp and the standing water. He started to lift the revolver.

Neumann didn't want to shoot. They would hear it back at the ferry landing.

There's nothing in my saddlebags you want, Neumann said. But now, we could trade horses.

Trade horses?

Yes, look here. There's money in this for both of us. Poth frowned and stared at him with small eyes. Neumann leaned down and grasped Poth's looped reins. Poth reached down to stop him but all he got was a slash across the back of his hand and a line of blood sprang up and began to run. Neumann whipped his penknife through the reins, and then jammed the smoking cigar up the sorrel's nostril.

Poth was lifting the revolver and Neumann opened the umbrella. The great fan of the umbrella, blossoming up out of nowhere, and the cigar up his nose, turned the sorrel to a lunatic. He reared up so high he nearly went over backward and Tom Poth's shot roared upward into the trees.

The sorrel gelding then squatted down on its haunches and sprang forward in a leap that was a perfect arch, and when he hit the water he was running. He was throwing his head from one side to another and so could not see where he was going.

The horse's cut reins were flying and sheets of water flew up from its hooves like fans, ropy with duckweed and stems. Tom Poth clung to the saddle pommel with both hands. *You son of a whore!!* he screamed.

Neumann sat and watched as the horse bolted onto what seemed to be higher ground and crashed against a water oak, slamming Poth bodily against the bole of the tree so hard his head flew back. Somewhere in all the turmoil Poth got off another shot but it too went wild and the thick puff of smoke lifted slowly. The horse charged on with Poth reeling and slopping side to side in the saddle, and then they disappeared.

Neumann sat and listened to the fainter and fainter sounds of hooves splashing, it sounded like a fulling mill. Then he couldn't hear anything but tree frogs.

Neumann quieted himself. He bent down to look at his revolver in the pommel holster and took a series of long breaths. After a while he rode on.

He followed the trail torn through the wetlands, for the sorrel horse seemed to know his way; he was going somewhere. Maybe he had been stolen from the people of the Ozarks and was heading home, back to the mountains and the high country. The horse had found one of the ridges, one of those snaking, meandering dykes of land a foot or so higher than the surrounding swamp, and was following it, and so Neumann and the bay horse followed it too. The wavering path he had slashed through was even now closing up again. The dark, four-inch-deep water was quieting now into stillness, the trefoil surface plant sliding back in, the wetland saw grasses springing upright. In the distance Neumann heard the clattering noise of a flight of ducks taking to the air. It told him that Poth was still on ahead.

The ripped trail of his horse was marked with things: Poth's hat, the pieces of leather reins, torn brush.

Overhead in the canopy of vines rare swampland birds sang and fought and announced the presence of human beings. The splash of the bay horse's hooves sprayed mud and water, and made it hard to hear anything, but occasionally he stopped to listen. There was the cry of a bittern, and then a slow whap-whap-whap as off in the trees a blue heron rose on its pipestem legs and beat its way upward with immense wings. After half an hour Neumann began to hear something like a tuneless singing up ahead.

As he drew nearer, Neumann knew it was a moaning sound. *Ohhhhhh*, the voice said. *Ohhhh God. Help me.* He heard the snorts of a frightened horse.

He stopped his horse again to listen, looking with a deep predator's intent through the trees, his hand closing on the revolver's grip.

Ohhh stop. Whoa fellow. Oh stop. Stop.

He splashed on and then ahead between the tree boles he saw a long deep light. A reflection. In the strange geography of the swamps there was a sort of lake, and the cypresses had sent up their conical root structures into the air, two feet tall, cypress knees. In among them was the sorrel horse with the U.S. saddle and bridle. He was leaning and pulling, for his stirrup seemed to be hung up. Sunlight fell from overhead in brilliant drapes of light, illuminating the shining sorrel hide in spots, and then a boot, and a leg in Federal blue hung up in the irons, stretched out long.

Tom Poth lay with his head caught firmly between two cypress knees, his face barely above water, calling out to Neumann. The horse had thrown him at some point, and his foot had gone through the stirrup iron, and the sorrel had dragged him pell mell through the runneling dark waters and weeds, and then Poth's head had caught up between two cypress knees as if the wetlands itself had taken him in hand.

Neumann came up and got off his horse, dropped into the ankle-deep water and felt roots crush beneath his boots. He walked through the sloshing water. Looked down at Tom Poth.

The Militia captain's head was firmly jammed between two large knees. His ears were nearly torn loose and blood was staining the water around his head. He gripped a tall cypress knee with one hand and the other, probably broken, dangled uselessly in the water. The pistol had twisted over onto his belly in its long-nosed holster and it was half under water, and so the powder would be useless. The horse was stomping as if he would stave holes in the water. He fought to be loose of this confusion.

Help me! Poth screamed.

Look at this, said Neumann. He stood there with his hands touching a cypress knee, amazed at the entanglement the man had got himself into. I'll be damned.

Help me, said Poth. He looked up helplessly, his eyes dark with mud.

In hell, said Neumann. I would help you on your way to hell.

Neumann sloshed over to the straining horse.

Don't scare him, said Poth. His voice was suddenly calm. I'm about killed. He's tearin' my head off.

Neumann turned and smiled down at the man. I could whip the horse, he said. It would likely pull your head off.

Before God, gasped Poth, from down in the mud. I am about to die.

Neumann patted the horse on the chest, between the front legs, and then on the neck, and the sorrel quieted a little. He slogged around to the far side, looking at Poth over the seat of the saddle. He took the Federal blue coat from the saddle strings.

Then he looked in the saddlebags and there he found an account book. He opened the pages with muddied, damp hands. It was in a dark red leather. Inside was written, Marquis L. Colley, Justice of the Peace, Jackson Township, Ripley County, Missouri. There were dark stains of old blood on it.

Look at this. What have you got here?

That's from some rich fellow, said Poth. He's got his money in a Cape Girardeau bank and I aim to confiscate it. I can do that kind of thing. Martial law. I'll give you it, I'll give you all of it, look there, he had thousands of dollars. I think there's more than two thousand dollars.

Where is Marquis Colley? Neumann's hat was pulled tight over his forehead. Where is Judge Marquis Colley? He turned cold eyes on Poth, it was as if the blood within him had turned cold and so he became slow and deliberate in his speech.

Cut me loose, said Poth.

Neumann stared at Poth for a long moment. Where is he?

I let the boys have him, said Poth. I never did nothing to him. The boys wanted him, before God, I never did a thing to him. I swear, he could be free somewhere.

His leg was stretched out in the stirrup iron and it seemed the iron was cutting through his boot, his foot was badly twisted, maybe the ankle was broken. Neumann stepped a muddy boot on Poth's throat.

I will drown you, he said. Where is he?

The boys! he screamed. The boys took him, it wasn't me! They was mad about something before the war! The boys shot him!

The leeches were already nestling into his neck, like gray kisses.

No they didn't. A raccoon chittered in a long purring stutter from a tree and wavy lines in the pool marked where cottonmouths spun off into their holes.

All right, I shot him, I shot him. Now look, look, that two thousand dollars is easy got, said Poth. He lifted both hands to the cypress knees and fought to get his head out of the crotch. I can show you where they lived.

Where is he?

You get me loose, Major, I'll take you there.

Neumann looked down at Poth and knew that Poth would never take him to Marquis Colley's grave. Nor could he force him to. As soon as they got out of the swamps they would be back in the hands of the Militia and under martial law.

Neumann took his revolver out of the holster on his saddle, and then searched through Poth's saddlebags where he found a box of ammunition. He worried it out between his bad hand and his good one.

Oh yes, you can have that ammunition, said Poth, and the horse too, the horse too. Just cut me loose.

Shut up. The watery and hollow silence of the wetlands closed around them. Neumann felt the strange glacial surge in himself that he did before a battle. He sat and watched as Poth sank lower and lower into the water. Listened to him beg. The horse started forward again and again.

Finally Neumann heard Poth's neck snap. He looked down into Poth's eyes. His hands had fallen each to one side in the tea-colored water.

No use now, said Neumann. You're paralyzed. Your neck's broken.

I could still live, said Poth in a small voice. I could still get along.

Neumann watched as the face sank below the water and its eyes began to bulge like eggs with white all around them, and he waited until all was still, and then he turned the sorrel loose. He got on his horse and rode away.

AFTER A WHILE HE CAME TO A PLANK ROAD RAISED A FEW INCHES ABOVE the water. It sank and wavered under the weight of the bay horse. It sloshed as he drummed along. The sycamores and cottonwoods now turned bright green, scattering leaves like largess, like green shillings. The willow oaks spilled off tumbles of grapevines weighed down by emerald unripe grapes. There were flocks of red-beaked Cumberland paroquets that made noises like doors being broken open by burglars. In their thousands they launched into the upper canopy and they all cried out together with a noise like nails being torn out of wood.

He rode on mile after mile into the dim golden sunset light. The low land was juicy with water. His horse sounded like a drum orchestra on the plank road. Neumann knew he would not hear horses if they were to come up riding behind them at a distance. And so long into the night he went on.

31

The people of the southern highlands would become famous in the nineteenth century for the intensity of their xenophobia, and also for the violence of its expression. In the early nineteenth century, they tended to detest great planters and abolitionists in equal measure. During the Civil War some fought against both sides. In our own time they are furiously hostile to both communists and capitalists. The people of the southern highlands have been remarkably even-handed in their antipathies—which they have applied to all strangers without regard to race, religion or nationality.

—FROM *Albion's Seed*, BY DAVID HACKETT FISCHER, OXFORD UNIVERSITY PRESS, NEW YORK, 1989

Other travelers have recorded descriptions of solitary old women who wandered alone through the American backcountry. . . . Rhoda Barker remembered an aged female named Mary Pitcher. "I have heard my mother describe her as wandering through the woods leading an old horse, her only property her knitting in her hand, and her dress mostly sheepskin."

—RHODA BARKER JOURNAL, MANUSCRIPT, HISTORICAL SOCIETY OF PENNSYLVANIA, QUOTED IN *Albion's Seed*

I remember as a little girl we always used to go and decorate those graves on Decoration Day. It was our Baptist Church over there, and people around this neighborhood. We would take a picnic lunch and go and pull weeds and whatever needed doing. Now at that time you could see the Union graves on the other side of the road clearer. We took care of them like the others. I guess they

were just put up at the time when they had that battle with whatever people
had; just rocks. Just piled up those stone slabs. That was all they had.

—INTERVIEW BY THE AUTHOR WITH MRS. ALBERT SISK,

BEAVERDAM CREEK, RIPLEY COUNTY

Life is like a mountain railroad
with an engineer that's brave
He will keep and he will guide you
from the cradle to the grave
Watch the curves, the fills, the tunnels
never falter, never fail
Keep your hand upon the throttle
and your eyes upon the rail

—TRADITIONAL MOUNTAIN HYMN

ADAIR CAME AT LAST TO THE HEIGHT OF LAND BETWEEN THE CURRENT and the Little Black Rivers. She came to the Military Road and took it toward her home. Whiskey walked along with a halting step, for she had run him too hard on his injured leg, but after a while his ears came up and he looked about himself eagerly. Soon they came to Ponder's Steam Mill and Store on the Little Black. The wheel was still and the pond undisturbed and the stone house on the hillside empty. There was no one there and so she went on.

She passed the Military Graveyard where they had buried the soldiers in blue and gray on opposite sides of the road, their graves outlined in limestone sills with stones raised up over them like ancient monuments from some distant age. She rode past their nameless gravestones. Confederate and Union alike.

Up the Devil's Backbone and past her mother's grave. Whiskey called out and tested the air with his nose. He lashed his tail and did not regard his injured leg but began to dance around in the road.

From the clear space on Copperhead, Adair saw that the house was still standing. She saw a buckboard at the rails in front of the house and it was painted a rusty, fading red with indecipherable lettering. Smoke boiled out of the chimneys and human voices called to each other from room to room of the house in careless ease. She sat on Whiskey for a long time listening and watching; a man's voice was singing lines of song. The trumpet vine devoured the veranda and it had blossomed out, and blankets hung out the windows to air from the second-story windows.

She crossed Beaverdam at the rocky ford and continued on past the Shawnee Oak. She tied Whiskey to the rails beside the buckboard. Watching cautiously. The cat Lucy ran along the veranda roof and then sat in the trumpet vines to stare down at Adair.

Daddy? she called. Papa! John Lee!

Adair dropped her tow sack and walked up the steps. In the doorway to all she had known of home, stood a man in a yellow vest. He smiled at her from under a silk top hat much the worse for wear. He carried a carbide lamp in one hand and a screwdriver in the other.

Well! he said. Ha! Well! And who might you be?

This is my house, said Adair.

Your house?

Where is my father? Marquis Colley. And for a moment Adair thought he still might have come home and that he might be behind the house digging in the heap of burnt barn timbers or just about to whistle something or on his hands and knees looking under the bed for his glasses.

Why no, said the man. He took off the silk hat and put it on again. Why, a ha, no, this place was abandoned. The abode of the owl and the wood mouse. Clean empty.

Adair walked straight at him and he turned quickly out of her way. She walked into the hall and then into the drawing room and saw painted stiff muslin on lath forms laid over the chairs which were still marked with charring. She came upon a triangular piece of her face in a fragment of the Tennessee mirror that remained in the ornate frame. The china cabinet had been righted and the shattered china swept up.

She opened her mother's old clothes trunk and saw there were still things inside but not much, and she let the lid fall shut. *The Horse Fair* hung askew in its frame, rippled with damp. *Holland's Pictorial History of the World* and two volumes of Dickens and all her father's law books lay jumbled in a corner.

Adair turned and pushed past a woman who wore a frilled pink dress, to her father's bedroom.

Those were our dresses, she said. My and my sisters' dresses. These people had cut up what dresses the girls had left behind and had sewn the pieces together for a coverlid over her father's blankets.

She walked out to the back where the heaped black sticks of the burnt barn were now grown over with milkweed and purslane. There at the hog pen rails Adair saw a young pig in a pink-and-blue-checkered skirt. It was walking toward her with expectant, begging grunts. The skirt flounced over its pink behind.

Get away! she shouted, and turned into the house again. She went on to the kitchen and saw all the blackware in use, the kettle hissing with its iron lips pursed and some of her mother's dishes stacked up in the dishpan.

You all get out, said Adair. She turned on the green brocade slippers and jerked her hair out of her eyes. I don't know who you are. Pack up all your stuff and get out.

It was entirely abandoned, said the man.

A young woman with a baby on her hip walked in. She said, There wasn't nobody here and hadn't been for a long time.

I'll go to the law, said Adair. If you all are not out of here by tonight.

You better tell her, Mr. Walker, said the woman in pink.

You'd better do some good telling, said Adair. Tell me what?

Miss, it's been, a ha, sold, said the man.

No it hasn't, said Adair. None of us sold anything. You show me where it's been sold.

Well, we didn't buy it either, said the woman. It ain't ours, either. She sat down on one of the Colley kitchen chairs and her idiotic pink dress like a hot-air balloon surged around her. The frills had been made by folding squares of white muslin and cutting diamonds and tri-angles in them, the way children make snowflakes of sheets of paper.

Of course it's not yours, it's ours, said Adair. She coughed into her hand and cleared her throat.

It belongs to the Vandivers now, said the man. They bought it for taxes. There hadn't been no taxes paid for three years and nobody here for half a year. He waved his hand around the kitchen as if to the entire place. They declared Marquis Colley deceased and his heirs not to be found.

But I am found, said Adair. I've come home.

But it's sold already.

Adair stood stubbornly and crossed her thin arms. Stood in the middle of the kitchen floor. She heard the minute thumping of Lucy running across the kitchen roof and knew that she would come down by the peach tree outside the west window.

I'm Jeth Walker, the man said. My wife, Sarah, and our daughter Pru Lester and baby Jim. I sure am sorry about this, Miss.

But there was nobody to pay taxes *to*, said Adair. For three years. They burnt the courthouse.

And what is your name, Miss? He bowed and put the hat on and took it off again.

Adair Randolph Colley. She turned to the fire and stared at it, bit her knuckle.

Well, they got a new courthouse a-building now. Go see for yourself.

Who is at the courthouse?

Well, a ha, the Union Militia. The man danced from one foot to the other. This part of the country is under martial law for the next two years. They run the courthouse.

Adair didn't say anything for a while. She sat down and regarded her feet in the stolen green brocade bedroom slippers.

Can I get you a cup of coffee? The woman in pink took up a blue spongewear cup.

Yes, said Adair. She put her feet on the broad hearthstones in the kitchen fireplace. Laid one after the other in a bed of sand by her father and John Lee and Speece Newnan when she was ten.

Well, I've got to get it back, she said. There has got to be a way they made a mistake. They can't have sold it. We have twelve hundred acres here.

The Walker family stood in silence and waited for whatever else she would say.

Adair stood up again and with a yearning, lonely gesture ran her hand down the fireplace stones, the faces that lived in the stone. There were seashells in it and on the bottom stone a fern leaf. She said, How much were the taxes?

Jeth Walker took his silk hat off again and turned it around in his hands and then drummed his fingers on the top. Outside the lazy July day was swagged with orange daylilies and leaf shadows.

The Vandivers went and paid the taxes is what they, a ha, say, he said. And they paid for Coleman as an administrator of the deceased's estate in probate and so on is what they said. The Vandivers said we could tarry here awhile to rehearse our performances before we went on, since the place was abandoned.

Who in the Militia is at the courthouse? Adair got up again and clutched her hands together. She did not know what to do with herself. Is it that Captain Poth? Tom Poth?

No, him, ha, I heard he was drowned in the Great East Swamp, no, him, we had him up in Wayne County same as here. It's Garner, about just as bad, Lieutenant Garner, the one that killed the Parmalee boys and the Goforths and them back in '63.

Adair thought for a while and watched the turnips boiling in the pot. Well, there is no use of me going to the courthouse, I guess. I'm not even of age. She turned the colander over in her hands and the carved meat fork and the big sycamore-wood ladle. Found her name carved in the kitchen windowsill.

We lost our place too, said Sarah Walker.

Adair sat down again and then got up and went into her father's bedroom. On the floor beside the bed she found the leather case that had held his folding magnifying glass and held it in her hand in a tight grip. Then she went up the Daughter Stairs to the girls' room. That young woman Pru and her baby, Jim, were evidently nesting up here, she thought, and despised the sight of a stack of folded diapers in her linen basket and a nursing corset that laced up the front draped over a chair and some sort of blue bodice with spangles.

She put her hand on the homespun blanket spread over her own bed where it was drawn up against the window, where she used to sleep to be by the open air and to be able to see out, to watch the moon rise over Copperhead and pass the squares of the windowpane over her bed both summer and winter, as if the rectangles of moonlight were rare white pages of books written by nocturnal magic, containing stories of great mystery. Adair sat on the bed and gazed out the window to the open prairies on Copperhead's crown, at the tangle of black timbers that had been the barn.

She sat on the bed in silence. Away from the crazy people downstairs. On those nights she had thought of herself as a person that wonderful things would happen to because she was uncommon and marked apart. That a clear light burned inside her that nothing could extinguish and it would always illuminate her way. That then before the war she had held this light between her hands as she had taken the candle out to see Whiskey led in through the snow. And that no wind would ever put it out. It seemed to her that at that time she had been a very pure person and had not wanted anybody to die nor led anyone to their death, nor had she stolen anything or lied or hated as she had hated. But now her name was written in the Book of Dirt.

Adair took up the homespun blanket between her fingers for its familiar touch and found the place where the ocher yarn had been woven in instead of green because they had run out of green. She knew there were many others also who had hoarded their light against all trouble and all assault and had gone down into darkness as well, without a word spoken and their names were known to no one. You would think this could not be true but it was.

She went back down to the kitchen.

Well, was that your room? asked Pru Lester. She jumped baby Jim up and down on her hip.

Yes, said Adair. Me and my sisters. But I guess it's not now. She drank the last of the coffee from the blue spongewear cup that she had used for many years and put it back in the dishpan. The only way ever to get it back is to find my father, but I have come to believe he is no longer alive. She rinsed the cup. And at the courthouse they don't think so either. And of all people they would know.

Well, I'm sorry, said Jeth Walker.

We lost people too, said the woman. Everybody has suffered.

Adair pressed her hair back from her face. She went to the veranda to look at Whiskey and for the view from there. Then she turned and regarded Copperhead Mountain and the Devil's Backbone. Now their land was gone, and somebody else would gain their living here. Adair walked down the veranda from one end to the other, her head in her hands. Finally she picked up her tow sack and went back to the kitchen.

Well, she said. I came traveling a long way thinking I was coming home. But I could have just stopped off anywhere.

They were all respectfully silent, as if at the scene of a fatal accident, and watched her walk from room to room and back again, not able to go or to stay. She went again to the back kitchen door.

Go on to the courthouse, said Jeth Walker. He held his silk top hat in front of him like a stubby toy cannon. You'll never feel right about it until you see for yourself.

Not with the Union Militia there, she said. They would find something against me.

You can come with us, he said. We're, a ha, going on the road. We lost our tavern there at Greenville to taxes same as you.

We had performances and music there for fifteen years before we lost it, said Sarah.

And so we're just getting up a traveling show. I taught that pig to dance and I do Master of Ceremonies.

Adair said, That pig dances?

Ain't that skirt cute? Sarah said. I made it myself out of a tablecloth I found just lying around. And Pru sings.

The young woman said, I'm the one who sings the last song about "comin through the rye" in a kilt. It's real short. I wear silk tights and lace-ups. You just do what you have to do. We don't pretend to be quality.

Adair watched the pig in the tablecloth skirt come to the back kitchen door and stand on the sill stone. It waved its snout in the air.

Watch this, said Jeth Walker. He began to whistle "Arkansas Traveler." The pig stood up on its hind legs and shuffled uneasily toward them. It made pig noises and the skirt dangled around its hooves. Jeth Walker put on the top hat and did a few dance steps himself. Now, we are doing a short excerpt from a play as well, so that we have cultured and refined things as well as mere sensations for the masses. We do short scenes from *The Hermit of Gervais*.

I never saw it, said Adair. Performances always made my hair stand on end on the back of my neck. I get too excited and I end up crying.

You could come along, said Sarah.

Yes, you could be in it. The young woman gave baby Jim a handful of cooled boiled turnip. We all have misery to face up to, girl. I lost my husband in Price's raid and here I am with the baby and everything. So you just got to get along how you can.

She could be the Saucy Girl, said Jeth. You see, there has to be the Aristocratic Girl that he marries, and then the servant is the Saucy Girl, and she says smart and impertinent things.

Pru Lester said, then the Aristocratic Girl, she isn't saucy. She's easy to do. She never does anything, she's just real refined and snooty. I'm her because I don't have time to learn scripts because of the baby. All I have to do is say Brigit I Want You and Oh Help Me, Sir and Please Don't Cut My Hand Off and such as that. Please Don't do whatever they are doing.

There's not much other way to get your living here, said Sarah. People losing their land to taxes and you couldn't have done much here alone anyway.

I couldn't go onstage. I get too agitated, said Adair. What do you do? Adair turned to Sarah and made herself smile.

Oh, I'm a guard and a messenger and I play guitar, and make cos-tumes and scenery. I get to wear britches a lot. I find them handy.

Can you sing? Jeth asked Adair.

Well, I used to, but anymore I start crying. I don't know what's wrong with me.

The young woman handed baby Jim to Sarah and sized up Adair with a measuring stare.

Well, she could let her hair down and stand in front of the Noble Ruins and sing Oh Frail Lamp of Love Extinguished and cry. She would do very well.

Her eyes, said Sarah. They're so black, they would show up well onstage.

No, she couldn't stand up to it, said Jeth. The people adoring her the way they do with the Saucy Girl. And us traveling to the cities, Pocahontas and Poplar Bluff and Cape on the steamboats.

Sarah Walker nodded. Regretfully. And the Saucy Girl lines are hard because they're so smart, they get the best laughs. People scream.

Adair let all this fall into silence as a fire dies down.

I better go on, she said. I might come upon some news of what hap-pened to my father one of these days. She took herself in hand and turned to Pru and smiled. I am sure you are very beautiful as the Aris-tocratic Girl, she said. I know you all make people happy.

Well, said Sarah.

Who was your father? Jeth took off the hat and laid it on the table as if to make it sit still, and sat down bareheaded.

Marquis Colley. He was the justice of the peace and he taught the common school.

Well, we're just plain old people, said Pru. She rocked baby Jim on her hip again.

Adair said, And he and my mother came here from Tennessee in 1845, and he helped set up the school board and the county court-house. She listened for a moment to the mockingbird singing with wild joy over her new nest in the sycamore. And he loved to read in his law books and he was very mild with us. He died somewhere alone without ever sending a last word to us or knowing what become of us. She stopped and wrapped her hands together in her lap. My mother is buried up there on the Devil's Backbone.

A hot wind moved over the valley meadows and poured through the Shawnee Oak as if through a reeded instrument in a long, blooming hush. Lucy the cat slowly stalked in the back door paw by paw and came and sat before Adair. She gazed up into Adair's eyes in a searching, intense stare and then gathered herself and sailed into Adair's lap.

Go on to Vandiver's, Adair said. I can't take care of you.

My grandmother died in the bale shed of the Mingo gin, said Sarah Walker. Nobody knew she was gone for a week.

Well hush, Mrs. Walker, said Jeth.

ADAIR TOOK WITH HER THE LAST FRAGMENT OF THE TENNESSEE MIRROR wrapped in burlap, and a few other things of use in a traveling and solitary life. She found articles in her mother's clothes trunk—a haversack, stockings, a shawl—and took the blankets from her bed upstairs. She told the Walkers they could take whatever they wanted or could find. They were disturbed and regretful and tried to press other things on her, but Adair had learned the specific gravity of possessions and how they weighed a person down.

She walked back up Stanger's Steep, leading Whiskey, to search for the Log Cabin quilt and the silver dollars and other things she had been forced to leave there, traveling mostly at night. Against the high ridges of the Irish Wilderness she thought she saw the mournful spirit of the soldier in the snare and how against the pale barrens above Pike Creek he hung upside down like the Hanged Man, swaying in the moonlight, and then he was a woman upside down with her skirts tied around her ankles but Adair turned her head away and walked on with Whiskey behind her.

She went back along the Steep until she saw at a distance Dolly's bones beneath the oak tree and the skull hanging in the halter, and did not go any farther but turned back to search the trace. She didn't find anything nor did she expect to very much, because of the soldiers coming down the Steep to the surrender points and others on the road who were poor and desperate, and someone had found the silver dollars. Maybe they needed them more than Adair did.

After a week she came back to her home place and sat up on the barrens at the ridge of Copperhead Mountain. The traveling show people had gone on. It looked as if the Vandivers were storing hay in the house now, and more of the windowlights were gone. She stayed there three days and let Whiskey graze in his slow, limping walk.

On the third day at sunset she was combing out her hair when she saw a man in civilian clothes and a broad hat ride down the road and past the Shawnee Oak. He rode a bay horse. He got off and stood before the empty house, holding his horse's reins in a bandaged hand. There was a folded umbrella tied to the pommel of the saddle, suspended there like a sword.

Major Neumann called out, Adair? He waited. Adair! he shouted. Adair!

He walked into the house and after a few minutes she saw him in her bedroom window looking out. One side of his face was bigger than the other. After a while he came back out again.

Adair! he called. He turned to the hills around. I said I would come for you! Adair!

The light of the world failed to gray and shoals of lightning bugs drifted down the valley in white, insubstantial fires, millions of icy bone-lights.

She sat with her long hair flying loose and the silver brush in her hand and Whiskey grazing nearby. She watched as ghosts watch from the other side of a looking glass, come from a distant place of being and not of the same world.

Adair! I will not stop looking until I find you!

Over the folded blue mountains an evening wind came up, stroked over the trees in silky rushes. She saw the thin edge of a new moon glinting through the trees over Courtois and then it rose with the old moon glowing in its arms, as if to present to the summer night this dark, mysterious gift.

Will Neumann sat on the veranda and Adair saw the flash of a match, the deep glow of his cigar as he settled to wait.

She rose to her feet and laid the silver brush down on her bundle. She gathered her skirts in her hand and began to walk down the hill, hurrying, before the light failed.

(((Listen to)))

Enemy Women
A Novel

by Paulette Jiles

PERFORMED BY
Karen White

ISBN 0-06-053522-9 • $34.95 ($53.95 Can.)
14 Hours • 10 Cassettes • UNABRIDGED
Includes a Reading Group Guide

HarperAudio *An Imprint of* HarperCollins*Publishers*
www.harperaudio.com